THE CALL

Book Zero

The Village

PETER WALKER

The Call - Book Zero of The Village

ISBN: 978-0-6450838-1-1

Original Photographs by Peta Hood
Front Cover Graphic Design by Jessica Wigg

Website: www.thevillagematrix.org

Published with the assistance of Angel Key Publications
https://angelkey.com.au

Contents

About the Author

After a successful career in commercial radio and television, Peter Walker founded and operated the world's first environmental and conscious radio network, Planet Radio, from 1993 until 2008. In 2005 he began teaching personal development and sacred sexuality, including the powerful and life changing "Quantum Leap" retreats and the ancestral cleansing of his "Dragon's Breath" workshop.

On December 21st 2012, Peter literally walked away from "normal" life, leaving behind his partner, daughter, family, career, possessions and friends. He walked 13,000 kilometres in nine countries both to learn about and develop community and as a personal investigation of Balance, Peace and Freedom underpinned by love.

Through a series of lucid dreams, Peter began creating "The Village", a template to redesign our failed economic and social system. "The Village" community gatherings began in 2014 described as a "movement" to reshape society for the 3rd millennium. This is the first book composed to provide a cryptic template to that design.

Peter is an author, orator, master of ceremonies, teacher and student of the possibilities and opportunities of life. Peter currently resides in a converted school bus in the Byron Bay region of Northern NSW, Australia.

"The Call" is Book Zero of a series entitled "The Village".

Acknowledgements

For Zoe, the extraordinary young person who became my daughter. Though I walked away from Zoe to experience and learn, I also walked because I was inspired by them to be a part of designing a magnificent future which extended beyond my tiny lifespan, built on balance, peace and freedom underpinned by love.

Zoe has never strayed from our pact to adopt one another as family. We became Father and Daughter in 2010 and it continues to be my privilege and honour.

For Kyle Winn who took me through a meditation which sparked a profound realisation that I was here to embrace my magical mystical character rather than live a comfortable but essentially dull life.

For the Creator of All Things, ultimately the writer, the written and everything I am blessed to participate in, my endless gratitude for speaking through me.

Dedications

Dedicated to all the courageous souls who answer The Call to co-create The Village.

Special thanks to Gregor Drugowitsch, Chris Brown, Kathy Reed, Scott Collins and the many others who continue to empower the dream.

Deep gratitude to Gregor Drugowitsch, Bernadette and Jason Darnell, Alexandra Moshonas and Glenn Hall for writing retreats in Australia, Kefalonia and Wales.

Eternal Love and Respect to Glenn Hall, Clare Hopkins, Olive Burnell-Molyneux and Jessica Wigg for believing in me and this vision I hold.

Jessica, you have been my muse. Thank you.

Cover image humans: Gavin and Peta.

Prologue

The night became preternaturally dark, but still he kept moving. He had been walking for around four hours. When he stopped for a moment to look up, he could make out the lightless form of the mountain. A firmament of brilliant stars, the Milky Way, stretched across the sky.

The few tools he needed for ceremony were swaddled in a multi-coloured cloth, pushed deep into a soft, leather bag that hung on a broad leather strap across his right shoulder. The bag bounced comfortably on his hip.

His mouth was dry, but the dryness was more about the knowledge of the work he must do on this lightless night than a lack of water.

He was sure he had remembered everything.

In his right hand was a staff of hard, straight wood that had been his constant companion for the past two years. He had taken it from the forest in the mountains near where he had been living with nature, communing with the earth, soil, rocks and stones, the wind and the clouds, the streams and the rain, the sun and the fire of the rough camp he had called home.

The staff had been present at every moment, every ceremony he had performed in preparation for this night.

Every day of those two years he had also woven a web, danced a pattern into the staff so that it could become the primary tool for this work.

Without warning, Elias swung the staff in an arc around his head and completed the movement with a flourish that saw its tip extended at arms' length in front of him. The muscles on his upper arm and shoulder rippled with the effort, and the

wind picked up as the movement came to a close. He dropped the staff back to touch the earth and began using it to assist him in climbing the slow slope under his calloused feet.

A fresh breeze carried the scent of the surrounding eucalypt forest to his nostrils and gave a gentle push at his back, urging him onwards and upwards. The undergrowth began to change shape and scent as he passed the concealed entrance. This was the first clearing. His beginning ceremonial place, selected for him by the elders on an earlier journey twenty years ago.

From this mountain, there were hundreds of invisible threads running deep underground to similar sites all over the planet. Elias could feel the thrumming of these tendrils of power, these 'songlines' underneath his feet.

They excited him, added energy to every step and he lengthened his stride to arrive at the power spot a little sooner.

More time spent in meditation before he began the dawn ritual would just add to the impetus of his work, so it was worth the effort. The ley-lines under him were sending him a surge of energy, coursing through the muscles of his legs, filling his first chakra and pouring upwards to his heart.

He marched on and up as the slope became steeper.

The undergrowth gave way to giant crystalline boulders and tall, white-trunked eucalypts that sang a rustling, clacking song in the wind. It sounded like the rhythmic clatter of clap-sticks around a fireplace where the ancestors had burned black-wattle bark and travelled, to gain wisdom from the Dreamtime.

Elias swung onto the first level place on the side of the hill and paused for a moment. Though the night wind was cool, the pace he had been going left him bathed in a sheen of shining sweat.

He flipped the staff to his left hand, lifted the strap of the leather bag over his head, placed it on a flat rock back a little from the edge and peeled his shirt off.

The wind had been a good travelling companion to this point. For the main ceremony at dawn, he would need it to

be calm. Beginning with the staff in his left hand he began weaving a series of intricate patterns in the air. He passed the stave from hand to hand. Considering his powerful frame he danced in a surprisingly agile way.

Then he brought the base of the stave down with a dull thud on the damp soil and muttered a few unintelligible words.

In that moment, the wind dropped.

A smile creased his face. Being attuned with the weather was a favourite of his. Elias' natural place, his mastery, was with fire and earth, so having mastery of the wind and water had taken him longer, had required more discipline and a more torturous accessing of his ancestral memories. Now, they too recognised him and respected his ministrations.

He sent a silent prayer, thanking the spirits of the land, the Rainbow Serpent and his spirit animal, Dirawong, the goanna.

With the calming of the wind came silence. Even the animals of the night felt his power.

Elias pulled his shirt back over his frame and picked up the bag. He eased the strap over his shoulder, weighed the staff for comfort in his hand and set out once again to the final ceremony place. Not far now.

Further down in the low hills and the valley, with the wind now absent, a mist began to gather, shrouding the dank, tree-covered hills in a grey cloak.

The only sound was the padding of his bare feet on the stone as the mist rose. It remained several paces behind him as he climbed toward the summit. The highest point was soon the remaining piece of the earth still visible above a sea of grey-white brume.

Almost there now.

He glanced from left to right, shivering despite the mild exertion of his climb and activated the 'seeing' that opened other worlds to him. On both sides now he could see the wraith-like images of those he was about to summon. Nothing frightening for him, nothing to fear, just the semi-opaque

images of each of them going about the business of their day or night, not yet aware of the call.

Ah, perhaps not all of them were unaware. The shaman woman, Tisa was wide awake and doing some of her own work, with all that paraphernalia she used. He smiled at that. She did weave her magick with great skill and beauty. All those things she used as tools suited her somehow. Feathers and crystals, things wrapped up in swatches of cloth, plant parts, animal skins, bones and sigils. Different choices, same direction.

His smile broadened. It would be very good to see her face-to-face once more.

There was the muted 'ooom, ooom, ooom' of a Tawny Frogmouth and a disturbance of wings. He smiled again. Tisa was sensing him too and had sent her messenger to visit him, to let him know she was aware. So at least one of the twelve would need no further invocation.

The others though were not so present, perhaps choosing to be so, for any number of reasons. Ah, there. Petra saw him.

Some would be cloaking themselves, some had no idea and others had many things to do in everyday life. Still others were sleeping and this would come to them in the dream. Victor was already taking the steps they had both agreed would be needed to bring the next generation up to speed.

Ariah had become too old and unwell to make the journey, but her daughter Rena didn't have any knowledge of this or the changes that were coming. Victor would remedy that in his usual abrupt manner.

Elias paused in his solitary march and took a moment to take a deep inhalation. He held his breath for a long count. When he exhaled his warm breath misted into the forms of his spirit animals before morphing into the mist approaching him from behind.

The place he was seeking was now a climb up almost vertical rock. A cold, steel chain was pegged into the stone to aid the climb when it became too steep. He barely needed to

touch it, but it was a reminder to collect all of his faculties as he lifted his frame up and up, his staff more hindrance than help, scaling the steep, stone wall to arrive on a plateau. It was covered by low, patchy grass, scratching scrub and the twisted trunks of a species of acacia tree.

He turned around to face the valley.

It now seemed a much greater rise than it looked from below, but perhaps that had to do with the rivers, tendrils and dervishes of mist that flowed and danced where once there was solid earth.

Elias sat. The cool stone chilled his backside, thighs and feet as he crossed his legs. He removed the bag, laid it at his side and placed the staff across his lap. Closing his eyes, his hands went to the two places worn a little deeper on the staff.

At best estimate he still had four hours before dawn, so there was plenty of time to find his centre. The mist rose even further, breached the summit and wove around him so that he was shrouded in its cloak of cool wetness.

Breath in and out, slow and measured, brought his attention to also shrouding the energy that welled in him. It wouldn't do to announce his intention before time.

Visioning that point just behind his navel, light in the darkness of his physical body, he realised that containing it until the time was right had been the principal work of his entire life.

The mountain, the boulders, the soils and rocks and sand and stone could feel him. A shudder ran through the bedrock, perhaps reaching all the way down, and all the way back in time, to when this mountain had last spewed lava and life. She had been one of the colossal volcanoes of the Dreamtime.

What might have been hours, but for Elias was a timeless experience, passed as he sat in that meditative pose. His staff thrummed with the energy channelling through it. Now he must go to the ceremony place.

He rose in silence, stretched his back, arms and legs then shook his body from head to toe to get the blood flowing.

While the air was now quite cold and damp, his skin steamed a little, following the trail of steam that was his exhaling breath. Elias checked that he had everything.

His staff held firm in his left hand, Elias pushed through the sparse brush to the open space hidden from the view of all but the few who climbed up to this place. This was the ceremony place, hidden in plain sight by the words and the dreams of the sisters, the Aunties who tended the mountain.

He placed the bag on the ground and laid the staff nearby, pointing to where the sun would rise in just an hour or two. The mist swirled once and the ceremony space became totally transparent, the air alight, cerulean sparks tinkling in a dome over the space for those with the eyes to see.

Elias frowned in concentration. There must be no doubt that it was right timing for this. He lifted the soft leather flap of the bag, drew out the coloured cloth and unravelled it with care as he had done so many times before. The blade of the knife glinted blue in the sparkling light.

With his right hand, Elias embraced the carved, wooden hilt, spread the cloth out in front of him and placed the knife with the blade angled to the place where dawn would break. He collected the hard, wooden staff, lifted it to the sky and began to wend and weave in a dance, round and round the full circle.

Sometimes he whirled so fast that everything was a blur. Sometimes he was still, as if frozen in time. In every moment it was a dance of incredible beauty and extraordinary power. Mother Earth and all her children danced with him.

The thicker end of the staff emitted an almost impercep- tible sound that could have been voices of the people of this land, could have been the rush of wind or water, the roar of a fire, the rumble of stones cascading down a mountain, the song of a cathedral choir, a solitary catbird, wildcats fighting or a child's sleeping breath.

From that same place came a light like lightning and fire, dragon's breath and dying breath, mist and madness. That light, that sound, wove a magnificent, intricate dome

above the space, above the man – locked tight to the earth in an astounding geometry of lines and frequency.

Elias, the Conjurer, the Caller, the gatherer, then drove his staff deep into the solid rock, both hands reverberating with the effort of his dance and that final impossible thrust of timber into solid bedrock.

Now he dare not release.

At the apex of the dome there remained a hole into the sky, perhaps a metre round. It began to glow. As Elias stood there gripping his staff with both hands it increased in brilliance until he was engulfed in an effulgent glamour that bound him and his staff inextricably in rock and air in the one moment. It was impossible for him to move, but he remained relaxed, for he had no need to move.

Not yet.

Still as stone, Elias was the rock and the ether. The light poured down over him and that staff of wood and was drawn into the stone beneath his feet. He remained that way until the inky blackness of the night began to give way to the soft light of dawn.

As sunlight began to pierce and dispel the mists that shrouded the land, the light pouring through the dome diminished until it blinked out. Summoning all his strength, Elias broke free of the thrall in which he was held, drew himself and his staff out of the stone, and laid it down.

He sat cross-legged on the stone and reached for his knife. In perfect alignment with the distant horizon, he drew the blade one hundred and eighty degrees, from precisely north through the eastern, lightening sky, and finally direct to the south.

The dome folded back until it formed an arc above and behind him. In front, from where he stood, Elias could now see each of those he was summoning but for one, positioned equidistant from each other across the one hundred and eighty degrees of the arc. That one felt closer somehow. He saw others too, those who would not come.

Placing the knife back on the stone, he faced the rising sun and in a voice rippling with the power he had just experienced, he said,

"It's time my friends. Be bold and come."

CHAPTER ONE

B right sunlight flickered off a sparkling, aquamarine sea that rose and fell against the rocky outcrop where Petra stood naked but for a knife and bag attached to a wide belt resting on her hips.

Her eyes squinting against the glare, she took a moment to savour the sun's warmth, check the blade and burlap bag, fill her lungs and plunge in. Diving deep, the pressure increased, holding her in the way she enjoyed so much.

With long, slow strokes she was soon fanning along the sand-covered ocean floor, pushing plumes of white sand behind her. She unsheathed her knife just before she reached the ledge where she always found abalone. The local people called it 'loco'. As she drifted, she felt the first twinges of need for a new breath. Flicking the tip of her knife under the flat shellfish, she upended a dozen, turned to collect them and floated them into her bag.

As the last of them clicked in, the call for air came with renewed intensity. She smiled, slid the blade back into its sheath and kicked upward. When she broke the surface, she took a deep breath. It was an easy harvest this morning and no real stress on her breath for this dive. A quick double-check reassured her that bag and knife were secure.

It always amazed her how far she could travel underwater. The current today must have been strong, helping her cover the distance from the rock ledge to the underwater shelf where the abalone were abundant. She rolled her tanned shoulders and struck out for the shore.

After thirty or so strokes she paused and lifted her head to see how close the rocks were.

"Damn," she muttered, spitting salty water and finished the sentence in her mind, 'I don't seem to be any closer.'

She wiped the water from her eyes and peered at her diving ledge. Was that a man squatted on the rocks? She felt the current tugging at her bag as the shore slipped further away. It was a man, indistinct but certain, squatted on the stone ledge with a wavering ripple disturbing the air above him.

In sharp contrast, as clear as this bright day, she heard his voice.

Petra relaxed and swam with, and across the current, until the drag eased. The water swelled under her. She plunged down the face of a two-metre wave that took her all the way to the beach, strode out of the surf and sprinted back to the rock ledge, half expecting to see him still sitting there. But she knew better. Elias wasn't anywhere near here in any physical sense. She spoke out loud.

"It seems the time has come then, Petra. I guess this party had to end sometime."

She loosened the belt, bag and knife and sat for a few minutes in the sun to dry. Her brow furrowed a little as she pondered what needed to be done. Pulling a simple, white, cotton shift over her shoulders, she removed the bag and knife, slipped the knife into the bag and stood to draw the belt secure once again around her waist. She stepped down from the rock ledge and strode along the perfect, white sand, leaving the only footprints that beach would see for a long, long time.

CHAPTER TWO

A scorching, dry wind screamed around the eaves of the old colonial house. Sleep had been impossible, though a night of wakefulness hadn't diminished her energy. Maybe it was the wind that brought the message to her. Maybe it was the vast, clear sky.

Whatever it was, Tisa Emem heard it distinctly. Felt it. She had been waiting for it.

She had known it was coming and knew it would arrive on a day and night when the wind was tossing the dust into every corner, singeing the pollens from the grasslands into inflamed and reddened eyes.

The message was clear so she sent an animal spirit messenger in reply. What to do next was also clear, but how to do it? She had been living here for thirty years. There were so many people to consider, so many friendships to unravel now the message had come. For all of those thirty years she had anticipated this day almost with a longing, with a yearning. Now it had come, the yearning was amplified. There was also regret. What to do next was evident and Tisa knew it must be done with haste and without fuss. But first, she must leave them a message. She owed them some kind of explanation. She owed them that much.

Tisa walked to the simple wooden table and scraped the left-hand drawer out a few inches, reached in for pen and paper and laid them on the table. Without sitting in the rattan chair that had begun to unravel years ago, she paused for a moment, or was it much longer, and noticed how the light-blue paper shone

in the early light as it sat on her old table. A cup of tea was what she needed. A cup of tea would settle her nerves.

When the pot boiled, she lifted it from the fire with a cast iron hook. Kesari had made it for her all those years ago. She tossed in a handful of tea. That hook had been fashioned the first time Kesari had visited. The first time, when she came because she had heard of Tisa, had heard what she could do. Just over ten years ago. Kesari would be thirty five now. Memories of her visits wandered through her head and painted pictures of their laughter, their sombre visits to the grasslands and the gentle silences when they travelled home again, the smell of horses on everything.

It was four years since Tisa had seen Kesari. Her visit had been brief. Was it six days? She called it a flying visit, to ask what could not be asked in any way but face to face. Ten years ago she had stayed almost eighteen months, her first and longest visit. Smiling with the memory, Tisa recalled the birth of that tiny child. Kesari had had no doubt and named him Max. Tisa had sweated and chanted and used her calm, strong, gentle hands to draw Max from Kesari's body into this strange world. That time, that dreaming time of laughter, long conversations and intermittent sleep had seen Max become a strong baby, present in the world and learning things he could have learned nowhere else and from no-one but Tisa.

Steam rose and the smell of strong, black tea filled the room conjuring another rush of memories for the old woman. A big cup was required because this was to either be a long letter or a letter that would take some time to extract. It was a letter that had to say as much as possible while not saying anything at all. Those who read it would need to see different things, make different conclusions and take different actions. Some would never forget her and would wonder why. Some would be very glad she was gone. Lowering her body into the tattered wicker chair, she set her cup near the blank page and picked up her old silver pen. It was cold in her hand. An unopened envelope, its window crackling a little, enclosing her name inside, became a

scribble pad until the ink began to flow into a half dozen black swirls. She wrote her name on the envelope. Tisa Emem.

Ninth born child. A chaotic time for her family. A family known as the people of peace. She could only hope that would continue to be so. Tisa knew what she had to do next.

First though, the letter must be written. At least she would soon see Kesari and Max. This time they would be together until it was done. This time they would come to know one another as never before. This time they would depend on each other to stay alive. It was a long way and across some difficult country with even more difficult people.

"My Family," she began because, in their own way each of them was family.

"My family" perched there at the top of the page. She lifted the mug of black tea to her lips and blew gently, like a zephyr whispering through the long grass after the rain. As she took her first cautious sip, she began to write.

"Today I have to leave you. Today I begin a long journey. At the very least I will be away for a long time, measured at least in years and it may be that I never return to this place that I love and to all of you that I love. Yet I take this journey with full intention and nobody is forcing me to go.

Those of you who were there at the beginning will recall what it was we began to create here.

Over the past thirty years we have made genuine progress, but the job is not yet done and will never be complete. Sometimes it feels as though we are inching forward and sometimes we seem to lose ground, but if you look back now across those thirty years it is easy to see what we have all achieved and to take some real pride in our efforts. There is nothing more important now than to keep moving forward, to redouble your efforts, because the time has come that we have been preparing for all this time.

Many of you older ones will remember what hunger was like back when we began. Today, we have overcome that hunger by working in harmony with our land, remembering the isunde

to help us grow food for ourselves and remembering the old ways we used to live here. We have had the good sense to know that the old ways could not deliver everything we needed, so we have reached out for wisdom from others as well. So now all of us eat well and our children are healthy and strong.

The animals have also returned. This last year we have seen more of our magnificent lions, zebra, many thousands of wildebeest and our beloved tsessebe. They are all growing in numbers and we have played our part in making this happen while we live here amongst them. There are many things we can be proud of and many things for us still to do. Alas, I cannot be here to watch you go on to even greater success.

I don't want to even begin to speak to each of you individually, because where would I stop if I were to do such a thing. You are all such a part of this beauty we have created. You all know what needs to be done to keep it happening.

Can I remind you to pay attention to each of the different aspects of our way, to never permit one to continuously over-ride the importance of another? Can I remind you that each and every person must have their right to contribute in the way that we have been practising now for these many years, a way that is so similar to the old ways, yet has changed to mean that we no longer need nor desire a 'Litunga'? All of us must be heard. All of us have our place.

Can I remind you of something that we have always known? We are a part of this place and this place knows how to hold us and in return we know how to hold it. We are not the enemy of this place and it is not our enemy.

I would like to be able to say to you that I will leave in six months or one year or perhaps even longer, or that I will never leave, but I do not have that choice. Soon the rains will come and you know that I cannot find my way from here once they begin. I have such a long way to travel and so I must go this very day.

You all know and remember Kesari and beautiful Max, her son. You all remember how she, and then they have come to

be with us over these past years. Each time they have come to us and become a part of this family of ours. This time, though they are not my final destination, I must go to them. It is a long journey and until I reach them I must travel alone, but you know how well I love this land and this land loves me, so do not fear for me or come looking for me. By the time you read this, I will be long gone and I will leave no tracks.

Once I have reached them we will remember each of you before we set out on an even greater journey. From then I will travel with both of them, for it is quite clear to me that we are all called and we must all travel together, so they will help to keep me safe and I, them.

Continue our work here. That is the best thing that can be done. Continue as though I was never here and I am always here and one day perhaps I will be able to return. Never forget those pillars on which we build everything that we do here and never forget each other for each of you brings your own unique offering to our effort and to this way of life.

Because I know that it is now time for me to go, I can tell you that how we live here and how we are together with each other and with the land, animals, sky and water – there has never been a more important time to continue, to keep on. To embrace what we are living, being and doing here as completely and beautifully as we can. Never has there been a more important time.

This is enough for now.

I must go. I hold each and every one of you with love."

The sun was streaming through her window and drenching her bed in golden light. Despite her gentle composure, warm tears trickled down Tisa's cheeks. She shifted the page away so that no drop would fall on the light-blue paper. Knowing what she needed to do, the practical necessity of it was not the problem. Taking the steps to leave all these people, this family behind...

Folding the pages into three, spending a little too long on getting the edges straight, sliding the paper into a clean, bright,

white envelope and writing 'To My Family' on the outside were all done through silent tears. She stood and walked to the shelf near the cooking fire to lean the letter against a small brass elephant she kept there.

It was time to go. Picking up the brown pack and her walking staff, Tisa stepped out of her two-room home into the wind and felt it wash across her body and blow her hair all about her face. She leaned the staff against the wall and pulled a black elastic from her left wrist to fasten it around her unruly, grey-black hair. She looked around one last time.

Her shrewd gaze took in the fields and gardens that had fed them so well for years now. The water storage tanks that Munjita had designed and tended to the construction of, near fifteen years ago, had held them safe through all those dry seasons since. She smiled as she took in the grove of trees that, in just a few short years, now provided shade. She remembered that for so many years before, no tree would grow there. She brought her soft eyes to the cluster of small houses, still quiet at this time of the morning because the people were resting. It had been a late night talking and deciding, sitting in circle together in the unique way that she and Elias and some of the others had dreamed, back when this all began. They deserved to rest.

Tisa picked up her staff and walked with determination from her home of thirty years, out of the village. First, though it was a path filled with danger, she must go north.

On her desk, a forgotten cup of cold black tea.

CHAPTER THREE

A single jazz trumpet weaves its melancholy like grey mist through the hum of soft drink coolers in a retro Greenwich cafe on a cloud-lined Friday lunchtime in late September. Overstuffed leather lounges that have seen better days are comfortably empty. There is still the impression of a broad backside imprinted in one of the dun-brown cushions echoing the ghost of a cafe dweller not long returned to their hiding-hole of a damp room below the pavement on the high street.

On the footpath outside a mother and daughter are filling their mouths behind the silence of glass, mouthing old news and gossip at each other as only those who intimately know each other's ugliness can permit.

A shining teapot reflects framed fame through a fascia of fingerprints and wafts the scent of peppermint though the noisy air. Waiters scurry and stand, scurry and stand like foraging rats, toadying to a few ragged customers. The grey-clad locals are sipping brooding coffees under shadowed, brooding brows; extending their stay because there's no good reason to go home.

Rena twisted a tendril of her unruly mop of hair and lifted her eyes to scan the street. A man of indeterminate age limped past. His gait somehow reminded her that there was a need for her to walk the few blocks home very soon to begin preparations for dinner for her mother and herself. She shifted heavily in her chair, scraping it back across the timber floor as though to make a move but then settled again and plunged back into the rag-eared novel she was reading. Rena was loath to break back into reality, loath to meet what must be done, so she read on to escape into someone else's imaginary drama.

Outside it began to drizzle a little, dampening the street, blackening the tarmac, silencing the occasional footfall of passers-by. An uneasy feeling gnawed at the pit of her stomach as it had since that day.

It had been a Saturday when life had become less constant, less predictable. Since that day when the strange dream (was it a dream) had woken her, pulse racing, from a fitful sleep into a bright, sun-filled morning.

The brightness of the day felt starkly at odds with the niggling sensation sitting deep in her gut.

Something was happening or was about to happen. Something that would bump her unceremoniously out of the fugue she had been living in for the past twelve months, since she moved back in with her mother to care for her, to return the favour of childhood. She could feel it.

"Well, damn it, just get on with it," she said out loud, glancing around, self conscious to see if anyone had noticed her outburst. No-one seemed to pay any attention but for a slim faced man with perceptive eyes. He raised his head to give her a brief nod, as though he knew her, or knew what she meant. Then he stood, gathered the notes scattered about his table and walked the few steps to Rena's table in the centre of the room. Without asking, he sat down opposite her.

"It's disconcerting, isn't it? It sits in the pit of the stomach and it's not going away. If anything it feels like its bedding in. We may have to do something about it," he uttered, in a tone that felt gentle and forceful in the same moment.

With his words, Rena felt a shiver of apprehension run the length of her spine. Her eyes scanned his slender face, shrewd eyes framed by long lashes, three deep lines furrowed across his forehead and he wore a rough stubble of beard. He could have felt threatening, but for some reason she had no alarm at all. Rather she felt that she should remember him, though there was also a certainty they had never met. His words were unnerving.

"I don't know what you mean." Rena said in an undertone, almost a whisper, wondering why she was whispering.

10

"I think you do. It started on that Saturday. It wasn't a dream, as far as I can tell. It feels more real every day, and the sensation gets clearer rather than drifting away. Dreams tend to fade out. This isn't doing that, is it? Seems we'll have to do something about it. My name's Victor."

As he finished speaking, his hand darted out across the table. Rena took it and shook it. His hand was warm and dry.

"Rena. Not sure why we're meeting, but hi. Not too sure what you're talking about either, but I have the feeling you're going to tell me. Best get started. I've got to go pretty soon."

Victor smiled, and with that smile, his face made such a radical shift that Rena was, for a moment, startled.

"Then let's go. I'll walk with you." He rose and dropped some cash on the table, walked out the door and stood just outside, pulling a hood over his head against the misting rain. Thoughts whirled in Rena's mind, but there were no alarm bells ringing. She felt calm.

Soon they were walking down the hill towards her home, side by side, their shoes squishing on the wet pavement. He was tall. She came up to his shoulder.

As they walked, they both looked straight ahead. Rena was silent. Victor followed her lead. The silence, for some inexplicable reason, was comfortable. Soon they arrived at Rena's apartment building, climbed the stairs, their footsteps sounding hollow in the stairwell. When they reached the door, she found her key and swung it open. The agreeable, yesterday scent of some kind of incense drifted past them with a rush of warm air.

"You'd better come in".

The door closed with a click and there was the sound of keys turning and two bolts being driven home.

11

Grey

An inky gloom more impenetrable than Dr Grey Symes had ever known.

A sense of agonising sadness clung to him and tore flaps of his skin in a hundred places, adding to the forlorn sensation with an excruciating pain. An unholy shriek issued from somewhere. Was it from his throat? Was he so disconnected from his own body that he couldn't tell if that was his own scream of agony and loss?

Sweat beaded on his face then ran in tiny rivulets down his smooth-shaven cheeks and found their way into the torn skin on his neck and shoulders to add even more pain, as if that were possible. Grey took a deep, rasping breath, his throat parched.

In that moment, the cloying blackness gave way to a malevolent, shadowed figure that clutched what appeared to be a broad scimitar in its claw of a hand. Terror gripped Grey, and he tried to run, but his legs were encased in a thick sludge.

The figure faced him, brought the tip of its weapon to his belly and began to edge forward. The blade punctured his gut just below his breast bone and made its way upwards, slicing through skin, muscle and bone, bringing pain beyond imagining.

The creature reached its claw-like hands to either side of his chest and tore it both ways, exposing lungs and heart. Were it not a dream the pain and trauma would have meant that Grey would be, by now, unconscious but the dream forced him deeper into the experience, galvanising the agony.

The claw of the beast reached down and grasped his heart, squeezing it without mercy. With one almighty pull his heart was torn from his chest. He screamed and flailed and screamed as life

drained from him, yet death was somehow evaded. Something fetid and glutinous invaded the bloody cavity and a paralysing possession tore its way into his soul.

Sweat-drenched sheets clung to Grey's twisted torso as he woke.

A thin grey light eked through his bedroom window. He could hear the rattle of a twig scraping a repetitive rhythm on the glass. His heart was pounding so hard he thought he might die at any moment. With an almost superhuman effort he dragged in a deep breath. Then another.

With his third breath, his heart began to steady and slow.

CHAPTER FOUR

She was sure it hadn't been there before. A small adjustment to the focus on her telescope brought the tiny, greenish dot into focus, almost as though it had moved a little closer. What the hell was happening? So much of what Raniyah had learned about astronomy was being overturned by this. She had trained her scope onto this part of the sky, not for any 'rational' reason, but because she 'sensed' that it was what she needed to do. When she first positioned the telescope onto that random place in the night sky there had been nothing out of the ordinary. She wandered off to bed before midnight, wondering what that 'sense' had been.

But tonight, at eleven forty-seven, thirteen minutes before midnight, the scope still in the same place, she saw something come into view that piqued her interest.

Stars didn't just appear, didn't look a particular colour and certainly didn't move closer. Three hours later it had become even more certain, more radiant. Whatever this thing was, it was moving fast and seemed to be on a trajectory to Earth.

Toby would be more than interested. Perhaps it was a little too soon to invite him to look. Raniyah didn't want to appear to be foolish, but this felt important. She decided to leave it just one more night before asking Toby, sharing her discovery with him. She was tired.

Night after night of gazing into her scope until the early hours of each morning was exhausting. This could make it worth the effort. Maybe she had actually discovered something. For some reason, in these strange times, that didn't seem impossible. Something significant felt like it was shifting in the world.

Stepping back into the warmth of her front room she sat at the antique table that served as her work desk. She tapped the computer keyboard. A search of the major astronomy sites showed her that there was nothing unusual being reported.

Could that mean that she was the only person who had noticed this? That seemed doubtful.

She searched some more, but there was nothing. Yes, she would ask Toby to come over and look tomorrow. Tomorrow? To be clear, it would be later today. At four am the day was less than an hour away. The first light of dawn would soon show in the eastern sky. It was time to get some sleep.

She stripped her shirt and shorts off and dropped them where she stood, then drifted into the bedroom and lay on the square of foam rubber that served as her bed. She was tired, that was certain, but her mind was whirring with all the possibilities that this tiny, green spot might represent. Sleep didn't come until the sun began to light the room. It looked like it would be a beautiful day, the sky clear but for a turbid mass of clouds off on the horizon, far in the south west.

Raniyah slept. That was the morning her dreams began in earnest.

Morning meditation done, Toby began to place each of the items set out before him onto a square of red cloth, which he then folded about them. He had dropped a lot of the paraphernalia he had once used when he had been studying a whole range of old teachings. There was something solid about the few pieces that remained. A crystal that an old Nepalese woman gave him when he was sitting at the south end of the lake in Pokhara, Nepal, a heart-shaped stone he found on a beach near Inverness in Scotland, a tiny glass flask of water that his friend Alice claimed had some special healing properties and an abalone shell were all he had retained. In the shell rested the sage stick that he used to set the space. There was nothing quite like the smell of sage smoke.

Once it was all wrapped and packed, he rose and paced the stone-walled room. He stopped to gaze out the front window at

the trees and ferns that screened this place from view. Then he paced again. Most days his practice gave him a sense of relaxation in its simple repetition. This morning he found it something of an otherworld experience. It was not quite the empty place that he aspired to, but it was interesting. He smiled and walked into the bedroom, emerging into the open space outside the front glass wall. He began to dress in the traditional Hakama of Aikido. As he unfolded the garment he could almost hear the voice of his sensei explaining the seven folds of the Hakama.

"These seven folds represent the seven virtues of budo," Sensei Michael had intoned.

"The first of these is jin which is benevolence, gi which represents honour or justice, rei is courtesy and etiquette, then comes chi for wisdom and correct use of your intelligence, shin is then sincerity in all your life, chu is loyalty and the seventh fold is piety and devotion. Aikido is born of the bushido spirit of Japan, and in our practice we must strive to polish the seven traditional virtues, both in our daily practice, and in every step of life."

His Hakama in place, Toby drew his body into the first of his poses. There was nothing better he knew to remain calm and aligned, than Aikido. His body shifted with ease, catlike from pose to pose, his feet positioned to perfection and his frame balanced throughout each of the moves. While he had only practised at Sensei Michael's dojo for a little over eight years, he had found aikido very natural and had learned fast. As he danced across the floor Toby let his mind wander to Brianna and the years they had spent settling into their bushland hideaway. Their first meeting was at the dojo.

From the outside, the house looked small, no matter what direction your approach. Inside it was spacious and cool, with a surprising, high ceiling for an underground dwelling. Solid posts and accurate hand-laid stonework supported an earthen roof that masked its presence from above. The rear wall was underground. Toby recalled the huge machine he had used to complete the carving of a giant hole in the slope years ago. Though he and

16

Brianna had dug much of the excavation by hand, the hardest physical work either of them had ever done, there had been a few outcrops of basalt that just wouldn't budge with hand tools, so they had called in a friend to break and shift them. Toby's younger sister and that excavator driver were only two other people who knew the building existed, as far as they knew. The driver was a good friend, and trustworthy, so they assumed he had kept their secret.

Every post in the place came from the tall, straight trees that grew here. Toby had selected and felled just a few of them, cured the timber for two years and cut the lengths needed to fashion the posts and beams that were the supporting structure of the place. It needed to be strong to support almost a foot of reinforced concrete. The stonework had been a heavy and laborious task, but they had managed to complete it in their self-imposed, eighteen-month construction time. The hand-hewed timber floor and all the fittings that completed the building, including the glass panels and door made it their home. Decorated with wall hangings, mats and cushions, it presented a distinct, middle-eastern flavour. It suited them well.

Though his mind was busier than ideal for Aikido practice and though his eyes were not focused on anything in particular, Toby noticed a movement down the slope. It was just a shift in the sunlight, like something had flashed through a sunny spot and back into shade. Brianna would be almost ready to come up from her garden. She tended it with a very similar discipline to his daily practice. On most days he could see the validity in her claim that it was more useful as a practice. Today was different.

A sharp message flashed across his mind, "Toby, HELP!"

One person could jump without effort into his head and that was Brianna, but Brianna calling for help, now that was a surprise. She was more capable of looking after herself than he was. He grabbed his aikido jo, a short, hard staff of ash wood. Even without this simple weapon, Toby was a fearsome opponent. Brianna was lethal. Move....fast....now.

Toby steamed out the door, then paused for just a moment to drop his Hakama as it dragged on brambles alongside the gravel path he and Brianna had completed a year earlier. All his senses were on high alert.

No sign of her yet, but she wasn't far away. The fact that she wasn't calling out was no reason for concern. She could reach him without spoken language, so if she hadn't said anything more than 'Toby...HELP!' she would be in the garden.

He moved swift and silent along the path, scanning his peripheral vision from edge to edge.

When he reached the garden he soon discovered why Brianna had called. Four men were doing their best to manoeuvre her into a corner against the rock wall at the rear of the garden. To this point she still had lots of fighting room and looked to be unharmed. Her garden shovel had become a weapon, held relaxed in both hands. The four men, though still confident, were reminded that she was not going to be easy prey. They hadn't considered that she could reach out to Toby with her mind.

Toby dropped the man on the left at the same moment Brianna struck the one on the right and he fell, clutching his groin. The other two didn't know where to look or move first, but they recovered well, stepping back from both Toby and Brianna, who now presented in unison, training evident in their posture. The attackers were two metres away from them now, giving them room to move. In a second they took in the scene and decided to retreat. Toby saw the shift in their eyes and noted how their muscles moved. The biggest of them grunted,

"Clear".

He and the smaller man backed away. The other two picked themselves off the ground and also retreated a few paces. In a few moments they vanished into the bush. Both Brianna and Toby noticed that they moved fast and efficient over rough ground. They had training. Toby had taken them by surprise, giving him, and Brianna, the advantage they needed. It was

certain that this didn't end here. They would be back and nowhere near as polite next time.

"You OK, Bree?"

"I'm fine. What the fuck just happened?"

"I have an idea. Let's get up to the house."

"Yep, just give me a second."

Brianna walked a few steps and reached down to the path between two neat rows of the garden. She collected a wicker basket full of fresh-picked vegetables.

"I can't leave this lot here," she smiled.

Toby shook his head and turned back to the house. Together they strode back up to the hill, retrieving the black Hakama on the way.

Once inside, Toby folded his Hakama and returned it to its place in the bedroom. When he came back into the lounge, he reached behind a tapestry on the wall and pressed a small black button. A metal security grid slid into place across all the glass panes. Moving back to the door he wound a circle of steel in the centre of the door and bolts slid into place in eight places around the door. The house became a fortress.

The aroma of fresh-made coffee announced that Brianna was still on point. She brought a mug to Toby and they savoured the first few sips before Brianna said,

"You have an idea, you said. Is it what I think?"

Toby nodded.

"In that case, I'm going to miss this place."

Toby grimaced.

"Yeah, me too."

He took a gulp of coffee then added, "Did those guys put a mark on you?"

"No, I heard them coming, grabbed the spade and just turned to meet them. When I saw there were four, I gave you a call. Four is a lot, if they're any good."

Brianna put her coffee on the counter, "The big guy was familiar somehow. Can't recall where I've seen him before, but it'll come to me." She smiled, walked over and leaned forward

to plant a kiss on the tip of Toby's nose. "Thanks for coming straight down, lover."

"Well, it seems pretty certain they'll be back, so we best get to work." Toby drained his coffee.

Brianna's gaze followed him as he walked across the room to what appeared to be a blank wall. He pressed the wall at shoulder height and a square panel slid out. Toby lifted the base of the panel, reached into the space behind and brought out a small journal, bound in grey. He flipped open a few pages and grunted his satisfaction. This was what he wanted.

"Where do we go first, Toby?"

"We go to the top of the mountain. We've prepped the cave for just this sort of thing and it'll be safe. From there we can try to make contact with a few of the others to ask some questions."

"Great. So we do a full pack down here?"

He nodded, "Yep. We're going to be away quite a while."

For the next two hours Toby and Brianna worked in almost complete silence. Both of them knew what had to be done and had a very clear plan as to who did what. Most of the contents of their home would stay in place, just put in storage. The few things that were to come with them fitted into two bags, purpose-made for this day. Strapped across the back of each of those bags was an Aikido jo.

Raniyah tapped the screen of her phone for the tenth time in three hours. She waited and listened. Message bank again, but this time the message had changed. In Toby's clear, deep tone she heard, "Thanks for calling. I'm off grid for a while so if you've got my email, reach me with that."

That was what she had been waiting for. When the first hour had passed and she had no response from Toby, she wondered how long it would take before his message changed, and to which one. She had not expected it to shift to this one so soon. She clicked her phone open, pulled the sim card out and tossed the phone on her bed. Stepping over a pile of discarded clothes she walked out to her balcony and started dismantling

her telescope. If she could manage it, this would come with her, for the first bit at least.

Soon it was packed down, bagged, still bulky, but as manageable as possible. She brought the scope inside and placed it next to the coffee table, then disappeared into her bedroom to pack some clothes and the few bits she would need, if that message meant what she thought it did. Who was she kidding? If that message was on his phone, it meant exactly what she thought. She took a moment to grab a couple of extra sim cards, retrieved her phone and slotted one in.

The door clicking shut as she left her apartment made her wonder when she would see the place again. She strapped her kit and the scope onto the seat of her Kawasaki, lifted her leathers over her shoulders, climbed aboard and kicked the motor to life. First walking the bike backwards down the drive, she pulled on helmet and gloves, then gunned the bike and roared off towards the mountain.

The last of the light, tough aluminium screens slid into place. With that, all trace of sunlight was gone inside Toby and Brianna's underground abode. A single lamp glowed on the kitchen bench, casting a low, white light. The tapestries and mats looked dim and mysterious. Both Toby and Brianna were dressed in sombre clothing, their feet in solid hiking boots. They would need them. In unison, they shouldered their packs. As Toby cast a final look over the room, Brianna deactivated the eight-way lock to release them into the late afternoon. They squinted into the light as their eyes adjusted. The press of a button reactivated the lock behind them.

The day was beginning to fade. They had about an hour and a half to make it to the cave. That should be enough time. Toby reached into the pocket of his trousers to retrieve his phone, tapped it a couple of times and waited. Brianna threw him a quizzical look and tipped her head to one side.

"Almost forgot to change the message. That's done now. For Raniyah."

Of course, Raniyah would have to know. As soon as she heard that message she would go into automatic. Brianna and Toby knew they would be seeing her soon.

"Best be off then, Bree. The light isn't going to last much longer. I don't want to be wandering about up there after nightfall. The place is hard enough to locate in the daytime. Are you ready?"

"You know it, Toby. Let's go." She smiled at him and took off with a loping stride. He stepped into it with her and they began making their way past Brianna's garden, and across the small orchard. Pushing the scratching undergrowth and brambles aside, then drawing them back into place behind them, they walked along an almost indiscernible path that snaked its way two hundred metres down into the valley.

They followed the path for most of its length. Just before it ended, it opened onto a small clearing near the creek. They turned a sharp left and disappeared behind thick undergrowth into a forest of towering white trunked trees.

CHAPTER FIVE

R ena pointed to the sofa. "Make yourself at home." She continued through the lounge and climbed the spiral staircase
to visit her mother's bedroom, to see her propped up on thick
pillows, sleeping. That's what she did most of the time since
the accident. Rena backed out and clicked the door shut. Not a
word came from Victor as she descended the stairs, stepped up
to the kitchen bench and began preparations for a simple dinner.
She looked around to scan him, sitting upright in the soft lounge
chair, his ankles crossed and eyes closed. Was he meditating?
She took a few moments to examine him.

A slim, yet solid physique, he looked slender, fit and
strong. His face exuded peace. A high forehead with premature
lines rose above definite brows and an aquiline nose. His face
was framed by shoulder-length, wavy, black hair, scattered with
grey. The one-week stubble on his face was not quite a beard,
though it fashioned two grey flashes on his chin. She guessed
he would be around forty-five years old. He was still wearing
his hooded jacket, though the hood now rested on his shoulders,
which were straight and square. Khaki cargo pants and a pair of
solid hiking boots completed the picture. He spoke.

"Looking at me won't get dinner made for your Mum,
now will it?"

Rena felt blood rush to her cheeks. She turned to select a
pot and muttered,

"Cheeky bastard, I thought you were meditating or something. How the fuck do you know about my Mum? Take your
jacket off. You can hang it on the back of the door."

Victor smiled as he removed his jacket. He stood to hang it then turned back to Rena.

"I know quite a lot about you, Rena."

Over the next four hours, through dinner, tending to her Mother, cleaning up, sipping wine and then late cups of tea, Vincent told Rena everything he knew.

"Man, that's a lot to take in," said Rena, when the silence reached into the last dusty corner of the room. She shook her head and rummaged one hand through her hair, "We both need sleep. I'll get you some blankets. You can sleep here. I'm getting some rest."

She retrieved two thick blankets from the overhead cupboard in the corner of the lounge-room, tossed them to Victor, collected their mugs and took them to the kitchen sink. As she was running the water, waiting for the heat to come through, her legs began to give way.

She gripped the edge of the bench hard and heard a voice, which sounded like her own, cry out, "Victor!" The whole world dropped first into an infernal abyss, then swirled with a million brilliant colours. Still gripping the edge of the bench, she dropped to her knees on the ice-cold tiles of the kitchen floor. There was a brief sensation of warmth around her shoulders, of strength and of being held, lifted and carried.

In that instant she was sitting on stone on top of a mountain. The wind cut through her light clothing. She was not cold. She had known cold all her life and this felt warm to her. It was dark, a more stygian night than Rena had ever experienced. In this place she could stand with no effort at all. Here, her legs were strong. She knew this, felt this. She stood. Inside her there was a mass of energy, gathered up in her very core, a rush of some faculty she had never known before. She felt powerful. Capable. Adept.

The wind stopped at the same moment she opened her eyes. She could hear some kind of birdcall. A night bird of some sort was shrieking at the heavens. She didn't recognise the call. There were millions of stars but they were not the

stars she knew. This was somewhere else, where the stars were extraordinary, beautiful and stretched in their majesty across the blackness of the night sky.

Billions of stars.

Rena gazed upwards in awe as galaxies stretched across the night sky. It was as though someone or something had thrown them there, a great glittering wash against the aphotic blackness. With genuine difficulty she dragged her eyes away to look around and to look down. Low trees with twisted trunks cloaked the ground behind her and on both sides. In front there was a clearing with low patches of spiny grass. Below the peak on which she stood, the whole world looked white. It couldn't be snow. If it was snow, she would be freezing. It swirled and moved. Mist. It must be mist or clouds, blanketing the land underneath this peak. The mist was rising.

She saw a taut-muscled, dark-skinned man come into the clearing and put a bag on the ground. He sat for what might have been a long time, if time could be measured in this place. He placed something else on the ground then began an intricate and enraptured dance that wove a filament through each of the elements. The staff of wood that he bore whirred in the still air. Rena saw him bathed in a light that came from a point in the sky above him. She gasped aloud when he plunged his staff deep into the bedrock under his feet. A shaft of brilliant, incandescent light poured from the star-filled sky. He stood as still as stone.

The image began to fade. Rena felt a gripping nausea roiling in her belly as a caliginous gloom took hold of her. Blackness, bleaker than death as consciousness failed her though she heard words that were a susurration through every cell of her being.

Eight words, both an invitation and a command.

CHAPTER SIX

Living alone had its challenges, every one worth his privacy and freedom.

Wolf upended his third scotch. The eighteen-year-old liquor slid down his fifty-four-year-old throat and a warm glow suffused his body. It had been an unusual day, demanding things of Wolf he had spent a large part of his life avoiding. He could only reframe, knowing that there were good reasons for everything that had happened thus far. Pouring a fourth deep scotch, he sipped this one. Years ago, Wolf had been able to drink a lot of scotch with very little ill-effect. As he grew older he felt the call to drink with a lot less frequency. It didn't sit as well with him. Tonight, there was tomorrow to consider and he couldn't hitchhike. Tomorrow, his sole option was to walk, north-west, up into the mountains.

He picked up the book and thumbed through its well-worn pages one last time. On the last day in this place, this book was a real find, pushed back on a bottom shelf in the antiquarian bookshop where he had become a regular. Wolf was more than pleased he had interrupted his list of chores to call into John's bookshop.

It would have escaped his notice, but he had dropped his pen. Leaning down to retrieve it, he had noticed that one volume stuck out a little. He had pushed on the spine to shift it back into line but something prevented it from sliding back into place. He dropped to his knees, removed half a dozen books and peered into the space. Shoved into the back of the shelf he saw the small book that was now in his hands. Maybe a little over a centimetre thick, it didn't look in any way special.

He had reached in, retrieved the book and flipped through the pages. It was filled with text, drawings and diagrams. There were handwritten notes and ceremonial designs scrawled in red ink across almost every page. That claimed his attention. He took it to the front desk of the shop and placed it on the counter.

Over the past few years, the bookshop owner had become a friend. He was a balding man named John, over seventy-five, confined to a wheelchair. Wolf remembered asking him how he managed to reach the higher shelves and the old guy had chuckled and called,

"Max, come and say hello to Wolf."

A slender young man wearing round, wire-rimmed glasses emerged from a back room and introduced himself to Wolf,

"Hello, it's nice to meet you, sir."

"No need for the 'sir' Max. My name's Wolf. I'm a bit surprised I haven't seen you in here before now. Do you spend all your time back there?"

"Yes sir, um Wolf, during the day at least. Most of the time I spend here is after business hours. John has a couple of height limitations which means I get a job. I prefer working when no-one else is around."

His voice had a pleasant tone about it. Not soft-spoken, but a kind of non-intrusive lilt that spoke of studiousness and introspection.

"Well, good to meet you, Max. I'll see more of you in future. I plan on spending quite a bit of time here. It's a great collection of books hey?"

"Sure is. I'll get back to it."

That had been over a year ago.

Wolf switched his mind back to finding this book earlier today.

"I can't find any price on this, John. How much do you want for it?" Wolf had said.

"Never seen it before," replied the bookshop owner, running his hand across his balding scalp. "I thought I knew every book in the place. Err, say five?"

Wolf had pulled his wallet out, found a fiver and placed it on the counter, then picked up the book and slid it into his backpack.

"Thanks, John. See you next time."

The old man had inclined his head then dipped back into the book resting on his lap.

Wolf felt elated as he waited beside the road to thumb a lift from one of the locals. They often picked him up and were more than happy to drop him at the turnoff to the gravel road that led the few last kilometres to his place. Today his lift came from one of the old men who had farmed in the valley all his life. The old guy loved to chat about everything from the weather to the sorry state of the world. When Wolf settled into his small cabin, obscured from the road by trees and undergrowth, he had a chance to look at the old volume.

He couldn't be sure just yet, but he'd had a distinct feeling that this book was important.

CHAPTER SEVEN

Cole was pretty sure he was becoming addicted to adrenalin. He loosened his shoulder and extended his arm in a final stretch to reach the small nub of jagged rock jutting out from the cliff face. He wrapped a finger and thumb around it, took the weight off his left foot and lifted the final few centimetres to gain a secure grip. Hauling his weight up onto a narrow ledge, he felt every muscle strain. A breeze cooled the sheen of sweat on his face. As he stood on the ledge he allowed his muscles to relax a little, gaining strength for the final ten metres to the summit. He looked up and began to climb, cautious in every movement, till he was able to rest his right elbow on top of the cliff and swing his legs up.

Breath coming hard, he stood on the very edge of the cliff and looked down. A strong wind gust shifted him on his feet and he teetered on the edge for a few moments. His heart skipped a beat and he stepped back a pace. That was unusual. Imbalance was not part of his vocabulary, but that wind brought both a moment of vertigo and some other message he couldn't quite unravel. There was a whisper of some secret, living in that moment of uncertainty. He shook his head twice, brushed his hand across his short-cropped hair and drew a deep breath. Turning to look across the grass-covered plateau to his cabin in the distance, he decided. 'Enough for today, time to go home and time for food.'

Striding out in the direction of the cabin, he felt his muscles relax to add a spring to his loping gait. The wind was cool already. He'd need to make a fire tonight, both for cooking and to keep the cabin warm. Maybe there was a storm coming. He

looked to the south and saw obsidian clouds gathering on the horizon. It was strange for a storm to come up at this time of year. Strange too, that errant gust of wind but there was no time to worry about it now. Better to cut some wood, put some logs under cover, and get food organised. His stomach rumbled in agreement.

Hunger almost masked the uneasy twinge sitting deep in his gut.

The fire cast a soft glow through his cabin. An empty bowl sat on a low table. Cole reached out for the poker and stirred the embers a little till a flame caught and flickered. He placed the poker back on the hearth, pushed the bowl to one side and drew the laptop closer. Flipping it open, Cole clicked on David's profile picture. It looked like he was online, but David often left his computer on, but unattended. Worth trying, he double-clicked the picture and heard a faint ringing tone. David's lined face and genuine smile appeared on screen.

"Hey Cole, what's up?"

"Hello, Dave. I just wanted to check in with you about some things that seem a bit unusual."

"Like what?"

"A strange wind, a bit of vertigo and a storm coming," Cole grinned. "Not much I know but my gut tells me there's something happening".

"Is there nothing clearer than that for you?"

"No. I just have a strange feeling that there may be a couple of glitches in the matrix."

Cole shifted as he felt this gut twinge again, "and my gut is talking to me".

"Are you willing to make a guess?"

"No, I'm not. It's why I called you, Dave. I thought you might have a better idea than me. You are way more across stuff like this. Any connections you can make?"

"Tell me what happened."

Dave folded his arms and leaned in a little closer to the screen. Behind him, in shelves that reached from floor to ceiling,

Cole could see part of the immense library he had marvelled at when he had last visited his friend. So many books. He knew too that Dave had read and re-read every one of them and could quote paragraph and line from many of them. Cole remembered being attracted to three sections of his extraordinary library.

An entire wall was filled with the teachings of every mystery school, religious instruction and magical path you could imagine, including twelve leather-bound volumes that claimed to contain the age-old secrets of hermetic practice.

Another wall was dedicated to connections, relationships, family, from age-old texts describing the traditions and practices of ancient civilisations to futurist writers of today and every step in between. One winter weekend, the two of them had laughed their way through relationship advice books from the nineteen-thirties to the nineteen-sixties. They had also investigated the wares of several boutique whisky makers from the island where Dave lived.

The last section was much smaller, yet had a far more powerful impact for Cole. Just a single row of rare books dealt with what Dave had catalogued 'Lore'.

Dave interrupted his daydream.

"So are you going to tell me, or do I have to guess?"

Cole smiled. Dave was nothing if not straight. Direct. Some even described him as abrupt. It was his way. Cole liked it.

"Huh, oh, sorry, my mind was wandering. There's not much more to tell. A strange gust of wind, vertigo that I don't usually experience, storm in the distance that's way out of season and this weird feeling in my gut. That's it."

"Did you hear anything?"

Hear something? Like what?"

"Elias has been busy, my friend. Might be worth doing some elemental ceremony and see what you can find there."

"Elias. You mean......?"

Cole felt a shiver run down his spine. Elias being busy could mean a couple of things. Neither of them added up to a peaceful life for Cole. Neither of them would sit well with Ivy

and Robin, and if things didn't sit well with them, they didn't sit well with Cole.

"Maybe I heard something, like a whisper. Nothing I could make out for certain."

"Do the ceremony. Call in your ancestral line. My guess is that you'll find what you're looking for. Maybe talk to me afterwards to let me know what shows up for you."

"That's all you're going to say, isn't it?"

"You know it, brother. I can't do it for you. Give me a call tomorrow, same time."

"OK. You got it. You'll be there?"

"Depend on it."

The screen blinked out as David ended the conversation.

Cole closed his laptop and looked around. He rose out of the chair and crossed the floor to a steel chest in the corner, near the fire. Taking a key from its hook behind the mantel he released the lock. 'OK then, time for some ceremony.'

But first, call Ivy. The call rang out with no answer. He left a message. She would understand.

"Sweetheart, I'm going to be out here one extra night. I'll see you both, tomorrow morning."

David paced around his lounge-room, deep in thought. His grey eyes scanned the spines of many thousands of books. The learning of many a lifetime was contained in these volumes. This could be the last time he would see them arranged like this, at his fingertips. There had long been a good reason to commit every word that he could to memory. Now he would learn how well he had managed that. He moved over to the northwest corner of the room, pulled the mat away to curl the fingers of both hands under a heavy brass latch. He pulled with all his strength. Though the door was heavy, it was still well lubricated. As he strained, a sucking sound announced air rushing into the sealed space. He leaned over and peered into the darkness. Even after all this time, it smelled dry and clean, just as it was designed to be.

Kneeling, he slid his fingers around the perimeter of the opening till he came to a notch. Stretching his entire forearm back from there on the underside of the floor, he located the switch. He flipped it and a dull, orange glow lit the purpose-built bunker.

As he put his foot on the first rung of the ladder, he thought back twenty-five years to the time when he first met Elias. Together they designed and built this place. Elias had been un-wavering in every detail of the construction. Tonnes of concrete formed the first layer of walls, one-point-six metres thick. After that first layer, the entire construction was wrapped in tough, thick plastic, then a centimetre of pure lead, more plastic and a final pouring of concrete to fill it out to the desired mass. There were no windows, no way in or out except for the airlock. David had just opened it for the first time since they set the space, protected it and sealed it.

As he descended the stairs onto the rubber-covered floor, he looked around. Every wall from bottom to top was racked with empty shelves. Looming in the centre of the space sat a set of sliding shelves. Each of these was stacked with books, but for one. All of the books were books of Lore. The few he had upstairs, the ones he had shared with Cole, were the first volumes he must return to the bunker as he transferred the library into this place. He spoke out loud to the thick walls of this purpose-built basement.

"I guess I'd better get started then."

The walls swallowed the sound of his voice.

CHAPTER EIGHT

Another late night and the skyscrapers across the city, even at this hour, were lit like beacons. Even through the triple-glazed glass of the twenty-third floor, Carter Nelson was certain he could hear the persistent rumble and hum of endless traffic. He leaned back in his chair and stretched his arms high above his head for a moment, eyes shut tight against the glare of the screen. When he opened his eyes, the screen still glared. He hunched down and began flicking through the pages and pages of legalese he was required to comprehend.

The reward for topping his class at Georgetown just five years ago was a key research role at Rothstein and Kill. This current project was one hell of a development plan running from the Catskills in the north to Valhalla on the Kensico Reservoir. The numbers had to be right. Abel Rothstein, senior partner, had appointed him to the task. That was a huge vote of confidence.

Carter pushed his glasses back onto the bridge of his nose and squinted at the page. There was nothing obvious he could find that would stop the development going ahead as Nanjing Development Co intended. His job was to find every one of those things that weren't obvious. Locate the small stuff and alert the firm so they could eradicate every possible factor that might stall a multi-billion dollar investment.

There were a couple of small environmental matters that would need some attention, but nothing that Nanjing couldn't handle. Both Nanjing and Rothstein and Kill had powerful connections with the White House. The law firm also boasted strong links with both the State Governor and the whole of New York State administration. Carter could see nothing that

couldn't be facilitated with relative ease. He flipped to the next page but at this late hour, his eyes failed him. The words blurred and ceased to hold meaning. Just then, the door swung open and Katy Reid stepped into the room. Carter looked up.

"Are you still going, Carter?"

"What do they say, no rest for the wicked."

"Thought you might be interested in getting a drink, maybe some food?"

Carter scratched his nose, pulled his glasses off and tossed them on the desk.

"My answer is yes, why not? I can't see properly anymore so, time to shut down."

Katy had been at the firm for the same time he had. Hired in the same intake, a friend since college, she was doing quite similar work, poring over documents and previous cases, looking for loopholes. She sat on one of the black swivel chairs opposite his desk, leaned back with her hands behind her dirty blonde hair, crossed her ankles and beamed him a smile.

"Have you found anything to worry about?"

He paused for a moment, collecting his thoughts, then sighed and started packing to leave.

"No, there's nothing much. Maybe a few eco matters, but they can all be pushed through. I still have quite a way to go, though."

Together, they left the office, silent in the elevator as they descended to street level, past the security guard in the foyer to emerge from a plate-glass doorway into Manhattan south, one block from Wall Street. A calf-length Burberry overcoat kept the chill at bay for Carter. Katy never seemed to feel the cold, having grown up in New Hampshire. The sounds of the city kept them silent throughout their two-block walk to a bar which the partners of the firm frequented. The barman had their drinks in front of them before they uttered a word.

Sipping her vodka and lime, Katy ventured, "Did you see the news reports about the protester's blockade up at the lake?"

"I haven't seen a thing. I've been head down in all the paperwork. Protests huh?" he replied.

"The TV said there were about a hundred people. They had banners, got national news coverage and made statements to the media. They got quite a bit of attention for just a hundred people."

"What's their story?"

Katy shrugged and screwed up her nose a little, "They seemed to be about water, you know, not poisoning the water supply to the city, that sort of thing."

"That's nothing too serious then. All our environmental reports say the same thing. This development has nigh on zero chance of doing that."

While Carter hadn't seen the latest news, small protests were nothing new in the short history of the project. There had been quite a number of direct actions since the announcement of the development plan. Every report and environmental impact study Carter had read about unconventional gas extraction had come through with the same conclusion. The project would deliver zero or next-to-zero impact.

"The damn protesters should just go away and get themselves a job. In my opinion they have way too much time on their hands," Carter added. He took a long draw on his Siberian Night and signalled to the barman to refresh both their drinks.

"Well, you're thirsty, then? I should have interrupted you a while ago. We don't have much night left." Katy finished her drink, smiled at Carter and said, "Do you want to eat something?"

"Er, OK yes. Here? Or did you have somewhere else in mind?"

"I was thinking pizza. There's a great new pizzeria maybe ten minute's walk from here that some friends were telling me about, if you've got the energy for the walk. You can get those there too," she said, pointing at his glass.

"Yeah, OK, suits me. I've been sitting all day. A walk will do me good. Will you be warm enough?"

"Not a problem. It hasn't even begun to get cold."

They sat together in a comfortable silence, both tired from their intense, focused day and possessing the ease of having known each other for most of their adult lives. Working together had put them even more at ease. When Katy finished her second drink, she slid off the stool and excused herself to visit the washroom. Carter nodded and continued to sip his stout. The door to the bar swung open bringing with it a rush of cold air and a solid, square-framed man in a wide-brimmed black hat with long, straight, black hair to his shoulders. He wore a pair of out-of-fashion jeans, a fur-collared woodsman jacket over a plain, black t-shirt and practical, brown boots.

In New York there's nothing if there isn't variety, but in this part of town, he looked a long way out of place. With the exception of two or three New Yorkers ensconced in one corner of the room, chatting and drinking – and the barman, leaning down to wash glasses at the far end of the bar – Carter and the casually dressed newcomer were the only people in the place.

The man removed his hat and jacket and hung them on the coat-hook inside the door. He walked the few paces from the door to the bar. Without a word to Carter, he sat on the stool that Katy had vacated. He didn't ask permission. He didn't order a drink. He wasn't drunk. He had arms like the gnarled roots of a tree.

Carter said nothing and continued to sip his beer. The man turned his head and looked straight at him. Neither his face nor stance held any threat or malice. He spoke with a veiled intensity in a calm voice, low but without menace.

"What you're doing, my friend, is never going to happen."

"I'm sorry?" Carter's eyes lit in astonishment. Was this guy talking to him?

"I'm sorry too. You are wasting your time. The land you're looking at has been sacred land for longer than you can imagine and that is not going to change. What you are doing is never going to happen."

"Do I know you?" he sputtered.

"You will come to know me, friend. We have a lot of business in common. Right now, we are just approaching that business from vastly different places. Right now my job is to tell you that you are wasting your time and that you need to visit the places you have all your focus on. You cannot know what you are dealing with from a tower office in the city. You have to visit and see what it is you are interfering with. This weekend would be a good time. Balsam Lake Forest. You come and look."

He pushed back the stool and stood, looking down on Carter's astonished face. "Bring her too. Bring her. She needs to see." Then he turned and walked back to the coat rack, lifted his hat and jacket down and put them back on, taking more time than any New Yorker would ever take. He left the bar without another word or glance. The cold night air rushed in as the door glided shut.

"Who was that?" asked Katy as she came back to her seat. She noticed the shocked look on Carter's face.

"I have no idea." Carter was stunned. He shook his head as though trying to dislodge something solid that wouldn't shake loose.

"Are you OK, Carter?" Katy asked. She felt protective and concerned for her workmate and friend. He looked as though he had seen a ghost. His face was pale and he looked shaken by what must have been quite a brief interaction with the long-haired man she had seen sitting with him. "Should I call the police?"

"No. No, I'm fine. He didn't do anything to me. He just spoke a little. Let's just get out of here and find that pizza place you mentioned. I'll tell you all about it over some food. Let's go, Katy." Carter threw back the rest of his drink and tossed two fifties on the bar. "The rest is yours, Ted." The barman looked up and nodded, "Thanks. I'll see you next time."

Ordering ahead, even at this late hour, was always a good idea to avoid a long wait. As they left the bar, Katy made a call and ordered one vegetarian and one pepperoni and ham, gourmet pizza. She and Carter had eaten together enough times to make

her pretty certain that she would have the order close to right. She wondered about Carter's silence as they walked in the cold air, crossing streets and dodging late night cabs. Whoever that guy was, he had had an undeniable effect on her friend with one very short meeting. She hurried to keep up with Carter's determined city stride.

When they arrived they discovered that they weren't the only New Yorkers to have discovered the place. It was close to 'standing room only', but the call ahead had secured them a small cubicle near the swinging door that led to the kitchen. Carter moved straight to the bench that gave him a view over the packed restaurant to the front door, where more people were trying their luck for a seat. Katy signalled for two beers from the waiter she had met here on a previous visit, hesitated a moment then shuffled in beside him.

The pizza cafe was warm and loud. The delicious aroma of wood-fired pizza wafted into every corner. It didn't seem to make a whole lot of difference to Carter's paleness.

"So tell me," she looked expectantly at him. He shook his head and smiled a little.

"It was pretty weird, Katy. He just turned up, sat in the seat you were in, like I'd invited him over, then spoke to me about us both looking at the same thing from different directions. Then he told me I needed to go to some place in the mountains and check it out. Said something about what we're doing is 'never going to happen'. He said that a couple of times. Yeah, then he told me to visit some forest and said you should come too." He paused and took a deep breath. He searched Katy's face for reaction. She looked flushed and wide eyed from the change of temperature.

"He said something about not knowing anything from an office building in the city then told me the name of some forest," he repeated, trying to recall the details of the exchange. "You know, Katy, it wasn't so much what he said to me, I've just been feeling strange since he came by. Maybe anxious, something in my gut, a bit, er, shaken up or something?"

The pizzas appeared, landing on the table in front of them courtesy of a pretty, young waitress who smiled a broad smile and said, "One gourmet vege and one ham and pepp and two beers. Will that be all folks?"

Katy dealt with the waitress as Carter pulled out his smartphone and began skipping through the apps.

"You folks don't mind if we put a couple of people here on the other side of your booth?" asked the waitress, looking like she knew the answer already.

"Actually, yes we do mind. We'll keep the booth to ourselves, thanks. We have some business to discuss," Katy replied, and tossed her bag on the bench opposite.

"And yes, that's all we want right now thanks." As the waitress wove her way back to the counter, Katy turned back to Carter who was peering at his cell-phone, glasses perched on the end of his nose.

"Balsam Lake Forest. That was the place he mentioned. The place he said we needed to visit. It's up in the Catskills. Balsam Lake Forest," he repeated and tapped the screen several times.

"Ok. Balsam Lake Forest, let me see," she said, sliding in a little closer and looking down at his phone. He had shifted it to satellite view and all she could make out was what looked like a lake in the middle of a forest. "Catskills is a big place, Carter. Where exactly is it?"

"From here it's just under a hundred and forty miles. Way up in the mountains." He paused to choose a large slice of pizza and began eating. Katy scanned the map from New York City to the lake in the Catskill Mountains. Last time she had been out that way, she wasn't yet ten years old and had gone on her last annual camping holiday with her father and brother. She recalled that it was cold, rugged and the best fun she could recall from childhood. The memory of roasting marshmallows around a campfire with her Dad and brother whisked her to a far different place than poring over legal documents in a city tower.

Carter finished his slice of pizza and reached for another. He looked sideways at his friend and said, "You not hungry?"

"Er, yeah I am. Just getting a bit lost in some memories, that's all."

She selected a slice of the vegetarian pizza and took a big bite. "Mmmm, it's good".

"What memories?" mumbled Carter through a mouthful of pizza.

"Good memories. My Dad and brother and I used to go up that way at least once a year when I was a kid. It's a beautiful place." She gave him a quizzical look.

"Feel like going for a drive in the morning?"

"What... you mean to the Catskills? You want to go there tomorrow?" she said, incredulous. Was this the Carter who worked like a demon suggesting a weekend away in the mountains?

"What did that guy do to you?"

"I'm not sure. How do I look?"

She took a moment to scan him. The warmth of the cafe and the pizza he had eaten seemed to have restored some colour to his face. In every other way, he appeared to be the man to whom she was accustomed. But he had just suggested a weekend in the Catskills.

That was not the man she thought she knew.

"You look fine. You were pale before, but you look fine now. It's not how you look that's worrying me. It's what you just asked."

"Well, I'm going in the morning. I'll be back by Monday. Do you want to come? I've been hard at it on those documents for a damn long time, so I'm thinking some fresh air will do me good." He reached for his third piece of pizza and started eating while looking at Katy, the question still in his eyes.

"Uh, OK. Why not? What time were you thinking?" she asked.

"Well, it's almost two now so sleep isn't going to amount to much tonight. How about we set out at seven?" He smiled at her, then looked away to get his beer and take a long drink.

"So we just go from here and get some things and meet where?" she asked.

"Why don't you come to my place and we'll drive from there. I've got a Nissan SUV that you've never seen, so it's a better car to take into a place like that. Once we're done here it'll be about two-thirty, we'll both be home by three. You can come to mine any time after that. There's a spare bed at my place you can use if you come straight around, maybe we can get a few hours rest." Carter sipped his drink and almost sputtered. "We'll stay somewhere in a local town tomorrow night. I can't imagine the place will be crowded at this time of the year." He looked around the restaurant and saluted to a friend on the far side of the room. "So, that's my plan. We get up at six, toss everything we need into the SUV and be on the road no later than seven."

"Great. I guess. OK. Ok, yes." She wasn't sure what had just happened, but from no plans for the weekend, she made an immediate addition to her non-existent social calendar.

For the next half an hour they made plans more like a couple of school kids planning to escape boarding school for the weekend than two executives from a major New York legal firm. By two-thirty they were done, though all trace of the weariness of their working week had vanished. Katy checked the bill and left eighty dollars on the table, though the bill came to less than sixty. In a popular spot like this it was good practice to leave a tip for the person who gave you privacy on a busy night. Carter pulled on his coat and opened the door for them both. A cold rush of air blew hard through the open doorway, scattering menus and napkins onto the polished floor. They left, agreeing that Katy would come around as soon as she had a few things packed. The door clanged shut behind them.

He hailed her a cab, packed her into it and set off to his apartment on foot. As he walked, Carter noticed that he hadn't felt this alive in a very long time. It felt like a good decision, this

spontaneous adventure. He also felt a light-headed strangeness and could not, no matter how he tried, get the face of that man out of his head. Nor the words he had spoken.

"Balsam Lake Forest, you come and look. You bring that woman too. Bring her. She needs to see."

CHAPTER NINE

It had been a long time since Ruslan Adiputera had managed an opportunity to enjoy time alone. His was a busy life. He sat in his well-appointed home office, draped in a crow-black cassock, surrounded by over three thousand volumes that taught, unveiled, discussed and prodded the principles and intricacies of every major religion and philosophy on earth. A small crystal decanter of liquor sat beside him on a finely crafted, three-legged side-table. The long, slender fingers of his right hand twirled the matching crystal glass, half-full of the liquid. On each revolution his ring sang a single crystalline note into the cool air of the silent room. Behind him, soft light filtered through a massive pane of glass in an ornate French window and cast indistinct shadows on a pile of volumes. These were stacked on the wide boards of the floor of the Cardinal's residence. He had called this mansion home for the past twenty-one years.

So very much had happened across those years and in the years prior, the impatient time in what he called 'the powerless priesthood'. He could still recall the moment when he had been accepted into the fold, the moment when the bishop had approved of him, laid hands on him and ordained him. He recalled going to his knees as a novitiate, a nothing, rising a little while later as a Priest of the Holy Roman Catholic Church. Since the age of fifteen he had yearned for that moment and since the age of fifteen he had worked to achieve his ordination.

From there, his career had moved with surprising rapidity considering the slow turning, intricate and bejewelled cogs of the machinery of the church. Sometimes he had needed more patience than his true nature craved. More often he had needed

to shift and slide in a hundred different ways, like a sinuous, writhing serpent, crushing its prey to curry favour. To raise his head or his hand at just the right moment - or to cut one of his fellow priests down a little, so that he stood out above them. So that it was always he, Ruslan Adiputera who would be considered. In that regard at least, little had changed, though the manoeuvres needed a good deal more subtlety in his current circumstance.

That too was not difficult. Experience combined with his natural competence in negotiating his way as a powerful strategist meant that he was well regarded in the circles where it mattered.

Twelve years ago the Pontiff had made him Cardinal Ruslan Adiputera. That was the minimum mantle he felt he deserved. In some ways, that felt like an age ago, the whispering of a different life altogether. In other ways, it was just a moment away, as though time had no relevance at all.

He lifted the heavy crystal glass from the table, appreciating the weight of the glass and of the smooth, golden liquid it contained. He tossed the liquor back in a single movement, shifted his frame in the chair and poured another generous measure.

Earlier today he had received the missive from Rome. The Holy Father had called the Cardinals to the holy city. It could mean one of two things. Cardinal Ruslan Adiputera lifted his frame from the chair without making a sound, bar the rustle of the vestments he wore almost every moment of his waking life. He took eight steps to reach the bookshelf on the far side of the room.

He took down a carved, mahogany-wood box on the shelf at chest height and withdrew a large, fat cigar. Twisting it between thumb and forefinger, he picked up an ornate, solid-silver cigar-cutter and clipped the tip from his cigar. He replaced the cutter with a sleek, black lighter decorated with an inverted crucifix and lit it, puffing clouds of blue smoke as he cast his

eyes across the spines of the books closest to him. He always smoked with his right hand.

Stretching a little to a shelf just above the height of his head, he drew out a leather-bound volume covered in the insignia of the occult. As the book slid into his hand, three photographs dislodged and fluttered to the floor, all face up. The Cardinal pushed the cigar between his teeth, making him look like a caricature gangster, a squinted snarl on a giant of a man in a black ecclesiastic frock. He bent down to claw them back together, to scoop them up.

His face became a mask as his eyes scanned the first photo, then the second and third, the fingers on his right hand shaking almost imperceptibly. There was nothing in any of these photos that could mean anything to anyone but him. Three different years, three different groups of boys that had chosen to accept the Lord Jesus Christ as their personal saviour. All of them had taken that immense step, making the commitment before the age of thirteen. He had been in his early thirties.

In each photograph he stood behind the boys, his hands resting on the shoulders of those nearest to him. He was dressed in much the same clothing as that which he wore today. Taking the cigar from his mouth, he flicked ash onto the plush Persian rug then pushed it back between his florid lips to draw in another lungful of smoke. He reached down to his groin and adjusted his genitals. Perhaps it would be better to keep the photos in one of the bibles, rather than with these books. Yes, that would be better.

The Cardinal walked back to his chair, his eyes never leaving the age marked photos. The boys looked back at him across the years, unable to change the expressions caught in the moment the shutter clicked. Depositing the book on his oversize desk, he sat in his chair once again, holding the photos by their stark white edges. He rested his cigar on a holder near the crystal glass then picked up the glass and once again, downed its contents in a single swallow.

CHAPTER TEN

"We can say to you with almost complete assurance and in the most exhaustive process we have ever employed, Ms Claesson that there is no-one who will even come close to you," Ambika Rouse said, "all five of the permanent membership have indicated their willingness for you to hold the role."

Anita Claesson was facing the windows of her office in a high-backed, leather office-chair, dressed in a charcoal-grey Armani suit, honey blonde hair coiffed, her hands folded, left across right in her lap. Ambika Rouse had been in the company of many powerful men and women in her time, so was capable of not letting anything faze her, yet this woman still gave her a prickle of unease that just wouldn't quit.

"When we started this campaign it looked as though Raphael Werner had some small chance, but with all we have done to lobby and intervene, his reputation is nowhere near what it was three months ago. The straw polls have seen you without any 'discourage' up to this point and on the basis of that, subject of course to the final straw poll proceeding without a significant deflection from its current course, we can almost guarantee that you will be the next Secretary-General of the United Nations."

The chair spun to bring Ambika face to face with Anita Claesson.

"Almost guarantee. What does 'almost guarantee' mean, Ambika? It's a guarantee or it isn't."

Her head tipped a little to the right to punctuate her question, and Ambika, always watching, couldn't help but notice the small, vaguely reptilian, folds of flesh on her client's neck.

"There is nothing that we can do that will one hundred percent guarantee your selection, Ms Claesson. You are well aware that we are dealing with those who are among the most powerful people in the world. Yet we have been able to be very influential in shifting several of them into your favour. The veto of any member of the permanent members of the Security Council remains, no matter what steps we take," said Ambika with smooth assurance, holding her gaze, "but that is the one small possibility that remains in the view of our team. That is, your team."

In just over fifteen years, Ambika Rouse had plotted and followed a precise course to the seat in which she sat. After publishing her thesis on 'Political Marketing & The Power Lobby' she had soon found a place with Ogelsby Multi, the largest and most successful advertising agency in London. Two years later she was their principal Senior Account Executive and eighteen months further on, she founded Rouseabout, bringing three of Ogelsby's major accounts with her. They had not been happy. That was their problem.

In the intervening decade, Ambika had guided her team to open Rouseabout offices in seven cities around the world. Although the company was nowhere near the size of Ogelsby, her client list was blue chip. She had first heard of Anita Claesson when she received an invitation to attend a function in Paris five years ago. Her host, leader of the party she had just manoeuvred into power, the newly elected President of France, had been terse and polite when introducing them to one another. Since then, it had been the aspirant Secretary-General that had maintained contact. Just the way Ambika liked it.

She had added the account to the Rouseabout elite client list three years ago and in just a few weeks she felt quite sure she would be ticking off another successful campaign. That campaign would be noticed in the halls of power in every part of the world. The payoff for this particular success was not limited to the ripple it would send through the advertising and political world. Within the terms of her contract, there was a

further five-year appointment of her agency to the account of the Secretary-General of the United Nations and a five-million-Euro Bitcoin bonus.

"In your opinion, who is the permanent member country most likely to renege on that, Ambika? Who might surprise us?" The Secretary-General-elect shifted her gaze, turned her chair to face the window, then stood and took the few steps toward the glass.

"There is little chance of any surprise, Ms Claesson. You will be nominated, that is without doubt. All five permanent member states have indicated support for your nomination. All five have stated their support in public."

Without turning, Anita Claesson said, "Which one?"

Drawing a slow breath, Ambika leaned forward a little, straightened her back and settled into the chair.

"How is your French these days, Ms Claesson? You told me that you were now fluent but I haven't had that confirmed in person." Her question hung in the air like stale cigarette smoke.

"Thank you, Ambika. That is all I need to know." She turned her head to reveal a taut, joyless smile that rather reminded Ambika of a picture she had once seen of a Komodo dragon. "I'll see you at the same time next week. I believe the appointment is already set."

She turned back to the window.

Though it was similar each time, Ambika had never quite felt at ease with the manner in which Anita Claesson dismissed her. Without another word, she stood and left the room, clicking the door shut behind her. Her client remained where she was, back to her Advertising and Campaign Director, motionless.

The Aston Martin DB5 Vantage convertible flashed along the autobahn, growling like a panther on heat. More than fifty years vintage and it still topped two hundred kilometres an hour with comfort, if not quite ease. Ambika loved this car. Shifting gears back down and bringing the car into city speed limits was its own brand of blasphemy, but the Aston Martin didn't

seem fazed by it and continued to purr underneath her as she approached Vienna.

Schonbrunn Castle passed on her right as she rolled the top back and let the wind rush over her and toss her hair about as she idled her way into the heart of the city. Soon she was standing at the window of her executive suite in her favourite boutique hotel, the Vienna Astoria. Her car was safe and secure, ensconced in the hotel parking station. While her luggage hadn't yet arrived, the bottle of chilled Louis Roederer had been deposited in her room in advance of her arrival.

Two glasses were perched on the bureau near the window, small beads of condensation forming on them as they warmed in the air of the room. As soon as she walked in, Ambika filled one of the glasses, raised it in a toast and gazed out the window at Vienna, a fragile smile playing on her lips, her body still buzzing a little from the high-speed drive.

A knock on the door interrupted her reverie and she called out to room service, "Come in." The door swung open and a short, neat Austrian man bustled in with her single bag. He set it down on the baggage rack just inside the door.

"Will you have your normal table in the restaurant, Madame," he enquired in English with a strong Viennese accent.

"No thank you, not tonight Henri. I'm going out in the city, so it won't be necessary," she replied, with some warmth in her voice. Henri had been porter for the hotel for as long as she could remember and had brought her luggage to her room every time she visited the hotel and the city. She passed him twenty euros with a smile.

"I would appreciate you reserving it for tomorrow night please."

"Of course, Madame, welcome back."

He disappeared quietly as she turned back to the window, sipping her champagne. This would be a brief visit to her favourite European city. There was some business that needed her personal attention with an American client that happened to be in the city. Since she had been attending to some matters in

Munich, it was a perfect opportunity to take the Aston Martin for a longish drive through the south of Germany and into Austria. She had stayed two nights in Salzburg near the border before the final drive through to Vienna for her weekend meeting.

Tonight, she would spend some time catching up on emails and communications, bathe and rest, then head out to wander the Naschmarkt in the morning. Once upon a time she would have been seen in the dance clubs and bars on a free Friday night, but for the past four or five years, she had found a great deal more satisfaction in private time and rest.

She finished her glass of champagne, poured another and walked barefoot to the bathroom. Soon steaming, hot water was burbling into the huge claw-foot bath. As steam rose to fill the room she removed the rest of her clothing, padded out to the door of her suite, opened it a crack and slipped the 'do not disturb' sign onto the outside handle. She clicked the door shut and returned to the bathroom, tossed in rose and lavender bath salts and lowered carefully into the steaming, bubbling water. Now that was good.

When the bathwater began to cool, Ambika got out and drew on a white robe. But for the reflected light of the city eking through the window that overlooked the street, the room was dim. She stood watching the lights of the city come on one by one, each one brightening the room a little more by the tiniest degree. A small frown creased her brow as she stood.

No matter what she did, those last few comments from Anita Claesson would not leave her alone. She knew better than anyone that it was impossible for anyone to make a guarantee that the voting system for the United Nations would deliver the result you intended. She knew better than anyone how much finesse needed to be employed to shift the politics in subtle enough ways to have an intrinsic influence on the outcome, but a guarantee? It wasn't possible. There was always a weak link and the best strategy was to align oneself with the weak link so, at the very least, you knew the measure of your most vulnerable point.

Ambika was sure she had done everything her reputation demanded to ensure Claesson would become the next Secretary-General. Sure of it. Those final comments troubled her still. She had long been willing to recognise her intuitive self as a guide. She picked up her cell phone and pressed a single digit. Holding it to her ear, she could hear the international dialling tones as the call found its way. It answered before she heard it ring.

"Melanie, can you tell me what's in the news for the past couple of days. I haven't even been online since I left Munich, let alone watched TV. Everything I'm going to get here is in German and I just don't have the patience for it."

"Hello, Ms Rouse, yes of course," replied her UK personal assistant from the Rouseabout head-office in central London. "Just a moment and I'll give you the full rundown. How's Vienna?"

"The inside of my suite is a delight thanks, Melanie and the drive here was great. What's in the news?" She was rarely abrupt with her PA, but the feeling in her gut was becoming more and more pronounced. She hoped it was just champagne on an empty stomach.

"The US President is visiting western China. There are quite a lot of earthquakes in the Pacific earthquake belt. Officials have noticed a disturbing increase in the radiation output from one of the reactors in Fukushima in Japan. The EU is getting tough with Spain. A new black leader in South Africa looks like banning GMO everything. Japan is poised to approve mandatory human medical tagging. Does any of that mean anything to you?" she asked as she scanned the international news site.

Ambika allowed her shoulders to drop a little. Some of the tension eased from her neck.

"No. None of that is what I'm looking for."

She raised her hand to massage her neck then said, "Anything else on politics in Europe? Anything on Anita Claesson I should know about?"

She almost imagined that she heard Melanie huff at the other end of the line.

"No, Ms Rouse. There is an opinion or two in various editorials, all of them glowing and everything in order. You would be the first to know if there had been anything at all on that."

It was a fair call.

"Sorry Melanie, of course you're right. My apologies, but I have this uncomfortable feeling going on and I'm trying to work out why. Thanks. I'll be in touch. Enjoy your weekend." She ended the call and tossed the phone on the bed. Maybe it was nothing.

She decided against heading out into the city. Perhaps she needed something to eat. She lifted the receiver on the in-house phone and dialled nine. Reception connected her with room service. She ordered a snack. They told her it would be ready in twenty minutes.

In Paris, the French President paced up and down his office and listened, his private cell-phone pressed to his ear. He nodded and uttered single-syllable responses from time to time, easing tension by clenching and unclenching his other fist. Before Ambika's meal arrived several countries away, the President's face had shifted to a pale, steel-grey and his lips were tight with fear and fury. When his call ended he had agreed with his caller that he had a distinct preference for one of the outcomes presented to him than the other.

"Yes. I understand," he murmured into the phone.

He sank into his chair, his eyes passing over a small framed picture of his wife and daughter. He rested his elbows on his knees and dropped his head into his hands.

Ambika still experienced the same thrill.

It had never been quite the same gaining a major client when she was working for someone else. Bringing clients over to her own agency was just an uncomfortable necessity to facilitate start-up. In stark contrast, securing a new major client provided her with a rush that endured.

That was the plan for her meeting tonight.

It was experience that found Ambika at the markets on Saturday morning, not buying much, but marvelling at the

colour, smells, tastes and general rush and tumble of humanity. It was true that it was a restrained bustle here in Vienna, when compared to the Asian and Indian markets she had visited, but it was exciting nevertheless. Also, she could remain anonymous here. She had dressed for just that anonymity, looking like a local shopper.

She sat at a small cafe and sipped her second strong, black espresso while she tapped away at the screen of her tablet. She was never able to fully relax her attention to her mission, even on this sunny Saturday morning in Vienna. The crowd bustled about her outdoor table as she reviewed the pitch she had been preparing with painstaking thoroughness for the past six months, working in tandem with her US sales department head and his polished team. That had been a real pleasure, she reflected, discovering just how good a team had been assembled by Kit Lawrence, her head of business in the USA. It had been Kit who had made the recommendation that Rouseabout pitch for the account. So far they had been well received.

This meeting tonight would be key. It had happened that the Chairman of the Board and his primary ally on the board were both visiting Europe to make an initial pitch of their own, so timing was perfect. Ambika wondered for a moment whether they had come to the city in similar style and then set the idea aside. They would have flown in from Paris or Brussels or wherever it was they were presenting. Corporate leaders weren't known for adding fun to their business.

She looked up from the tablet in her lap and signalled the waiter. He came over, brandishing a dazzling smile. She asked for a menu, which he proffered with a flourish. She couldn't help but smile. There was still something attractive about the old-style service of Europeans. She chose a croissant with salmon, watercress, Swiss cheese and capers and yet another coffee, then changed her mind about the coffee and ordered tea instead. It was not a sound idea to be too wound up. She reminded herself to stay in touch.

No alcohol, limit the coffee, get some exercise this afternoon, take a break from everything electrical for at least an hour before the meeting, meditate for at least thirty minutes. Drink plenty of water.

"Please bring me a bottle of water as well," she said to the waiter just before he left.

"Certainly, Madame. Would Madame prefer Perrier or Tibetan water?"

"Um. Fresh water from the Himalayas sounds good. Tibet water, please. Make it two bottles will you?"

"Certainly, Madame." He disappeared back into the cafe.

Ambika leaned back in her chair and looked around the square. It was a perfect Viennese morning. She had seen that there was some superb opera on in the evening. Of course there was always superb opera in Vienna but she had never taken advantage. She picked up her tablet to type a note into her Sunday morning calendar. If this meeting went well, and she could see no reason why it wouldn't, she would call Alberto, an old friend who lived near the city and ask him to accompany her to a Sunday night performance. She knew how to work hard and stay focused, but once the meeting was done, she could spare twenty-four hours. So many times in Vienna and never once attended the opera. It was time to strike that off. She smiled again. It would also be very good to see Alberto. It had been a long time. Business could wait until Monday morning. In any case she had no ticket to anywhere, just her Aston Martin to drive back to Munich. The thought of that was pleasing.

The waiter returned with her croissant, pot of tea and two bottles of water, decorated with a striking full-colour depiction of the Himalayan peaks. She drank the first bottle of water before starting her meal. Staying hydrated helped with everything else and she was impressed. This Tibet water tasted good.

Out of habit she tapped the screen on her tablet and began to search which agency held the Tibet Water account. That would be another worthwhile coup. Secure a brand that already had powerful distribution and sales all over the world. She

made another calendar note to speak with her Client Account Department head in London about considering how they might go about making an approach.

Ambika's tablet opened a password protected online database which flashed onscreen the clientele of every major advertising and marketing agency in the world. She nodded when she saw the name Ogelsby come up alongside Tibet Water. Well, in reality, it didn't come up beside Tibet Water. The water was in the product listing of Meranto Corporation. Could that be true? Meranto were into water?

She picked up the empty bottle and turned it over in her hand, checking the label for evidence. No sign of Meranto anywhere on the label. As she read through the fine print, looking for information about the companies associated with the water in Austria, her eyes also scanned the ingredients. Since when were there ingredients in water? She read the information again. It was a long list. Some salts, sugars of some sort, some additive numbers and several other markers she had never heard of. Strange, she had never thought to look at the ingredients of her bottled water. Ambika had always assumed it would be one hundred percent water. This was worth keeping on record.

Using her cell phone, she photographed the bottle, first the eye-catching, almost garish design, then the ingredients and other information printed in minuscule type on the rear label.

When she returned to her hotel suite, Ambika dropped her clothes piece by piece, leaving a trail from the entrance of the suite to the bathroom door. Her bath on the previous night had been such a relief. She decided to repeat the process. She twisted the hot water faucet on and as the bath filled, began to prepare for her meeting. She checked her phone. Not a single call. She couldn't decide whether that was a good thing or not. She collected the clothing she had dropped and laid out fresh attire for her meeting. A charcoal grey business suit, black high heeled shoes, black stockings, gold jewellery, a gold Raymond Weil watch and a Hermes leather portfolio that could be mistaken for a handbag.

All were understated and acceptable anywhere in her business world. All were part of the process and the theatre. She slipped her cell phone into the portfolio and padded across the carpet into the bathroom, feeling the contrast of cold tiles on the soles of her feet, turned the flow of hot water down and the cold water on. Closing the door part of the way, she gazed at her body in the full-length mirror.

So far, life had not done too much damage. Long legs led to fashionable, flared hips, a flat stomach defining that she had chosen to have no children. She liked her breasts and the slender neck she had inherited from her mother. People had often complimented her as beautiful. Until the last couple of years it had never meant very much, but she was aware that beauty in her world seemed to remain the premise of the young, and that she was moving past that. If there was anywhere that Ambika's sparkling intelligence shone through it was in her deep green eyes. She had used them to her advantage many times.

Above her high cheekbones there were some fine lines which faded as steam began to fill the room. Even noticing this made her smile and they became a little more noticeable. Despite all she had experienced, the driven lifestyle she had chosen, she had maintained a sense of humour and laughed with ease. For some inexplicable reason, she didn't feel much like laughing today.

She shut the water off and climbed into the bath. It was the perfect opportunity to combine bath with meditation. Shutting her eyes, she began to relax every part of her body, step by step from toes upward. She could feel the pressure, which had been in her head since sitting at the cafe this morning, begin to ease. It was when she was telling her arms to relax that her phone buzzed twice on the bed, interrupting the near silence. Damn phone. Poor timing. That was a text message from who knows who? She took a decision to check it when she was finished, but she was determined to have this personal time.

Starting at her feet again, she followed her meditation relaxation discipline until she was in a self-imposed deep trance,

made all the more luxurious by water at the perfect temperature. Less than thirty seconds after it had buzzed, inside the leather Hermes portfolio, the screen on Ambika's phone shut down.

In the same moment Ambika Rouse forgot the message had arrived at all.

CHAPTER ELEVEN

Thousands of multi-coloured deck chairs arranged on the beach were stretched far into the distance on dun-coloured sand. Even here on the beach, the noise from people and commerce flooded the senses. The insistent hooting horns of tumbling cars, skittish, wobbling scooters, rented auto-rickshaw taxis, lumbering buses and over-laden trucks decorated by a thousand gods, assault the ears as they wended their way to Main street and into the myriad lanes and alleys of Arambol. On the beach the sound was somewhat masked by small, pounding waves whipped up by a tropical storm that had pummelled the coast two nights ago.

Even the wash and flurry of the waves could not drown out the rumbling, mumbling motion of the ocean of people plying their daily trade. Tourists murmuring in English, traders calling out in Hindi, German, English and occasional French created a cacophony, each of them eager to collect a few hundred rupees more from the passing parade.

On the beach, a vast mixture of nations including brown-skinned Indian men, moving with a practised languor, carry burgers and chips, piled high for the European appetite. Others bore trays of genuine Indian curries, flanked by all-you-can-eat roti bread and Tiger beer for the visitor wanting a 'real Indian experience.'

White as snow English girls just arrived in the mother country prepare to sample Arambol night-life for the first time, applying layer upon layer of sun-cream, one day too late, to ease the livid burn from the poaching sun of their first day in the land of Shiva and Shakti. Fair-haired Swedes and Germans huddle

together doing their best to make sense of each others' language. They give up, in peals of laughter, reverting to English, thick with accent.

Fine-boned French girls, who stay more to themselves than most, speak French and seven words of Hindi as they flick hair back from their faces with a languid, liquid flourish and flirt with fit young Indian men who have come for two weeks from Mumbai to play in this place that isn't quite India.

Suntanned Australians look more at home than most, familiar with the heat, the women swathed in electric coloured saris bought at local markets or faded sarongs from their recent trip to Bali or Thailand, flashing more of their bodies than any Indian woman would dare. The men paddle around in knee-length board shorts, the cracks of their arses lurid and profane, sharing obscene jokes in loud voices while clutching the neck of a bottle of beer in one hand and what's left of a six-pack in the other. Here and there a mid-western American girl is getting lessons in debauchery she couldn't learn at home.

At four in the afternoon, the cloying heat begins to ease as the sun, disguised in sad mimicry of an iridescent orange ball, toys with an indeterminate horizon. The sky is dirty-brown with pollution, thick like the sewerage seeping into the ocean two hundred metres from shore.

This is Arambol Beach, where youth has been coming to play, dance and get 'fucked up' on everything from alcohol to ecstasy, hand jobs to heroin since the first trance performers partied hard right here. That was two, almost three, generations past in the early nineteen sixties.

Today however, no-one is interested in the history lesson. There's a party on tonight.

A warm wind blustered past Ethan's tight-bound dread-locks and buffeted Saffron's face, tangling her long, blonde hair. Underneath them, his Royal Enfield 550 is rumbling like recent thunder as they flash past open fields, dashing and swerving around innumerable cars and garish, decorated lorries. They scare scooter riders with the roar of their exhaust. Saffron could

never tire of this. Anyone wanting a dose of freedom in India can get themselves an Enfield.

Traffic began to build and back up as Ethan turned sharp right, then left and dropped through the gears. The bike slowed to a growling crawl in the market street, turning left to the beach.

He parked the Enfield just past the point where the last coffee shop and clothes stall gave way to deckchairs and sand, finding a slot between two other similar motorbikes, glistening in chrome and black paint.

Saffron eased out of the saddle and hauled her long leg over. With her hands on Ethan's warm shoulders, she pushed off to stand, beaming a smile brighter than midday. He sat there a moment, the bike grumbling. When he switched it off he turned his beaming face towards her, his straight white teeth framed by an untamed beard and moustache, his eyes a little bloodshot but twinkling. Fine lines at the edges of his eyes accentuated the shine. On an impulse she leaned down, grabbed his beard on both sides and pulled his face to hers, planting her soft lips on his.

"You enjoyed that then?"

"I did. Let's do it again," she enthused, her mouth still close to his, "let's ride it to the party tonight."

"It's the transport I've got with me Saff, so your wish is my command. Come on, let's find the others." he said as he lifted his lanky frame off the bike, disentangling his leg from the next bike to avoid the hot exhaust pipe.

Side by side the two of them look good. His thatch of light brown dreads and messy hairiness seemed the perfect counterpoint to her long, straight, blonde hair and the slender, elfin smoothness of a striking, pretty face.

Saffron is blessed with surprising green eyes, though they can't be seen right now as both she and Ethan sport expensive sunglasses. Both slender, he well over one hundred and eighty centimetres tall in black cargo pants, Doc Martens, a blue t-shirt with psychotropic mushrooms scattered across his chest, a single

band of tarnished silver around his left wrist and one silver ring with Celtic etchings.

She is just over one hundred and seventy centimetres with a turquoise, silk scarf holding her hair back to reveal a face and neck that conjures 'pixie' in an instant. She has light tanned skin, unshakeable dedication and a faded lemon-yellow linen shirt buttoned once at the waist and draped off one shoulder, over a white bikini top and a golden Ganesha pendant.

As the Hindu elephant god dangles between her breasts, thirty or more fine, multi-coloured, Indian bracelets rattle on each wrist. Her tan highlights white Indian-cotton shorts and, in one hand, her brown leather sandals. She's taken those off already, choosing risk over safety to have her bare feet on sand, feeling heat between her toes.

Traipsing along the beach arm in arm, they draw attention from all sides.

People call out; people they both know, people who know him and a few who know only her. Both of them twist and turn to smile and say hello, but stay on track to meet with close friends further down the beach. They arrive as the burning heat of the sun begins to ease, everybody hugs everyone, orders are taken and they eat together, passing stories backwards and forwards in quiet voices. They take time and temper with ease because tonight will become tomorrow soon enough.

And tonight, there's a party on the mountain.

Through mouthfuls of half a dozen shared curries, high piles of steaming hot roti's and dishes of yoghurt and chutney they talk about rain coming, crowds of people, riding Royal Enfields, music and, most important of all, who is in the line-up at the party tonight.

"What time is your set tonight, Ethan?" This comes from the deep-tanned Israeli guy named Asher who sports black, curly hair, a sharp nose and arms tattooed in patterns and sworls from wrist to shoulder. Ethan has been friends with him for the past eight years here in Goa. His new French girlfriend, Marcelle shifts a little in her seat and smiles at Saffron, her eyes doe-like

and her toes resting on Saffron's feet, moving infinitesimally. "One forty-five. I'm headline for an hour-and-three-quarters. Should be fun." He replies and smiles a half smile that belies the intense excitement he's feeling. He will have the crowd at the best time of the night. Ethan's high has already begun with nothing to enhance it but a headline gig, two beers and a motorbike ride with Saffron.

"When do you plan to head up the mountain?" asked Asher.

Ethan turned to look at Saffron and lifted an eyebrow in question, "Does midnight sound about right, Saff?"

"Yes, that suits me. I just have to get a shower, a change of clothes and some shiny things back at our place. I'm not going to take anything until after midnight. I want to ride the wave while you're playing, so I'm just going to relax and hang out at the house until we go. Mind you, I am going to dance myself crazy tonight." Saffron smiled a tiny smile and flashed her eyes at Ethan. "Meantime, I'm taking it easy."

She turned to Marcelle.

"You want to come and hang out, Marcelle? Ethan's got things to do and he and Asher can both come by and get us from my place at midnight."

"Yeah, I'd like that a lot," replied Marcelle, brushing her feet across Saffron's feet and ankles under the table.

"Sounds like a plan then, people. Asher and I have to do some business, so we'll see you later. Are you OK to get back to the house, Saff?"

Saffron looked a little distracted. It took a few moments for her to focus once again.

"Oh sorry, Ethan, yes, I'll be fine. I'll spend some time with Marcelle, get myself a new dress or something on the way, you know, some shopping."

A couple who Saffron didn't know very well was sitting at the far end of the table. They stood up together, chairs scraping through dry sand. They said their goodbyes with promises to reconnect at the party at twelve. That shifted everyone at once.

Ethan stood and came round behind Saffron where she sat, leaned down and kissed her neck.

In a whisper he asked, "All Ok, Saffron?"

She looked up at him.

"All perfect, Ethan, I just want to take it easy so I can party through till dawn. I want to see the sunrise from up on the mountain."

"Great, I'll pick you up close to twelve then." He kissed her on the temple and turned to Asher, "Let's do this, bro."

Suddenly it was Marcelle and Saffron, gentle flirtation in the summer heat, and three-thousand revelling travellers on Arambol Beach late on a Saturday afternoon.

CHAPTER TWELVE

The house was set back a few hundred yards from the coastline, surrounded by low trees that did little to obscure a wide expanse of sparkling aquamarine, the Pacific Ocean. A wide, open, timber deck, interspersed with random sized and placed terracotta pots, stretched out in front of sliding glass doors, framed in oiled timber on the old cottage. The weatherboards lived up to their name, grey-white with years of rain and wind and sun.

Sticks of driftwood decorated the front wall, strung together by coloured strings, shells bound in too, rattling in the breeze. Five green-glass, fishing net floats hung on timber rails surrounding the deck. Perched on the seaward end of the deck, a light wind cooling her on another warm day in paradise, sat Petra. Her head was down as she wrote in her notebook with a short pencil, making lists.

She had found this place almost two years ago. Some of those closest to her had called her absence an 'escape' but Petra knew it was a self-imposed sabbatical.

She had come here to prepare for this moment, to prepare for the call. She had known it would come after meeting Elias that Sunday morning, just four years ago at a weekend gathering at the base of the mountain where the band had played till dawn. Her memories of that weekend were crystal-clear to this very moment.

It had seemed such a slim chance that she even turned up there. Almost a coincidence with a last minute invitation from a pretty Portuguese backpacker she'd just met, sharing a backpacker dormitory with her the previous night. The girl had

run out the door of the hostel. Petra followed her and asked to know more. The tousle-haired girl had pushed a small slip of paper into her hand, kissed her on the cheek, then jumped into the back of a van full of people and called out, "See you there."

Much later that night, she did.

They called it a 'Village gathering'. Over two hundred people had come, it was cheap to come past the front gate and everyone had the biggest smiles Petra had ever seen. She remembered thinking, "I have found my place". At first she had wandered about the space, a kind of bushland campground, to see what it was she had found. People greeted her, smiled and waved, shared stories, joints and laughter from the moment she arrived until dusk.

She realised that she hadn't found a place to set up her small tent. Never too much trouble because of its size, she had begun looking around the campsite for a square of grass. She'd had invitations as she went from one or two new friends, to set up in their cosy community clutches of canvas, but she felt like making her own camp. She was firm but polite as she refused each of them, saying she needed some space.

As night began enshrouding the camp and the lights and lanterns came on amidst the flickering of campfires, she remembered thinking, 'Well, I might need the smallest space, but I hate setting up a tent at night' and then, 'I wish I had a joint,' had flitted through her mind in the same moment she first heard his voice.

"You can camp here, sister. There's a space right here near the creek." His voice was deep, warm and friendly. A dark-skinned man was balanced on a sawn log perched in front of a camp that looked like it had been there a long time. His tent was an old fashioned thing, once white walls and a green roof, now stained by mould and tea-tree. The front flap was held up by two twisted branches with the tattered colours of a string of Tibetan prayer flags strung between them.

For the first time in her life, Petra had noticed that when she heard him speak, she also heard him in some other way she

couldn't quite describe. It was as though she heard him both through her ears and somehow, inside her head.

Inside her body.

"My name's Elias, sister. It's a good spot and it'll give you a little space." He had smiled his big smile, ebony skin accentuating a row of fine, white teeth. He had pointed to a flat patch of grass, sheltered from the lights and noise of the main camp behind a natural mound of earth, "No fun setting up a tent at night".

It was a good spot.

"Thanks, Elias, was it?" she had said, questioning her own memory more than he.

He nodded, picked up a small tin box, took something out and began rolling it between the palms of his hands.

"Thanks, Elias. You sure you don't mind?"

He had just smiled again, inclined his head a little and kept up the gentle motion of his hands. Without another word, Petra tossed her pack on the ground and made camp. By the time she had everything laid out, her sleeping mat and sleeping bag ready and all else easy to hand and sure to stay dry, night had fallen. She stood up, pulled a deep-green shawl about her shoulders and looked across to where Elias had been. She couldn't see him for a moment. Then a red glow lit the lines of his face and made his eyes shine.

"What's your name, sister?" he had asked before taking another long drag. As her eyes adjusted to the darkness, she noticed he was holding the glowing ember out towards her. She had taken the few steps closer to him to accept the smoke.

"Petra. My name's Petra. Sorry. I just had to get that done before the light went."

"There's nothing to be sorry about." He had nodded his head at the joint in her hand, "That's local, from the bush here. Home grown. Clean. Don't let it burn down."

Petra had taken a long drag and felt the effect of the sweet smoke, held it in her lungs for a few moments before puffing it into the warm night air. That was the beginning. They had talked

from then until well after eleven, when drums and didgeridoo called her to the dance floor and Petra made her excuses and went to dance.

"Hey Petra, you came!" It was the Portuguese girl, flush-faced and draped in fairy lights, sarong and a bright yellow bikini top. "I thought you might."

Petra had hugged her and thanked her for the invitation, then a crowd of four loud boys about twenty years old, eyes bright, tripping into another world, had scooped up her friend and dragged her to the centre of the crowd of dancing bodies, gyrating sinuously to the drone of didge, drums and weaving keyboard. Petra had become part of the ecstatic crowd and become lost in the music with everyone else.

It was past three in the morning when she found her way back to her camp and Elias was sitting in the same place, with three or four others, passing around another large joint. The small campfire lit them all in a flickering, orange light. After introductions she sat with them awhile, listened to them murmuring to one another in a language she didn't understand, then said goodnight and crawled into her tent to sleep. When she woke the sun was already high in the sky. There was no sign of Elias, though his camp was still there, a pair of boots upended near the ashes of the fire.

She had wandered out to buy a coffee at the gypsy caravan where a sign said, 'the best coffee in the world'. A dozen others blinked like startled owls in the sunlight. It was good coffee. It was free, like everything else. Everyone here contributed everything. Nothing for sale.

The day had passed quickly. She had splashed in the creek to wash sweat and dust off then found food that could have been lunch or brunch, a couple of vegetarian pakoras and a big mug of sweet, spicy chai tea.

Just after midday the Portuguese girl had found her and she had spent the afternoon at a weaving workshop, a singing workshop and sitting in the shade chatting with a small crowd of tired, happy people who seemed devoted to saving some

energy for another night of dancing and playing into the dawn of the next day.

As the light began to leave the sky and the shadows lengthened, she had wandered off to her camp, thinking to change clothes and spend some alone time before another night of dancing.

Elias had been propped in the same place she had found him the previous day.

She sat with him and took a deep drag on the smoke he offered, feeling that same instant effect that had encompassed her the day before. Then they had talked... and talked.

He spoke of things that Petra had not even begun to imagine. He spoke of the Dreamtime of the land and the natural order of things. He spoke of the history of the place they were sitting. Not some potted history with dates and fights and explorers, but a history that spoke of the valleys and the mountains, the trees and animals, the water and air and the people that lived within those things. He spoke of how the land had been formed and was still being formed. He spoke the history of the place but without time, a history that was the present, the future and the past all at once.

Petra had listened, more attentive and more present than she had ever listened to anything or anyone before. As he spoke she had been able to see, almost touch, the things he described. She had felt the struggles of the mountains and the rivers, flown into the high places with the birds and slithered on the earth, belly to the ground as diamond python. She scrabbled and scratched her way up the trunks of giant trees as goanna and sat in tribal circles, lit by a flickering campfire, to sing and dance up the animal spirits with her brothers and sisters, the songs of the ancient people.

When the light of dawn had begun to soften the shadows and the flickering fire no longer etched sharp lines on their faces, his talking had ceased and he had sat there with his eyes red from smoke and no sleep, smiling his broad smile at her. She hadn't felt tired at all. She had felt more alive and more

energised than ever before in her life. He had rolled and lit one last, long, fat joint from a glowing ember, holding the end of the stick gingerly, as though the embers might jump to burn his fingertips. As he had passed it to her, he said,

"Not too long time now sister, people of all nations, all colours, from all over the place are gonna have to gather. It's close. You hear me huh? You hear me?"

She gazed at him. "I hear you, Elias."

"No I mean...." he paused to take a big draw on the smoke and pulled it back into his lungs, then let it drift out into the lightening air, "I mean you hear me in here." He tapped first his heart and then his head and ash fell from the tip of the joint and landed on the ground in front of his folded legs.

"You mean?"

How could he know about that other way she was hearing him? That 'hearing inside' thing, he couldn't know.

He had chuckled, "I know, Petra my sister. When I call, you come huh? You'll hear me. Maybe you'll even see me. You just make sure you come, doesn't matter what else you're doing. Just come." He leaned forward. "And sister, for the first bit, you need to walk from wherever you are and expect things to guide you. Don't resist. There are many perspectives and experiences you will need to have on your journey to me." He sat back again. "I'm glad you came out to this gathering. We almost missed you but for that young one from Portugal. Hey, we'll see you again when the time is right."

The memory was so enticing that she had been visualising it in intricate detail as she remembered, as though it had no particular place in time. She felt almost as though she could have reached out and touched Elias from right here on this wooden deck in Colombia. It was as though it was past and present and future all at once; distance too, meant nothing at all.

'Write the damn list,' Petra thought. She scraped the legs of the chair across the hard planks of the deck and shifted in closer to the table. Her pencil scratched another few words onto the page. It was a basic list. Just the things she would need to

put in her pack. From passport to toothbrush, she had always written lists like this when she travelled. When she became a nomad, she travelled light but that was the best reason to have a list. Everything on it was essential.

When the list was done, Petra went inside and packed everything into a single, army-issue rucksack and leaned it against the wall, under the wide eave just outside the door. She could not justify delaying any longer. It was a week since she had received the lucid message to "be bold and come".

She turned to face the ocean then walked off the deck, between twisted shrubs on a path you'd never find unless you had made it yourself. Soon, she stepped onto a long, white, empty beach. Stripping off her sarong, she dropped it on the sand and plunged into the wildness of the waves, loving the feeling of the salt-drenched water on her body. She swam out to where the waves were forming, slick glassy greenness and water lifting into liquid walls.

The offshore wind had been blowing hard all night and a good part of the morning. The swell was at least two metres. In the late afternoon sun she frolicked like a seal, diving through the walls, popping up with gasping breath time after time as the waves crashed behind her. Once in a while, swimming fast, chasing the suck and pull of the water, her body slick and smooth would plane down the face of the wave. Arms stretched out in front of her, steering and directing, she tumble-turned to exit tonnes of crashing liquid, her hair streaming and tanned arms flashing and ploughing to whisk her once more behind the break.

It was here that Petra belonged, somehow. Her ancestors had been close with the water for as far back as she could trace them. They had been fishermen who risked their lives on danger-ous seas; or pearl divers, diving impossibly deep with just the breath in their lungs. One great-grandmother had given up a life of comfort to live her life with a man who owned a riverboat. She had birthed eight children on the water, not even pausing to go ashore for any of the births.

Petra lined into the peak of a big right-breaking wave, swam hard onto the face of the wave then plunged down it. The power of the water thrust her body out of the wave almost to her hips. Just to her left, foam spat and crashed, threatening to engulf her but never quite catching up until, with a whoop of pure pleasure, she plunged straight down the wave, into the calm of the deep water. Bubbles warbled all around her, charging for the surface. The wave passed and she floated upwards to gulp a big breath. She swam for shore, walked straight up the beach, stooped for a moment to collect her sarong and disappeared in the scrub, back to her house.

Now it was time for a long night's sleep if she was able. Tomorrow, up early, leave the key for Tommy, the local guy she'd been friends with for all the time she'd been here. He was the least likely person in the world to ever leave this place. Tommy would keep the place safe until she returned, if she returned.

Coming Elias, coming brother.

Next morning dawned fresh and bright. Quartz crystals dangling in the windows flicked tiny pieces of rainbow all across the room. One on Petra's forehead, just between her eyebrows, danced around as the crystal shifted in the moving air and came back to rest there. Petra continued to sleep, eyes flickering in a dream. When the sun rose above the eaves and the rainbow dance was done, her eyes opened. It was a later start than she had intended, but there was nothing to be done about it. Better to get on with the business of the day. Plenty of fresh fruit was the best thing she could think of for breakfast today. Petra pushed the remaining fruit into her rucksack. She made a mental note to stop by the supermarket when she got to Buenaventura.

Her list was on the hardwood, kitchen bench.

Leaning over it, she scanned her way down, ticking off each item in her mind's eye, then scratching a line to make it clear that each item was checked. She had everything. Nine-fifteen. Three hours later than she planned. She walked to the door, collected her rucksack, stepped out to the deck and slid

the door closed. Once she'd tied on her boots, she stepped down from the deck, walked to the side of the house and dropped the key into a combination-lock, key container fixed to a steel grid. She snapped it shut. At the back of the house she turned off the gas bottle, rattled the spare to be sure it was empty and shut off the power supply. Tommy would do the rest. Knowing Tommy, he would be living here in less than a week. It was sure one hell of a lot nicer place than that little hut he'd been living in. Good luck to him.

She shouldered her backpack, strode out through the scrub onto the beach and turned left. There was a light wind at her back. That brought a satisfied smile to her face. Funny, she'd be wishing for an offshore breeze on any other day but today, this was much better. After walking a little more than a kilometre, she disappeared for a moment into the scrub and emerged dragging a camouflage-green, two-seat kayak. She tossed her socks and boots and pack into the front compartment, hauled the craft down to the water's edge and waded out a little until she was knee deep in the cool water. She reached in to the rear compartment and drew out a double-ended paddle.

Petra climbed in and set out for Buenaventura, the blades of the paddle flashing in the morning sun.

Mid afternoon on that same day, Petra's canoe scraped softly onto grey sand under a crumbling pier near the city yacht club. She stepped into the shallow water, made a little murkier by a constant wash of boat traffic and storm drains, and sniffed the air.

All her senses railed. The smells were overpowering because of the purity of the place she had lived for the past two years. A neighbour who often visited the city had saved her the trouble of visiting this noisy, smelly, busy place. The first thing she noticed were exhaust fumes. The first sounds were boats, cars and grumbling trucks rushing backwards and forwards, motors roaring. Hundreds of lorries and trucks were parked in service bays along the docks, engines running, rollers up. Box after box of everything imaginable were being packed and

unpacked, piled into storehouses, added to a billion other things ready for sale.

Underneath was the insistent smell that followed humanity. The smell of sewage, rotting garbage and the pungent odour of food cooking. In this city, most was seafood with the dank aroma of pork, beef, lamb and chicken woven in. This afternoon, every grill in the city must be heating meat, preparing dinner for people who had no time to prepare their own.

Petra hauled her kayak up the wet sand to slide it under a tiny, ancient boat-shed twenty metres from the pier. Dragging a heavy security chain through a stainless-steel eyelet, she lashed the canoe to a post and snapped the lock shut. If there was a need, it was better to know it would still be here.

Shouldering her pack, she climbed crumbling concrete steps, half buried in sand and made her way up to street level on cracked and uneven flagstones, part of a path that led to a pale brick building. Stain marks persisted where the letters BYC had once shielded parts of the wall from the sun. No-one had taken the time or had found the energy to update that sign for years. Most of the sailors Petra knew from this club now raced each other in the consumption of rum, dry red wine and cheap local beer. They drank with a passion once reserved for sailing, propped on low stools inside concrete walls.

Petra sat down to pull on socks and boots before making her way to the back door of the club. She fished in her pocket for two dull, brass keys. She tried the one she thought would work. It slotted in and she swung the door inwards to a dark corridor. The rumble of drink coolers, ancient refrigerators and male voices replaced the muffled roar of traffic. Stepping inside, Petra navigated her way to a wooden door on the left-hand-side of the corridor. The second brass key let her in, to be assailed by the musty smell of stale, damp air. Reaching up to the right, she flicked on a light. The small room contained an iron-framed, single bed, a bedside table and a high, dirt-encrusted window. On the wall above the head of the bed there was a dog-eared poster advertising a sailing regatta from 1989. On the wall to

Petra's right, two more peeling, ragged posters and a cracked, timber-framed mirror above a narrow, brown-stained, porcelain basin. Petra wrinkled her nose and tossed her pack onto the bed. She unlatched the window and pushed the panel up with a loud creak. The aroma-filled air outside was still better than the air in this room.

Looking into the cracked and dusty mirror, she grimaced at her reflection. The tap squeaked a little as she turned it. Dirty brown water coughed and sputtered into the bowl but soon gave way to clean, cold water. She leaned down, cupped her hands and splashed her face three times. That would have to do it. Petra wiped her face on a small towel attached to her pack then left the room, locking the door behind her.

The sound of mens' voices carried from the bar. They were louder than before. When she entered the room, the big Colombian barman tilted his head and gave her a genuine smile. He continued to serve a couple of ragged-looking grey-haired, bearded men. She walked to the bar and sat on a high timber stool. The barman came to greet her.

"Petra darling. Haven't seen you in here for the longest time. How you doing, sweetheart? How's that old place on the coast? This is a nice surprise. What can I get you?" he blurted all at once. She answered the last question first.

"Just a Negra thanks Pablo, a big one," she said.

"Coming right up, mujer hermosa," the big man poured her beer and returned with a pint glass of the dark liquid. "So what's happening? How come you're in the city?"

She paused a moment. "I'm just moving through Pablo. You recall I told you that one day I'd be likely to breeze through on a mission? I told you about that man I met when I was travelling."

He nodded.

"Well, today's the day. I got his message, believe it or not. Not on the telephone. I was out collecting some loco's off the point and a message came through loud and clear that it was time to make my move. So I'm off."

"Give me a minute," Pablo said as he shifted along the bar to pour drinks for two young men. When he returned he was frowning. "When did you get that message exactly?" he asked. He looked as though he already knew the answer.

"Last Saturday. A week ago. Why?"

"A woman came in here last Saturday. She gave me this. Said you'd be coming through in one week. She told me to give it to you, chica. That was this time last Saturday. I thought she was crazy because I haven't seen you here for so long. Here. For you." He handed her a long brown envelope sealed with a red-wax seal. Petra turned the envelope over. Her name was scratched on it in freehand, underlined with a flourish.

"What's this, Pablo?" she asked, looking up at her friend.

"Only one way to find out, chica. Open it."

She slid a finger under the flap and tore the envelope away from the seal. Inside was a single sheet of yellow paper. She unfolded it to read, "before you go to Phoenix as Elias has instructed, you must come to see me. I have gifts to aid your journey. You will find me at Aguas Calietes near Machu Pichu." The note was signed with the name Evita Huamani.

CHAPTER THIRTEEN

Things had become a whole lot clearer for Cole in just twenty-four hours. He had wanted to call David twenty-four hours later, but it was not to be. One-year-old Robin knew that there was nothing more important than her needs. Cole was never going to argue with that. Never.

He was more than an hour late to make the connection. When he answered, Dave looked exhausted. Behind him, the shelves, which Cole had been so accustomed to seeing bulging with thousands of books, were near empty. 'Empty space where once there was knowledge,' he thought.

Now he saw yawning chasms in the story of that immense library.

David had been busy, pausing for a few hours to sleep, barely pausing to eat, busy transporting every volume into the bunker under his home. Every book categorised, labelled and sorted by topic, author and genre. It was a big task, yet would have been far greater a trial had they not already been well organised on the upstairs shelves. His face looked drawn, which may have been the light in the room or the flickering connection, but was primarily his physical and mental exhaustion. In twenty-four hours, more than three-quarters of the job was done.

The plan that Dave and Elias had hatched all those years ago was being played out. Elias had predicted that by the time he made the call, there would be no time to lose. It was important to be swift, though there was nothing else to indicate the need for haste at David's remote home. There was nothing but the warning from the dreams of a dark-skinned man on the side of

a dormant volcano. It wasn't much to go on, but David knew more than most about Elias and the role he was destined to fill.

Outside, the wind howling around the side of the mountain and shrieking through the eaves of David's small house, sounded like sadness. Inside, the fire blazed in a big steel and glass burner, coffee bubbled on the stove and David sat in his soft lounge, warm and exhausted. Cole smiled at him with the fondness of deep friendship.

"You look bloody awful."

"Thanks. I've been busy," he said, taking a mouthful of scotch from a thick-bottomed glass, savouring it before continuing, "How did you go, young fella?"

"Elias has made The Call, right?" replied Cole, "and I'm one of the people expected to answer it?"

"I knew you'd get it. I'm part of it too," David gestured around his room, "but I have to get this lot sorted before I set out. Reckon I'll be heading off in about four or five days."

"That's easy for you, Dave. I got some things that make it a little more challenging." Cole pinched the bridge of his nose between his eyes and looked up.

"Ivy and Robin," David said flat-toned, knowing the answer.

"I can't just get up and leave them. I don't even want to get up and leave them," Cole said, "They are what my life is about. I'm not going to go off wandering to some black guy who just sends out the call. Am I supposed to abandon everything I've committed to in the past five years? It's not going to happen."

"Elias will support that, Cole. If you can't do it then there's nothing more to discuss. Just go with your heart, my friend".

Cole sat in silence and stillness for a full minute so that David wondered whether the screen had frozen.

"Are you still there, Cole?"

"Yes. I'm just sitting with that. So what happens now, if I don't set out? What happens? Do I mess the whole thing up? Do I break some sort of chain or process?" He looked lost. His shoulders hunched down and his face exuded a palpable sadness.

David laughed out loud. "Cole, give me and you a break. There are bigger things happening here. Just imagine for a minute that everything will just shift into place no matter what you decide, or have already decided, to do. Looking after your family, staying true to the things and people you've committed to, is just as likely to add the right energy to this thing as dropping everything and heading off for a mission." Dave stood and walked to his fire. He chose a glowing ember to light his cigarette.

"What's your choice? Choose what that is, though it seems you have already done that, and rest easy with your decision. It's indubitably not about leaving the people you depend upon with no support. It's quite the opposite I'd say, quite the opposite."

He shifted in his seat and took a big mouthful of whiskey.

"Have you read any good books in recent times?"

"What?" Cole peered at his screen as though that might help him to discern the random nature of David's question.

"Have you read any good books?" he repeated.

"Er, no, books? No, I've been doing a lot of climbing, trekking and being a Dad. I love all of that, especially being a Dad. Robin just had her first birthday, by the way. She's growing up so fast."

All the features of Cole's face shifted and softened as he spoke about his daughter and his tone of voice reflected that gentleness. "Dude, how is whether or not I've read any good books relevant right now?"

"There's a couple I'd like you to read, if you'd take the time. Since I'm leaving here in the next four or five days, I thought I might drop by, stay a couple of days on my way through and give them to you."

"I'd love that. You can come by here anytime, you know that." Cole was pleased. He had spoken a little online with David, but there was nothing, for either of them, that quite matched spending time in the same place, face to face.

"Great. Well, it'll take me a little while to get there, because apart from one ferry ride and crossing the ditch, I'm walking, so it'll be at least a few months. But keep a spot for me."

Always welcome, David, always. And you genuinely believe that if I don't respond to this 'Call' thing, it will all turn out OK?" he asked, absentmindedly twisting his hair as he spoke.

"Yep, it'll be fine. Elias always said that what is occurring is far beyond the players. I'll bring the books for you and I'll bring some of this fine brew," he said as he raised his glass in line with his camera, "we can solve the problems of the world one night."

"I'm looking forward to that Dave. I had better let you get back to work."

"Ah, no more work today. It's time to rustle up a feast, do some light reading and shuffle off to bed. Another cold, wet, windy night here." He leaned forward to tap on his keyboard and the picture disappeared, "Goodnight Cole. Call anytime. Give my love to Ivy and the little one."

"Yeah, I will. Night, Dave. Thanks for the chat."

Cole snapped his computer shut and sat back, looking relieved. When he started the conversation there had been some wild thoughts running, thoughts that had worried him in a way that nothing else could. Everything had changed since he and Ivy had decided to make little Robin. Everything had changed, and yet, the call of that dark-skinned man was a powerful motivator. He was a hard man to resist or deny. He had a kind of underlying power that defied description. It seemed to have little to do with this physical, three-dimensional realm.

He had felt him during that last climb up a sheer cliff face. He had felt his influence, but wasn't able to unravel the code. Maybe that was because he was so focused on hanging on. Earlier today he had visited him in that place where he seemed to have a greater presence than here in the material world. When he visited that place, the realm where everything morphed and changed with such fluidity, he had significant influence.

Cole stood and walked up five stairs to the main floor of the house. He pushed the door to his daughter's small bedroom slightly ajar and listened to her gentle breathing in sleep. Soothed by that sound, leaving the door just open, he stepped quietly into the master bedroom, slipped out of his clothes and slid between the sheets, feeling the warmth of Ivy's body beside him. She stirred and rolled over to face him. In the dim light of the night sky, she looked at him with a sleepy softness. "Everything OK?" she murmured as she reached out to encircle him in her arms and slide her body closer to his.

"Everything's fine. Dave sends his love," he replied.

"Oh, that's nice. Hold me, babe."

"Yeah, I've got you. I've got you." He wrapped her in his arms and leaned in to breathe the scent of her hair as she rested her head on his shoulder.

In a few moments her breathing settled again and she had drifted back into sleep. Cole lay there drinking in a sense of worth he had not expected from the love of a woman and the birth of a daughter. In the midst of that, he found he was still unable to release what he had come to understand in his ceremony. From bed, he watched the sky and did his best to relax and rest. Sleep visited just before dawn, as the new day cast first a grey light then mixed it with orange, red and violet as the sun battled to shift heavy storm clouds.

Looking around the bunker, David sighed with relief. It had been a bigger job than he thought, the final stages taking longer than he anticipated and the storage space less generous than he imagined. Now, five days after his conversation with Cole, it was done. Every single volume that was of any importance at all was stored in this impregnable bunker. Deep references of lore and magic, religion and science to copies of what could be argued to be the greatest examples of storytelling and fiction literature the world had yet produced sat side by side in a bibliographical sarcophagus.

Rows and shelves of tall tales and children's stories that fashioned world views at the most influential time of life sat

below the musings of philosophers. Neat rows of the unalterable recorded 'written word', some deeply at odds with one another - rested in familiarity, side by side. The straight spines of religious texts in military ranks glared at them across the narrow corridor in this vault, mutely disapproving. Soon they would all be closed, as tight and airless as their dogma, in an impregnable bunker full of words.

On other shelves, the memories of time in photographic volumes that captured momentary beauty, atlases drawing a picture of the vision of the geographical, social and political divisions of several ages, reference books and textbooks that reflected the bibliography of the finest universities across the globe.

A significant section for poetry, ballet, arts and expression, yielded to a specific sector dedicated to music in all its forms, not limited to the lyrics and scores, but well over five hundred thousand individual recordings stored both on their original medium and as digital copies, marked and stored alongside one another.

It could never be described as a complete collection of human knowledge and art, but it was extensive and in these times of change, of immeasurable value. David rechecked the digital reference and the manual card reference one last time. Both were in order. He climbed the ladder back into his warm lounge room. Lifting the heavy trapdoor, he lowered it into place and it closed with a hiss of air. He locked it and spun the combination dial a few extra times for good measure.

It was done.

The storage system and content that he and Elias had hatched all those years ago were complete. It was time to take the next step. In many ways the next step was even more challenging for him. The time had come for him to walk his talk, to leave this place and answer the call.

He walked down the narrow hallway from the lounge to the staircase leading up to his bedroom. As he climbed the steep stairs, he collected those few things lodged here and

there, things he knew he must not leave behind. A small knife, mild steel blade and hardwood handle, a pair of solid hiking boots hanging by the laces from the stair rail, his deep-green thigh-long waterproof jacket and two flint fire-starters. Each of these he collected one-by-one as he climbed the stairs. Each of these he deposited into pockets and spaces in a full-packed rucksack. He would still be leaving a lot behind, but that could not be avoided.

He needed to travel light, taking only those items for which he had genuine need. He knew that even this small haul would diminish if anything was found to be extraneous, unnecessary weight. By the time he zipped up the pack, it was after four. Drenching rain and wind hadn't let up in almost a week. Everything outside was saturated. He discerned that it was unlikely that he would make a great deal of distance in the remaining hour of light. It would be better to get a good night's sleep in a warm room after a decent home-cooked meal. He decided to set off at dawn the next day.

His pack landed with a muted thump on the boards of the lower floor. Following it down, he dragged it into the lounge-room and deposited it beside the door. David turned to begin his last supper at this hideaway on the side of a mountain. The fire was still burning and popping as he dropped into a dream-filled sleep just after eight.

When light began to suffuse the sky the following morning, the remaining embers came to life with the addition of three small logs. The aroma of coffee soon permeated the air, bubbling and spitting on the gas, speaking of comfort. There was still a strong, cold wind coming out of the south-east but the rain had stopped. A few windblown clouds rushed across a pale sky. In the east the sun was announcing its plan for the day but hadn't yet breached the horizon. For reasons he wasn't able to identify, David stood gazing out the window for almost an hour, pausing several times to top up his coffee, witnessing the light waxing on this cold morning.

The first shafts of sunlight streaked above the lowlands and lit his home with a golden hue, casting stark, dark shadows across the landscape. The valleys below were still bathed in a kind of molten reflection, but his house shone with a brilliant, golden light. His face, behind the pane-glass window, was bright in a similar way. So was his spirit.

In his youth he had felt this same thrill each time he was about to set out on an excursion into the wilderness. Each time he had been testing his preparedness, feeling more connected and alive than at any other time.

Today's beginning felt like that.

Whether it was the sun or the coffee or a great dream-dance of sleep, his whole body felt wide-open. He was ready, receptive, on-task, fresh and fully alive. He watched the sunlight crawl down the side of the mountain to slither into the valley. It cast a lazy reflection off the surface of the river, winding its way through the valley, conjuring a sense of calm. That river would be his companion for at least a few weeks, always as close to his right hand as he could navigate without upsetting the local farmers and landholders. 'The water of the river is a potent entry point to the journey,' thought David, smiling. The sunshine lit his face, accentuating the lines that life had etched there. It was time to go.

David took his empty cup, washed it with unnecessary thoroughness, dried it and placed it back in a cupboard above the sink. He rinsed the small, metal percolator and stuffed it into the top pocket of his pack. He ran the water one last time, cleaned the sink with the towel then tossed it into the fire. Hoisting the pack on his shoulders, he slid the door open to breathe the fresh, cold air. Frosted grass crunched under his boots as he took the first steps of a long journey. There was no point in looking back.

He strode down the mountain, under gnarled trees that clung to the chilled earth and made his way toward the river. The straps of his pack bit into his shoulders and the waist-strap pinched and chafed. He smiled at the discomfort, knowing that in three days, at the most four, the weight would feel normal.

The track was slippery and wet. Leaves and branches slapped his face, wetting him through, but, at the pace he was descending, he still felt warm.

The heady sense of beginning was still with him, driving every step. Day one was always a good day for the well-prepared and David had prepared very well. He climbed through scrub, getting wetter still, noticing that here, nothing ever dried out.

Green-and-brown moss and grey-green lichen covered everything. Above the wind still howled through the tree-tops. They looked tall and straight though their upper branches swayed and swung, soughing as only she-oaks can. Somewhere in the sound he could hear a different background, the sound of water rushing down a creek, splashing on rocks, heading downwards faster than he. He hoisted his frame over the trunk of a huge tree, felled over a hundred and fifty years ago. What must this valley have looked like before these mountains and valleys were stripped of their thousand-year-old timber?

The creek was bubbling and burbling in front of him. It was better to cross it here than wait until it was wide and impossible to ford without swimming. Stepping onto slippery, moss-covered rocks, he made his way gingerly across the stream. He slipped only once but corrected in time to avoid a boot-full of water and a thorough drenching. Once he made it to the north side of the stream, he continued downward on a path that became wider and easier to travel with every step.

Half an hour later, the land levelled out. He was off the mountain, beyond the tree-line and on the edge of a wide-open field. It looked to be a field of boronia. He snatched up a few of the small, round flowers and crushed them between thumb and forefinger. Yes. The capacity to identify plants was a source of pride for David. Maybe it was a skill that would be helpful on this journey. He sniffed the sweet scent of the bruised flowers and turned to look back up the mountain. Though he couldn't be sure, it looked like sunlight was reflected from the windows of his home. He could not be sure what he was seeing but he

was sure of the exact location of his home. One day, he hoped he could return.

The records, books and knowledge were as safe as he could make them. Turning his back on the mountain, David set off along the left bank of the river and committed to his journey.

First, rendezvous at Cole's place, spend some time with his new family then continue to walk. He was determined to join Elias, to answer the call.

CHAPTER FOURTEEN

A heavy steel-and-glass door slid back with a hiss the instant the laser identifier completed mapping Alva's iris. She stepped into the dust-proof, air-conditioned offices of Verity Global and walked along the corridor which took her past communications and marketing to the boardroom. Pausing for a few moments to check her electronic portfolio, she touched the pad on the wall with her index finger. The door swung inward with a sigh.

"Ah, Alva, welcome."

Simon Chant, Chairman of the Board of Verity flashed his brilliant smile. He had a genuine liking for Alva, his company Vice President. She had worked hard and smart to become an active, valuable member of the Board of Directors. Alva smiled in return, "Apologies, Simon, I'm a little behind schedule." She took her seat just to Simon's left and placed her matte-silver digital portfolio on the French-polished surface of the huge, oaken, boardroom table.

With a glance Alva took in the meeting. A brief scan informed her that they were the only two smiling. The entire board of twelve were all present. Considering today's subject matter, all of them were required to be present. It was now Alva's job to engage even the most sceptical of them in supporting Simon's push for the new technology that was contained in her portfolio. To her left, Allan James was already on-side. None of the rest of them had given any clear indication, so this meeting would expose alliances and allocate power. As a new Chairman, Simon needed his strategy to proceed. It was the first

crucial step to taking genuine control of the company, offering it fresh guidance into the future.

Simon was an impressive man. Standing straight and at full height, he was just over one hundred and eighty-five centimetres tall. He sported a shock of curling, brown hair which he refused to cut. Short hair was a long held tradition for the role of Managing Director at Verity Global. Speaking plainly and with a nested confidence, he outlined an introduction to the work that had consumed Alva's time and effort for the past fifteen months.

He was dressed in designer jeans and a loose, pale blue shirt. A neat but casual jacket hung askew on the back of his chair. Articulate and well educated, Simon had started life in middle-America. Even as a boy he had a plan. He began working toward it in earnest at the age of fourteen. Reaching the role of Chairman of Verity Global at the age of thirty eight was a major achievement, though it hadn't been without its challenges. Some of those challenges now sat in this room.

Her name on his voice broke Alva's reverie, and she looked around the room once again then stood to address her fellow board members.

"Folks, this is the sharpest of cutting-edge technology we are about to investigate. The reason I know this is that it has been in our own research and development division that the idea germinated, was developed and perfected to the place we are now confident is a fully marketable product."

Good so far. The room stood stock-still and Alva felt the heat of the attention of eleven exceptionally skilled business minds, preparing themselves to dissect every word, every figure and every assumption or projection in her presentation. Whether she liked them or not, Alva both respected and appreciated the company she was in, some of them active and astute in boardrooms such as this for the past forty years, some almost as meteoric as she and Simon. At thirty-three, she was the youngest director in the room, but not by much. She continued.

"The concept of RFID chips has been around for some time, yet it has also faced some pretty stiff opposition from

social activists, including some respectable scientists and a whole plethora of academics. The idea of a 'chip' being introduced into the body that has the capacity to track an individual as well as contain medical and identification data meets with concerted disapproval from a whole range of fronts, not the least of which circulates around freedom of movement and the right to privacy," she intoned, "so there is a firm pressure to advance the technology to a place where there is no introduction of an alien item into the human body. That is where the focus of our research has been for the past five years." She paused, aware of the theatre of the moment.

"We are now confident that we have devised the perfect solution."

Alva owned the room. It was as though everyone held their breath waiting for her next word. Although each of the directors knew that the research division of Verity Global had been working on identification strategies, most of them had no idea where that research had taken them.

"Fifteen months ago we decided to look with greater thoroughness at alternative ways in which we could facilitate an identification procedure that would avoid the injection or other introduction of a foreign body into the recipient." She lifted one of the folders from beside her portfolio and waved it at her audience.

"Nine months ago we had what we thought to be a breakthrough, and following that line of investigation, we have designed and perfected a technology that we believe will revolutionise the entire RFID industry because it is no longer RFID but DNA identification."

She spoke with the fluency and confidence she had developed with practice since age fifteen. She flipped open her electronic portfolio. A holographic image appeared above the centre of the boardroom table, misting and morphing for a moment then seeming almost solid. All eyes locked into a multicoloured image of human DNA, twirling on its axis in the conditioned air so that every member of the board was able to

witness the image from every direction. Alva glanced in Simon's direction for a second. He inclined his head infinitesimally without shifting his gaze from the suspended diagram. Alva continued,

"Human DNA contains a five-carbon sugar. At a basic level, sugars are molecules made of carbon, hydrogen and oxygen with molecular formulas that are almost always some multiple of CH_2O. In DNA, the sugars are closed to form ring structures. DNA contains the five-carbon sugar deoxyribose which provides the name deoxyribose nucleic acid or DNA."

Alva spoke a little faster than she might with another group. She was aware that some in the room had little time for the science behind their work and just wanted to know if it worked. Still others remained intent on the financial projections. Nevertheless, this audience was required to possess at least 'broad brush' knowledge of the science of their latest development. All of them were quick-witted and intelligent.

She continued, "The relevant science is available to you from R & D if you have the time and inclination. I can forward it to anyone who wants to read it on our secure system, but I don't intend to wade through all that today."

She smiled around at each of them, holding each pair of eyes for just a moment to reassure that she still had every iota of attention. Satisfied, she continued, "In this presentation it is sufficient to provide you with a simplified diagram of the outcome, and this is it."

The image in the centre of the room wavered a second, then vanished, so that all of them were confronted for an uncomfortable moment by each other gazing into space. A new image appeared which looked like a portion of the double helix of a strand of DNA, but the connecting material between the familiar double helix had been enhanced. A small portion of it glowed and flared to gain attention and draw the eyes to it.

That is just what happened. As it did, Alva softened her tone just a little to lure her listeners.

"It is this connecting material that is of most relevance to our work. The two helices of DNA are held together by hydrogen bonds. It is through these weak bonds that we have been able to access a doorway to the helices, to the identifying material of DNA."

The hovering image shifted and turned, then morphed to a closer view of the structure of the bonding material, which pulsed a little in the projection. Alva had made a personal request for that additional touch when she was having the holograph designed. Nothing like some living theatre to move things in the direction she wanted.

"In accessing the DNA in this manner, we have gained access to every aspect of that individual's genetic structure, their uniqueness, similarity, aberrations and so on."

She paused for a moment, picked up her glass and took a mouthful of water, then replaced the glass on the table before continuing.

"But this is the standout exciting development for Verity Global and for each and every one of us. Our team has synthesised an organic tag that can be introduced to the DNA helix via the hydrogen bond that not only provides us with all of this information, but enables us to add as much information as we could ever need to add. Medical records, legal history, family connections, criminal record, banking and finance can all be transferred in a simple and efficient manner. This can be done remotely."

The interest and growing excitement in the room was palpable, but Alva wasn't finished. She strode around the room so that she was able to see each face of each and every director. When she completed the circuit of the boardroom, she spoke again.

"In addition, with this organic tag in place, every financial transaction no longer requires cash, cards, RFID or anything else."

She added. "Once this technology is in place, nothing other than the DNA signature of the living person making the

transaction is required, which of course is an indelible encoding in that individual, not able to be copied or reproduced."

Now she was warming to her task.

"Every living, breathing human becomes their own bank, their own personal record, their own personal computer, storing every bit of information about them within the DNA code of their own body."

This was beyond ground-breaking. Every identification corporation on the planet had been investigating these sorts of possibilities for at least a decade and all of them had failed, until now. Alva and her team had cracked the uncrackable.

"This means also that everyone can be traced and tracked with ease. Thus we find ourselves with a process that means each person can only purchase via their DNA code and it MUST be done by THAT living person."

Alva took a long, deep breath as she caught Simon's eyes. "The tag can and will be subject to continuous satellite monitoring, keeping a real-time trace on everybody, anywhere in the world, all the time."

A series of images hung for a few more moments in the cool air of the boardroom. As the last one faded and the helix returned, Alva almost whispered.

"Finding lost or missing persons, escaped criminals, crime suspects, children - will no longer present any genuine difficulty. The computer that will keep all of this on record will be in the very body. It will be contained in the genetic design of the person."

Her voice gained volume in tiny increments.

"No banks of computers, clouds, storage banks; all of these instantly become antiques. The body of the host and every other living body becomes the storage system of itself and connection to everything else. The capacity of DNA to store information is immeasurable." An image appeared to enhance her words with a vast visual map of the expansion of memory storage since the mid-twentieth century. "I don't mean that in a figurative way. Nothing we have in the world has the ability to measure

the storage capacity of DNA. Our best guess at this stage is that if all the information in the world were to increase fifteen to the power of ten, we still wouldn't have begun to scratch the surface."

The image changed again, punctuating her points.

"How can I know this? Well, that's as far as we have been able to take it so far and there is no sign of storage lag, no sign of 'filling' the available space."

Alva paused once more, to add to the dramatic effect, and because it was somewhat beyond her control. What she had to share was dramatic. She picked up her glass of water, took a mouthful, then twirled the glass in her hand and looked at it quizzically.

She switched the holograph off, though there were several images still to run. Perhaps there was good reason to bring this presentation back into the world of gas and liquid and solid. As the holograph faded, she raised her glass as though in a toast.

"The most important discovery is the way in which we have identified we can introduce this technology to the world. It's as simple as this."

She brandished the glass, then brought it to her mouth and drank the remaining water.

It was a moment she enjoyed. Simon already knew what she was telling them. Every other member of the board looked a little mystified. Then one of the older members, Joe Steen spoke.

"You mean we introduce it orally?"

"Yes, that's true. But what else?" said Alva, her voice flat.

The next youngest in the room, Anna Bernstead shifted a little in her seat and looked around at all the faces before piping in with, "It's introduced in liquid form?"

"Also true but there is a still more important feature." The whole room went quiet. Alva let the silence hang in the room a moment before adding the coup-de-grace.

"It is tasteless, undetectable and is contained on one of the hydrogen atoms in water. Any water, all water! H2O. And I have outright certainty that it works. Not just because it has

been trialled on over twenty thousand animals in our labs. We have also trialled this technology, this 'giant leap' on over two thousand University Students. In addition, because I like to be certain, I have trialled it on myself. You may rest assured that this technology has been tested with scientific rigour. It works. It's faultless, one hundred percent accurate and as far as we can determine... irreversible."

CHAPTER FIFTEEN

At a precise fifty degrees centigrade and ninety percent relative humidity, the air was so thick it was difficult to breathe.

Vivid green plants of a thousand different varieties stretched into the distance, perfect straight lines in frosted aluminium channels, exactly eight hundred millimetres from a floor composed of twenty millimetres of hard, rubber infused concrete that helped to keep the temperature and humidity precise. Three thousand hectares divided into fifty-hectare sections, each a micro-controlled environment. Three additional levels towered above the ground-floor planting, under a steel-framed, triple-glazed, bulletproof-glass roof, twenty-five metres above the ground.

It was an impressive research centre.

Seventy-five percent of the funding was provided by three major corporations, all of which had an annual turnover greater than the gross domestic product of any nation in the world. The other twenty-five percent was provided by the governments of the top twenty industrialised nations of the world.

There had been some argument between nations about where the facility would be located but Meranto Corp, the biggest and most aggressive of the corporates had put a stop to that by declaring that it would be located on their property in China, in the centre of a parcel of land that was bigger than most European nations.

Once they stepped in, arguments ceased. They were, after all, responsible for forty percent of the funding and the three major trade agreements in place across the globe had been

brokered by their CEO, Mara Lin. No politician wanted to risk being on the wrong side of that. Though Europe and the US were not happy with the decision, it was final and incontestable.

Right now, Mara Lin was struggling to breathe the thick, moist air in TropPlus5. A sheen of sweat covered her face and dampened the top of a light scarf, tied in a loose knot around her slender neck. Her white, silk shirt clung to her skin while her navy, silk trousers showed deep creases where she had been sitting. She travelled in the electric people-mover the centre used to ferry everything from seedlings to VIPs.

It was irrefutable that today was a VIP day.

"Is there any improvement on the growth rates of any species in these conditions?" asked the slight-built CEO, in perfect English. She walked along the aisle between the aluminium growing lanes, brushing her hand through the leaves of the nearest plants as she advanced into the space, "This is one of the most crucial trials in my estimation."

The principal biologist for the research centre, Dr Flynn O'Reilly was today both her driver and guide. The two of them had been working together for the past twelve years. Both had been educated at Tsinghau University in Beijing. He shook his head and took the few extra steps to come into pace with her as she continued down the corridor. His worn, khaki shirt was saturated with sweat.

"Quite the contrary regarding growth rates, Ms Lin. The best we have been able to achieve is two points less than we were achieving this time last year. Some of the strains are exhibiting significant signs of stress. Some are exhibiting some quite serious wilting. We're not expecting yields to match those achieved earlier this year. We haven't been able to isolate the problem just yet, but I believe we're close."

"How close?" She stopped and turned to face him, looking him in the eyes. "You do understand how important this is to the overall result?"

"Of course I do. I expect the research team will isolate the problem before the end of the week. If we are able to recover

the existing specimens, that will delay the project by ten days. If not, no more than four weeks."

A combination of sweat and the cloying moisture in the air dripped from Flynn's nose and chin. He drew a cloth out of his trouser pocket and wiped his face, annoyance showing in his movements. "We've had replacement samples growing for the past twenty-three days in similar conditions to limit the delay."

"Similar conditions? How similar?" Her voice was devoid of emotion and sounded equally devoid of stress.

"Five degrees cooler, ten off the relative humidity."

"That's a significant difference,' she said, "will the results still be valid, in your opinion?"

Flynn paused before answering. She was as close to as good a biologist as he, so misleading her was impossible. He chose his response with appropriate care.

"Ms Lin, we have made every effort to bring the temperature up to the trial site and match the humidity. It begins to give us the same result within forty-eight hours, so I decided to ensure we had samples rather than damaging our replacement stock. The chem research team are working on a chemical alteration of the Xs5D hormone composition but they haven't been able to provide us with an operable product to date."

"That doesn't answer my question."

"The results will still be valuable, if not valid within the perimeter of the trial restraints."

She gazed at him silently for almost a full minute.

"Show me where it's failing, show me the plants." Her voice was ice.

"Yes of course. Come this way."

Flynn walked ten paces to the end of one of the long silver trays and turned left with Mara Lin two paces behind. He crossed twenty rows before taking a right and continuing down the new corridor, indistinguishable from the corridor they had left but for an identifying number stamped every three metres on the sides of the trays. They walked for five minutes. With each step the problem became transparent.

Where they had been, the plants were a vibrant green, copiously leafy and vigorous. Here many of them were in an advanced state of wilt, the leaves sagging on the stems, yellowed and unpalatable. Some exhibited a rim of burnt brown on the tips of their broad leaves. In the section hardest hit, one in twenty plants were nothing more than a blackened stem, leaves rotting down into the base of the stem and white fungus forming to complete the process.

"How did fungus get in here?" she asked. The muscles in her neck tight, the first sign of her recognition of the potential enormity of the problem.

"I don't know." Deadpan. Flynn knew it was the wrong answer, but had no other answer to give. Mara Lin turned on him.

"You have to know, Doctor O'Reilly. We pay you damn well to know what the hell is going on in this multi-billion-dollar research centre." Now her voice was hard, cold and pure business.

"I'm aware of that. It's being investigated as we speak. First thing we checked was vehicles, staff, clothing and the health of everyone who came in here. The growing agent has had thorough investigation. All those investigations have yielded nothing. All show to be one hundred percent clean and clear. Currently we're doing a progressive analysis of the air conditioning filtration system, starting with the closest one to this location, those four units." He pointed to each of the four massive air conditioning units in direct line-of-sight of the corridor in which they stood. "Results are expected back on those in forty-eight hours and on the rest of the units in this pod forty-eight hours after that." He paused and took a deep breath of the stifling air.

"I'm in the process of knowing right now," he continued, "It first presented just after two yesterday morning. That's the first time there was any sign of it at all. It formed without warning and the process seems to be accelerating".

Mara Lin looked up to the rows that towered above them. Flynn spoke before she had the chance to voice her next question.

"It's affecting all the levels. An approximate area of four and a half hectares is now affected and that is growing at a rate that we are able to measure every ten minutes. Twelve hours ago we could only take a valid measurement once an hour. It's escalating fast."

"Shut the whole pod down immediately."

"Ms Lin, that's fifty hectares of product, not to mention the opportunity we have to investigate a whole range of factors, including the origination of that fungus. The scientific implications are going to be invaluable. If we shut it....."

Flynn wasn't allowed to complete his sentence. Chief Executive Officer Mara Lin was brutally accustomed to having her decisions actioned the moment they were out of her mouth. She spoke without emotion. "You are also terminated here, Doctor O'Reilly, effective immediately. We have no further use for your services. I'll find my own way out. Please do the same."

It was as though one of those heavy wooden things that they used to set on the shoulders of bullocks had been removed. Flynn could see pictures in books from his childhood. He recalled them in rice fields. He recalled them from further back in history, when white men pillaged the forests of nations where trees had been growing untouched for thousands of years. Sepia stained photographs of a dozen hard-looking men slouched around a fresh sawn tree whose trunk had a diameter five times their height. There was usually a bullock team in there somewhere too, all wearing those things, dragging timber out of rough country.

'Yokes... That was it.' Flynn felt a surge of elation.

It felt as though a yoke that had been growing in weight by the day had been lifted swiftly and painlessly and placed on the shoulders of some other poor fool. He could have been feeling sorry for himself, but Flynn O'Reilly could not stop smiling. The front window of his apartment overlooked the Luban Reservoir,

shining water stretched almost to the horizon, dotted with sails and surrounded by grass-covered hills. He was more pleased than ever that he had insisted on separating from the research centre accommodation he had been offered when he first took the position as Chief Operational Biologist at Meranto.

Flynn had always honoured a deep sense of privacy. Choosing a place that he was to lay his head each night was critical to that freedom, and right now, his choice felt good. He had seen other Meranto people find themselves out of work without notice. That had meant they were also out of house and home, all benefits instantly removed, with no other choice than to get to the airport as unobtrusively as possible and fly somewhere else.

Anywhere was better than being near to Chengdu once Meranto was done with you, because everything 'business' in Chengdu was Meranto. Banking, housing, media, travel, enforcement, health and even tourism made useful asides to the principal business. Meranto boasted two primary streams – supplying industrialised genetically altered food to a fast-growing global population and siphoning massive amounts of fresh water from the area once known as Tibet, adding a range of additives and selling that to the same market. But that was far from the end of the reach of its groping tentacles.

Typical of the company, it had secured worldwide rights to the name of the overthrown nation and had branded the water with that name. Rumour had it that over ninety percent of the people on the planet had consumed Tibet Water, Meranto branded spring and glacial water. Meranto had literally consumed Tibet's greatest gift to life on earth. The cleanest source of water in a world where clean meant something quite different to what it had less than thirty years ago and of course, Meranto branded water was loaded with additives. They were this year bottling over three hundred billion litres of water in a world market that showed no sign of slowing down.

Despite all this, Flynn O'Reilly could not stop smiling.

Damn the whole bloody affair, damn the company that had made him a quietly wealthy man and damn that cold, soulless woman called Mara Lin. He was glad to be out and had plenty of time to sort things out and decide what to do with his career and, come to think of it, with the rest of his life. Funny that he was one of those rare people who had taken a decision many years ago to never consume a single bottle of Tibet water.

Not one bottle, not even one mouthful.

Since he'd managed to hold to that promise all this time, even the past twelve years while the company compensated him for his expertise, he took a silent decision to continue his personal pact.

He looked around the room, trying to locate his personal water-bottle. It was a beaten-up metal container, once blue but now worn, scratched and beaten to the silver sheen of stainless steel. He'd had it for so many years now. The replaceable filters inside the lid meant that he could drink almost any water from any source, anywhere. He'd had the same kind of filters installed in his home. When he first arrived, he'd tapped his plumbing out of the city water supply and straight into the lake that lay in front of the house.

His practice before he began working for Meranto had been drinking local water from wherever he was through those filters. For some reason he'd been even more disciplined about that since he had begun working in this part of the world. The Chinese may well be leading the world in environmental innovation these days, but only after they had partnered with companies such as Meranto and drowned every fresh water source with more heavy metals, glyphosate and other poisons than any reasonable scientist could imagine. That was why Meranto and the Chinese government had to have Tibet.

It was all about the water.

Flynn, on the other hand, had a particular distaste about drinking water stolen from the Tibetans.

He made a conscious choice for the only other option, water from the lake, filtered by the best filters in the world.

Where could that bottle be? He walked through the front room, searched kitchen and bedroom, turned the place upside down. He looked in places he knew it couldn't be, then looked again. Where the hell was it?

He grabbed a glass and filled it from the filter tap above his sink to quench his thirst, but it was going to take longer to quench his need to find that bloody water bottle. Flynn cast his methodical mind back over the previous few days. Blessed with a razor-sharp acuity, he could fashion a clear memory of every waking moment in almost any time-frame. On this occasion, he could not remember. That was extraordinary. The remaining possibility was that it was still at the research centre. If that was the case, it would have to stay there. His clearance pass had been revoked within a minute of his dismissal leaving Mara Lin's mouth. The pass-code let him out, but it would categorically not let him back in. Damn that woman.

He reached under his bed and slid out a small metal box, unclipped the lid and opened it. A half dozen blue stainless-steel bottles lay inside. He chose one and twisted it open to check that the filter was in place. Satisfied, he closed the box and went back into the kitchen to fill his new bottle. He must have left it at the research centre. No problem. It was time for a new one.

Now, plans for the future.

Tibet. Not the water, the country. It didn't have 'official' recognition as Tibet any more, but Flynn liked to remember a time when it was. Keeping the name alive in his head helped with that. Tibet. He would go to Tibet and maybe just keep going from there, down through Nepal and into the north of India. The Chinese had built several roads all the way through to the Indian border and though the landslides continued to disrupt the flow of traffic they had hoped to achieve, the road was still quite often passable. Well, that was easy. Rugged, magnificent Tibet was the destination but not quite yet.

If he was going to head off into country like that he would need to have more physical strength than a research scientist before he went. He sat down and spoke out loud to the wifi-alert,

wide-glass screen that looked to be hovering above his desk. "Fitness programme, altitude above four thousand metres on motorbike and on foot."

The screen answered him. 'Searching.'

CHAPTER SIXTEEN

Today was going to be a full day. Not that it was different from almost any day on Grey's schedule. He tumbled out of his king-size bed at five o'clock and began dressing for his morning run. It was still pitch-black outside. He pulled on black shorts, a maroon, sleeveless sweatshirt, socks and runners. In the kitchen he poured a glass of water and drank it slowly. He stirred glucose and protein powder into a second glass and drank that too. Grey possessed the habits of a methodical man.

He wrapped the band of his heart monitor and pace counter on his wrist. Stepping outside, he stretched his arms back and forth, up over his head and reached down to his toes, stretching his back. At the front fence, he spent five minutes stretching his legs, feeling his muscles warm and the sleep shift out of his body.

He would run ten kilometres again today. In the biting cold, ice still slow melting on dirt-brown puddles in the street, he began to jog past an array of houses. In the semi-dark of street lights, they all looked so similar to his own, the houses of the well-to-do. A line backed by so many other lines of neat buildings with neat yards and neat front doors providing barriers to who knows what lay inside? His years of medicine had taught him that the mask people wore had little to do with the lives they lived.

These neat and tidy facades had no bearing at all on the reality of people's existence.

Grey had his first appointment at nine-thirty. There were a whole range of matters to attend to before that, so the run must take no more than one hour. He increased his pace and felt the

familiar discomfort of pushing his way into a rhythm. Turning into this street and that, following a path that he'd travelled many times before, he soon came to the enormous park. It was just a seven-minute run from his home, at this hour, a landscape of light and shadow.

As he passed the gates, he increased his pace, muscles loosening to find that all-important rhythm. He had disciplined his mind to think of nothing at all as he wove his way into a landscape of short-cropped grass, neat lines of rose bushes, clumps of trees, over-arching oaks, tall, slender birch, towering, expansive pines and all the smells that accompanied them. With nothing to think about, his shoes making a slight, slapping noise on the pavement, his body beginning to step out without conscious effort, Grey's mind travelled of its own volition to the dream that woke him. He tried to shake it off, drop into that empty place which running invoked, but to no avail. The dream persisted so that free flow evaded him, making every step an effort.

He increased his pace still further to feel his muscles protest and his breath labour. The parkland flashed by almost as quickly as the visions of the dream flashed through his mind. As he came to the place where his pathway led onto a circular track, the majestic, brightly-lit Chateau de Kaeken stood to his right. He scanned the rest of his surroundings. Light was beginning to push the gloom away. His body began to respond. Each step became a little easier, a little more fluid. If given the opportunity and patience, it worked every time.

Even at fifty-two, he was in fine form, his body responding well to the effort, his heart strong. As the first streaks of dawn lightened the sky his mind relaxed, went blank and permitted him to pace easily around the track. There was not another soul to mar his way on such a cold, early morning. Steam streamed out behind him, his sweat misting in the freezing air, his breath a repeating cloud. He made an infinitesimal increase in pace for the final two kilometres. As he pulled onto the track in front of

the Chateau, his wrist monitor beeped twice to tell him he was done, ten kilometres.

He slowed his pace to a gentle jog and began to wend his way towards home, jogging easily through the park, now lit by a soft, dawn light. The sun was not yet over the horizon, but the darkness had been dispelled in more ways than one. Soon he made one final turn into his street with breathing steady, pulse steady and bad dreams pushed back into the night where they belonged. It was six-fifteen when he arrived back in the warmth of his home and seven by the time he had showered, eaten and dressed.

He finished the last of his coffee as the morning news flashed headlines on a giant screen with the sound muted. There was nothing new to report. Every story was a re-run from the previous day, re-packaged and touted once more. 'They are always the best days,' thought Grey. Even politics seemed quiet. He checked his watch, grabbed the keys to his Lexus electric and headed outside. As he engaged his home security system, he felt a sharp twinge in his chest.

Dr Grey Symes had been stationed in Brussels for twenty-two years. Though his marriage hadn't survived the push and pull of his role with the World Health Organisation, his career had flourished. Thus far he had managed to resist the continuous pressure to relocate to Copenhagen, and with the vast improvements in immediate communication since the beginning of the second decade of the new millennium, there had been a significant easing of that pressure.

It was soon to be the twelve-month anniversary of his appointment to the Director-General role, replacing Dr Ghebreyesus. It had been a time of enormous challenge working with the assembly, though he was accustomed to the climate of the organisation. As always, shifting the direction of such a complex and public entity was a complex task.

It had taken its toll on Grey, his hair colour now matching his name and far too often, his complexion. Still, he felt that he was doing well in a competitive, high stressed world. There

were not too many of his fellow doctors and scientists who were still jogging ten kilometres almost every day of the week. If he looked at his personal process, he noticed that he had a judgement that a good number of his peers would do well to take some of their own medical advice.

He turned his Lexus onto the motorway on-ramp and let it glide into the ever-present traffic. He adjusted the volume on his favourite classical station and let his mind wander. He traced the past year of his role as Director-General and smiled at his own implacable, relentless drive to expand and enhance the influence of the World Health Organisation to include every nation around the globe.

Much progress had been made, though the machinations never shifted fast enough for his complete satisfaction. Still, with his underlying agenda for medical micro-chipping and what many saw as quite a radical approach to birth control on a planet that, in his mind, was over-populated and running out of time, he was satisfied. The meeting this morning could well shift some of those plans forward much more rapidly than even he had dared to imagine. His first appointment would take up most of the day. His personal assistant had instructions to be prepared to delay every other meeting if this one proved to be as productive as its promise.

He was looking forward to meeting with Simon Chant, Chairman of the Board of Verity Global.

At seven forty-two, at the wheel of his car, to the cymbals clashing in Debussy's Le Martyr de Saint Sebastien on his favourite classical radio station, Dr Grey Symes heart stopped.

CHAPTER SEVENTEEN

Flipping from page to page, Wolf sat on a timber chair pushed up to a green-topped card table in his tiny cabin. The dim, yellow glow of an old kerosene lantern was his only light. His solar light had given up after four hours. Wolf pored over several faded symbols that might have been the same, but seemed different enough to muddy the meaning. Investigating the ancient knowledge contained in this volume would not be a simple task.

Though he had been studying such things for over twenty-five years, it was still challenging to unravel the codes embedded in the glyphs and sigils that covered each of these pages... They were scrawled in an imperfect freehand by what looked to be a single author. It seemed that way simply because the style and design, the drawings and marks of each page had a striking similarity throughout. Some of it was made extra difficult by the scrawl in red ink left by what he could imagine must be some thorough, investigative student of the craft.

Wolf turned another page, squinted to make out the first few characters, then brought his thumb and forefinger to his eyes and rubbed them as gently as possible, so as not to blur his vision any further. He was tired.

In the soft light of the lantern, the pages had begun to swim like the ripples on an ocean beach on an almost still morning. Smiling, thinking about the sunrise on the ocean, Wolf took care to pack the small volume in a square of soft, beige deerskin, folding the edges to contain and protect it and tying it off with a twist of brown leather. The metal box in the corner of the room needed a four-digit code to be opened. He knelt beside it, dialled the code and opened the lid. The hinges squealed a little

as usual. 'Must get oil on those hinges,' he thought as he cast his eyes over the contents.

A small compartment in the underside of the lid contained five thousand dollars in cash. There was a series of thirteen notebooks, each labelled by his neat handwriting in black ink on dark green covers. Five old-style cell phones, brand new, lay beside them. Not smart-phones, but presenting simple numeric pads, a tiny screen and suitable for calls and texts, nothing more. There was a well-honed bush machete with a two-foot blade, sheathed in black leather. A hunting slingshot and a small steel box which, Wolf knew contained three hard drives. It also contained an acid pouch that would destroy them if anyone opened it without knowing how. Only Wolf knew how. Even if someone managed to breach the box and get to his notebooks, the information would be useless without the disks. If these ones went, whoever took them would assume they were the originals as they had been copied with painstaking thoroughness. The originals were safer still. Secure, stored and buried. It would take the partial knowledge of Wolf and two others to work out where.

He reached in and took up the machete to feel the weight of it in his hand. Placing it on the bench beside him, he extracted the slingshot and a clear plastic box containing hundreds of shiny, steel ball-bearings.

Thirty of the ball bearings went loose into a trouser pocket. The lid back in place, he tossed the rest into his well-stocked backpack. He counted out four thousand dollars, put the last thousand back, and the rest went into a cash belt that would fit close to his body. Who knows, if he made it back here that thousand could well be useful. He put all the phones but one into the pack. The machete lay on the bench. He picked up a sheet of white paper and ran his finger down the list he'd compiled over the past few days. It was all done.

Lifting the glass shield on the lantern, he touched the corner of the page to the flame. The paper flared and caught. When all that was left was a tiny corner of paper he dropped it onto a candle holder nearby and watched it burn to nothing.

He closed the metal box, picked up the deer-hide package and the lantern and took a few steps to reach the bottle of Welsh whiskey he'd been saving for this day. He poured the first long shot. Stepping onto the deck, he sat and looked up at the silver sliver of a crescent moon.

Wolf spoke out loud to the surrounding bushland.

"Here's to you, Elias."

He raised his glass and threw the scotch back in a single practised movement.

"I happened across a nice surprise today that I think you'll like. In the morning, I'm on my way brother."

CHAPTER EIGHTEEN

"Did you see the look on Keith's face?" laughed Alva. "It was completely priceless!"

"He wasn't the only one, Alva, the whole room stopped. Jaws dropped all over the place. I think we may have just taken that giant step to bring the board all the way with us. It was a great presentation."

The two of them had retreated to a private, luxurious room attached to the boardroom which offered a 'king and conqueror' view of the city.

Simon reached over the armrest of his Italian leather lounge chair and scooped up the small mirror dusted in white powder, tapping out some more of the finely ground dust from a matchbox-sized, silver container. He fashioned two long lines and snorted his share of the cocaine with a long, loud sniff, passing the paraphernalia across to Alva as he finished.

"Watch our share prices skyrocket once this news gets out. We really can do anything with this on the market."

Almost the instant Alva sniffed the long, white line of dust a deep shudder rippled through her body. She whipped back hard in her chair, blood rushing from her face. Sweat beaded on her upper lip and at her temples.

"What the fuck, Alva? Are you alright?"

Eyes shining and movements deft and smooth, Simon leapt up and perched over Alva like a bird of prey. She continued to shake, her face pallid and her hands twitching as though possessed, even as she gripped the arms of the chair with a ferocity that threatened to tear bare-handed rifts in the leather.

"Can't breathe," she managed to croak. "Help me."

Rushing to the bar, Simon twisted the faucet and pushed a large glass under it, returning moments later to her side. Alva's face had begun to change colour, from its earlier paleness, to a subtle hue of blue. He slammed the glass down on the coffee table, wrenched her forward in the seat and thumped her hard three times on the back. She coughed out once, her eyes pleading with Simon as her throat constricted still tighter and precious air failed. Her hands now clawed at her throat, at the chair and at Simon's hands and arms as he tried to wrestle her away, so he could continue to assist.

Reaching under her, he lifted her bodily from the lounge and stood her on the soft carpet, supporting her with one strong arm wrapped around her torso. With the other he began thumping her back. Alva blacked out and slumped, seeming lifeless, into Simon's arms. Despite the sharp clarity of cocaine, Simon began to panic. Dragging her behind him, he reached behind the bar and gripped the ivory handle of an old-fashioned corkscrew. Though he had no real idea what he was doing, he was not about to have Alva die in his arms and his office without trying everything. She can't get breath through the normal channels. He would make another one.

Pausing for an uncomfortable instant, Simon pressed the point of the corkscrew into her neck and drove that spike into his associate's windpipe. Blood spurted from the hole he made but still no breath. Simon picked her up and shook her, dropping her into his arms afterwards to squeeze her, on for three, off for three, on for three, off for three.

Alva breathed.

Halting, bubbling with blood, sharp with pain – but breath. Then another, coagulated with sobs, and another. Thank God. She is alive. What just happened? Fuck.

Heart racing, Simon lowered Alva to the settee and strode to the bar. He noticed how his fingers shook as he pressed on the intercom and counted the slow seconds until his secretary's bright voice chirped in, "Yes, Mr Chant?"

"Get the company Doctor here now. This is highly confidential, Sarah. Make it better than fast."

He didn't hear whether she responded because he was beside Alva, checking her pulse, checking her breath, noting the sweat on her face, the blood on her neck and blouse, the corkscrew, bloodstained on the carpet.

CHAPTER NINETEEN

Wolf's dream was awash with blood-red lines stretched across pages and pages of hastily scrawled text. It seemed that every line had been altered, updated and questioned so that the original text was almost obliterated. With an inexorable slowness, the lines covered the entire page, then every page until at last blood flowed in rivulets from the pages of the book, filling every crevasse and every cranny on his weather-beaten face, pouring into and out of his crinkle-skin eyes, his ears and his nose. It gurgled in obscene, viscous bubbles from his gaping mouth, down his chin, embracing him in deep red from chest to feet.

Wolf woke with a start, coughing and spluttering, the cough racking his lean body. He tumbled off the bed and onto the hard floor of his sparse, spartan room. When the coughing eased and he opened his eyes to the dim light of early dawn, eking through a single window, tangling itself into the crushed sliver of dusty cloth which served as a makeshift curtain, Wolf still couldn't stand. Anyone watching would have imagined he was shaking off the worst of a mighty hangover, but this enmeshment was no addiction.

The small book he had found was somehow influential, weaving an etheric web that encased him cocoon-like, yet without comfort. It was rather a 'binding' and extraction was difficult. Moving his head from side to side, Wolf listened to his spine crack all the way down his back. He writhed with the excruciating pain that rammed itself into his coccyx like a red-hot knife driven home with relentless vigour.

With that movement though, he knew he had taken the first step to breaking the hold this entity had on him. One finger at a time he raised his hand from the floor, pain bringing beads of bloody sweat to his brow. He grasped the deep-green crystal that hung, askew on a leather strap, around his neck. As his fingers wrapped around its verdant coolness he muttered some unintelligible words through clenched teeth and let every muscle in his body relax.

The curtain fluttered outwards as though a monsoon wind had rushed from the room. Breath came with increasing ease. His voice became a mantra, spilling out the words he had used to break the enchantment with greater and greater volume and rhythm until there was a sing-song cadence to it. Wolf drew up to his full height and stretched, upward, downward, side-to-side, forward and back. He was himself again, or as near to it as he needed to take action. Thoughts rushed through his head admonishing himself for not taking greater care. He scratched at the cupboard just above his head till he managed to open it a crack. Clawing around inside, he located a dull, grey, rectangular box marked with a delicate array of sigils and designs. The three small metal clasps which secured it were sticky but soon gave way. With a slight creak it was open.

The book just fitted but fit it did, tight and neat - as he had suspected. He closed the lid and re-fixed the clasps. His recovery was immediate as power flowed into his frame, his arms and his legs. Some of the fine lines on the box began to glow a dense maroon colour but otherwise it was now benign.

Wolf tapped his mobile phone. The screen lit, writing lines on his face to show him the messages that had arrived. Three were from random unknown people, one from John at the bookshop. He punched the screen with his forefinger and waited. Nine times it rang. Number nine was the number that, for Wolf, represented chaos.

"Harbinger's Antiquarian Books, John speaking."

"John, it's Wolf, you called me?"

"Wolf. Yes I called. Are you alright? We need to speak. We need to speak as soon as possible. Not on the phone. Can you come?"

"Yes, of course."

Wolf had not ever heard this tone of voice from the bookseller. There was fear in there.

"I'll be right there. What time is it?"

"It's about ten-thirty. What...?"

Wolf had already hung up. He took a brief cold-water shower to wake him and set out at a jog towards town. At this pace he would be there in less than forty minutes. It was also a good reminder for him to attend to his fitness. He would need to be at his best very soon. If he was going to make the journey to Elias, and that was certain, he had a long walk ahead of him. His breath came with ease and muscles loosened as he relaxed into his stride. By eleven he reached the outskirts of town and began to wend his way through the streets to Harbingers Book Store.

"John. Are you OK?" Wolf had made unconscious preparation for a sight he didn't want to see, but though John was drawn and tense, with a fine mist of sweat on his brow, it was clear that he wasn't under any personal or immediate threat.

"I'm fine, Wolf. It's not about me. It's young Max. I found him in the back of the shop this morning. He was out cold. I can't find anything wrong with him but his skin is clammy and his breathing is shallow. I can't call the authorities," John grimaced, "He's not what many would describe as legal here." The older man was also a little breathless.

"Where is he now?" Wolf said, exuding calm.

"He's still there. I couldn't move him."

The look on his face reflected a rare frustration with his disability. "I'm sorry to have called you, but there was nothing I could do by myself. Then I thought of you and remembered that you met him that one time. He doesn't permit that very often."

The young man's hand was cold and clammy. So was his forehead. Somehow John had managed to push a pillow under his head but the lad was laid out on a hard, wooden floor covered

with a threadbare carpet. Wolf did a swift check on vital signs to discover the same information the store owner had. Max was blacked out, unconscious, yet his condition seemed in no way life threatening. He was stable. John had made his observations over half an hour ago. In the intervening time, nothing much had changed.

With an unexpected gentleness, Wolf shifted the youth a little and held his left hand above the boy's chest. He closed his eyes and his face exuded complete calm and peace. Breathing slow and deep, drawing back from the physical exertion of getting here into a place of complete meditative relaxation, Wolf began to pour energy into the young man. Had anyone been watching they may well have seen nothing but a wiry older man crouching over the younger man's supine figure. Those with the eyes to see would also have witnessed a wavering but distinct blue-green light extending from the palm of Wolf's hand into Max's chest.

After a few minutes, Max's body twitched several times. Wolf touched his right hand to the younger man's forehead and drew his hand with a studied gentleness back over the crown of his head. He sat down beside him with legs crossed. The book-store owner rolled his wheelchair into the passageway lined with a thousand books to see Max lift one hand to his face and gingerly open his eyes.

"What happened?" he whispered softly as some of the light returned to his startling, bright eyes.

"Take it easy. There's plenty of time for questions." Wolf turned his head to John at the end of the aisle and spoke a little louder.

"John, get some water will you?" John disappeared faster than you'd have thought a man in a wheelchair could move.

As the moments slid by, colour returned to the face of the young man and his pulse and breathing steadied to something resembling normal. Soon, John returned with a glass and pitcher full of water and passed them to Wolf. As Max leaned up on

one elbow, he took the glass and drank a little then threw back the whole glass.

"More."

Max downed a second glass and lay back down. Wolf reached out to the shelf above and slid a thick volume under his pillow.

"What happened?"

"Maybe you can tell us?"

The young man shifted a little and closed his eyes again. Several minutes passed before he began to speak.

"I was sorting some of the books on the top shelf, just moving them about when the strangest sensation travelled through me. It began at the base of my spine and at first there was just a kind of shiver that went all the way to my skull. Then wham.....it felt like a flaming sword had been shoved all the way through me from base to head."

Max winced and writhed in Wolf's lap as though the memory had reached into his consciousness through a gap left in the veil to that other place. He breathed a deep breath through his nose then exhaled loudly and slowly through his mouth, symmetry of a sigh.

"I guess that's when I blacked out.....well, not really black......"

Wolf took a brief glance at the bookshop keeper. "Tell me about that, Max."

"In the centre of the pain there was light," he began, hesitant, "and in that light uncountable colours and hues. I was without a body. There was nothing physical about me at all."

Wolf noticed in this moment the startling nature of Max's eyes. His pupils were so large as to deny any colour, extending out to the whites with a fine rim of prasinous emerald. He had only once seen anything like it before, in the eyes of his teacher after a four day black-wattle ceremony.

"Go on, Max," whispered Wolf gently, cradling the boy's head with even more care.

"In this place I was nothing, all pain was absent. All pleasure was absent, yet... how can I describe it...?"

He paused again, his face softening and his skin morphing to resemble delicate porcelain.

"I was *everything*." He paused again inhaling and exhaling a long deep breath.

"Everything is me. I am everything and yet I have ceased to exist." Taking another long breath, Max continued.

"We are on the edge of realms of such incredible beauty, such... majesty... glory!" His face curled into a beatific smile. "There aren't seven dimensions, nor eleven, nor even one hundred and forty-four. It's endless and beginning-less. The old stories, the old ways, the narratives we have all been written with, have zero relevance now. It's time for us to scribe a fresh chronicle." Max looked startled, connecting his gaze with Wolf, then John and back to Wolf.

"It's time. It is, isn't it, right now? Time to jump into the river and move with the flow of what is happening to us on so many levels that it's impossible," he smiled, almost laughed, "Impossible and misguided to hold to the old ways. They haven't served us for so long, yet they are so familiar that they seem like pillars, like the structure, the bedrock of our authority."

Pushing his elbows downward onto the hard floor, Max lifted into a sitting position, his arms wrapped around his knees, Wolf pushed aside.

"They're not our authority. We are. It's time, Wolf isn't it?" He sounded sure and inspired.

"It is little brother. There is no question." He turned his face to John and said, "John, can you manage without this lad in the shop? I just got the strongest message possible that he is going to join me on a very long journey I have been committed to for some time."

One day late and with an unexpected companion, Wolf set out to follow the call from his old friend, Elias. The sun was beginning to light the clouds that stretched in a troubling, immutable pattern across a background of soft grey-brown. They

reminded Wolf of the magnificence of the opalescent blue he recalled from his years as a child and a young man. Sadness still persisted deep within him for the loss of those skies, but Wolf knew the work was now being done, the shifts were underway. The loss had been required to prompt this time in which he and hundreds of thousands of others were instruments of the most profound change that life on earth had ever witnessed.

At his side loped Max, a slight-built young man who had experienced an epiphany. That epiphany, which had enmeshed but remained mysterious even to an elder such as Wolf, powerfully implicated the young man in this calling. His summoning may not have been quite as explicit as for the others, yet Wolf now knew that this quiet lad, whom he had met by what appeared to be pure chance, had a significant part to play. What that role might be would unravel as it would, yet by asking him to be his companion on the journey, Wolf had stitched a significant thread into an already complex tapestry.

The dreams that had so troubled him were not forgotten. They had been relegated into a holding place. It was one of Wolf's particular skills. Through the discipline of practice, anything could be subjugated to that to which he chose to bring his attention. Anything. In the sigil-inscribed grey box, shoved deep into his pack, some well-chosen words spoken over it to ensure it remained in secure containment, was the small red-marked volume. Even in that box, Wolf was sure he could still 'feel' the diminutive compendium. Take a step and take another. Become present in the space between each step. Bring entire focus to the simplicity or complexity of taking the next step and the process would paint its exquisite design in perfect timing.

"Where are we headed?"

"We're walking North West up into the mountains at first. As far as I can tell we will head along the top of the ridge for a few days. Anything after that is too far out to make a plan. We just have to see what comes up and something always comes up," intoned Wolf between steady controlled breaths.

The younger man looked a little perplexed and went to speak several times but hesitated and remained quiet, taking his long paces with an ease that surprised Wolf more than he was willing to admit. Half an hour passed and the two had begun to make some distance onto the slow, sloping foothills just prior to the acicular peaks behind.

"What I meant was, where the fuck are we actually going? Not just today, but the entire journey. Some explanation of this thing you've enlisted me for would be greatly appreciated? You need to share some more information with me if this is going to work for us both." Max had taken his time to identify and employ his assertive persona. He had used the time well, through his natural introversion and introspective examination.

Smiling at the conscious control of the dream that such a shift required further encouraged Wolf to allow the boy in. Whatever his capabilities, they were significant, with genuine consideration of his lack of training. As far as Wolf could tell, he also possessed no knowledge of the world's and realms they would visit in the course of this pilgrimage.

As the spaces between the trees closed in on the two travellers, a storm began to brew in the peaks above. Immense black clouds coalesced in broiling masses with an occasional greenish hue. Neither Wolf nor Max had noticed as they climbed the steepening slope, at least not until Wolf realised that it was far darker than normal for the time of day.

"We need to find shelter, Max."

They stopped and both looked skyward through the sombre canopy, then cast their gazes to left and right to see if anything, even slightly, resembled cover. In the same moment both of them spotted their shelter. About eighty metres away, to the left of the increasingly indistinct path lay the shell of what had once been one of the giants of the forest. In the centre the remains of the massive trunk was a section of thick, iron-hard timber covering a space they would surely both fit.

"Race you." Max was off, running for the tree as the first pounding drops of rain began turning dry earth into slippery

mud. A shrieking crash, thunder and lightning in the same moment, plummeted into the tallest of the trees near them followed by creaking, a loud crack and a tumultuous crash as the tree was split in two. Both of them reached the hollow trunk within a millisecond of one another, tossed their packs on the ground and swung around to witness the rage of the storm. Max laughed a loud, excited chuckle and looked to Wolf who couldn't help but join in.

As the storm progressed, a section of green cloud passed above the tree trunk they sheltered in and cast fist sized balls of ice to the ground, tearing leaves, twigs and even branches off the surrounding trees. As the hail crashed through the forest and collected in random piles at the base of trees, making a wall against the old felled trunk, they sent their laughter into the fury of the storm. The insanity of the moment took over. Their laughter didn't ease until the fast-moving storm tore around the steep scree-covered face of the next peak, clattering against the exposed rock wall.

They sat in silence but for the sound of drops falling from the treetops and the splash and rattle of instant creeks and rivulets. These had formed to crisscross the side of the mountain, tumble between the curled roots of the older trees and cut swathes through the paths and clearings.

Max looked across at Wolf to see that the older man had assumed a trance-like state, sitting cross legged on the dry ground. His back and neck were straight, his eyes closed and his nostrils flared as he breathed deep, in and out. In the grey dimness Max couldn't be certain that he was witnessing a kind of energy pulse that emitted a bluish-green light from every pore in Wolf's skin. He watched transfixed for long enough to realise that when Wolf breathed in he could see light moving towards the older man, diminishing in brightness as he breathed out. Standing in silence, Max stepped out onto the wet earth free of the cover of the old tree. He sniffed the air and sensed a spark, crystallised ozone shimmering in the still air. Ice melting into

moss freckled earth meant the temperature had dropped almost ten degrees.

Max shivered as the sweat and dampness chilled his skin. After gazing about for a few minutes, Max stepped back to the hollow tree to find Wolf still deep in trance. Streaming straight through him Max could now see a distinct column of greenish-blue light, extending from the canopy above, direct through solid timber, through his new friend and deep into the earth. He shook his head a little with the realisation that he was 'seeing' deep into the earth. He sat down opposite Wolf and assumed the same position. Closing his eyes Max imagined that same column of light pouring through him.

Soon afterwards, he dropped into a deep meditation.

"I thought you might find your way here." It was Wolf's voice – translucent, crystalline and power-infused. "What you described back in the bookstore made it seem that you would be a natural."

"Where are we?" Max replied, though it was not exactly spoken.

"There are a whole range of realms that have not been available to humanity for a very long time. They were hidden from us with good intent and purpose but they also have their own purpose, so they have been assigning some of us to re-activate them."

"Why can't I see you?"

"You have your eyes closed, buddy. Prepare yourself, but open them."

The sight that confronted him was more exquisite, fragrant and beautiful than anything Max could ever have imagined. Everything emitted a sparkling patina consistent with the gleam that Max had already noticed in observing Wolf in meditation. Even more startling was that it was an enhanced image of the same scene as that in which they had taken shelter from the hail storm, but for that nascent glimmer, the scent of a lambent flower garden, colours so vivid they belied description and a myriad of exquisite life forms.

The hard destructive balls of ice that had been so threatening were, in this place, pools of translucent water from which indescribable, mythical and delicate creatures drank, skittered and played. The timber grotto in which they sat was etched with similar sigils and markings as those carved into the small box in which Wolf had contained the red-inked book. Draped all around them were a kaleidoscope of colourful flowers and intricately woven, smooth-barked vines intertwined so as to create a unique, entrancing framework for their sitting place.

The trees appeared to tower almost twice as high, forming a monumental colonnade both back down the way they had come and towards the peaks they must ascend. Beyond them, the summit of the mountain on which they travelled stood tall and gleaming in a myriad of shifting hues, foreground to a startling, azure sky more entrancing than any Max had ever seen. Across the sky sailed picture book clouds and six or seven immense birds, extraordinary, multicoloured wings spread wide, circling and wheeling, calling to one another, the sound echoing off the sheer stone walls of the mountains.

"Where are we Wolf? What is this place?" Max voice sounded, though his lips did not move. The air in front of his face shone a little less and ripples of energy moved towards his face.

Without moving or even seeming to notice that anything had been uttered, a shimmering wave of energy shifted outward from Wolf across the space between them and Max heard,

"This is the place that every path that has ever been imagined or practiced has aspired to, little brother. This is home. This is what so much of humanity has forgotten. This is the place of perfect peace. It is here that we are limitless." Wolf smiled at Max and in the making of that smile it was instantaneous in becoming a sensation in the younger man.

"What are we doing here?" The question came though Max couldn't discern from where.

Wolf shrugged and the space around him shrugged in alliance.

"I had a sense that you would be able to travel here if I gave you a little push my friend. Seems I was right because here you are. What we are doing here is getting clear between us, what we are to each other and where we are going back in that world to which you are accustomed. We have some travelling to do, Max. We go to connect in physical form with a very old friend of mine and back in that world he is a long way away."

Max looked mystified and all around him the air and everything else wavered and issued a dullish, burnt-orange hue.

"Why don't we go straight to him from here? I feel like we could do anything, travel anywhere we chose, from this place."

"It's true. We could do that. It's not the point. As we travel back in that relative world, we create a movement of energy that must move to completion. The movement has already begun and there are those on course, just as we are, to participate in that movement to completion. It's the grandest adventure we have ever experienced as humans. The journey must be made. That's all I can tell you right now." Gold and silver emanations floated outward from Wolf.

"Let's return. It's time for us to move on."

Wolf breathed a deep breath through his nose, lifting his shoulders and pushing his belly out as his chest filled with the sweet air of this exquisite place. Then he closed his eyes and began breathing out. Max felt his eyes close and a sense of complete peace and relaxation imbued every cell in his body.

When Wolf's out breath was complete, Max sat without utterance for a few minutes before he opened his eyes. The first thing he noticed was a cold, misted exhalation wafting out in front of him, reminiscent of the wavering energy he had experienced in that other place. Smiling his broad smile, with a deep-green shawl wrapped around his shoulders and sticks, twigs and logs perched precariously in his arms, Wolf was kneeling to feed a small fire. The smoke rose into the tops of the trees and a tiny lick of flame made the twigs crackle and pop. Wolf shuffled and fussed around the fire, looking like a woodsman from some time in the distant past. A viridian-green

woollen cap covered most of his shock of unruly hair and hid his ears. As he added the wood, the fire began to crackle a little more and the flames grew larger.

The remaining daylight faded until day gave way to night. Wolf added even more of the wet timber, creating smoking ringlets and showering bright orange sparks into the still, damp air. As the smoke curled into the treetops, Max shivered and moved closer to the fire, rubbing his hands to warm them. Wolf glanced up from his fire making and looked Max up and down.

"You look a bit shell-shocked. Are you OK?" He spoke with gentleness, his gruff toughness hidden away.

"It's a lot to take in," Max murmured.

"It is. That's true. I was hoping that the excitement," he paused and threw twigs into the heart of the fire, "the possibility, the magnificence would be a kind of foil to the shock. Perhaps I've misjudged."

Max gazed at him with a fixed thoughtfulness then spoke softly.

"No, you've judged well. It is a shock for sure but it is exciting. I'm not sure how I fit in though. Why could I just hop across from one place to another with ease? I've never seen anything like it before but I felt... at home." He rubbed his eyes as the smoke swung around in his direction, following the slightest breeze.

"I can't say that I'm sure about that either, Max. The first time I had any idea that you were implicated in this whole shift was when you described what you experienced in John's bookshop. It was a strong sign but still, I wasn't sure. This little journey we took tonight was a kind of confirmation for me. I'll need to connect in with Elias before too long and let him know what's happening. Let him know about you." He chuckled. "Knowing him, he already has some knowledge. Nothing much escapes him."

The two men moved closer to the campfire. Together they made a dinner that eased the cold out of their bones and prepared them for sleep. As Max lay down he felt his muscles relax. He

noticed his breath, inhale and exhale. His eyes were wide open, yet the darkness was intense, interrupted by the silent stars poised above him and one owl, much closer, issuing a soft but piercing hoot in the still air. He slept. Just a little distance away Wolf was motionless, his breath silent, in through the nose and out through the mouth, held just a little longer than usual in between.

Elias must be told, though it was almost certain that he knew what had happened. Elias had an intrinsic connection to the realm they had visited. Still, it was a courtesy that Wolf would not overlook. The morning seemed like a better time to reach out to him. Right now, Wolf was weary. As he closed his eyes, sleep came in a few moments, rushing him into a dream world of his own design. This too was Wolf's travelling place. Wolf could learn much in the dream. It had been his practice for many lifetimes and still served him well. Tonight he would dream with intention and the intention was a simple question.

What is the next step?

A hedge of rolling clouds blanketed the stars and the darkness deepened over the two sleeping figures. They were surrounded by a throng of imps and sprites and other beings that served to form a guard assigned to the protection of the sleeping men.

CHAPTER TWENTY

The sun had never lit this room and never would. Not a single window, not that a window would open the room to anything more than identical rooms and eventually, solid rock and stone, cold as death and diamond hard. Once the sun may well have blessed this place, perhaps fifty million years ago, before the mountains had shifted and worn, inch by painstaking inch, towering majesty yielding to the inexorable weathering of time. Now buried here, a tomb of sorts, she breathed in and out with all these other people, faces lit by the phosphorescence of thousands of screens.

If you listened for it you could hear the soft issue of air pumped in an endless stream into this tomb and back out, filtered beyond recognition. The air was gathered from well above ground level, eighty metres above the warmth of the earth and the inexplicable green township that clung like an oasis in the desert. Further afield the air hovered above cactus, snakes and stony ground.

The air for this place was gathered at night, when it cooled from around forty-five degrees to less than ten. Compressed, packaged, filtered, temperature controlled, moisture controlled and released by degree. This room was one of more than a hundred rooms much like it. At every station was another person, mirrors of each other.

Paying their rent, paying their mortgage, paying school fees, paying insurance, paying the butcher, grocer, doctor, dentist, orthodontist, teacher, politician, priest and snake-oil salesman with a job, a career that had them careening from year to year, locked underground. Most days they would emerge

when the sun had long gone, sometimes leaving a ravenous, red afterglow stretched across heaven, etched into the firmament before giving way to the endless blackness of the night sky, ablaze with billions of distant stars.

Gaze at the monitor. Pay attention to any aberration because that could be the one that couldn't afford to be missed. Ten hours were spent down here, six days a week with three breaks a day in another windowless room. Here workers could eat, watch some television, drink coffee or talk, listless and uninspired with someone who might have worked here for the past ten years without knowing anything more than their co-worker's first name. One week off every year, one week with three selected options for a dream holiday was the sum of all that was offered. Three options for each demographic; singles fun, couples fun, family fun and a retirement fund.

No-one on the floor was over forty. Those who sat up in the overhead viewing stations could be, often were, but no-one on the lower floor. The glass framed viewing stations were comprised of old men, suited and tied in regulation uniforms, grey and white or decorated in navy and khaki with gold and silver epaulettes. They were always serious, ever frowning, nodding and pointing to things about which those on the floor could only guess.

In that way Akashi Agola was out of the ordinary.

As her Saturday shift ended, Akashi shut down her work-station and sat back, her body heavy in the chair. She could smell the cloying scent of the aftershave of the last man who had come into the room today, his shoes tapping on the grey tiles. It wasn't all he had left behind. Set on the corner of her desk was a small black square containing twenty terabytes of information. He told her it was a copy of his 'won' files, filled with dossiers on terrorists and potential terrorists. From Monday she would occupy a new space in the bunker and would need to begin her research. Seems he was looking for correlations that pointed to a cell of people dotted across the globe who he had described as 'persons of interest.'

From Monday she would begin what she had joined the service for, the position that could put her firmly in the place for which she had aimed - if she got it right; if she was able to find the correlating data. She twisted her silver ring off her finger, pressed down on it so that it stood on edge on the polished surface and flicked it hard. It span so fast that it became a silver blur, a tiny globe of silver. She watched until it slowed and lost momentum, toppled and rolled down to a stop, sending a tinkling sound into the silence.

Akashi put the ring back on, lifted out of her chair and began to pack her few personal items into a small, unmarked, cardboard box. A photograph of the mountain, another of her trekking in the mountains of Nepal in that unforgettable October, a gold pen her father had left her, a notebook bound in royal blue and a double pointed quartz crystal followed each other into the box. They were nothing much, but these things reminded her that there was life after Saturday, even if it was only one day.

On Monday she would be in her new private office on level two. From level four to level two because the man with hard soled shoes, a haircut that matched the clipped way in which he spoke and too much aftershave, said so. She turned the ID clip over and gazed at her image looking back, in uniform, hair tied back, level two clearance chip etched into the plastic card and her ID number in bold black letters. She would need that to access the place, to put these things in whatever room she had been assigned.

She picked up the disk. Twenty terabytes of classified dossiers on people she had never met, whose lives would face significant change once she had done her job. But tomorrow was Sunday. She decided to take the whole lot home with her, to locate her new office first thing Monday rather than spend another minute in this place. The whole workforce had gone home. Some days, when caution waved its flag in the halls of power that simply meant a new team would file in to warm the seats of those who left. As it had been quiet for the past

month, Akashi looked out over work-stations abandoned and devoid of life.

She was the last to leave. It was time to go, time to have that precious twenty-four hours. Another operative would take this place tomorrow but Monday she would find her new office and begin. She clicked the door shut as she left and heard the lock roll into place. The click was only audible because she was alone. The hum of the air vents was background to that sound. She walked the long corridor to the elevator and pressed 'up.'

CHAPTER TWENTY ONE

Once the bike was concealed in the undergrowth to her satisfaction, Raniyah hunched into the straps of her pack, shouldered the telescope and set off. Crossing the border had presented no real problem, the guards giving her US passport just a cursory glance before waving her through. That at least had been a relief. So nothing had happened on a national scale. It must have been a more personal issue for Toby and Brianna. In a way, that felt like good news. Even better news was that Toby was able to change his phone message. That meant he and Brianna were both OK.

There was no real reason for her to be quiet but Raniyah had made a discipline of silence when walking in the wilderness so she had continued the practice. An occasional twig snapped until she found her rhythm, warmed up and the shake and shudder of the ride had settled. The scraping bushes and grasses down here would soon give way to open ground. She continued to climb, thinking that things must have escalated quickly for Toby to go straight to his 'I'll be off grid' message. Some sort of direct impact must have occurred. Soon she could ask them in person.

The straps of her pack pinched and rubbed, reminding Raniyah how long it had been since she had been on a genuine trek. No amount of pack-free training could prepare for the real thing. The telescope was heavier than she liked, but she was still glad she had brought it. There were not much better places than up at the cave to retrain it on the heavens to show Toby and Brianna what she had seen.

Raniyah pushed on. After half an hour of scrub, the ground began to shift to rocky scree. She slithered and scrambled over two hundred metres of terrain that threatened to slide her down onto a pile of rubble. She regained a path of sorts and began a steep climb upwards. An hour later she came into a clearing not far from the entrance to the cave. She stopped and quietly unloaded, hiding her belongings behind bushes at the edge of the clearing. It would be better to approach the cave unencumbered.

Up here the wind was cold. Raniyah felt goose-bumps almost as soon as she stopped and unloaded, which meant it was close to freezing. She leaned over her pack, unclipped and unzipped the top, hauled out a black fleece and put it on. That was better. It wouldn't take long for her to get a chill if she cooled down in these temperatures. Though it wasn't yet night, the sun had begun to sink towards the horizon. She could almost feel the temperature dropping by the minute. But what a view.

She stood for a few minutes, quite alone in the clearing to gaze out to the distant sea where Vancouver Island stood stark against the waning light. Turning her back on the sight, she walked out of the clearing and stepped across cold stone toward the cave mouth. It was a long time since she had visited this place. Each time she felt the energy of the site, wild and harsh, yet it always comforted her in an indescribable way. She pulled out a small flashlight. Switching it on, she bent down and stepped inside.

The cave looked empty, but Raniyah knew that part of the security of this place was just that truth. At the back of a cavernous first section was a small opening, concealed in darkness by the shadows of four large rocks. She dropped onto her hands and knees to crawl through then stood again in a second, smaller chamber. Just behind her and to the left were gaps and small ledges that served as footholds which formed a steep path upwards. She trained her flashlight at a spot about four metres above her head to shine on another opening in the stone. That was it. She began to climb, cautious to get her foot and hand-hold set each time before taking the next step. As

she eased into the opening, a light showed at the far end of the tunnel. The light assisted her to drag and shunt along without significant scrapes and scratches. She heard a familiar voice.

"You took your time then?" Toby called out, "Thought you must have got lost along the way."

"No such luck, big brother. You're stuck with me." Raniyah smiled her broad smile as a steel screen was removed and light flooded into that narrow place. Toby reached out to grab her hand and helped to lower her into the space inside. It had been a long time. She last stood inside this cavern when it was little more than an eight-metre by twelve-metre empty space, with a floor covered in guano, a very bad smell, the rustle of bats in the ceiling, a table, two chairs and biting cold. Bree and Toby had been busy.

Raniyah looked around. "Toby, this is totally awesome. Look what you guys have done here. Wow!" She was awed by what she saw.

The space had received a thorough redecoration. No smell, the bats gone, soft lit by a glow that seemed to emanate from the rock walls and roof from about two metres upwards. A decorative standard lamp, three ornate table lamps placed at strategic points around the room, an old-fashioned green-glass and brass desk lamp and an Himalayan crystal salt-lamp adding warmth. The floor was resin over polished concrete, scattered with similar Persian carpets to the ones that decorated their other underground home. These were a little more worn and a little less ornate.

A large double bed was part-hidden by heavy drapes to Raniyah's left, and outside that space, four fold-up rails, two-by-two, were bunks that could be lowered for sleeping. Alongside that, solid timber benches, storage cupboards and a double stainless-steel sink. Beyond that a semi-opaque, glass-brick wall that shielded what must have been some form of bathroom. Opposite her, Raniyah took in a lounge space with book shelves and a bench full of board games. A huge circle of glass perched on what looked like the root of a tree, making a fabulous coffee

table. Two big three-seater lounges and a fabric-covered standard lamp, depicting an English fox-hunting scene, had two ornate dream-catchers suspended from it.

Her eyes roved to her right where there were three workstations, desks, chairs, filing cabinets and computers at each. At one of these, Brianna beamed back at her.

"Hey, Ran, it's so good to see you. Where's your stuff?" As she spoke, she stood and walked over to embrace her sister-in-law with genuine affection. They stood there together for a long embrace. Raniyah made a muffled murmur into Brianna's shoulder that sounded like 'Good to see you too, Bree.'

When they moved apart, Toby and Raniyah also hugged. Brianna repeated, "Where's your stuff?" as she walked over and set a stainless-steel kettle onto a gas flame.

"Oh, it's just up near the clearing. I'd best go get it, now that I know it's just you guys here. Give me ten minutes and I'll be back."

"I think we can do better than that," said Toby. He reached above his head to slide the rungs of a ladder down to the floor. Raniyah looked up to see the ladder extending all the way to the rounded ceiling of the cavern, some seven metres up. The portal at the top resembled a steel ship's door.

It took Toby less than two minutes to scale the ladder, push the portal open, disappear and return with her pack and telescope. He tossed the pack down at her feet, descended into the cavern, secured the door behind him and gingerly climbed down the ladder with what he knew to be one of Raniyah's most valued possessions. When he got to the floor, he handed it to her in mock ceremony, smirking a little.

"Thanks. Pretending it's not important or not, I appreciate your care, Toby. Once we get a bit sorted, I want to show you both something with this. It's the one reason I brought it."

The smell of fresh coffee began to pervade the room.

"Coffee for everyone?"

The three of them sat in easy comfort with each other in the muted light of the standard lamp. Toby had ambient music

playing. Raniyah had no idea who the performer was but it was pleasant enough. After coffee, Raniyah showered and freshened up while Toby prepared a simple meal.

Now it was time to have the conversation that had to happen.

What on earth were they doing in the cave? Each of them was aware that it was a big step for them to take, populating the cave, so the conversation had been bubbling under the surface of every word and movement since Raniyah had arrived. It was time to get clear. Toby rolled a small joint, lit it, inhaled a deep toke and passed it to Brianna. She looked at him with a quizzical expression.

"No-one is going to find us here tonight. We are about as safe as we are ever going to be."

Toby sounded relaxed and at ease so, reassured, Brianna drew deeply on the joint and offered it to Raniyah. She joined in without hesitation. As the marijuana took effect, they all relaxed. Nothing was going to stop the necessary conversation. Raniyah began.

"Look, I don't know what it was that brought you guys up here. It must be something pretty serious because there's not much that spooks you two. But I have a bit of news of my own that feels important. It's the reason I lugged that telescope all this way."

"You go first then, Ran," said Toby, passing the smoke to Brianna once again. He puffed a plume of smoke into the air, "What's happened?"

"Well, you know that I spend a lot of time checking out the heavens. A couple of nights ago I had this strange notion to point my scope into a random spot," she paused to reconsider her choice of words, "at the time it felt anything but random. It felt like something was... I don't know how to explain, something was compelling me to look at the precise spot I chose. However it happened, at first there was nothing that made any sense at all, nothing striking, nothing to report. But then at around midnight the other night I saw something strange." Raniyah's hands were

shaking a little, not from cold because somehow, Brianna and Toby had managed to ensure that this massive cavern was warm and comfortable. She was excited and it bubbled through the mildly euphoric sedation of the marijuana.

"Toby, something just appeared. Something that wasn't there at all a few nights ago is there for certain now and it looks to have a colour. I watched it for just over three hours and in that time it got bigger, more obvious. It looks like it's getting closer. Can you believe it, getting closer in the space of three hours of watching, Toby, Bree? Three hours. That is totally and completely amazing. Impossible, but I saw it with my own eyes. So I brought the scope. I want you guys to see it too, even if it's only so that I can believe it myself. It's a spot about halfway between Sirius and Orion's Belt." Raniyah chuckled. "Bloody weed, I'm raving. Sorry guys, but I guess you can tell it's pretty exciting for me."

"That much is clear. So is the sky tonight last I looked, so let's have a look later on. Leave it till about midnight, the moon should have gone by then. Sounds a bit of a tall tale, Ran, but we'll have a look tonight." Toby smiled with unmasked affection at his sister. He was sitting on the edge of his seat as she spoke, so her excitement was infectious, though not so obvious for Brianna. She was lying back in the big lounge, her arms spread along the chair. There was a look on her face that even Toby found difficult to comprehend. She looked as though an idea had just become real for her, as though something had clicked into place. Toby looked at her, questioning.

"Bree, what is it?"

"Huh. What is what?" she asked, as if extracting from a dream.

"You have a strange look on your face. Is anything wrong?"

Brianna shifted in her seat, shook her head from side to side and said dreamily, "It... I'm not sure. Some kind of weird premonition maybe, lost and found in a dream. There was some kind of cave. Raniyah was sleeping or unwell. I saw an old woman."

There was silence for a few moments. Raniyah stood, walked the few steps to the kitchen and filled her glass with water. "Does anyone else want some water?"

"Sure, one for both of us please, Ran" said Toby. Raniyah filled the other two glasses from the filtration tank and came back to the lounge, placing the glasses on the table in front of her brother and sister in law.

"So what about you guys? Why are we up here? What happened?"

While Brianna and Raniyah listened, Toby spoke about the incident with the four men at their home. He knew that Raniyah liked the detail in things, especially stories, so he described everything that he could recall, right down to describing each of the men and the fact that one of them had seemed somehow familiar. He gave her details of how they had locked down their house and begun the ascent to the cave as an immediate priority after the attack.

He didn't describe how Brianna had called to him. Only he and Brianna had any knowledge of this development and it was up to Brianna to decide if she wanted to share that.

"So, four guys and they cornered you down in the garden? Didn't you tell me that almost no-one even knew you guys were there?" asked Raniyah of them both.

Toby answered. "Very few people knew. You are one of two people beside Bree and me. That's one of the reasons we're up here so quickly. There are three people who know about this cave and we are all here."

"So how did you know Brianna was in any sort of trouble way down in the garden, Toby? I've been inside your place and no sound gets in there. Do you have two-ways on every day or something; or just a sixth sense, or what?"

Raniyah was looking straight at Brianna when she asked and though her sister-in-law's lips didn't move at all, her voice was somehow in Raniyah's head.

"We have a special connection, Toby and I. If you can hear me now, it's the first time I've ever tried it with anyone else. Did you get that?"

Raniyah looked shocked and stunned. "What the fuck did you just do? Did I just hear that? What the..."

Brianna sat forward, peering at Raniyah. "You heard me?"

"I guess I did, but your lips didn't move. You spoke to me?" Raniyah was nonplussed. This time Brianna spoke out loud.

"I did. It's something Toby and I have been practising now for the past five years or so." Brianna laughed. "Never tried it with anyone else though Ran. What did you hear me say?" Raniyah repeated what she had heard inside her head word-for-word.

"Brilliant." said Brianna, "Nice trick, huh sis?"

"That's incredible, Bree. Where did you learn to do that? Can anyone do that? Can Toby do it back? Can I do it? That's awesome. Can you teach me?" Raniyah's questions tumbled out in a rush.

"So that's how I knew she needed me Ran. She called out to me like that. Like I said, I was in the middle of my aikido, so I just grabbed a jo and headed straight down. It gave us the element of surprise."

Toby smiled and began the makings of another spliff.

"It took us a while to get past just visualising a shape or a sigil or some visual thing to each other. It took us a long time to even imagine we could use sound rather than visual imagery, but once we did that, it began to work much better, much more quickly. I have to say though, it is a bit of a surprise that you got me with such clarity on my first try. I never imagined it would be something that would go beyond Toby and me," said Brianna, shifting her gaze to Toby to ask, "You going to share that, lover?" Toby passed her the freshly rolled joint. She lit it and took a deep draw then passed it to Raniyah, speaking as she passed it.

"It seems you have a talent for hearing that I would never have expected, Ran. You being able to hear is as much of a

surprise for me as it is for you. I wouldn't have even tried it if I hadn't had a smoke, but hey, we've learned something about each other. Welcome to our little club of three."

Raniyah looked from one to the other and back again at Brianna, her mouth dropped open in surprise. "Toby can do this back to you too?"

Brianna glanced at Toby then replied, "Well, so far Toby has proved to be better at hearing me than I can hear him or I'm better at sending out the message. We're not too sure which it is. But we have reached the point where we can have a private conversation without opening either of our mouths. We've practised a lot to get to that."

"That's so incredible, Bree, Toby! Whatever made you start even thinking that you could ever do it?"

Raniyah was shifting around in her seat with excitement, reminding Toby of how she had once been as his little sister when they were both just kids. He answered, "Like I say, it was a bit over five years ago when we took interest to start work on it. Bree first noticed that when we turned off all the electronics in the house and we were out of range of any wi-fi, or at least most of it, we seemed to be in sync quite a lot. It wasn't language at first." Smoke coiled in grey clouds to the roof as the three of them continued to share the herbal mix.

"It started with simple things like being at opposite sides of the room and both getting up at precisely the same moment to get the same thing from the same drawer. Remember that, Bree?"

She nodded with genuine enthusiasm.

"Then we began to notice some other random things. Four or five times in the one game of scrabble, I knew the exact word Bree was going to put out next and exactly where. In the same game, Bree thought she knew all the letters I had, all seven of them. In fact that was when we decided to test our theories for the first time with any seriousness."

Raniyah looked at both of them, still incredulous.

"You know, we'd laughed about it a bit and messed around with it a bit, but that night we ran our first real test. If Bree

140

thought she knew what letters I had, I thought we'd better see how accurate she was. Neither of us was serious about our outcomes, but we did it. The first time she got six of the seven letters. So we did it again. The second time she got five of the seven. The third time she got all seven. And the fourth. And the fifth. Then she got six again on the sixth attempt. It was pretty mind-altering stuff. So we reversed the process. Bree picked up seven letters. I got them all. She did that twelve more times. I missed one tile once on the ninth try. I got all the rest."

Toby brushed his hands through his hair. "It seemed like something worth investigating further and the rest is history."

Raniyah shook her head to clear it a little. A lot was happening in a very short amount of time. This latest revelation had her reeling. She remembered a series of events that had happened in her own life where she had been sure that she knew what was going to happen next. Times when she had heard things from people that she knew they had never said out loud, would never say out loud.

Sometimes it had felt like a gift. Sometimes it felt like a curse.

Once it had kept her safe from a good-looking, fair-haired man she met online. She had heard what he was saying about her in his head, was sure she had heard it and at the same time couldn't quite believe it. Then she learned that the same man had been arrested just three days later for doing to some other woman what she had felt he had in mind for her.

But now, she thought, it's time to get my scope out and have a look at that thing between Sirius and Orion's belt.

Toby stood, "I'd say it's time to get your scope out and have a look at that thing between Sirius and Orion's belt, Ran. You want to come and set it up with me?"

Raniyah stared, incredulous. Brianna did too.

"Did I just say that out loud?" said Raniyah

"No you didn't" answered Brianna, "but I heard both of you".

"Have this woman taken somewhere else, Brother," he snarled. "Make sure she has food and fresh clothing. Have the Sisters ensure she is washed and scrubbed well. She smells foul."

This he spoke to the shorter of his two companions, who drew out his mobile phone and began tapping on the screen. The other two continued on their way.

For the next fifteen minutes, the short priest stood with as much patience as he could at that place, pacing from time to time while he waited for the arrival of a small delegation of nuns and a large, strong man. He was very aware of the importance of following the instructions of Cardinal Adiputera to the letter and to their definite conclusion.

When the nuns and strong-arm arrived he pointed and said, "Take her and do as the Cardinal commanded."

To his complete surprise, when the big fellow reached down and lifted the shawl, all he uncovered was a pile of dusty, grimy rags.

CHAPTER TWENTY THREE

Since she could remember, Valda Balaz had been groomed and prepared for the life she now led. Her most abiding memories were not curled in comfort with her mother or her father – both people that she was taught to respect – as there had been very controlled and limited contact. As a child she was close to her personal maid, Ellen, and to her language tutor, Andreas. With no mother available, Valda accessed her instinct to fashion Ellen to be the nearest person to take that role. Andreas because, of all the things she was required to have the discipline to study and learn, languages were what she both excelled in and enjoyed.

By the time she was seven, in addition to English, she was as fluent as native speakers twice her age in Mandarin, Spanish, German and Hebrew. By the age of eleven, when she became a boarder at Eton, she had added Russian, Hindustani, Arabic and French.

Ellen had been removed as a source of comfort and support simply because of the chance of Valda becoming dependent or needy in any way. She was told the separation was to teach her how to fend for herself. In the world of social friendship and connection, that was all she knew. When she graduated from secondary school she was offered the opportunity of every University in the world. She possessed a brilliant mind and had been the highest performer in every subject. She chose Yale University in New Haven in the United States. Her father approved. Without that approval, she would have been forced to choose again.

Nothing about the life path of Valda Balaz was accidental. Every step had been mapped out, every move considered.

At fifty-four years of age, the time for responding to the wishes of anyone else were long gone, though her father still exerted a powerful influence, even at his advanced age. She knew that he would not let go until they lowered him into the ground in a plain timber box held together with wooden pins. He had made that clear at her ninth birthday and had repeated at every birthday since then.

Valda's mother died when she was forty-three. It made little difference to her life. She was no less unknown or missed in death than in life. Valda attended the funeral. She spent time with the mourners and delegates who paid their respects because that was what was expected. That was what was appropriate. Valda attended for the same reason.

Had her father died before she reached thirty, her reaction would have been much the same. Until then he had been an officious figure in her life, referenced by those who watched her every move and every decision, but their communication was rarely direct. She had no real idea who he was as a man, only that he had unassailable connections at the highest levels of power all over the world. She knew he also exercised that power with a ruthless pragmatism.

At thirty, when she had at last completed her extraordinary education, he entered her life in a dramatic manner. Her father had made a rare visit to the house that had been purchased for her in New Haven, Connecticut. She had lived there since her freshman year at Yale.

That ceased the day he made his visit. Her new position was understudy to the US Secretary of State. For five years, that is what she did. Her father then arrived once again to inform her that she had been assigned a new role. No questions were asked, no explanations given. She was to become First Assistant to the US Secretary of the Department of Defence. Eight years later, three months after the death of her mother Valda Balaz became the new Secretary of Defence. In this role she influenced the

international stage on a daily basis. Her influence was second to the President of the United States of America in the order, administration and assignment of the world's most powerful war machine.

Valda Balaz imitated the ruthless nature of her father and the President of the United States of America had so many other things to attend to.

On a clear morning, where the first streaks of liquid sunshine streamed across the Pacific Ocean, Valda Balaz sat on a sturdy and stylish chrome, steel and glass deck that stretched out to hover above a private, secluded beach in the northern region of New Hampshire. Her cell-phone sounded its distinctive tone. She reached for it and checked the caller before tapping her screen once.

"Hello Anita. It's been a long time. What can I do for you?"

CHAPTER TWENTY FOUR

A sigh escaped Carter's lips as the road opened its way to the outskirts of the city. A fresh, cool greenness began to surround them. He glanced across at Katy to see that she too seemed more at ease, drinking in the soft light reflected from trees and grass which replaced the gritty glitter of concrete, cold steel and glass.

"Coffee soon?" he murmured, hesitant to disturb the glow of silence.

"Sure." Katy seemed almost mesmerised.

The hum of the vehicle, wheels on tarmac, wind rushing past, green beginning to usurp grey and black and the sparkling lights of New York helped them slip with ease into a shared silence. At the next exit, just after seven am, the tick of the indicator sounded as Carter eased his car into the outside lane and stopped down at an old-fashioned diner. It looked like it could have been extracted from a road movie from nineteen-fifty-two. The waitress was dressed to suit.

She smiled and chatted with an irresistible animation while she made them each a take-out coffee, prattling on and on about weather and kids and life. It seemed not to matter whether they responded at all. One comment stuck in Carter's mind when he and Katy were back on the road and the journey began to shift into a slow, winding expedition through endless hills and overhanging trees.

As they were leaving the diner, the waitress called out,

"Be bold. This weekend is time for you both. Enjoy Balsam Lake."

Neither he nor Katy had mentioned anything about their destination and there were still a hundred different places they could have been going. What on earth did she mean by "be bold"?

Carter wiped his hand across his face, reached for his coffee and let his foot rest a little lighter on the accelerator. He lowered his window as the SUV slowed to half its previous pace. As that happened, all the trees slowed down with them. Single droplets of dew glistened on the grass beside the road, soft morning light refracting every drop. Before them, the mountains of the Catskills rose in glorious majesty into a brightening blue sky scudded with soft, white clouds.

"Wow, I'd almost forgotten how beautiful it is out here." whispered Katy as they wound their way into the mountains.

"It sure is. Look at that."

Suspended on a gracious thermal in the cool air were two eagles, floating easily on updrafts, scanning the terrain for their morning feed. Carter pulled the SUV to the side of the road, lowered both front windows and, even from inside the cabin, he and Katy were at once transfixed by the birds. They sat in the cabin in complete silence. Without warning, one of the birds called out its piercing shriek. The other responded with its own spine tingling call.

Suddenly Carter and Katy became the eagles.

Breathtaking views, the most extraordinary sight imaginable and the power of wings, sure, complete and at ease was their experience as they hovered without effort above the vehicle. Here they sought nothing but the joy of being suspended two hundred feet above the treetops, wheeling and swerving one with the other. Somehow they gazed down upon themselves, two pragmatic, practical New Yorkers in an SUV, but from the clearest possible perspective that they were also these majestic birds. They floated, hovered and gazed in complete wonder and awe through the eyes of eagles for what might have been one minute or might have been thirty. In this realm, time seemed somehow immaterial.

150

Then it was over, just as it had begun.

"Carter. Carter? Are you OK?" whispered Katy, eyes still glazed but conscious of herself as herself once again.

"Sure. Yes. Yes. Just give me a minute." He let out a big breath as though he had been holding it inside for too long. "Just one minute."

His left hand scrabbled at the door, searching for the handle as though he didn't know his own car. His fingers hooked onto the latch and he threw the door open to escape the confines of the metal and plastic box. He stumbled a few steps and almost fell, but managed to land in an awkward heap on grass and wildflowers ten feet from the car.

"What the fuck just happened?" Carter sputtered, a look of complete disarray in his face, his eyes shining.

"We were.......," Katy looked dazed and somehow beatific, "flying?!" She smiled at Carter, the broadest smile he had ever seen from her.

"We were flying, Carter. It was so wonderful. I've never experienced anything like it. I could see forever. We were flying..."

"Not possible. It's not possible." Carter stood, shook his whole body, brushed his fingers through his hair and stretched his arms above his head. As Katy watched, from her vantage, she was sure she could see broad wings extending from his arms and shoulders. Or was that just a trick of the light?

"You saw what I saw, Carter. I know you saw it. I was there and I know that you were too. Possible or not, it just happened."

"We're both tired. Some kind of optical illusion or something. Maybe it would be a good idea to rest for an hour, clear our heads, freshen up a little?"

"I don't feel sleepy. Not at all. The opposite, actually. If you need rest, can I drive your car for a while?"

Carter didn't answer for a few moments then shook his head as though that might help him to return to his senses. He muttered something about having strange visions, something about his parents, something about imaginary friends – then

looked straight at Katy, his eyes damp, tears rolling down his cheeks. He wiped them away with the back of his hand, rubbed his face vigorously with both hands and spoke.

"Sure Katy. You drive. Good idea."

Without another word he climbed into the passenger seat, leaving her standing, dumbfounded by what she had just seen.

"Give me a minute or two. I have to re-orientate for a bit." Katy replied in a soft voice. There was no answer, so Katy began to walk back the way they had come. Just one step after the other to freshen up, ease her heart rate a little, breathe in the fresh air, smell the pine needles and the wildflowers. Walking just a few hundred yards to remember what it could be like to walk on solid ground, mother earth. She took off her shoes, glancing back towards Carter to see if there was any sign of hurry or impatience but he was just sitting, head laid back on the headrest. Or so it looked from here. He was in no hurry.

Holding her shoes in her left hand, she sidled into the forest just a little and the woods enclosed her with a brooding silence. She was fifty yards from the road, but the trees behind her seemed to shift a little closer together with every step she took.

She remembered things from when she was just a kid, on camps and adventures with her Dad in these mountains. Such happy memories sprang into her mind. One vivid memory leapt into her awareness and stayed there. She had been nine years old. While walking through a forest much like this, here in the Catskills, she had felt a sense that she was not alone. Her father was not far away but far enough for her to know that it wasn't him she was sensing. It was something else. Even at age nine it hadn't felt frightening, just a bit eerie and unusual. Then the experience had deepened. She saw him, spoke with him, hugged him, bade him farewell and promised to remember.

She had not remembered until now, but perhaps now was the perfect time. Now her memory was detailed and lucid. So present that it was as though Katy were nine again and the scene being played out in this same moment. She remembered too her conversation with her father. In the evening, sitting by

the campfire with her father, she had spoken to him about her experience. He had simply smiled at her and told her it was time to forget about imaginary friends. It was time to become a big girl. So that is what she had done, until this moment. It might even be perfect timing. Katy remembered everything. Every detail. Every word if there were words at all.

He was not at all frightening. When he was present nothing was frightening. She sat on the leaves and the moss, her skinny legs folded underneath, hands resting in her lap over khaki hiking shorts. He sat with her, dressed in some kind of brown or green robe, his arms mirroring her. He sat on his legs in a way that Katy had thought most adults either couldn't or wouldn't do. Smiling, he reached out one hand to encourage her. She took his forefinger in her small hand and smiled in return. Without words, he had begun to speak with her, though sometimes it was hard to discern whether it was the wind washing through the leaves and branches, the soft sloughing of wind through pine or his voice planting itself direct into her mind. His mouth didn't move yet she heard words, she was certain of it. His chest rose and fell as he breathed. Wisps of his leafy hair moved a little with the breeze and she listened.

This is the story he told.

"One day soon all of these things will occur. I share it with you because you and many others will play a part in the centre of it all. You could not know about this until now. Once the telling is done I will ask you to remember it, but you will forget until the right moment. At that time you will remember as if it is happening to you once again, so clear will be every detail and every word, though no words will be framed from my mouth.

My name is Negyesydd. I have lived a long time. Though to you I appear perhaps as another adult, I have lived much longer than you can imagine. This story is one of those that I have carried in this life, though its origins come from a time far removed. Yet because the story is here with me now, it is never and can never be removed from this time."

He shifted his shoulders and the air rippled around him.

"There are two fabulous powers, appearing as two colours of the same light, one being the most verdant green and the other an incandescent crimson. These two beings came to this earth that we all know, or feel that we know. As was their nature, they began to dance. From this came a kaleidoscope of colours and images, creation and destruction, light and darkness woven together in a chaotic confusion. This left the earth scattered and disoriented. The two beings saw that this is what they had done. They sat together to speak and to decide. Both observed that the dance they performed sparked and maintained chaos.

After speaking together for what seemed to them like no time, but was one thousand years, they took a decision to dance alone. They agreed to dance in turn, sparking and spawning creation rather than spewing it forth all at once. One would rest, watch the other dance and prepare for the time when it would dance again. But now, in conflict with their agreement, the crimson dancer continued dancing for aeons, fuelling fire, melting steel and stone, building and constructing, burning and smelting. For too long, the green rested and watched, silent tears rolling down its enormous face.

The time is now.

There is no more waiting. With tears drying, the other, the green, the nurturer has ended the wait, has begun to stand, is beginning to dance once again.

With this standing, the crimson being cast itself into a flurry and a fury. On the earth, this has become the harbinger of great destruction, war and disaster. The earth has begun to quake, to vibrate with greater ferocity. Fire has begun to spew from suppurating vents. The air has become thick and dank, the soil barren and dry. Water flows in many rivers as a filth, dark and cloudy. The time of the dance of the crimson is drawing to a close. The being of nurture, earth care and natural co-creation is standing.

With that first movement, thirteen thousand one hundred and eighty-two human children opened their eyes for the very first time and remembered why they have come here. A great

war subsided into a cold and threatening peace and the children born with eyes open began their work. At this early stage, many of them weep as they work, feel the yoke of the dance of the crimson and struggle and choke. Some are lost. Some could not stand the agony and slide into forgetfulness once more.

Many have prevailed and many more have arrived. As the green begins to dance its first slow and stealthy movements there is a shift on the earth unlike anything ever experienced on this plane.

Never in living human history has such a change come, though there are humans who have journeyed for over nine hundred thousand years. For these few, memories of another dance of power reminded them that as this new dance begins, there is no turning back.

As the green began to move, 'something happened'. An energy movement has begun.

At once more and more humans began to dream of peace, live for peace, stand for peace. The balance of the dance begins to be restored; the people who have been enthralled, enmeshed, chained and imprisoned begin to feel the loosening of their bonds. The troubles of the earth begin to subside, though the impetus and the power of the crimson dance still flares all over the world, clinging to power. As that being feels the dance of the green take shape it casts deeper and deeper thralls, controls and illness. It is a final scrambling effort to persist as it has so many times before, always seeking to remain to wield its titanic influence.

Many of those being born were born into the new vision. This alone empowered the green to continue its dance. As the dance progresses many thousands more have opened their eyes and their hearts to a new movement, a shift in how the world must unfold. With the dance of the green is created a hope for the future in the face of bleakness and trouble. The birthing of the dance of the green is confronted with challenge and uncertainty. But with each human who begins to gain hope and takes action to empower that hope, the green is strengthened, sustained

and sated. The dance will become impossible in its burgeoning beauty, more sweet and flowing to weave an unimaginable tapestry of incredible magnificence in every single nuance of movement.

It is the dance of the green, verdant and plentiful that shifts the way the world works, moves life into the possibility and the reality of co-creation, manifestation, nurture and love. The dance of the verdant green has begun and it will persist. It must persist.

Know that in your experience and in mine it will be many thousands of years. That fantastic era has now commenced."

Katy smiled as she recalled the excitement of that meeting. Her eyes sparkled as they hadn't since that day so many years ago. She remembered Negyesydd standing to bring one of his leafy hands to rest on her head. She felt it as a simple blessing. He brushed his leafy hand across her pate in the way a father would, with love and care. She felt a massive rush of well-being descend upon her in that instant. She looked up to gaze at him, towering above her – but he was gone. She sprang to her feet and rushed along the path to find her father, to tell him everything that had happened.

Her father listened to every word, caught in her excitement. When she was complete, he had gently admonished her for holding onto imaginary friends. 'Katy, sweetheart, you are now too old for such things' he said, 'you must live in the real world.' Katy loved her father. She vowed never to see, feel, experience, imagine or create such a childish dream again. She locked it away in the deepest recesses of her mind.

Now, unbidden, without seeking permission, over-riding her vow, Katy's imaginary friend had returned.

"Let's go." Katy climbed into the driver's seat and started the SUV. Carter looked at her and was surprised how young and refreshed she looked. "What's happened to you?"

"I couldn't even begin to explain. Let's just get there, shall we? This is going to be interesting and I'm way out of my

depth." She pushed her foot a little harder on the accelerator and the car surged forward, wheels spinning.

Ahead, the mountains loomed, looking less imposing and more inviting as they approached. Surrounding them, the green was everywhere. Above them, in the place of the eagles was endless blue.

Windows wound down to allow the coolness of the air to flow freely through the car, Carter and Katy breathed deep breaths, filling their lungs with the freshest air they had experienced for a long time. The road wound through the mountains, one moment steep drops to the left and then to the right. They gazed at head-turning views between the sturdy trunks of trees that clung with stolid vigilance to the tortuous slopes, ever reaching towards heaven.

"Man, this is so beautiful. I haven't been up this way for ages. I used to love coming up here as a kid." Katy steered the SUV around bend after bend, ever upward, the air becoming fresher by the minute.

"It is," replied Carter, "And this is the place we are setting up to drill for gas. It seems a shame once you get up here, have a look and get the feel of the place."

"It does, it surely does." Katy brought the car to a halt at a crossroad and peered in all directions to find a road sign.

"I think it's straight ahead. Do you have any better ideas, Carter?"

"None. Just go straight. There can't be too many wrong turns we can make when we're this close." Both of them looked refreshed and somehow lighter. Five minutes later they rolled the SUV at a slow idle through the village of Livingston Manor.

"We could turn here towards the lake, but I'm thinking we go and have a look at the place you arranged for us to stay. We can get rid of some gear and then head out to the Lake. What do you say, Carter?"

"I'm easy. Sure, let's find the place. It's a bit further along at Roscoe." They passed the town limits and kept moving,

looking right and left at a genuinely quaint and beautiful town dropped into an even more beautiful landscape.

"The house I booked is just a cabin. We collect the key in one of those lock-boxes. It's you and me and whatever ghosts there are up here, Katy."

Soon they arrived at Roscoe, another quaint village. They passed through without stopping and continued half a mile before turning left to find the cottage.

"It's such a cute cottage, Carter, check it out." Katy sounded much like the excited little girl she had recalled earlier. Carter had not met this version of her and was entranced. 'Innocence and a light heart are attractive things' thought Carter as he noticed that the smooth, collected, New York City woman had left the room.

They eased the car onto a cobbled driveway alongside a small but well-tended cottage. It was fashioned from solid timber logs, hacked and shaped at each end to fit together. The weather had offered its services to weave one log with another so that they sat in a strange intimacy and comfort with each other. Sash windows revealed three rooms. The main part of the house was a substantial rumpus room with a rough timber floor covered with several rugs that might have been Persian. Alongside these, in an awkward adjacency to tanned animal skins and a mud-brown, leather lounge lay a book on Vegan cooking in front of a rough, stone fireplace.

To either side of this stood bookshelves filled to overflowing with fauna, geography, hunting, fishing and flora reference books. One shelf contained a small selection of Western novels alongside a variety of volumes of Stephen King and a dog eared version of The Lord of the Rings. There were extra stacks of books on the floor beside the shelves.

Decorative antique bric-a-brac, paintings on tanned animal hide and hunting trophy heads were strewn around the walls. One corner was dedicated to what looked like a basic but functional kitchen. An array of cooking pots hung from metal hooks on a round steel frame.

One open door at the far end of the room revealed a small bathroom. A claw-foot bath was perched against one wall. The wall and floor were both tiled in charcoal-grey and white. A closed wooden door with polished brass handle led to the bedroom. Carter carried a large bag from the rear of the car. He dragged a second along the path, its castor wheels rattling and protesting on the stones.

"Did you pack bricks, Katy? This damn thing is heavy."

"Some books would be all that weighs anything. I brought a few books," said Katy feeling a little sheepish. She flipped the rotors on a combination lockbox that contained the key to the cottage.

"We're here for two days. What on earth did you bring books for?"

"I like books."

She retrieved the key, slid it into the lock and opened the door. Carter hauled his load inside and dropped both suitcases on the floor. He looked around. "This not a bad looking place. I think we've done OK, Katy. Look, there's even a stack of dry wood. We can get a fire going tonight."

Katy walked through the room. She pushed open the bedroom door.

"Um, Carter, there's just one bed in here. It looks to be king-size I think. Are we supposed to share that?"

"Ah shit, I didn't think of that. No problem. I can crash out here near the fire on this super-soft lounge." He punctuated his comment by flopping into the lounge. It expelled a big whoosh of air. Katy continued to explore the bedroom, bathroom and at last, the crowded bookshelves near the fireplace. She drew her finger across the spines of the books in the top row until she came to one small volume dwarfed by all the other references.

"Heya, Carter. Have a look at this. This is a pretty unexpected little book to have amongst this lot, wouldn't you say?" She turned the small volume over in her hands and read, first the title, then the description etched on the back cover. The small

book was stained with age. It was marked as a 'first edition', published in 1937.

"*Three Thousand Years – History of the Muhheconneok*" *- In the annals of white history, there is little to find of the genuine story of the original people of what became New York state. In this volume compiled by seven families of the original Mohican tribes of the Mahicannituck explores and marks the contributions of the Muhheconneok to this exceptional region.*

Under the short text was a black and white photograph of around thirty Native American people, dressed in traditional clothing, frowning at the camera." She looked at Carter for a moment, surprised and delighted as she continued to read, flipping pages. "Wow, Carter this has got to be a pretty rare little book. It's a wonder it hasn't been taken out of here long before now."

He was less interested, "Great, slip it under your arm or something. Let's go, Katy. I want to have a look at this lake." Carter moved towards the door. Katy followed him, her head still buried in the book.

CHAPTER TWENTY FIVE

Just a little before the sun reached its zenith, bathing the landscape in the brightest of light, Elias rose from the ceremonial place, collected his tools and began to prepare for the journey home. Not a single wisp of mist remained. Sunlight glinted here and there along the river as it snaked its way to a brilliant, sparkling, blue-green ocean.

The Call, his responsibility, was done.

What that meant to Elias was the beginning of a long wait. Those he had called must hear him, respond and commit to the pilgrimage. Some would not take so long and others had massive journeys to negotiate. All must begin quite soon. There was much to do.

He padded barefoot on the cool stone and began his descent, watching the light play on that river and sensing its similarity to the travels that each of those 'called' must make. When he reached his home, a little more than three days walk from this sacred place, he would need to make a connection with each walker. They would require guidance and assistance. That wasn't true of them all. Victor would be fine. David was dependable, Wolf was unpredictable but capable and Tisa, particularly when tested, proved to need no help.

As he walked, he smiled at the thought of telling Tisa she might need his help. He missed her. Tisa had a way about her which appealed to a core place in Elias. She brought him into deep appreciation of this Mother of The Earth, this dreamer-creator of a new-old way. Her New Earth Village had thrived, against all odds for thirty years.

However, many of the others *would* need assistance. It was important for him to make his way home swiftly.

It took just one deep encrypted call and one similar encrypted email for Valda to start a process that within six hours, even she would not be able to stop. There were not many people in the world for whom she would move with such haste. Anita Claesson was a special case. She was an important and useful ally who possessed significant power in several realms.

Turning over the events of the day, Valda smiled at the prospect of the outcomes of every step. She had been trained well for this kind of interaction. Valda felt the power of her influence in a world still dominated by men. Though her mind was a powerful tool, it was not her mind that guided most of her decisions. She had access to so much more.

In addition to her comprehensive training she also possessed an innate 'feeling' sense she had honed over many years in her own body. It told her, though with less transparency, that while the decisions of the day would yield well, other influences were being cast. She felt these aberrations as a sharp, shooting pain in her left temple. For her, that particular sign had never been as simple as a 'headache.'

"I need to look into this," she muttered as she stood to erect a shade and arrange a yoga mat. Lowering her body into lotus pose, she sat on the mat, back straight, eyes closed and hands in a position of supplication.

One minute and eleven seconds into her meditation the visions began.

Soaring across a lightless sky flew giant creatures, horrifying in their distortion and mortifying to witness. Underneath this on a plane that might have been solid ground, lay an enormous network of crimson bands strewn in every direction, clamped upon the superstructure of this realm.

Valda moved here without fear.

That hadn't always been true. The first few times she had entered this realm without sufficient knowledge or preparation had been beyond terrifying. For the malevolent beings here,

sensing her fear was instantaneous. On both occasions it had taken an intervention to interrupt them from their voracious assignment to feed on that fear.

The first intervention had been mundane, a simple redirection around a flux of energy which felt magnetic like a swirling whirlpool. On this occasion Valda had no sense of what had intervened, only that she had somehow avoided great danger.

The second intervention was unexpected, uncalled for and dramatic. It seemed to arise from the issuance of fear itself. One moment the beings had zeroed in on her terrified energy and the next they had turned abruptly away, shrieking as though in pain or somehow challenged. Valda witnessed their unexpected trepidation as they addressed a tiny, fascinating, bright, green-gold light.

Each of her senses screamed when that entity issued its own power, challenging the beings to desist or cease to exist. One of the giant beings, its pustulant skin seeping a fetid putrescence, moved to engulf the challenger in its giant maw. A livid crimson energy poured into the cosmos ahead of its advance. A single pulse of verdant power brought the giant to an instant stop. That pulse of power, at a far greater distance was agonising for Valda. It was far more devastating to the giant being. Reeling and flaying, vermillion bursts of pure energy emanated from a massive gash which tore it from mouth to tail.

From the mortal wound that creature bore came an immeasurable wash of fear which permeated everything. That wash of fear prompted each of the other gargantuan beings into ferocious action. They all lost interest in everything but their damaged companion. In a sickening, bloodcurdling display, they consumed it in its entirety. Physical, mental, emotional, spiritual and energetic life force to the last tendril of its bilious auric power.

To her relief, Valda was forgotten.

Their hunger abated, the creatures retreated, faded and withdrew.

When she rediscovered the capacity to reason, Valda surveyed all that was in her awareness with studied thoroughness. Standing or perhaps floating, the intense, green-gold light faded. Valda was able to perceive the form of a diminutive human woman. She saw no more as the light and thus any form it seemed to present, dimmed to blackness.

What human of such power could or would intervene on her behalf? Even more surprising was that she sensed no malevolence at all from the being. In fact she had sensed something infinitely benevolent. Long ago, Valda had ceased all pretence that her work served any but her own agenda and that of her master. It was impossible for her to comprehend the 'why' of such an extraordinary intervention on her behalf.

She chose each of her tools for success and efficacy. Morality and compassion had no part to play.

This being on the other hand...? The experience was etched into her memory. The being and its motivations remained a complete enigma.

Nowadays, she knew this territory well. She moved through it without effort, scanning for each and every ripple of power. All who visited here could not avoid leaving a traceable signature in the matrix and the tapestry. This visit was already proving useful for Valda. She could see that there had been an inordinate amount of activity in the field. She continued her painstaking search in an effort to locate that one, specific stitch in the weave. That single, significant exercise of power continued to spike an agonising pain in her left temple.

Several times a glimmer of energy tasted almost right, but that was all, just a fleeting taste. A group of three power-filled beings had been bold or foolish enough to visit here together. They had stayed for quite some time. One extraordinarily ancient being with a signature she was familiar with had called by briefly. He appeared to have come with something or someone she could not identify. That alone was unusual and worthy of note. Whatever it was, it tasted of enormous puissance. Somehow it managed to effectively mask its identity from her.

She tried her best, extended tendrils of power but was unable to tear the mask aside. It was impossible for her to determine what had been present. Automatically, Valda made a mental note to further investigate a being with such potency.

Perhaps it was a long time that she searched in that world. In the world of form and time, Valda completed her meditation to the recorded sound of a Tibetan bell just thirty minutes later. She had found much of what she needed. The pain-filled sting in her temple was summarily banished.

Damn that bloody earth wizard. He had done it. He had taken the step that so many others had shied from. Elias had made the call. It was a bold and courageous move. His ceremony, his call to the knowledge-keepers and change-agents meant that, in this instant, everything must change.

So be it.

Valda's mind raced as she calculated the risk of bringing this news and knowledge to her own circle. Some of them had little idea that she held a key to other realms. Certainly all of them recognised that she possessed power and respect yet she was also acutely aware that competition was the nature of their beast. Some would hear whatever she shared to find a way to challenge her. They would seek to gain and distribute their advantage. Some would move with her because the hierarchy told them that they must. She decided it would be easier to keep her discovery confidential for now. She would simply act.

Valda stood, leaving all her detritus where it lay. The yard boy would get it. The Cardinal's boys were trained well to understand submission, compliance, orders and obedience once he was done with them.

"Speak."

He was the only man she knew who answered the phone in this manner. He also knew with whom he was speaking. That proclaimed an insolence she may well need to deal with at one point or another.

"There are some shudders in the machine. I need you to take action, radical collection. Do not terminate."

"Yes."

There was nothing more from him. She could hear him breathing.

"Locate and collect thirty-six, thirty-seven and fifty-eight. Canada."

She enunciated with intent so as to ensure there was no misunderstanding. The call ended as abruptly as it had begun.

'With those three collected we'll see whether Elias can bring his plan to fruition,' thought Valda as she paced backwards and forwards. She picked up her cell once again. She knew it would ring three times before it was answered or it wouldn't be answered. She listened through the third long tone.

"Adiputera." He was similarly abrupt.

"Cardinal, steps have been taken that will disturb us all. I first sensed and have just now confirmed that to be true. Elias has been proactive. He has taken the step we have always known possible. As a result, others have begun to move and there will need to be a co-operative strategy. Until further notice you will need to cease and desist your er...'practices' until we are able to deal with these matters."

She sounded calm, yet the firmness in her voice could not be mistaken. She continued.

"We will be facing enough challenge without additional confusion."

"I hear you. Do you have a timeline, dear lady?"

"Now of course." She barked.

With a determined effort to maintain or at least fabricate calm between them, Valda breathed several deep breaths. For the moment and as long as he toed the line, the arrogant prick was still more useful as a genuine ally than an automaton.

"Please Cardinal, as soon as you are able for your best interest and mine. Be assured that we are facing challenge and difficult times of great significance. We must be united".

"As you desire, Madame, I'll begin to dismantle immediately and apply the necessary covers." The Cardinal scratched

his groin with his free hand. He gripped his semi-erect cock through his cassock as he spoke.

"Thank you, Cardinal. I do assure you it will be for the best."

"That is without question, Madame. Thank you for the notification." The clergyman responded in the diplomatic tone he normally reserved for peers and superiors in the church. She disconnected. The cardinal gazed at the screen of his smart-phone for a few seconds after the screen blacked out. He slid it into his top pocket.

"Fuck her." He snarled.

Cardinal Adiputera was unaccustomed to taking orders from anyone. He was not going to start taking them now.

"Fuck her."

CHAPTER TWENTY SIX

"The corkscrew was quick thinking on your part, Mr Chant."

Doctor Mark Ellis, a slight sparrow of a man who looked to be inflicted by persistent illness, spoke in his chittering fashion to Simon. "Have no doubt that you saved this woman's life."

Simon shrugged and took his deep glass of cognac with him to the window where he downed half of it in one gigantic gulp.

"What caused it, Doctor? She was in perfect health one minute and the next..." He threw back the rest of the cognac.

"It can't have been the cocaine. I had much more than she did. We will do the tests in our own labs."

"I will do them personally, Mr Chant. It looks like a simple allergy response but I'll do all the necessary tests to determine what the allergy might be. She has no past allergic record that I am aware of."

The Doctor glanced nervously to see Simon Chant frowning directly at him.

"I will do the tests myself, Mr Chant, depend on it." Doctor Ellis said seriously.

"That is the only appropriate action, Doctor. Let me know the minute you have answers."

The doctor took a few steps toward the door of the apartment. Simon Chant's voice stopped him.

"Doctor, please ensure that those results remain strictly confidential. My eyes only, you understand?"

"Of course Mr Chant, consider it done."

The doctor continued to the door and left the room. The security-lock issued a soft click as it secured the room. It was the

only sound in the apartment. Triple-glazed windows blanketed all noise from the city far below.

Simon Chant punched the screen of his cell phone and waited for the call to connect. There was no answer, but for a shriek and whistle which sounded like an old style fax machine. He let it play for twenty seconds and hung up. That was the first step. It was not his preference to follow this path but the future of the company was dependent on the outcome of this unexpected drama. His role was to lead, so lead he would.

He poured another large cognac and made another call. He punched in the number of a local Indian food delivery restaurant and ordered the spiciest Indian food he could find. It was always this way once the cocaine and cognac had worn off. So bloody hungry.

Two days later, Dr Ellis presented Simon Chant with the test results. The testing was comprehensive. The results were clear.

Twenty four hours later, a tragic motor vehicle accident filled the headlines of every media outlet in the nation. The news affected a high-profile company, Verity Global, a household name across the United States. The report provided details of an accident which claimed the lives of a limousine driver, a highly respected medical research officer Dr Ellis, the personal assistant of the company chairman, Sarah Anderson and an unnamed junior lab technician from the Verity Global medical facility.

When the news had been pushed out of headlines, Simon Chant telephoned Alva Irving to inform her that her test results indicated she had fully recovered from her ordeal. Alva chose not to challenge her chairman about the vehicle accident. She felt the agony of her part in the deaths of people she had worked with for many years, peers, friends and associates. In her body Alva could feel the result of her own experimentation. She knew now that she would never truly recover. Other strategies would be necessary.

CHAPTER TWENTY SEVEN

Last time Tisa had heard from her friend and occasional protégé, Kesari and Max had been in Egypt. Kesari had posted her a photograph. It was one of those very few impractical items she carried with her on her journey. When travelling this way, without company and on foot it was the greatest danger of all. More dangerous than dark nights, wild animals, wild people and wild weather, was the danger of carrying too much.

She had a long way to go across several countries. She knew there were many perilous and troublesome places for any traveller. At least as an older woman she would draw far less attention from any militia. Perhaps some change had happened in the world. To be happier and safer in the world as an ageing, senior woman possessed a kind of simpering tragedy. Tisa had not grown up with that. As an older woman, most people would reach out to her. At least, that was the world she had known last time she travelled. Admittedly, Tisa hadn't travelled in this manner for thirty years, so much may have changed.

At least in this moment the world remained reassuringly familiar.

Tisa skirted around the edge of a wide-open plain of grass, stretching far into the distance. She hugged a line of trees, as much for personal cover as shade and relative cool. It was not the time to be witnessed by every living thing, nor to pass out in the baking sun. It was four days since she had walked away from what looked to be her life's work. She had met with no-one. It seemed village life had continued without her. No-one had tried to find her or encourage her return.

The call to be on the road was long expected. For many years Tisa had hoped for and dreaded the call. Neither she nor any of her companions had any idea that she would disappear one morning. No-one had imagined she would simply walk away with a brief letter of farewell. Perhaps one or two of them might understand – if they had ever listened, genuinely listened when she foretold this journey in children's stories.

Those children who heard those stories were now fully grown. Some of them might remember. Some might piece her stories together with the lives they were living. One or two may have had the sense to overlay fiction with reality to make the connection. In any case, she was alone now and she was making slow progress. She knew she walked around twenty-five kilometres per day. 'I have walked one hundred kilometres out of thousands,' she thought. She put another footstep behind her. This is the only way to do it, one footstep at a time. It was fast enough. It seemed interminably slow and it must be fast enough. She took some time to feel that. It would surely have been far more time-efficient to take one of the ancient vehicles parked outside her home.

No-one was following her. It was fast enough. She kept walking.

So far the days had been fine and clear. There had been an occasional threat of rain but at this time of year it would rarely form into anything. Unless a summer storm came raging through out of season. It sometimes happened, so best not to imagine it was impossible. Just keep walking, one foot in front of the other. Let's see what nature wants to deliver. Nature will have what she wants.

Tisa kept on doggedly, feeling a little better and a little stronger each day. Not a soul had passed words with her. Even the vague shadows she noticed in the distance several times had paid little attention to a single walking figure. The pack on her strong back seemed to lose a little bulk each day. Tisa knew it was she who was growing stronger. The change in her pack was not so significant. It seemed to become a little smaller, but that

too, was normal. With the constant motion everything dropped, bounced and shifted to the lowest point. That made space inside that was not available when first packed, but for the finely honed blade of a sharp knife with a simple, wooden handle.

She would fill that extra space with food and water. She must remain prepared for those days when no-one showed up or called her into their town, village or compound. When she had completed her passage through this grassland, she would need to be well stocked. She felt safe and held in this wild land, with the animals, the soft sound of breezes, open-skied nights and billions of stars.

When Tisa next stopped long enough to let her mind return she could see the northern end of the grasslands where it met a thick bank of trees. From this distance it appeared as a shadowy line but for the occasional larger tree that framed the sky. These stood out from the rest and said 'you are getting closer, Tisa. You are getting closer with every step you take. Every step makes a difference, old woman.'

Those big trees called her. She could hear her name whispered as she drew closer, one step at a time.

All of this land spoke to her all the time. She had heard a whisper in the sands and soils that Kesari was not in the same place, though she was still close by. She was close enough not to change direction. The earth told her this, as though it were counting Kesari's every footstep and keeping her in step with Tisa. She was not far. It was worth keeping on, to find her. She could always locate her somehow, that much both of them understood. Tisa knew that if she had felt the call so clearly, Kesari would also know and would be expecting her.

When she reached those trees, Tisa surmised, that distinct tree-line up ahead, she would also begin to meet people. By now that would be a good thing. There would be better water and better food than that which she could glean from the land. Standing still, she possessed the necessary skill to eat direct from this land. When she was moving, time became more important. When she began to move in this way, time ceased

to function normally. It sped up as soon as she did. She could feel it happening.

Tisa's thoughts went to those who flew in aeroplanes and drove fast cars. 'Time must rush by dangerously fast for them,' thought Tisa, smiling at how strange that would be. How unbearable would that be? Always rushing to keep up with time only to have it accelerate to match your pace.

One step after another, Tisa let her mind unravel the African grasslands to lay it out behind her like a waving sea of rustling stalks and leaves. A myriad of small animals slid silently below sight. The old woman knew them all.

When Tisa arrived at the village she approached with caution. A hot African sun blazed high in a perfectly blue sky. It was mid-afternoon, so there was time to ease her way in. It was more important to learn a little about this community rather than bursting in suddenly. As the sun began to soften, she watched people begin to populate the spaces between the buildings. The evening light was a burnished bronze across homes, dusty streets and endless grasslands. As she expected, the last of the local people to emerge were the older women. When they arrived, she stood and walked the final two hundred metres.

Holding her head straight and proud, she walked straight toward one older woman who had a brace of children running around her feet and clinging to her skirts. Without shifting her gaze for an instant she approached the woman as though no others existed.

Suddenly she was face to face with her. Crone meeting crone, their faces mirrored their experience with this magnificent, unforgiving land. The old woman's eyes twinkled like those of a child. The gaggle of children who clung to her skirts hushed when Tisa drew near. The old woman looked into Tisa's eyes and spoke to her in her own dialect. It was quite different from her own tongue but similar enough to understand.

"You have walked a long way, sister and have much further to go."

The old woman smiled at her then leaned down to lift a tiny child into her arms. Tisa smiled in return, nodded and spoke to her in the language of her own people.

"You read that right, my sister. So far I have walked a little way north. I have much further to go. Right now I am in need of rest. Is that possible here in your village?" she intoned steadily and cast her gaze around the children. These were quiet and attentive to both the old women.

"The children and I say you are welcome, sister. What name do we use for you?"

At this point the children loosed the skirts of the old woman and swarmed, still silent, around them both. Some hung from Tisa's clothing in the same manner in which they had been connected to the old woman.

"My name is Tisa. I thank you, sister"

"And mine is Cheelo. Come with me now. We go to see the women, to say hello and bring you into our place."

She reached out and gripped Tisa's hand with a grip as firm as steel. Tisa was well pleased with her strategy of entering the village. It seems she had met with the precise person she had hoped, the elder woman of the village. If this were so, according to local tradition, this woman held more power in the village than any other being, including the men. Even the chief would ponder before over-riding her authority. This made Cheelo an important first contact on her long journey through Africa. If she had managed to reach direct to the 'elder woman' her journey would be a simpler affair well into the future.

She shuffled along with Cheelo. Not a word passed between the two old women but the children broke their silence. Chattering with child-like animation, they telegraphed their excitement. Two small children were still connected, their tiny hands gripping the cloth of her shirt as though they would never release her. The old women and the tumbling mass of youngsters wove their way towards a long, low, mud-brick building. It sat at one end of what must be the village square, a wide-open, welcoming space. The yellow soil had been packed hard by a

billion foot-falls. There was a massive steel drum which served as a fire pit in the centre. Seats fashioned from logs, metal drums and upturned buckets surrounded the fire.

As they approached the longhouse, six or seven women emerged to greet Cheelo with wide grins and open arms. They called out to her, inviting them both to join them. Soon Tisa was surrounded by women and children. The women pressed food and water on her and offered a bitter drink in a small wooden cup. When she submitted to their call for inclusion, she discovered the drink slaked her thirst better than anything she had ever sampled. It may also have had ingredients that softened the edges of her consciousness. She began revealing many details of her story.

Cheelo interrupted her.

"Perhaps it is better for you to get some rest, sister. Let me show you the place where you can lay your head tonight and for as long as you need."

She took Tisa's arm with her iron grip once again. Leading her away from the flock of women and children she whispered with her as others prepared for dinner and talked, excited about unexpected travellers.

Cheelo made a clicking sound with her mouth when they reached the edge of the village square. She spoke with firm authority.

"It is best not to say too much to everyone all at once. Hold some of your story for the time it is right to share." She looked at Tisa's face, searching for any sign of disagreement.

"I understand, Cheelo. I have come a long way and I am tired. Thank you for extracting me. You are quite right. It is not my intention to share too much, yet I want you to know."

"Then tell me, Tisa. Tell me stories about finding your friends and travelling to far-off lands. Tell me more about Elias and your call. Tomorrow I will tell you some stories of mine."

She smiled a knowing smile. They stooped a little to enter one of the thatched huts. Together they sat inside, leaning into the comfort of a cool mud-brick wall. Tisa knew now

that she had chosen well. She had met exactly the woman she intended. This meeting would provide her with greater safety on her journey.

"You know of Elias?"

Cheelo nodded. "He has reached out to many. He told me you were coming and asked me to do what I could to assist. There is quite a lot I can do."

She smiled her warm smile once again and Tisa felt the protective nurture of this old woman. For an hour she spoke with open frankness about her history with Elias, the work she had been doing for the past thirty years on the grasslands to the south and the need for this journey. As they sat together, silent at last, basking in the comfort of being with one another, a small ten-year-old girl poked her head inside the door to invite them to dinner.

Though she had entered the village quietly, Tisa's arrival had created a stir. It rippled through each and every soul. Everyone in the village had been summoned to this welcoming dinner. They wished to honour, welcome and meet her. It wasn't quite the anonymity she had hoped for but there was nothing to be done. She and Cheelo stood and walked to the long-house, the pretty child holding Tisa's outstretched hand.

It was apparent that the whole village had gathered. The room was busy. No-one was eating as the first to eat must be the guest of the feast. A large man stood at the far end of the room. Almost the moment the three of them entered the building, everyone became quiet.

The big man spoke.

"Welcome to our home, mother. It is our pleasure to welcome and share with you. From this moment, our home is your home. What we have is also yours. As we eat together, we weave the threads of friendship. I thank the earth for the food we are about to eat. I thank you for coming to meet us. You are always welcome."

He sat down. When he was seated a platter was placed before him and the room erupted into chatter. Once Tisa had

sampled some of the food, the clatter of eating followed. At first Tisa felt overwhelmed by the welcome. She had been hoping to slip into the village and back out, barely noticed. As the evening passed, she relieved her gnawing hunger and talked with Cheelo. When her conversation extended to several other women sitting nearby, she wondered where all this might lead. She became aware of the large man who had spoken. He crouched behind her and spoke to her in a gentle baritone.

"Mother, I know that you have been walking and must be tired so I won't ask you to stay up any later than necessary tonight. Tomorrow I ask you to spend some time in circle with me, Cheelo and several of my brothers and sisters. There are important matters to address. Will you do that?" He beamed a big smile as he asked.

"Of course, brother, thank you for the invitation. How do I find you?"

"Cheelo will ensure our connection. My name is Kumbukani. Tomorrow we speak together. Sleep well tonight, Mother Tisa."

"Thank you Kumbukani, I am sure I shall."

The big man rose to his full height. He stood well over six feet tall. Smiling his broad smile, he left the feast and strode with purpose to another large dwelling at the far end of the compound. Tisa watched him lean down to disappear inside. Five or six other villagers followed him. If there was anything to disturb her sleep this night, it was the knowledge that she now must stay through tomorrow and that she seemed to be the centre of some sort of gathering, a gathering that had arisen because of her arrival. A small, bright-eyed child pushed under her right arm and snuggled into her. She looked down at the child and smiled. That brought her back.

Tasting more of the delicious food prepared in her honour, Tisa brought her attention to the young women around her who asked her questions, one on top of the other. Tisa did her best to answer them all. Time passed and soon Cheelo let her know it was time to rest. By then the child had shifted into Tisa's lap and

was asleep. A fresh-faced young woman reached down to collect the sleeping child. She brushed with familiarity against her, at ease with the contact, woman and child alike. Tisa noticed this intimacy extended to the men of the village. These people were natural with touch, with being close. It felt good.

As she made her farewells, Cheelo moved in to guide her to the hut where she would sleep. She was surprised to find that there were already a dozen children scattered inside. Space remained for six or seven adults. Tisa looked at Cheelo with a question in her eyes.

"They wouldn't have it any other way, mother. There is a place for you and me, one of the mothers of these children and three of the men of the village. They will sleep nearest the door. Your place and mine is here."

Tisa lay down between the sleeping children. Though the day had been exciting and there were many reasons to lie awake, Tisa Emem fell into a deep and dreamless sleep the moment her head touched her pillow.

In the morning it was children who woke her, but not as she might have expected. Seven or eight children had found their own way to be as close to her as they could manage. Their wriggling made sleep impossible for her. Cheelo was nowhere to be seen. She hugged the children one by one as she extricated from them to emerge, blinking owl-like in the morning light. The sun peeked above the horizon, sending long streaks of burnt orange light between the trunks of trees to set the swaying heads of grass on fire. It was Tisa's favourite time of day. At this village, on this morning it was also unique and exquisite in its beauty. She walked outside the circle of buildings to the edge of the grassland. On an open space of yellow-ochre soil between vast tufts of long flat-bladed grass, she sat down, legs crossed.

Tisa closed her eyes. Behind her eyelids her eyes rolled upwards to gaze at a spot between her eyebrows. The darkness morphed into a rich, indigo hue. She sat still, alone, concealed by the grass. Soon the indigo became pure white.

In this place of sight beyond sight, Tisa witnessed her soul-self sitting in a space on the summit of a hill, bare of vegetation and scattered with boulders bigger than she. She stood and walked to the largest of the boulders, an immense rock three times her height. She began to climb. When Tisa reached the top, she stood there alone and surveyed the scene. In the distance, as she faced the rising sun stood a massive tower, straight and tall between the sun and her eyes. As she gazed, she was sure the tower moved, shuddered and shook – or was that a trick of the light as it poured around that shaft of glass and steel.

She shifted her gaze to see an image of a vast, luxurious ship plying its way through a sea of blood. As it drew near she could make out skeletal figures on the deck, surrounded by massive wealth and luxury. The figures scrabbled and tore at one another, searching for something to slake their hunger and thirst. Now she turned to gaze behind her. Fields of green extended far into the distance. Massive machines trundled across them, harvesting the heads of billions of growing things. In one corner of that immense field, the earth was brown and dry. In that place, a small group of people were touching each other's foreheads and passing one to the other, gifts packaged in fragments of rainbow. She could hear people singing.

Turning to the north she saw a vast library, a tower of knowledge. It reached further into the heavens than she could see. It was filled with every iota of knowledge the world had ever recorded. As she watched, she saw black roots claw their way into the soil, gripping deep into the earth, thrusting into bedrock. From that, crimson coloured leaves began to form. They shrouded the tower of knowledge from base to apex. A ferocious wind howled. As the tower collapsed, the dust and detritus of knowledge and learning carpeted the barren ground.

The vision became an immense volcano, thrusting far into the heavens. Beneath it lay a vast network of catacombs. For one moment the volcano stood there, gigantic and splendid. As she watched she saw tendrils of crimson fire split the earth far underground. The last image she witnessed was an enormous

explosion which cast lava and stone, ash and gas into a blood-red sky. The mountain became rubble. The catacombs were sealed.

Tisa sat on top of that boulder on top of a hill and mourned for her loss and sadness until there were no more tears to cry.

To her surprise, when her tears had dried a great peace arrived.

As the images faded, Tisa Emem opened her eyes. She looked around at the endless field of grass. The sunlight played across the swaying strands and shone bright in her eyes. She heard the singsong voices of children calling her name. Her smile returned. She stood and walked with slow steps back into the village. The cries of the children became louder when they saw her and realised she was with them and she was safe.

After breakfast, Tisa went with Cheelo to the large roundhouse at the far end of the square. Kumbukani and eleven members of the village were already in deep discussion. Most of them were grey-haired or without hair, but perhaps two were in their forties. Another two would not have been more than thirty-five years old. To Tisa's practiced eye there was one who was under twenty-five. Tisa wondered at this. It was not what would be considered 'normal' in this part of Africa. The young were never included in such a circle.

When he motioned, Tisa sat to the left of Kumbukani. Cheelo sat to her left. As they settled, Tisa heard Kumbukani ask the other members of the circle to interrupt their conversation and bring attention to their guest. One by one they signalled their agreement by placing one hand face-down on the bare earth.

"Mother Tisa, would you tell us of your journey, please?" asked Kumbukani in his gentle, rumbling tone.

Tisa looked around at the faces in the room. Each gave a sense of peace and relaxation. It was not the 'look' of their faces alone. She had a strong sense of feeling them in her body. It was as though they emanated an energy or field which helped her to feel at ease. Each of them had a unique frequency but the group also shared an all-encompassing frequency. It encircled them. The power of it was palpable.

"I have walked from a community a few days south of here. I have lived and worked with that community for the past thirty years. We are dedicated to regrowing, regenerating and refreshing the region. Our goal is to learn again how to live with the world, with the elements and, the sky above and the earth under our feet. Once we knew this better than most peoples of the world. Alas, we have forgotten much.

With just a little prompting, the opening of a few doors, we have achieved much and remembered much. The knowledge is programmed into the blood of each of us, deeper than we can comprehend. We are recalling how to seek inside."

She paused, recognising that if she were to follow the full version of her story they might be here for days. 'Abridged version, Tisa,' she thought.

The youngest member of the group spoke.

"Mother, it matters not for any of us if we are here for days. Please feel free to tell us the whole story. There is nothing more important in our practice than to spend time listening. We have all our ears open to you." She smiled at Tisa.

Had she spoken out loud? Was she still half asleep and not aware what her mouth was doing? The young woman spoke again.

"There is much that we can hear and see when we open all of our senses, Mother. This has been our practice since we were small children. It has been taught to us by our elders and is supported by our stories and our lore. You are safe here."

"Forgive me. It is just a little unsettling. In my community we work close with the land and with remembering what we once knew to align with the soil, water, sun and air. We choose to heal and repair as we are able. We have not taken the time to investigate this human connection which is your mastery. It is both exciting and, as I say, a little unsettling."

The thirteen people in the circle looked at her in silence. The young woman nodded. Kumbukani cleared his throat. Tisa sat silent for a few moments. She decided to be in complete faith that these people would never be her enemies and were in

alignment with her calling and her journey. She imagined she would need to discern this many times in her coming travels. What better time to practice her discernment than right here and right now?

She spoke of everything she could, from her initial connection with Elias over thirty years ago, the work she and her community had been doing in that time to the mission she was called to right now. She spoke of her fears for the world, for her community and for her friends, especially Kesari and Max. She spoke of her fears for her own safety. She also spoke of hope. She explained that for the past thirty years she had been assigned to creating a solution to the darkness which threatened to engulf the world. She talked of the past thirty years of modelling a different way. She was certain that she wasn't addressing everything that needed attention. She was also certain that she was addressing enough to make a difference.

To the best of her ability, she spoke of the Call she had received from Elias and the journey she had undertaken to travel to him, across the continent, across oceans and across the world. By the time she was complete, to Tisa's surprise, shadows were cooling the ground and stretched far across the plains. The day was drawing to a close. In all that time, through her sharing and some prolonged silences, all thirteen of the people gathered to hear her remained silent and receptive. They listened in silence until the last words issued from her mouth, from her heart and from her soul.

One of the female elders spoke. "Thank you for sharing from your heart, Tisa. You will find that there are more people than you imagine on a similar journey. It is happening all across the globe. In this village we have made contact with many others. We are a little surprised that we had not, until now, made connection with you who have lived and worked nearby. But perhaps that is why. We haven't thought to look so close to home. It seems you have been working with practical matters like food, water and shelter. While that is essential, it is quite

different to that which we have been attending." She paused a moment to take a drink, then continued.

"With your blessing we will send a messenger to your village in one week. We will inform them that you are safe and we will open a connection with your people and the work you have all been doing. As you follow your calling we will join with your family so that we might share what we have learned."

"Of course, sister, it does feel right, doesn't it?" Nothing could have suited her better. These people seemed on a similar course to that which she had given her life. As she sat in the circle she felt held by them in a way she hadn't felt since her time in presence with Elias. Another elder spoke.

"Mother Tisa, would you please leave us now. Having heard you, there is a lot for us to discuss and digest, not the least of which is how we can contribute to your continued journey." The elder turned to Cheelo and said, "Would you take her, Cheelo and return."

Cheelo and Tisa stood together. Tisa thanked them all for hearing her and the two of them left the room.

After the grey shadow of the closed room, though the sun by now was almost gone, they blinked in the golden dusk. Three girls of about twelve years sat just a little way from the door.

"I will go straight back in, Tisa, so can I leave you with these three. They will take you to the others and there will soon be dinner."

"Yes, that's fine, Cheelo. Do you have any idea how long you will be in there? I guess you all have to eat too," said Tisa.

"We do, and for that reason I don't think we'll be all that long. Kumbukani in particular will not want to miss his evening meal, so I suspect he will ask for a pause in proceedings rather than missing or delaying dinner. My guess is that we will recon-vene in the morning. For now I will go back in." She smiled, "I'll see you soon."

Cheelo turned to the three girls and asked them to take Tisa either to rest or to the longhouse, whichever she preferred. Two of the girls came to either side of Tisa and took her hands. The

other girl walked in front of her. They set out for the longhouse. Cheelo turned and went inside. The circle of elders continued late into the night.

Next morning Tisa woke surrounded by children once again. She rose to walk into the grassland for her morning meditation. She had woken late so the sun was high in the sky. She found the shade of a gnarled but leafy tree and took pleasure in the cool of mottled shade. Before she had completed her hour of meditation she was called back to the day by Cheelo's voice.

"Tisa. Tisa! Where are you? Tisa?"

"Over here, Cheelo. Just one minute."

Tisa emerged from the shadows into the heat of the sun. She squinted across the tall grass to see Cheelo looking straight at her.

"Come, come. Will you please join us in the circle?"

"I thought that my part in the circle was over." Brushing the dust and twigs from her skirt she added, "Yes, of course I will join you."

The old woman gripped her hand and together they walked to the roundhouse.

"I thought your part was over too. We all did. Some things have happened this morning. Do not worry. There is nothing to fear but we need you to be with us."

Together they hurried back into the subdued gloom of the roundhouse where the same twelve village members sat in silence. Kumbukani sat in the centre of the circle. As her eyes became accustomed to the darkness Tisa saw that Kumbukani was motioning for her to join him. Cheelo took her place on the edge of the wheel while Tisa stepped into the centre. Kumbukani gestured for her to sit with her back against his. Soon she was settled in place. She felt the warmth of his back against hers. A rumbling sound and vibration came through him. She took a moment to relax and let that be. As she did, the images of the previous day's meditation returned with far greater clarity. In that instant she let go of everything her mind was telling her to

do. As thinking ceased, Tisa saw images inside the virtual dream. 'Was this a hallucination?'

"It's no hallucination, Mother Tisa," rumbled Kumbukani. He seemed to speak from inside her belly. She had no notion as to whether his lips moved or there was any issue from his mouth, "it's a vision that we all see and it has direct connection to the call from Elias and to your pilgrimage. Keep these visions in your heart and soul as best you are able. As you progress, the meaning will become clearer. The imagery will teach and inform you."

The images vanished and in their place, Tisa saw circles of people sitting as this circle was sitting. Hundreds of circles of thirteen people sat just as this circle, in this village a few days walk from her home. She had imagined nothing like this. Rather she had imagined that she would walk alone and unaided for many weeks, even months. She saw that these circles were linked together, part of a matrix of people practising connection, in communication with one another across the continent and across the world. She felt excitement rise inside her, felt too a tide of emotion rise and overflow. Just as she felt that overflow, tears of joy, love, awe and wonder washed her cheeks. Kumbukani rumbled again.

"Brothers and sisters, this is Tisa and she is travelling, thus far, alone and unaccompanied. She may well come to your place, looking for safe haven. As we all know, it is very important that she is kept safe. We thirteen here commend her to you and assign you to keep her safe, hold her, introduce her to all that you can, just as we have begun."

For Tisa this was the most telling moment of the strangeness that had erupted into her life. She felt an answer, not in words, not in emotion, nor even in her heart but at some deeper level of her being. It was as though there was a wave of love, of being held, of recognition that reached out from every member of every circle in the vision – direct to her soul. She felt every one of them. Every single one. She felt them in a fashion that

she could not describe. There were no words. This was pure experience, beyond touch, beyond any sense she could identify.

For many years she had explored what many would see as 'unusual' or mystical experiences. Through meditation, ritual, trance, ceremony, teacher plants and substance Tisa had travelled but this was unique and exquisite. This was all-consuming and all-embracing. Tisa could not stop the tears flowing down her cheeks. She had no desire to do so.

"Keep breathing, Mother Tisa," rumbled Kumbukani, "it wouldn't do if you were to pass to the next realm here in this circle because I forgot to remind you to breathe." His reminder and his humour vibrated in her belly, adding to the beauty of the experience. His almost laughter, his compassion and his care were all present and, they too, embraced her until she was overflowing. She took a deep breath and her body convulsed a little as more tears escaped.

In that moment she was sure she could see Kesari moving with haste, determined and thorough through the streets of a town she knew but couldn't identify. Hurried steps, head turning from side to side, agitated, controlled, tense, breathing deep breaths, she was calling out something that Tisa couldn't discern. In the vision, Kesari paused for a moment almost sniffing the air. She shook her head a little and continued her thorough investigation of every shop and market stall, every nook and cranny. Tisa almost called out to her but saw something she wanted to burn into her memory.

Kesari is in Cairo. She could feel with distinct clarity where her friend was. She recognised the place and felt immediate relief.

Her pilgrimage had its first mission confirmed. She would find her friend. There was still a long way to go, so far to travel, yet through this strange experience with these people she felt confirmation and peace. Her relief eked a sob from her as she drew in another deep breath. Tisa spoke.

"What is this Kumbukani? What is going on?" she whispered.

"Ah Mother Tisa, a lot is happening all over the world which is connected to your journey. There are also many people in alignment with you and you will meet many of them face to face. Today, you have had the opportunity to meet several and to experience their capability." He chuckled and Tisa felt his body shake a little. His broad back moved against hers. He spoke again in his reassuring rumble.

"It is time for us to return." The vision of the many circles faded and vanished. Tisa returned to the roundhouse with her back pressed against Kumbukani. Twelve faces beamed at her and with her as each of them returned to the shrouded room. It was hot. Cheelo appeared at her side with a pitcher of fresh, cool water. She poured a cup and placed it in the old woman's hands.

Her smile seemed broader than her face.

"Welcome home, Mother Tisa. We have just done all we can for your safety and care. Travel in peace knowing that you have many friends on your journey."

CHAPTER TWENTY EIGHT

When Rena woke, she was naked but for a long white t-shirt, bunched around her waist. She was in her own bed with a feather duvet draped across her legs. Sun streamed through the small casement windows high on the bedroom wall, lighting tiny dust motes which rose in a soft plume from her duvet as it shifted with her. She was warm and comfortable but for the troubling visions of a strange and demanding dream. That dream twitched a muscle that ran down the right side of her neck and extended into her core, just below her navel. As her mind began to arrange the day ahead, from the care of her mother to the strange man she had invited to their home, she blushed.

Someone had undressed her, dressed her and put her to bed. Unless she had done that unwittingly – Victor must have done it.

"Good morning." Victor looked relaxed and a little bizarre. He stood in front of the stove wearing her mother's floral apron. The smell of eggs, bacon and toast was suspended in the warm air. "Want some breakfast?" Rena continued descending the spiral stairs, unable to suppress a smile at the edges of her mouth. The scene disarmed her pique at having been undressed by this stranger.

"Did you put me to bed?"

"I did." Victor continued to attend to the breakfast cooking, the sizzle of bacon the only sound. Rena's cheeks flushed a little deeper. Victor seemed not to notice the question, let alone her reaction.

"Thank you, I guess. What happened?" She scraped a chair back and sat at the large, timber dining-table.

"Breakfast?" Victor turned and smiled at her, fry-pan in hand.

"Er......yes please." He began to dish out on two large, white plates.

"I can't say what happened, Rena aside from your physical reaction. You blacked out, called out for me and since that moment you have been out cold or sleeping. I can take a guess if that's any help?" He smiled a broad smile, set the two plates full of food on the table and sat down.

"Your Mum's fine by the way. I said hello and made her some breakfast earlier."

Rena's jaw dropped. "You made breakfast for Mum! What? Is she ok? She didn't freak out?"

Victor laughed out loud.

"As I told you last night, if you were paying attention, your Mother and I have had an association for a long time, Rena. She is the main reason I turned up here at all."

"My Mum? I don't recall any of that." He nodded and shrugged, ate a big mouthful of food, poured a coffee and offered to fill her cup. After a moment, Rena nodded. "Yes coffee. Yes. Thanks."

"You heard the call last night didn't you?"

"The call?" Rena looked puzzled but not gormless. She had been informed by her dream.

Victor described what she had experienced down to the finest detail.

"Yes I did. How do you know that?"

"The call was intended for your Mum but as you know very well, she doesn't have the health or strength to respond. She made arrangements to pass her responsibility to the person she most loves and trusts. That's you, Rena. I was assigned to help you integrate and I can also provide some companionship and instruction along the way. I am called too. Your Mum has already arranged for her sister from Wales to live here and care for her. The only thing remaining is for you to agree. If you don't, of course we keep looking."

Rena pushed her chair back abruptly and stood, "Mum, what the fuck!" She rushed up the spiral staircase to her mother's bedroom. Victor stayed at the table, eating his breakfast and sipping coffee. Rena's shouting soon diminished to a gentle thrum of conversation between mother and daughter. By the time Victor had cleaned the kitchen they were done. Red-eyed and dishevelled, Rena returned.

"When do we go?"

"Tomorrow morning. Early."

At six am the following day they were sipping strong, black coffee at the kitchen table. Victor told Rena he would cleanse the place downstairs so she had time for a final farewell with her mother. When she returned the entire space was polished clean. Rena felt a little messier, her eyes red and swollen. Victor went up to visit Rena's mother. It was five minutes before he returned, looking pleased and determined.

"She's good, Rena. She knows how important this is. She is far stronger than you think."

At seven-fifteen, Victor and Rena set out, backpacks as light as they could manage. Walking east, they would soon connect with the Thames Track to follow it downriver as far as Erith.

"I'm still not sure why it's so damn important to do this on foot, Victor? We could be there in no time if we just booked a flight. Unless I'm misguided we are also heading in the wrong direction."

"It's important that we get our feet on the ground. Establishing connections from each of the starting points is an important part of responding to the call. Most people have forgotten what it feels like to connect with the earth. Everyone called has set off from different..." he paused for a moment to find words, "let's call them 'power spots', though power has little to do with it and spot isn't quite accurate either."

Victor thought for a moment.

"It does have to do with moving at the pace of the earth, the pace of being human and walking ley-lines from where the

call is heard to the place of origin. Some of it is complex and some quite simple."

Victor stopped walking and rubbed his hands across the back of his neck, stretching and taking deep breaths as he did so. He leaned down to touch the ground with both hands then stood and stretched backwards as far as he could reach. Rena did her best to copy him, though she was less elastic.

"Ancient people all over the world followed the same paths. It was not because they could see it worn into the ground but because there were songs or stories about the journey. They knew how to translate the song into the journey including warnings, places of beauty, where to find food, water and a whole lot more. What we are doing is a restart of that. It's a kind of reboot to activate the field."

He paused again to adjust the straps of his backpack, shrugging it higher on his back and tightening the strap across his chest.

"Well, that's part of it at least. It'll become clearer to you, that is, clearer as an experience as the journey goes on. Best news for you is that we don't have to walk the entire distance. That would be impossible with a lot of ocean in between. Even on land, we have choices."

They walked on and soon came to the bank of the Thames.

"It's a nice walk in any case. I'm mighty pleased it's cleared up," mused Rena. "What do we do for money?"

"We don't worry about it. You'll be surprised how things flow. The fact that you could experience the call means your Mum's confidence in you was well-founded. There are hundreds of thousands, perhaps millions of good folk all over the world who have been activated by Elias' call. Most of them don't have any conscious idea what has happened or even that anything has happened. We'll be fine. Be conscious of that and keep walking." He smiled. Rena noticed that his smile was becoming increasingly disarming.

Late that afternoon, Victor still walked with vigour. Rena looked as though she might die any minute. He turned to her and

said, "Just a little further. I have a very good friend who lives at Shornemead Fort. That's less than an hour from here." With the mention of an extra hour, Rena looked crestfallen. "Hey, cheer up. You've done well. The first day can be difficult even for a trained hiker. We'll take a break tomorrow because I want to spend the day with Bear. You'll have a chance to recover."

She huffed her frustration and kept plodding. Something sat in the back of her mind that didn't compute. If her memory served her well, Shornemead Fort had been demolished back in the nineteen sixties. There hadn't been anyone permanent there since the Second World War. What could he mean that he had a friend that lived there? A man called Bear? Some homeless guy maybe. Rena kept walking, the straps of her pack pinching and rubbing. Her new hiking shoes strangled her aching feet.

As they approached the old military fort a dense fog rolled up the Thames, blanketing everything in its path. So thick was the cloud that Victor stretched a short rope between them, tied at their belts.

"We can't be too careful," he grinned and pushed on. It was a good thing he used the string line as Rena realised that when it was extended, as it often was with Victor striding ahead, she couldn't make him out at all.

"Hey, slow down. This is all new to me. I'm exhausted. Victor, slow down."

"Sorry girl, you're right," Victor puffed, "I don't want to miss Bear. He's been expecting me." He slowed his pace a little. "It's important that we connect."

Rena noticed she could not make anything out with clarity, not even her own hand in front of her face. She tried it several times. Each time the blur became deeper.

"Victor. I think I need to rest. I might black out. My vision is blurring." She was breathless and confused. Victor came to her side.

"Let it happen, Rena. Just keep walking. I'll make sure you don't fall. It always happens the first few times anyone meets Bear. It's a good sign. It means he's close. Keep going, I've got

you." He linked her arm with his and walked beside her. The closeness and his solidity helped her balance.

"Just a little further."

"Hello Victor, what took you so long?" A deep, disembodied voice found its way through the fog. Rena's discomfort grew. Not just dizziness but a deep aching arose in all her joints. If it had not come on with such impact, she might have thought it nothing more than the result of her long day's trek, but this was different. While the ache was painful, Rena also felt an unexplainable elation and exhilaration.

"Bear, it's good to hear your voice. It's been too long." Victor's voice brimmed with emotion. It was a complete surprise to Rena. She peered through the fog, trying to make out a face, identify the form of this man who wielded such profound influence with her new companion.

"This is her then?" His ethereal voice sounded once again.

"Yes, the daughter of Ariah. Bear, meet Rena." It was at this moment that a shape emerged from the mist. What Rena saw was not what she had imagined. He was a powerful looking man, dressed in clothing that could have placed him in an ancient time. He looked like a member of an old religious order. She could still not manage a clear visual of him. The closer she looked at his face, the more it morphed and moved, becoming a thousand faces in one. The closer she looked the deeper the ache and the higher her emotional elation.

"Hello, Rena and welcome." His voice was mesmerising. They reached out a hand to each other. As their hands clasped he drew her closer. Without resistance, she stepped forward and they embraced. In the same instant, Rena felt a bolt of energy charge through her from foot to crown, warm comfort and excruciating pain in unison. She was no longer herself, no longer a body.

An exquisite sense of unity pervaded everything, from this place of pure consciousness. The universe was perfect in place, agony and ecstasy one and the same, distinctions between life and death impossible and impertinent. Everything awe and

wonder. He released her. She stepped back. Vincent reached out to steady her.

"My apologies, Rena. I'm sure that was a surprise but we don't have a lot of time to determine several things. One of those is now confirmed. So again, I offer a warm welcome. The ache you feel in your joints and bones will diminish with a little time." He turned to Victor and smiled. "Looks like you could both use a place to rest and a decent meal."

"That's certain. Lead the way, shiny one." Victor looked pleased. For some reason Rena felt that he was pleased with her. As they began to follow Bear, she looked sideways at Victor and issued a sharp whisper,

"Who or what is this guy and what the fuck just happened?"

Drawing her close, Victor kept his eyes on Bear's back as though to avoid losing him.

"He's an enigma. You are in the company of some powerful and useful humans Rena, me and your mother included. Bear is in a place all his own. I'm not sure even Elias has a complete understanding of his role or why he even seems to give a shit, but I was not going to miss meeting with him as we set out on this journey. I recommend that you stay alert and listen a lot. Much will be revealed."

They walked on, Rena and Victor trailing the misty image of this man who had emerged from the fog at a long abandoned fort beside the river. In less than five minutes he ducked his head down in front of them. He turned to warn them to do the same.

"I guess they thought they could knock out the first few invaders if the fort was ever overrun. They built the doors pretty low." His smile made Victor's grin appear dim by comparison. They bowed as they entered an expansive, round room. A bright fire flickered to the right. A large cast-iron pot bubbled above it, sending the scent of beef broth throughout the room. Rena realised that she was ravenous.

"Help yourself, little one. Bowls are near the fire and spoons too." Bear and Victor moved across the room and sat together, exchanging quiet words. Rena spooned broth into a

wooden bowl. She filled two others for Bear and Victor. They each took the bowl she offered, though Bear did not eat but placed it beside him. She and Victor ate while Bear's voice rumbled, blanketing the room like the warmth from the fire.

As she finished the broth, slurping the last few dregs, she took a closer look at Bear who sat opposite her. Victor sat to his left. There was something not quite human about him. She couldn't get a fix on it. It was as though there was a weird filter that shifted focus an instant before it became clear. She tried again and again as he spoke with Victor. Then she burst into their conversation.

"What is it about you? I keep trying to work out what it is that you have going on, but it seems impossible. Are you some sort of ghost or something? It's making me nervous and thank you for the stew."

Both men looked up at once and surveyed her as they might a noisy child interrupting adult conversation.

"...and don't do that shit to me either. He brought me along on this crazy journey," she pointed at Victor with her spoon, "that I know almost nothing about and you have just shown up, so none of that looking down your skinny noses at me. I need to know what's going on or, I am serious, I will go back home right now."

She stopped as suddenly as she had begun, wide-eyed and expectant.

"That's fair, little one." Bear rolled a cigarette, lit it and blew a cloud of sweet-smelling smoke toward the curved stone roof.

"As to the broth, you're very welcome. As to me, well that is a bit of a longer story. If you were to go back into the history of this land you would get the best clues. There is quite a lot of myth and legend that might help you identify what or who I am. I'm a bit distant from where most of the stories about me originate, but close enough. Suffice to say that I've been around these parts for aeons and I'm not feeling to go anywhere else for a long time. I like it here on these islands."

He rose from the fireside and took several large paces around the room until he was standing behind Victor. Somehow they looked like they could be brothers.

"Second part is, what you have just begun to participate in isn't any real surprise for me. It's come through on this plane before and worked out quite well for a while. This time around I suspect it'll stick around for much longer and be more widespread. If I'm right, the truth is I'm pretty happy to lend a little support to the degree that I am able. That might all sound like a lot of extra riddles and if so, so be it."

Rena was as confused as ever. "So you don't have anything to do with this thing that Victor and I are part of?"

"No, though I can be influential if there is genuine need. In my estimation, it would be better if I left it to you, Victor, Elias and the rest because my experience is marred by history and reshaped by the stories that have been told about me and everything that happened." He took a long drag on his rollup and passed it to Vincent.

"That's the power of stories, Rena. In some ways it doesn't matter much what happens. It is much more important how the stories are told because that becomes the truth. That becomes the illusion we all create for ourselves."

Victor reached over to Rena to pass the smoke. She took a moment to take it and have a tentative puff. She passed it to Bear.

"So why are we talking to you then? Seems like it's just Victor catching up with a friend?" She felt the 'ganga' take immediate effect and congratulated herself for her caution. She didn't want to be wasted while speaking with this man. He was already disconcerting.

Bear laughed a hearty laugh. "Well, there's no doubt that you are blessed with the kind of spirit you are going to need, little one." He winked at Victor and addressed him. "She seems to have adjusted to me already." Then back to her. "You don't have any joint pain or confusion any more, Rena?"

She took a moment to check in with her body and found that to be true.

"No. I'm fine. Thanks for asking." She was a little sur-prised that she now felt quite at ease both being with Bear and being in such close proximity. Even the shifting faces seemed to have settled and she could look at him without difficulty. "In fact, it's a relief. That was more than a little uncomfortable. Does that happen with everyone you meet? That must be murder for your social life." She giggled a little and realised that the joint had already had an effect. "I'm just wondering, Mr Bear," still smiling a broad smile she continued, in that strange place between seriousness and mirth, "If what you say is true, couldn't I just make up any old story, let's say one with a happy ending for me and keep telling that story to myself and anyone who wanted to listen and it would come to be?"

He nodded in enthusiastic agreement.

"Yes, that's it. At one level we can achieve a lot by just creating our own story and sticking to it. That has enormous power. So you can imagine that if you were to enrol a group of others to grasp your story, to own it, to align with it – you amplify the power of the story. That makes it very important to share your story."

He became intense and animated. With this came a greenish glow that extended from every part of his body. Rena watched, transfixed.

"Tell others the direction your story takes. People would be surprised what a close match there is with many individual stories. Most of us would be willing to make some minor changes to come into alignment with a strong story. 'Share your story' is the best advice I could give anyone. Make sure you and everyone else doesn't feel alone. In these times in particular, when there are so many people connected in ways that any other era could not imagine it is so important not to isolate." Bear moved again, crossing the room to collect a flint from a corner shelf. He dragged it down the stone wall. It sparked and ignited. He gazed at it for a few moments, re-lit the joint, took a deep drag and spoke once again.

"Connect and share your stories. Make close connection with as many as possible. Speak your truth without fear and discover that there are many more wanting to do the same and wanting leadership from whoever is willing to speak first. Share your stories so that you can gather together in this realm and begin to fashion the society and the future about which your stories tell. It's a pretty simple first step. To this point, in this particular drama, it is still a simple matter. Before too long you will discover that there are forces at play that will step in to diminish you and everyone. They will do everything they can to silence you and to separate you. They are accustomed to great power and have several thousand years' practice. They will cling to power with every ounce of everything they can muster."

Bear took another deep draw. An orange glow lit his ruddy, ageless face.

"The Call, the summoning of beings from all over the wheel of life is a bold and frightening move that begins a massive process foreseen in stories from many millennia. What Elias has done is a direct challenge to those who have misused their power. It cannot be ignored. It is certain that it will not go unnoticed. I should say it HAS not gone unnoticed and they will step up to the challenge. Elias was ordained to face the timing of that decision. Of all beings, he knew what a storm he would conjure. Even with all his power he is now required to succumb to the stories that others are writing. That is when the power of everyone's collective story will be tested. If you are wondering when to make your choice I can say this...."

He paused to inhale the smoke once more.

"Don't hesitate even for a day." He fixed his gaze on her to emphasise his point.

"Tell your story to everyone you see, everyone you cross paths with in every way. The most important part of telling your story is to 'be' your story. The stories with the greatest collective energy will be the ones that prevail. There will be all sorts of dramas occur in this theatre piece we are in and they will seem of incredible importance as they happen."

"They are nothing compared to the importance of holding true to your heart and soul-felt stories. They will create and co-create the ultimate outcome of all the drama."

As he spoke he emanated a palpable aura that seemed to grow with every word. While he no longer affected Rena in the way he had, she was now able to observe and make note of his power. Somehow she could be present with him as this arose. Somehow she was able to allow that power to wash over her without influence. Rena looked at both Victor and Bear and was just about to ask.

"That is the reason I brought you here, Rena," said Victor, "it was impossible for me to know what you might have inherited from your mother. Meeting with this being and sitting with him provides me with knowledge I required."

Bear walked back to the fireplace. He filled their bowls with stew and broth, sat down and passed a bowl and spoon to Rena and Victor. "If anything, she is better equipped than her mother in my opinion," Bear said to Victor. "The pace at which she transmutes what I bring is nothing short of astounding. Elias said that it was so but I argued with him. He was right and I was wrong. The future is in good hands and Elias made a good call." Then he turned to face Rena.

"It's impossible for you to possess a full comprehension of the role you are going to play in this Rena. I can tell you that from the place I bear witness most of the time, you will not be overthrown. While you haven't had any call upon you just yet, that time will come. With the capabilities you present, you'll be just fine. I can provide you with a forecast that may be of some assistance."

He shuffled his feet and frowned.

"In this journey on which you are setting out with Victor there will come a time when you will be tested. You will be challenged by some matters that you won't comprehend at all. You are well equipped to prevail, though the power you face will seem undefeatable. It is at the time you feel most lost that

you will reveal yourself, first to yourself and then to those with whom you co-create."

He began to spoon broth and stew into his mouth, slurping and smacking his lips as he ate.

"Ah Victor, if there's one good reason to incarnate in this world, its food." He kept eating with gusto. Soon his spoon was scraping the bottom of the bowl. He rose again and returned to the fire to ladle more soup into his bowl.

Victor and Rena also ate. There was silence in the room but for the clatter of spoons and the crackle and pop of bright flaming faggots in the cooking fire. When they finished Bear took the dishes and placed them in a pile beside the fire. "I'll get those later." He turned to Victor with an odd look on his face.

"Victor, I'm thinking it would be worthwhile to introduce Rena to some things she hasn't experienced yet. To give her some idea what she could be dealing with. What do you think?"

Victor rubbed his hand across his forehead and smoothed his hair down the back of his head. "You think now is a good time, Bear? Everyone and everything will be looking around now for traces of visitation. For the moment no-one but me, you and Elias have any idea about Rena. If we go visiting we'll leave distinct tags of her for those who know how to look."

"That's true but I'm known for taking risks. I think this is important. At one time or another she will have to be able to access without us. Who can be sure when and where we will be as this unfolds? So yes, I think it's the perfect time. If we all go, you and I can mask her, I'm quite certain. Anything or anyone seeking already knows to look out for you and me. I'm sure we will be able to provide sufficient confusion in the message of the tags. She needs to see. From tomorrow morning it will be you alone. Both of us can make it a much safer experience. Combined we can shield her while we show her."

Rena looked peeved. She stood up to face Bear, standing over Victor. "If you are going to speak about me as if I'm not here, I will not be here. When you have finished deciding where

you plan to take me maybe you might include me in the decision. You will learn that I will decide for myself."

It was Bear's turn to witness the flare of power surrounding his guest. Victor was chastened.

"Yes, you are right Rena. Please forgive." He turned his face up to Bear. "You saw that too, didn't you?"

"I did. It supports my suggestion, though masking her may be more difficult than I imagined." His smile was broad and warm. "Elias did say she would be a force to be reckoned with. I'm guessing even he may have underestimated what we have here."

"You two are doing it again," Rena said as she reached for her coat.

"Let's do it, Victor." Victor nodded.

The three of them sat facing one another. Victor had created a circle of stones around them and had spoken some words of protection that finished with, "All those who are not dancing in the light and the magical potential of all that can be, be gone from this space. I command it to be so; it is so and shall remain so. I command the presence of the Dream Teachers and the Enlightened Masters and I open the gates to our higher selves and our individual circle of souls. Creator of all things, be here now." He sat to the left of Rena and to the right of Bear. They joined hands, right hands face down and left hands face up. Bear spoke.

"Rena, please be assured that in our presence you have nothing to fear in this place we are visiting. Both of us have familiarity with this realm and have learned how to navigate it over many lives. You too have power though you may not comprehend it yet. Relax and witness."

Rena nodded, nervous.

"Shall we go, my friend?"

Victor also nodded.

It was as though the warm room in which they sat vanished in that instant. Bear transformed into the image of a strong warrior, clothed in regal garments from another era. Victor was

still clothed in the same attire he had been wearing but his entire body seemed to thrum in an almost musical cadence. He was surrounded by a light resembling the light of a golden sunset reflected from tumultuous clouds. That vision alone had Rena unable to believe her eyes. She was even further awed when she looked beyond her companions.

They were standing on a precipice towering over the entire landscape from Pembrokeshire in Western Wales to Margate and Ramsgate in the east of England. Across the width of the United Kingdom there was a tight net, a matrix or a web that bound almost everything in a crimson thrall. In several locations, such as the one they had just occupied a healthful green showed, a break in the completeness of the binding.

Without words Bear said, 'Let's take a closer look,' and he stepped off the precipice. Rena gasped and was astounded to see Bear still right beside her. "The rules are different here, Rena." Victor stepped off too and drew Rena with him over the edge of the mighty terrace.

And so they flew.

As they traversed the land, Bear close to one side and Victor close to the other, hand in hand, Bear told her the story of the land. Underneath the crimson web there was another matrix. This one possessed no malevolence. Rather, it linked place to place, place of power to place of power, standing stones to barrows, ever-flowing fresh water springs to underground ceremonial grottos, cliff-side passes concealed to all but their eyes, networks of catacombs older than time, fantastical creatures nurturing the remnants of ancient forest. Rena was in complete and utter awe and wonder. This place could not be comprehended in the rational mind, not even described.

In what felt like just a few minutes they travelled from one side of the United Kingdom to the other. As they turned in a long sweeping bank, rolling upwards on one side to swoop down towards the Thames, still gripping the hands of her companions, Victor laughed with complete abandon, a loud joy-filled whoop

followed by a mirth that seemed to echo all across this strange land. Both Rena and Bear joined him.

The two men brought Rena down towards the place they had eaten dinner and she was once again awed. The land when viewed with this proximity possessed an exquisite beauty. Somehow there were an unlimited number of shades of green and every other colour was imbued with an impeccable hue so that it was magnificent to witness. The water of the Thames was crystal clear and sparkled like a fresh mountain stream untouched by industry. Rena was sure she could see fish teeming up and down the river. While the river sparkled, everything else, even the air in which they were suspended, emitted a soft glow, the pulse of life itself.

"It looks like heaven." She had not spoken but both Bear and Victor looked to her and smiled. She 'heard' a response from Bear in his rumbling tone, yet again not spoken, "Heaven is so much closer than most have ever dreamed, Rena. So close that if people would shift their perspective a little they could live there right now."

Still holding her hands, the two men made a slight move in unison. The trio rose high above the landscape once again.

"Come and take a look at this, young Rena. Perhaps it will explain a few things for you."

Hand in hand they whisked across the sky in the direction of London city. This time they moved at a slower pace. The closer they came to the city the more complex the matrix of crimson became, ensnaring everything beneath it. As they approached Rochester and looked on to Dartford it obscured land, buildings and trees, so complex were the windings.

'Are you certain about this Bear?' Victor expressed a genuine concern.

'Nothing is ever certain, my friend but she will need to experience this at some time and she is well protected between us. She could be here in much more dangerous circumstances.' Bear replied. 'Let us give her some notion of what she has been called to deal with. I cannot imagine that there will be a better

opportunity.' They flew on, though both men edged just a little closer in order to provide a thorough masking of Rena.

Gliding over the city was not the same experience as witnessing the Thames and the countryside near Shornemead Fort. Here the air lost its lambency and felt more like a cold, wet and insistent, invasive fog, sending chill into everything it touched. Even these three were affected, the chill intruding into the circle of shared warmth that Victor and Bear had been maintaining since their arrival.

"What is happening here, Victor," Rena could not remove the forlorn sadness in her voice, "It feels so sad, so dense?"

Stretched out across the entire city was a blood-hued, crimson web gripping everything tight in its pall. Each building, each feature, even the struggling city trees dotted in parks and gardens across the vast urban landscape could be seen standing there labouring under the oppressive mantle the web maintained. Rena could see people too. Trekking in mechanical order from building to building, hailing cabs, climbing into cars, disappearing into the tube which looked so enmeshed in the web that it was almost impossible to imagine breathing in there. Without warning several strands of the web disentangled themselves and reached upward, stretching through the sky in the direction of Victor, Bear and Rena. One of these strands touched a point perhaps a hundred yards below the three travellers. A green flash sparked at that point and Bear reacted.

'Damn, I should have felt that sooner. It's time to go, my friends.' He angled his head towards the clear sky above. Victor responded to follow his lead. They soared skyward leaving the coil of web hanging in the air. They watched it drop in a kind of slow motion sworl back to the earth, re-entangling in the web that encompassed everything below them. Under the direction of Victor and Bear, the three of them sailed across landscapes and cityscapes all over the UK. As they approached each city, Bear and Victor would gather themselves and screen Rena's presence while still permitting her to see all that lay below.

In just a few hours they had visited cities as far north as Inverness, flowed awestruck over the magnificent lochs of Scotland and marvelled at the glorious beauty of The Lakes District. They glided like eagles over much of the Welsh countryside and saw the density of the web increase each time they approached even the smallest of cities. From time to time they would scan a small town or village and notice there was no sign of the web. Bear would smile on these occasions and mention the name of some familiar. Victor would repeat their names as if to grant just a little encouragement to whoever was resisting, to persist, to maintain their work.

They followed their earlier journey across the south, skirting around Cardiff to avoid the discomfort of the web but taking a little extra time to drink in the effulgence of the mighty Severn River and the Bristol Channel. Though the web extended into the water it became much less intense and felt as though it contained less power. Rena was transfixed in every moment, gazing across the ocean to see that the tendrils of crimson extended from nation to nation as though on a giant internet blanketing the entire planet.

As she opened her eyes as though from deep meditation, Rena felt the warmth of the fire on her back. Her hands were clasped with caring gentleness in the hands of these two men. She felt safe yet troubled. First Bear then Victor loosed her hand. They sat in that cavern looking at one another. Bear was the first to move. In silence he stood to collect and place a blackened pot on the edge of the fire. He tossed a few extra sticks of dry wood into the embers.

"I don't understand what just happened." Rena shook her head and looked from one man to the other. "What on earth...?" Shifting his weight a little Victor spoke.

"There are very significant matters occurring right now across this planet Rena. It is all part of an immense plan. Of that you can be sure. Bear and I have perhaps a little more idea of what is happening than many, yet there are others who are

awakening to pieces of knowledge that have been concealed from humanity for a very long time."

Rubbing his eyes, Victor took several deep breaths.

"This place, this earth has such enormous potential and yet for the past several millennia or more it has, with slow and painstaking intent, been transformed into a kind of prison. Because that has been so for many generations, most of humanity has forgotten just how blessed they are to have chosen to be on this plane."

He took two steaming cup of strong, black tea from Bear and passed the second cup to Rena.

"This is the realm that you will be influencing as you walk with me to join with Elias. By the way, it's not so much about us having to take a random walk for this journey. It is about treading those other lines you saw, following the lines underneath."

"Those lines that joined the power places, you mean? The greenish lines?" said Rena in a voice hushed by her recent experience.

"Yes. Those lines are far more ancient. They represent the truth of this planet. Those lines cannot be overpowered without the complete annihilation of this form, this being called Earth. But this time they have been sorely tested. The realm we just visited is the realm in which you exert the highest influence when you walk along the ancient lines." Victor looked wistful, recalling a time when the lines were singing their truth without interference.

"Some call them 'song-lines'. Some call them 'ley-lines'. It is not important which name they are given. Suffice to know that they are the original matrix of this earth. When they are revealed and revered, this earth is the heaven that humanity seeks." As he spoke in that room, warmed by the fire of his friend, the Bear, tears rolled down Victor's face.

"Tomorrow we will set out again, Rena. It's been quite a day for you and for us all." He drank his tea in several big gulps. "It's time to get some sleep."

Rena felt exhaustion seep into every muscle and bone in her body. Bear took her cup and helped her to stand. He guided her to a warm nest he had set for her adjacent to the fire, which flickered and danced a soft light across the walls and ceiling. In a few moments she was asleep.

"She is more than I expected, brother." Bear sat with Victor and reached for the pot to refresh both cups with hot, strong tea.

"My sense is that she will be sufficient for the role and may well add some nuances that her mother would not have been able to contribute".

"I agree, Bear. I spoke at length with Ariah about Rena and she assured me that she had witnessed many examples of her ability since she was a small child. In my opinion, it's a credit to her that she is here with us right now. There are many that would not have come." A cloud crossed Victor's face as he continued, "That tendril that reached us, Bear do you know what it might have achieved?"

Bear shrugged a little and scratched his nose. "There will be certainty that you and I have been observing, my friend. We were quite thorough in our journey. That trail will be able to be witnessed and I am quite certain there will be some questions that come up as to why we would do such a thing. It will be obvious that we would not do that for entertainment."

"Do you think she was perceived?"

"I know that she wasn't, at least not with any certainty. It would take more than a touch to penetrate beyond the glamour that you and I erected, my brother. That being said, it is also clear that there would be awareness that we were conducting some kind of tour. While they would not know who was on the tour it would be quite plain that a tour was going on. She is also a powerful being, so there would be knowledge that she exists even though she will not have been identified."

"So it was worth the introduction?"

"Of that I am quite certain, Victor. It is apparent to me that she will be drawn there at least several times during her travel, both with you and when you are not present. I'm not at all

concerned if you are with her but I rest with more ease knowing she now has at least some awareness. She will without doubt, question you without mercy when you are back on your journey together. I would see it as quite important that she is prepared if she visits alone. I predict that this will happen many times."

The two men sat together speaking in undertones until the first rays of sun began to colour the landscape. As this happened Victor rose to embrace his friend. As the mist cleared on the river, Bear faded from sight. The fort once again became the broken relic of a long past battle. Victor prodded the fire and placed some fresh sticks of gnarled and twisted timber on the flame.

The fire flickered and grew, casting warmth across to Rena's sleeping form. She stirred, rolled over and faced Victor, looking around the old fort, searching for familiar things – pots of tea, stew and broth and a man called Bear. She saw Victor huddled over a small fire, stirring the ashes to prepare breakfast for them both. There were just tumble-down walls of the old fort and a few of their things scattered about.

"Victor?"

"I'm here, girl."

"I had the most incredible dream."

"That was no dream, sister. We went on a journey that needed to happen. I can tell you every detail of your so-called dream if you'd like. It was no dream. It was a major part of the reason we came here."

He lifted a pot onto the flame. "I'll have coffee for you in a few minutes. After that there is some porridge to ease your hunger pangs and maybe help those aching muscles a little."

"Not a dream........?" Rena closed her eyes again. "But that's impossible."

"So much is possible, Rena. There has been a story told for an age and more that contains and constricts what is perceived as possible. The time has come to reveal that there is so much that is possible if we have the courage to imagine and create it together. We'll speak more about that later, I'm quite sure.

Right now it's time for breakfast. Get up. We have a long way to walk today."

After a wholehearted breakfast, prepared by Victor, the rush to move disappeared without explanation. He washed the pot and plates before approaching Rena. She sat in a classic meditation pose, her eyes closed.

"Rena, I need to sit for while at the side of the river. I need to be alone. Perhaps you also feel what I feel?"

Pushing out a little from the stone wall of the fort, she inclined her head a little then looked up at him.

"I'm already there, Victor. I felt it coming. It called me as soon as they walked into the grove."

Without another word, Victor turned and walked toward the river, already shape-shifting.

Rena sat back to resume her meditation. The ancient rocks in the stone wall at her back began to record the memories of all that happened, both there at Shornemead Fort and beside a simple campfire on the other side of the planet.

CHAPTER TWENTY NINE

It wasn't until the third day that a car pulled over to offer Petra a ride. She was heading in the opposite direction to the one she had planned. Something about the note from this stranger, Evita Huamani seemed to justify the diversion. The first day she had so many reasons to reconsider. A storm announced itself early in the morning. Rolling storm clouds collected in the west toward the ocean. It continued to build until just after one when lightning streaked the sky, thunder roared through the surrounding hills and the heavens opened with drenching rain. There was nowhere to stay dry. At first Petra searched for cover. After half an hour of fruitless search, she just kept walking. The rain was so heavy she was sometimes not able to see more than a few metres in front of her footfall. She kept on. The distance dropped away as she walked in the warm rain. Just after six pm it stopped.

The skies cleared.

She set up her tent and cooked a meal of vegetables and rice before collapsing into her tent. She managed to fall asleep, though she was still wet. Sleep was fitful. At last Petra gave up any idea of refreshing slumber as dawn brought first light into a windswept sky. Dragging out of the tent into the morning, she drew on her remaining dry jacket and climbed a hill rising east of her camp. From the summit of the hill, through the moss-etched trunks of the twisted trees that grew there, she watched the sun rise over the mountains that had been sentries to her progress. She watched as fingers of light reached across the land. Soon they touched and warmed her too. Steam rose from her clothes and skin.

On that misted morning she could feel, more keen and defined, the inextricable pull of Elias' invitation. Even when the beach house felt like it could be the perfect place for her to stop, relax and live a simple life, she knew that she must make the journey, drop everything and become a traveller again. With her elevated sensitivity to everything, from smells to sounds and even people, it had suited her. She loved the time to think, slow down and drop off the radar.

Her mind wandered back to Evita Huamani's intervention into her journey. Heading south to Machu Picchu felt like quite a long diversion. She wasn't sure why she had accepted such a long delay. What on earth could this woman, this Evita, want to gift her? Did she even understand that Petra was on a kind of pilgrimage to meet with Elias?

As she considered this from her perch on the crest of the hill, she reached the conclusion that Evita must know and that alone justified the diversion. It wasn't logic so much as an inner knowing. Petra gave authority to her intuitive sense. She 'felt' that this woman Evita was somehow connected into this matrix, this web she was navigating.

As the sun climbed higher into a sky that was now fresh-washed and clear, Petra walked back down to her camp, ate a sparse breakfast, packed her damp belongings into her wet pack and set off.

On this second day her pack felt heavy, but bearable.

She walked with stolid determination for three hours. Twelve kilometres passed under her feet. She rested, munching on chocolate and oranges, drinking deep draughts of cold water, as though it was the stuff of life itself. Just over an hour passed and Petra woke to find she had dozed a little. Though the short rest refreshed her, the place where the straps sat on her shoulders still ached. She reached into a pouch in the top of her pack to draw out a small pipe and some weed. She packed a loose pipe, lit it and sucked the sweet-smelling smoke into her lungs. She held it in, counting to thirteen before exhaling. She packed the paraphernalia away, stood and drew her pack onto her back. The

ache in her shoulders already felt more bearable. She began to walk once again.

All through that sun-drenched day Petra's experience of the land felt deeper and more connected with the simple motion of one step following another. Each step became her perfect next step, no question as to which way or why. The sun shone from its blistering zenith as she marched on. Several times she paused for a few moments. Once to extract a crushed and lopsided straw hat from her pack and perch it on her head, the other to take the weight off her feet for a blissful ten minutes. She drank copious amounts of water, refilling at every stream she could.

Under her feet the land spoke to her.

The trees and plants on either side provided welcome shade and reached out to her with stretching fingers. They reminded her that what she was doing was all that mattered.

The sweltering sun bore down on her for hours before softening into evening. A breeze cooled sweat on the back of her neck and her brow. Birds called to her and her alone, wheeling and shrieking above or flickering from branch to branch in the undergrowth, sharing their amiable chatter. As she walked she listened, watched and emptied her mind. Their message felt the same as speaking with Elias at that gathering several years ago. Their message felt like earth. Their message felt like home.

A little after five she sent a prayer to ask for a safe and comfortable place to rest for the night. By five-thirty she was edging her way into a nook that felt protected and secure. After setting a fire and cooking a simple meal, Petra sat pondering what she had been gifted from the day.

The rising sun is a daily miracle. Water is life. Taking the next step is the only alternative to being stuck in the one place. Everything is conscious. Rest is blessed.

By eight o'clock she slithered into her tent and fell into a deep sleep.

On the third day, before she set out, before she lifted her backpack onto aching shoulders, an old car stopped opposite her. The driver called out. She heard the car approaching, felt the

shift in the peacefulness of the morning, almost wished it had just kept going. She was tempted to say no. Then she looked up to be greeted by two smiling adults and two beaming, excited children in a beaten up Peugeot sedan. They all smiled at her as though they had found a long-lost family member. She decided to take the ride. A few minutes later her bag was in the trunk and she was in the front passenger seat. The car barrelled and rattled along the road at thirty kilometres an hour.

Though it was a Colombian family, they all spoke English, the man with such a strong accent that he was difficult to understand. The enthusiasm with which he spoke made up for misunderstanding and often turned into shared laughter. His wife and children were easier.

He was a clean-shaven, young Colombian man and though not yet forty, he had rough working hands that rested like roots in dark earth on the steering wheel of the car. His face exuded innocence and naivety. Thick, black, curly hair was plastered into control by hair-oil. He possessed an energetic yet easy physicality and that incomprehensible accent.

The woman who sat in the back of the car had birthed two children, a striking girl of about eight years and an equally attractive boy of around five or six. She said her name was Maria, her husband's name was Jose and her daughter and son, Ana and Felix. Just in that simple sharing, Maria established that she had a much less imposing, indecipherable accent and was thus the channel by which much of the conversation could happen. The children were shy at first, clinging close to their mother, but their reticence soon disintegrated.

The girl, Ana, found her way into Petra's lap, asking one question after another without pausing for an answer. Petra did her best to keep up until Maria intervened with a few stern words. Ana settled and they continued their shared journey along the narrow road.

"Why are you and your family driving south?" Petra asked when the noise of the children had subsided, soothed by the thump and rattle of the old car.

Maria replied, "My husband is going to pick the coca. He takes us with him so that our family is still together."

Jose nodded profusely and turned his head towards Petra to beam one of his bright smiles. "Buen dinero para recolectores rápidos", he said in Spanish.

"Aha, good money. I see."

"My brother, he buy coche, er auto, so we can go," Jose explained, still beaming his broad smile, perhaps proud of his brother's wealth or pleased to be driving his family to Peru. After about an hour travelling, there seemed nothing left to talk about. The five of them settled into an easy silence. Young Ana slept in Petra's lap, her head resting on her shoulder.

The road wound its way through magnificent country, mountains all around and fresh, pure air. They travelled in brilliant sunshine some of the time, interspersed with deep shade from trees and undergrowth. These grew right to the side of the old carriageway, plunging them into instant darkness and cool for good portions of the journey, even as the sun rose higher in the sky.

When those few hours had passed, Jose pulled the old car to a halt in a shaded spot on an otherwise open, gravelled space near a bridge spanning a fast-running creek. They tumbled out and headed in different directions to relieve themselves, as though Jose had possessed some strange barometer for the need to wee. When Petra came back to the car, Jose was busy hauling packages out of the trunk to make lunch. The children were splashing and shrieking on the edge of the creek under the watchful eye of their mother. She stood alert, hawk-like against the stone buttress of the bridge where she could see both of them without obstruction. Petra walked over and leaned back against the cool stone.

"You have beautiful children, Maria."

"Thank you, Petra. I am very proud of them."

"Ana was in my lap in next to no time. So sweet. Thank you for allowing her to connect with me in such an intimate

fashion. I wonder what kind of world they will grow up into? Does that ever worry you?"

"What is the point of worry? My husband and I had parents that were always so worried about the terrible things that might happen to us, to me and to my husband. Colombia is not an easy country to grow up in. Both Jose and I have seen much of the danger of being Colombian and not having great riches. But, here we are."

Maria turned her gentle eyes and gave a shy glance to Petra then renewed her gaze on her children, not wanting to lose sight of them for more than a moment.

"Both of our children are people filled with love as we have taught them and shown them, though many times I have thought that it is they who teach us. Worrying about what their lives might be will not change how their lives are, unless it is to limit them and make them afraid. How could I want that?"

"Your children teach you?"

"Both of them, yes. And we teach them. Together it is quite perfect."

"How do they teach you?"

"In many ways, Petra, in so many simple ways we learn. Right now we are stopped on a small road in an area where not so many people come because it is not considered a safe area to be. But we stop because the children need us to stop, for their comfort, to eat without rushing, to let them have time to play, to connect to the earth and the water. We choose to come this way because of the children. There are faster ways, faster roads but why would we go that way if we think about what it is to be a child."

Maria smiled down towards her children. They remained oblivious to her gaze, yet flourished in its protective balm.

"Every day is an excitement, every day is an adventure, every day is discovering something new and if we were to go the other way, down the new roads, going faster, all they would have to do is sit in the car and watch the world go flashing past without them. They would become bored and restless. This

way, though there may be other risks, provides very little risk of boredom or restlessness. This way they might remember for a very long time."

She reached up to her long, thick hair and refashioned the tie to make a loose bun. Her smile was wistful and full of joy.

"This creek, this meal we have together, this road, these mountains and this bridge all add beauty and colour to their lives. They will also remember you for a very long time. It is true too that we would not, and could not, have stopped for you on one of the new roads. We would not even have found you had either one of us decided upon the new roads. As the children enjoy this journey, so too do they show us, you, me and Jose how to relax and enjoy this journey. It is a great gift they bring."

"When you put it that way, I wonder why I asked the question, Maria. Thank you."

Maria and Petra leaned in silence against the bridge while the children explored the creek bank. Jose made lunch. These back roads were not recommended for travellers. They were barely encouraged for locals because of the presence of bandits in and around the mountains. On this day, however, this shining day with the murmur of the creek and the children, there was no sign of bandits. What happened was much older and much more common on old back roads in the mountains.

Connection and friendship happened. These things needed no particular reason, nor explanation.

Once the meal was complete, Jose rustled the children to action clearing up and ensuring that nothing was left behind. They all piled into the car and continued the long drive south. Every few hours they took a break, ate fruit, breathed fresh air, paddled in a creek, talked and laughed. Often in the car, the rattle and hum of the old Peugeot would first lull the children to sleep, then Maria and at last, Petra too would succumb.

At least four times on that first day of travel, Jose waited until everyone slept, then slowed down to little more than walking pace to take the time to look around at everyone. He took the time to look at his children, his wife, this friendly

stranger and he smiled a big smile that no-one else would ever see, that no-one else needed to see. Satisfied, he shifted in his seat, refocused and sped up once again. The smile would stay with him as he watched the scenery vanish past the old car his brother had bought for him. Soon he would have more money for his family. Soon he would be picking the coca and then he would have more money for his family.

Just a few weeks from now.

It was three nights later when bandits descended from the hills.

There were six of them. After a dinner of chunks of tasty, hard bread dunked in a huge pot of steaming vegetable soup that Maria had extricated from some hidden cool place in the car, Ana and Felix seemed to have even more energy than usual. They insisted on sitting around the small campfire to play games that made little sense but gave them reason to stay awake and stay with the adults. When that ran out, they played their final ace and Jose extracted a small, beaten up guitar from the Peugeot to play and sing. That turned into another hour for them both to remain awake. When enough time had passed, Maria stepped in.

"Ana, Felix. It's time for bed right now." Ana moved off to find her own toothbrush and cup and put herself to bed. Felix had fallen asleep in Petra's arms. She looked up at Maria.

"I think maybe he is already well gone," she smiled. Maria reached down and scooped her son from Petra's arms and carried him to the other side of the car, out of the firelight.

"You sing well, Jose, though a few more in English would have been a help for me."

Jose smiled at her and was just about to respond when he turned his face to the shadows at the other end of the clearing.

In a low voice he said, "Petra, stay calm please. We have some company. Can you do that?"

He spoke better English in these few words than she had heard from him in the entire journey up till this moment and it added to the attention he gained from her. She looked into his face and gave a small nod.

"Good. And please just stay where you are. Ok chica, let us see how this goes". He smiled at her again.

By now Petra wasn't sure whether to be terrified or reassured. Jose speaking English so well was more than a little disorienting but the careful controlled manner he had delivered the words felt ominous. She didn't have a lot of time to process what was going on, just a few seconds. Jose sat at her side facing into the gloom, the firelight flickering across his swarthy features. He spoke in a language that sounded quite different to any language she had heard from him thus far.

Six men in drab, grubby clothing stepped into the circle of firelight.

Each of them was armed, three with handguns strapped to their hips, one with a short shotgun and two with machetes and hunting knives. A small, wiry man seemed to be the leader. He responded to Jose while his eyes roved over the camp, taking in the old car, the remains of the meal, the campfire, Petra and Jose.

Petra couldn't explain it in any way that made any sense to her reasoning mind, but in just a few moments she felt something radiating from Jose that she had only felt once before in her life. It was a sensation that had nothing to do with any of her standard senses. It felt powerful, calming and peaceful. She felt the tension in her body begin to ease, her muscles relaxed and her breathing slowed. One other person she knew exuded such a rush of energy and that man was Elias. When she had spoken with Elias, when she had agreed to answer the call and had dedicated her life to having a choice, this kind of energy had been palpable.

Maria emerged from behind them and the sense of ease that Petra felt increased. What was that? Maria moved with slow steps to the big pot of soup, more than half of which remained. Lifting it back to the edge of the fire, she sat down on the other side of her husband.

The eyes of the six men followed her every move. To Petra all the sinister eyes of these men were paying a dangerous level of attention to looking at her rather than at what she was doing.

She realised this unease was present for her because she felt to be under the same scrutiny.

The small man spoke in an abrupt tone, a language that was unintelligible to Petra but must have been the same language as that which Jose had used. He spoke direct to Jose, who didn't take his eyes off his face for even the slightest instant. To Petra, the next five minutes were a bizarre glitch in time. She watched Jose and this ominous little man speak in a language foreign to her, yet she was aware of being rushed through a whole range of experiences about what was going on in the exchange.

At one point, she watched the hands of two of the bandits move toward their weapons. A few seconds later, their shoulders drooped once again and the moment had passed. Jose was unreadable. He was also still as stone. That is, he moved his arms and he tilted his head and he smiled and moved his mouth and face – but something about him was solid and implacable. Maria was the same.

It was after five minutes of observing all that was happening that Petra decided she too would become still.

She drew upon her meditation practice and invoked stillness into every cell of her body and every part of her field. It was at the exact moment that Petra felt stillness engulf her that Maria took a big breath of air and spoke for the first time. But she didn't speak in a language that was strange to Petra.

She was certain Maria had spoken in English. What was she thinking? Would these men have any idea what it was she was saying?

She didn't speak to the small man who had been talking with Jose. Instead she addressed a big man who stood furthest away, concealed by the night, the light of the fire fluttering on his round face. Her voice sounded like water tinkling over cool stones on a steaming, hot day.

"Senor, you look hungry. Would you help me take this soup off the fire and wash this spoon and bowl?" She reached down to pick up one of the bowls that the children had been using earlier and held it, her left arm outstretched to the tall man concealed

by the gloom. He moved forward, leaned his shotgun against the front wheel of the Peugeot and took the bowl and spoon.

"Thank you. There is water just over there in that dish. We can get the soup in a moment."

He shuffled off to wash the bowl and spoon. The small man looked perplexed and shifted his eyes from Jose to Maria.

"I am sure you are hungry too, Senor. We have five bowls and all of them need to be rinsed a little, but we have a large cup that perhaps will suffice for one of you."

She passed the bowl that Felix had been using earlier to the small man. He took it and looked unsure of what to do next.

"Just over there, Senor, the dish for cleaning. And would you all please just leave those weapons you are carrying there at the front of the car. I have children here," she intoned with a hypnotic gentleness, firm in her suggestion that no other action could be deemed in any way acceptable.

One by one the men placed their weapons against the wheel hub and collected a bowl and spoon. The last, a man who was just a little past being a boy received a big metal drinking mug that would contain more soup than any of the bowls. He muttered something that must have been "thank you" in his incomprehensible dialect.

Maria dipped the ladle into the big pan and stirred the hot vegetable soup, then filled the young man's cup to the brim. Steam wove its way into the bang of hair that threatened to obscure his right eye. He mumbled something once again as she broke him a large chunk of hard bread and handed it to him. Jose did nothing more than sit back a little. There was still a deep sense of peace emanating from him. Petra did the best she could to match his frequency.

The last man to have his bowl filled with steaming soup was the small man who had confronted Jose when they had first arrived, held his gaze, felt the most malignant. Now all he could do was smile. He nodded, smiled a big gap-toothed grin then bowed to Maria as she filled his bowl and handed him the final piece of bread. Petra could not help feeling as though it

was a living ceremony happening right in front of her. She had just enough of her normal self still present to wonder about this other dimension she seemed to inhabit.

As the men finished wiping their bowls clean with the last scraps and crumbs of bread, Felix appeared from behind the car, rubbing his eyes and looking for his mother. She reached for him and he snuggled into her lap as she sat in the firelight. Every one of the men watched and Petra was certain she felt the whole scene 'soften' somehow.

The small man spoke in a whisper to Maria.

"His name is Felix," she answered. "He is my youngest, yes. Earlier today he told me that you would be coming. He often knows such things."

He looked across at Petra and muttered something to Jose, who then turned his head to face her and looked her square in the eye and though his lips did not move she was sure she heard "have no fear".

"This is our companion who travels with us to visit Evita who has called her to Machu Picchu. She is under a far greater protection than I possess my friend, but mine also."

While she was certain that Jose had spoken in the strange language of these men, she understood every word as though spoken in perfect English. She thought that she must ask Jose about that at some time. The small man nodded and for a minute or two there was silence. Then a soft conversation began between several of the men and Jose as they shared stories about life in these hills, life in the cities, children and wives, coca and the weather. Petra would have joined in but had no idea whether her strange ability to understand extended to being able to speak in a way that these men would comprehend. Instead, she did her best to listen and to watch everything that was happening on this strange night in the hills of southern Colombia.

It was past ten when the small man called a halt. He motioned to his men to gather their arms. Then each in turn approached Maria, who still sat holding the sleeping Felix, to thank her for her hospitality. Next, each filed past Jose, shook

his hand and gripped him in an embrace before vanishing into the forest. The last to leave was the small man, who left with the brightest smile and a deep bow.

By the time they had been travelling together for a fort-night, Petra was enmeshed in the lives of this young Colombian family who had stopped for her. It would have been a long walk of almost three and a half thousand kilometres, so Petra was grateful and a little amazed that Jose, Maria and the children had taken her on with such ease. She did her best to over-contribute to the food they ate together. Jose and Maria watched that too and insisted that her fair share was all that was needed.

Each time she tried to pay for fuel, Jose would say that she must not, as his family were going south anyway, so it made no difference. Petra could see that this was not a family that had money to burn or waste, and yet she could find no way to break through their smiling, insistent refusal.

At the end of the fourteenth day, as Jose navigated the old car up a rough, winding, gravel road into a small forest, pro-tected from the winds that had been jostling them and everything around for the past two days, Petra plotted the next leg of her journey. She felt a certain impending sadness at the separation from her new friends which she knew must happen soon. Jose had let her know that he and his family would be driving as far as Ayacucho. In comparison to the whole journey it was close to where she needed to be, leaving her with around two hundred kilometres to walk, or should she find another ride, five hundred kilometres by road.

As Maria went off with the children to collect wood, Jose unloaded the car and busily set up the family tent. Since the second day it was the sole tent they had needed as Petra was invited to share with them, saving time and effort and giving them all that feeling of the security of each other, together in sleep. Jose always slept nearest to the entry, a kind of zipper sentry in a castle that couldn't be defended. Still it felt better for them all.

Petra drew together dry leaves, bits of browned grass, tiny twigs and a few small branches. She broke them into small pieces, with loud cracks, ready to feed them into the flames once the fire had begun to take. She arranged the small pile of flammables in the centre of a circle of red soil where she had cleared away the detritus, struck the red phosphorous against the scratch on the box, watched it flare and lowered it to the base of the kindling. The flame caught and began to consume the fuel, so she piled bits and pieces on top until she had a flame flicking tongues of red and orange into the dimming dusk.

When he finished making their home for the night, Jose wandered over to Petra's fire and stood there, rubbing the dust from his hands. He smiled down at her as she blew on the embers to fuel the fire and the light flickered across his face.

"You go er, solo el manana, we stop Ayacucho." He spoke with gentleness.

"Si, Jose. I don't know how to thank you for this journey."

"No necesita, senorita. It has been good adventure, yes?"

"Yes it has, Jose, a fabulous adventure. I'm very grateful. This would have taken me such a long time if you hadn't found me beside the road."

Jose smiled another small smile, a flicker in his eyes that might have been the fire but might have been something else. Petra noticed it.

"What, Jose? What is that about?" she asked.

"You wait. When children sleep. Wait tonight."

Petra looked at him with a questioning expression, but he would say nothing more.

From further down the hill came the sound of the two children talking excitedly with their mother. Loaded with sticks and logs they all stepped into the light of the fire, babbling over the top of one another, tossing the fuel into a pile near their father's feet and brushing bark and dirt off their clothes and hands. Both of them then rushed over to hug Petra, one on either side. She beamed at the attention from these two who had invited her into their lives as only children could, without

any reservation whatsoever. Well, at least that was still possible because Jose and Maria permitted it, encouraged it.

When they finished dinner, Ana and Felix continued to stay close to Petra. Though she had said nothing about the imminent parting of ways, the youngsters had determined that something was about to change. She concluded that they must have known that Ayacucho was close by now, though she could not recall seeing any road sign saying so. Perhaps it was just that children were still tuned in to such things.

Jose and Maria were cleaning up after dinner, washing dishes, burying scraps, pushing a few bits into a box they kept in the car for waste. Petra sat leaning against the trunk of a fallen tree that lay across the clearing, near enough to the fire to keep her warm. The biting chill had increased as they drove higher and higher into the mountains over the past few days. On either side of her, huddled into the soft curves of her body, Ana and Felix looked as though they would never leave her. Felix shifted a little and looked up at her. He said, "How long before you see Uncle Elias, Petra?"

Petra stiffened and a wave of incredulity flashed across her features. "What's that, Felix? Did you say Elias?"

He turned his innocent eyes up to her, "Uhuh. I said how long till you see him?"

"How do you know about Elias?" She was sure she had not spoken about Elias to any of them. The subject of anyone or anywhere further than Machu Picchu and Evita Huamani had never come up between any of them.

Ana piped up, "We both know Uncle Elias, Petra. Didn't you know that?"

Her jaw dropped open a little wider.

"You wha....? What is going on here?" She raised her voice to reach their parents.

"Maria, Jose – I do not believe what I am hearing."

The two of them rushed over, looking concerned.

"Something is wrong, chica?" said Maria, "what could be wrong?"

Petra stood and perched on the trunk of the tree. The two children looked aghast as she removed them from the closeness they had all been enjoying. Jose moved to the right of his son and put a reassuring arm around his shoulders.

Petra looked at each of them, incredulous.

"What is happening here?"

CHAPTER THIRTY

There was a long-missed sense of freedom in every moment. It had been a long time.

When he was just eighteen years old he had set out to trek as many countries as he could manage in eighteen months. Now that he had freedom from study and from the job his father had always wanted him to strive for, Flynn realised how much he missed the thrill of waking to make plans on how to spend the day.

Right now, though it was no more than a week since he had been dismissed from Meranto, he also found that there was a lot of planning to do. The sun sparkled across the lake as he drew his tablet toward him. He ran his eyes down the 'to do' list he had been compiling.

At the top was his motorcycle.

It was past time for a thorough service of his Yamaha 660. He climbed down the staircase to his ground-floor utility room and lifted the dust-cover off his bike. It was almost a year since he had fired it up. Purchased two years ago to give him the freedom to explore the region surrounding his home, it had been well used for about six months, used on the odd occasion for another six and under a dust-cover since. It had been fun for a short while, heading off across weekends, alone into unknown territory. Flynn had found the pleasure short-lived when there was no-one to share the experience with. The bike had since languished in the utility room. It looked like that was about to change.

He opened his well-organised tool cupboard and chose some tools, spread out a calico drop-sheet and began. By four that afternoon he was done. It was time for a test ride. Flynn

dragged on a jacket, boots and helmet, pressed the door opener, started the bike, pulled on gloves and took off down his drive to the open road. It was cool but not cold though he was pleased he hadn't let the warmth inside his home cloud his judgement about what to wear.

Around here, far from the city it was underpopulated, so he gave the bike some gas and took off on a circuit around the lake which he knew well. He gunned it on the long straights, backed off and accelerated hard out of one corner after another, testing his skill and the bike. Both were a little out of touch, but by the time he was halfway through the second circuit, Flynn felt confident again. His bike felt natural to him and was performing well.

Freedom flashed into his mind once again as he streaked along the shore of the lake. He geared down to make the series of winding corners. A broad smile creased his face, though without witness inside his full-face helmet. Flynn felt the best he had for years. He wondered how he had managed to slip into a numbed-down, dumbed-down state. It had crept up on him. This ride was blasting it out at over one hundred and sixty kilometres an hour. It was exhilarating. He powered down and eased the bike back into the utility room. It was ready. So was he. Flynn went back upstairs to finalise preparations.

When light first began to brighten the sky, Flynn rose and ate a big breakfast before filling his panniers and strapping his pack to the bike. He had no real idea how long his self-planned adventure might take so he had arranged a friend to care-take his home, visiting just once a week to ensure everything remained in order. A little after five-thirty he said goodbye to his house and to everything he knew and roared out onto the highway towards Chengdu. There would be plenty of opportunity to stock up food for the journey ahead. His kit contained all he needed for survival camping.

First stop Chengdu, then on to Ya'an, a full day journey of three hundred kilometres. Cool air rushed past him as he flashed along the road, weaving in and out of traffic. As he drew closer

to the city he could see the massive structures that had been his workplace. Lines and lines of enormous buildings covered thousands of hectares. In every one of them grew the very latest in genetically-modified plants, but for the last enclosure. In that, another team were raising experimental, genetically-modified animal product. In his mind he couldn't justify calling them genetically-modified animals because he had, across the years, seen some of the animal protein product line. It bore little resemblance to any animal he knew.

Soon he was passing the gigantic structures, in their imposing shadows, one by one. It seemed an age, even at speed, before he passed the gap between the first and second buildings. The air grew colder. So much of this region now saw no natural sun at all and Flynn knew the magnitude of the controlled environment inside. He gunned his bike a little more. The sooner he was past this place, the better. As he passed the last of them, there was a buffer space where there were no buildings but for a few old stone barns and an abandoned temple.

Beside the variety of other vehicles on the road, the first sign of life he saw in the distance was a wooden fruit and vegetable cart perched at the rear of a gravel space off the shoulder of the road. A mournful, grey donkey stood tethered in the grass behind it, chewing with haughty indolence. Flynn throttled back, pulled off the road and drew up beside the cart. An ancient Chinese man sat on a three-legged stool smoking a long, brown cigarette. When Flynn killed the motor, the man coughed twice, took a long draw on his cigarette and shifted in his seat. He did nothing more to indicate that he was in any way aware of Flynn's presence.

Flynn spoke to him in the Chengdu dialect of Mandarin he had taken the time to learn over the years.

"I want the freshest home-grown fruits and vegetables you have, sir. Nothing altered, just those things grown fresh in your own garden. Do you have some things for me, sir?"

The old man's eyes opened wide with delight and sparkled at Flynn, "Yes of course, mister. I always have some." He rose

from his seat and reached into a concealed drawer in his cart, drew out a box full of a selection of fruits and vegetables and placed them in front of Flynn.

"I'll take them all." Flynn passed some notes to the old man who began to count it.

"Don't worry about it. It's more than enough and you can have it all."

The old man smiled at him and pocketed the cash. "Enjoy your journey, mister. It will be quite cold where you are going. Take this with you too."

He passed him a flint and striker, in a case decorated with an intricate design.

"How much do you want for this?"

"Nothing, my friend," said the old man, the cigarette hanging from his mouth, wafting aromatic smoke into Flynn's face, "It's a gift. You will find it very useful along your path. One day it may even save your life. Take it, mister. It is my gift to you. You are embarking on a journey that will have far different outcomes and consequences than you could ever know."

He smiled again and his eyes twinkled with merriment beyond any reason Flynn could imagine. Sliding the gift into the pocket of his jacket, Flynn reached down, undid the straps, flipped both panniers open and loaded his fresh produce into each and strapped them down tight and secure.

"Think of me when there is smoke in the room, mister."

The old man sat down and while still puffing away at the last of his cigarette, began the making of another, as if to ensure that there was no gap between inhaling the sweet, acrid smoke.

Flynn threw his leg over the saddle, started his bike and pulled back onto the road, glancing in his rear-view mirror to see a contented old man puffing away on that next cigarette, alone on his patch of earth with his cartload of goods for sale.

The bike roared closer to the outskirts of the city and traffic became heavier, causing him to slow a little and to weave more. With the supplies he had, some of the need to visit the city had eased. There were still a few necessary items that he must

collect before he carried on. The city would be his last opportunity as beyond its limits on the south-western side, there was not much more than wide-open space and the foothills of the Himalayas, drawing into the distance of the highest mountains in the world. With the increased traffic he had no time to even begin to consider what the old man had meant by his parting remark. In this way it slipped by Flynn's consciousness into a dark space in his memory, waiting for the chance to lift itself back into awareness when the time was right.

When everything Flynn could think of including an extra fifteen litres of fuel had been loaded on, he checked the time. It was a quarter past one. Plenty of time to continue the journey to Ya'an and make it well before the sun dropped out of the sky and the temperature plummeted. Flynn did a final check that everything was secure, pulled on his helmet, started his bike and slotted into the traffic, headed in the direction of Ya'an. He had around two hundred and thirty kilometres to cover in that afternoon. Memories of earlier adventures as a twenty-year-old flooded in the moment he passed the city limits.

The sun had been long gone when Flynn rumbled into Ya'an. It wasn't late, but the sun had been absent for more than an hour. Black thunderclouds roiled in an unkempt sky. The wind and a road pockmarked with potholes made riding more difficult than expected. It was so cold that ice began to form on his glove. As he climbed off the bike, Flynn stretched his arms above his head to ease the biting pain in his shoulders and back. He couldn't feel the fingers of his right hand. His left hand was better. He had ridden one-handed, one gloved hand buried deep in the folds of his clothing. Walking and stretching, he stepped with an awkward gait towards the bridge across the Qingyi River and felt the ire rise in him once again as he watched the trickle of water that this once mighty river had become. The long arm of Meranto reached into almost every part of this region, sucking the rivers dry and ripping the land out of the hands of the local people, who were now urban and dependent.

Flynn took a deep breath. The air here was sweeter by far than back in Chengdu and exquisite in comparison to the stale conditioned air inside the grow-zone buildings. He couldn't be sure what the fragrance was that hung in the air, but it reminded him of happier times. He was transported to his childhood when he and his younger sister had built a secret haven under the boughs and blossoms of an ancient jasmine vine that curled and cloyed its way up the stone wall of their family home. Flynn shook his head and drew his attention to the present moment, watching two women, bent over and fussing with something on the left bank of the river. He let his gaze rest on them. One of them stood straight, turned and looked at him.

'You will stay at my home tonight. Lhasa is a long way and you will need some help to make a safe journey. You will stay. Wait there and I will come to you.'

He hadn't exactly 'heard' it but it was as plain to him that he was being spoken to as any face-to-face conversation he had ever had. He could still see the two women picking at the package on the river bank, but the one who had looked up at him was now gesturing at her companion. They both began to climb up the bank towards him. His head swimming a little, Flynn made his way on unsteady legs back to his motorbike and sat sideways on the saddle, stretching his neck muscles and waiting, though for what, he couldn't be sure.

The two women arrived a few minutes later. He had been unable to discern much from the bridge and though their clothing was quite similar they could not have been more different in face and feature.

One was perhaps twelve or thirteen, fine-boned and small in stature like most of the women from this region. She shone with an innocence and softness of feature that seemed out of place in this harsh environment on a cold, grey day. A fine, almost porcelain quality in her oval face framed long lashes under straight, neat eyebrows and the largest, greenest eyes Flynn had ever seen. She held Flynn's gaze for just a few moments before lowering her eyes and avoiding his stare.

In stark contrast, the old woman at her side was round-faced, her skin announcing deep lines and a persistent tan, weathered to a deep brown. Her eyes were hooded and black as pitch. She exhibited no shyness at all and held Flynn's gaze stoically, even as she lowered the basket from its perch on her back to the ground at her sandalled feet. When she smiled and held out her hand to shake his, in a Western manner, he saw the origin of that estuary of wrinkles.

"You can hear me, Mister Flynn. That is good. I am Chodak and this is my great-granddaughter, Jungney. You will come with me and rest at my home. We have little time, it will soon be very dark and," she looked for a moment at the sky behind him, "also very wet."

Her tiny claw of a hand gripped his like steel wire. Though she was no more than five feet tall, she somehow managed to meet Flynn eye to eye. Nothing of the world seemed quite normal when she was close to him and her touch was an intense exacerbation of that sensation.

The names she had given him and her appearance made him quite certain that these two were Tibetan, rather than Chinese. Traditional Tibetan as well, with names like that spoken in such a direct manner. Brave people or foolish, or perhaps something else, the introduction left him quite speechless. He didn't register that she had greeted him by name. Flynn recovered by reaching into his pack to draw out a map of the city and unfold it onto the tank of his motorbike.

"Yes, it is a good idea. I will show you where to find us and you can come very soon. But please be sure to come very soon. We will walk now and you come with...." she pointed a tiny claw at his bike. Flynn's world swerved and shifted as Chodak stepped forward to point to a place on the map and peer at his face to see that he had noted the location. She stepped back, hoisted the basket onto her back, hooked her arm with the young woman and they both began to walk away. Flynn realised that in the entire encounter he had not uttered a single word.

"Thank you."

He called after them. Though neither of them looked back, the old woman's hand lifted in farewell. As if to punctuate their parting, lightning cut a sharp, angular tear through the pitch-black sky. Thunder cracked and rumbled. After double-checking that he was sure he had noted the place they would meet, Flynn folded his map and threw a leg over his bike. When researching his intended journey, he had come across several references to road closures west of Ya'an. Wet or not, he was determined to check before stopping down for the night at Chodak's home.

CHAPTER THIRTY ONE

If Akashi Agola didn't open her eyes she could enjoy listening to the sounds of morning. She kept them closed. Apart from the hum of the refrigerator there were no other sounds of motors she could discern. Then the refrigerator stopped its mumbling. At first that seemed to be silence but then her hearing began to identify the most enticing of a thousand different sounds.

In the distance someone's music was scantily audible. If she listened with a little more intent, perhaps it was Vivaldi. In between was nestled the sound of several different songbirds greeting the morning, though most of them had ceased their regular dawn chorus as they had been awake for a long time.

Akashi could hear that someone was singing. It was a man. Again this sound seemed to be quite distant or perhaps they were closer and singing quietly. She brought the full focus of her attention to the sound of that sole voice. From behind closed eyes she thought that it was a pretty sound, not because it was perfectly sung, but because someone was singing.

It sounded like freedom.

Just after ten, Akashi struggled out of bed and made a strong black coffee. On most Sundays, this would be the first of perhaps four coffees before midday. Sun streamed through the kitchen window and splashed light into the sitting room, casting sharp relief on the kitchen floor. Grey shadows flickered into the corners of the adjacent room. She stepped out through sliding glass doors onto the landing and cast a languid gaze across the township that had never and could never announce itself. It existed as a 'hide-in-plain-sight' smokescreen for the

massive development underneath it, perched incongruous green in a scorched landscape.

From this vantage point she could look above the trees which towered over snug, ordered homes stretched across ten square miles of desert. It looked emphatic in its illusion of peace as it disguised the underground war machine. Beyond the limits of the manicured suburbs the desert stretched off to a distant horizon. She knew that was true whichever way she looked.

One of the greatest challenges in her life was the complete lack of friends and a social life for her one day off each week. Though she had learned how to fill the day in isolation, there were still days, like today, when she missed the fun, randomness and excitement of school days and university. Fun times before she received the letter informing her she had landed the career opportunity of her dreams. Her phone jangled and buzzed. She picked it up but let it continue to ring.

On most Sundays Akashi's mother would call her. It helped to ease the loneliness that both of them felt since the death of her father five years ago. It had become a tradition for them to speak for hours, emptying the thoughts and disappointments of the previous week, exchanging inconsequential minutia for the want of anything important to say. Today, Akashi let the phone ring out. She listened for the gaudy tone of message bank. When it came, she relaxed. There had to be a first time that she didn't connect with her mum. Today was that day.

Though there were intense, strict and policed rules about making social connections outside the bunker, there were more limited restrictions on exercise within the town limits. Akashi stripped out of her nightwear and walked naked around her apartment, gathering the things she would need scattered here and there in almost every room. She retrieved a white singlet emblazoned with a bold red tick from a basket of fresh washing she hadn't had the energy to empty. After a few minutes searching, her shorts showed up in a chest of drawers full of clothes she rarely used. Underwear and a pair of short socks were retrieved from the drawers of her bedside table.

Dressing in front of the mirror she noticed that her body shape had changed since she had been here. Even if the opportunity was available just once a week she could still address that. She opened the door into her garage and dragged an expensive, designer-labelled, silver-grey bicycle from behind a pile of cardboard packing boxes.

Her helmet and cycle shoes were still there with the bike, covered in a thick layer of inescapable, desert dust. Removing that dust with an oiled cloth took just a minute. Akashi was soon teetering down the driveway, her matching silver-grey helmet askew as she pedalled onto a tidy, clipped and manicured street. Her cell-phone was strapped to her left arm with earplugs connected and the cycle app she had downloaded flickered on the screen. Akashi liked to keep records. It was part of what made her very capable at the job she was required to do. As she touched the screen to start it, an audio recording app also launched.

Even at this time, the breeze off the surrounding desert was warm but it felt invigorating to be outside, breathing air that hadn't been through filters. She breathed the dust, pollen and bacon-scented air and smiled at the perfect imperfection of it. Though it had been her dream job Akashi had never realised precisely what she had been enlisting for. Her father had achieved the rank of Major in the US army. He had encouraged her since the age of seven to follow him into the armed forces. She had such love and admiration for her father that she had never considered anything else. Now she was committed and contained, holding a role which her father, even with his senior rank, had not been permitted to know.

He died thinking his daughter had achieved a mediocre military career. In fact, since this last promotion, she so far outranked what he had achieved in his long career that he would have been beyond proud.

Turning into Main Street, Akashi dodged and wove between orange, metal traffic-bollards. She coasted into the paved section of the mall, under the shade of trees collated in

metal frames and around raised garden beds, bright with flowers she had never taken the time nor had the interest to identify. It was true that once you had learned how to ride a bike, you never forgot. Revelling in the feeling of looping through the mall, she ducked out the other end and continued past shopfronts blazing with signs to buy this and that until she came to the end of it. She pedalled further, past the signs that cautioned traffic to slow down and onto a wider road that signalled town limits. She brought her bicycle to a stop and stood astride it, still seated on the saddle, turning her head to left and right to see desert stretched all around.

Her phone rang again. This time it wasn't her mother. The screen announced an unknown caller and there was no record of the number underneath. This call came with a requirement to answer even during her day of freedom. Akashi ignored it and stepped up onto her bicycle again, pushing hard on the pedals to flash past the large signs on either side of the road announcing town limits. Out here there was emptiness with endless wide-open space to either side. She pedalled still harder, bringing to her skin a sheen of sweat which dried almost as soon as it appeared. Telltale marks clung a little longer on her singlet.

Almost five miles passed before she realised how dry she was becoming, her mouth parched and the strength eking out of her with each additional push. Still cycling, she reached down for her bottle of Tibet water. She popped the top and slaked her thirst. The wind rushed past her. Drops of water escaped to cool her neck and chest. The phone rang again. Once again it was an unidentified caller.

She slid the half-empty bottle back into its cage and pedalled harder still, rushing away from everything. She pedalled to escape her father and his constant prompting of her to achieve rank in the military. She pedalled to escape the melancholic prattle of her mother, lost in the hopelessness of her life, edging by in slow-motion increments, interrupted once a week by a phone call to her daughter. She pedalled to evade the all-pervading miasma of her underground work station. Even

the new office gave her no escape. She pedalled to escape the rules and regulations that threw her off balance every single day, made her nerves jangle and shudder as though at war with her nature, enclosed her in self-imposed chains that rattled and clanked but never let go.

Over the sound of wind rushing past her, over the clatter and squeak of gears and chain, she heard a motor. A vehicle was coming from behind and by the roaring sound, it was coming fast. Akashi pedalled harder again, breath coming in gasps, hot air rushing past her, hair streaming, sweat drying faster than it could form.

In less than three minutes the camouflage-green, all-wheel-drive vehicle passed her and five hundred yards further came to an abrupt stop. To Akashi's surprise, three heavily-armed military police, helmeted and sinister, emerged from the rear of the vehicle and deposited themselves at even intervals across the road, weapons ready. As Akashi slowed to a stop, the front passenger door of the vehicle flew open and an officer stepped out holding a small metallic device.

"You're outside regulation space, Ms Agola. You need to come with us." His voice sounded almost warm but Akashi wasn't seduced. She looked him over to determine his rank.

"You'll stand down, Captain, and call these men off. I'm taking my day off and this is my recreation. It's none of your business how I spend my day. Regulations insist that I get sufficient exercise to remain fit for service and this is my choice." Her voice shook a little with the exertion of the ride and her rising anger with the confrontation. The officer made no move to respond to her but turned the small metal device over in his hand.

"Stand down now, Captain. That is an order." With her latest promotion to the second level underground she outranked him with ease.

"I'm afraid not, Ms Agola. You are outside regulation space and this is my jurisdiction. Your rank plays no part here."

He motioned to his soldiers. "I trust I will not need to ask these men to encourage you."

"Captain, I'm not sure you comprehend who you are addressing. I received a promotion just last week which means I have just attained a rank equivalent to Colonel. I will give you one last opportunity to stand down or face the consequences. Get out of my way." Akashi pressed one foot down on a pedal and began to move her bicycle forward.

The Captain lifted the hand in which he clasped the small metallic device and pressed once. The result was instantaneous. Akashi braked and stood astride her bicycle. Inside, something that might have been her soul – twisted, struggled and screamed in agony as it made one final effort to overcome a command that permeated every part of her being. Her body would not, could not, respond. The three military police approached her, weapons at ease. One took each arm and the third helped her to dismount from her bicycle. He put it into the rear of the vehicle.

"Thank you for your compliance, Colonel Agola. Nothing further need be said about this incident. We will return you to within the town limits and you may continue to cycle. You will not breach the perimeter again. Is that understood?" His voice was now cold and permitted no argument.

"I understand, Captain. Cycling permitted inside the town limits only. That's clear."

The military police released her. The Captain motioned her toward the vehicle. Akashi complied, climbing into the rear seat without further encouragement. Two of the police clambered in the other side. One jumped in the back with her bicycle.

After closing her door the Captain twirled the small metallic unit in his hand, shook his head in amazement and climbed into the front passenger seat. From there he reached down between his legs and lifted a bottle watermarked with the 'Verity Global Tibet' water insignia that had become so familiar.

"Have some water, 'Colonel' Agola." His lips curled around the epithet. "You look as if you could do with it." He

passed the water back to her. His voice was once again warm and relaxed.

"Thank you, Captain. You're right, I am thirsty."

On Akashi's mobile phone the audio recording continued. It captured the hum of the vehicle and every moment until she was back in her apartment, where it ceased without prompt, a record of the whole morning.

CHAPTER THIRTY TWO

The instant he opened his eyes he knew that there had been an intrinsic change in him. His body was restrained in such a way that he could move nothing more than his eyes and mouth. His head had a restraint that extended across his forehead and somehow latched into his skull behind his ears. His neck was thus held in complete stasis. A bond also lashed his shoulders and arms to the bed upon which he lay. Another held his pelvis still. It felt as though his legs were encased in something like a cast which prevented him from even wriggling his toes.

His chest was exposed to the open air. The air was warm. There were a hundred ways that Grey Symes experienced agonising discomfort as he lay on that bed in a stark, white room. He could see no window. He could see recognisable medical equipment and to his surprise there was also medical equipment he did not recognise in that room. He was alone. The sounds he could hear reminded him of operating theatres and the tools for monitoring life signs. He was accustomed to those tools but unaccustomed to them monitoring HIS life signs.

He could feel that intrinsic change in every aspect of his being. Something intense and fundamental affected everything about him. It was far beyond the hard restraint that tied him to the bed. He tried again to move his left arm. The restraint was immovable. He tried his right arm with the same result. Even tied down in this fashion Grey Symes felt extraordinary strength and fitness yet he knew that this was not possible as he lay here on this bed. He explored the room once again, flicking his eyes from place to place, scanning for evidence of........a door. Yes, that line in the wall was the top of a door.

In that cognitive moment it opened with a hiss as though breaking the seal of an airlock. Why would that be so? Three figures approached him. He tried to speak and found that although there was no physical restraint to speech, a reptilian croak was the best utterance he could manage. He tried again and once again heard a strange, disembodied croak. How long since he had spoken?

"It would be sensible to refrain from speaking for the moment, Dr Symes. You have had a very significant operation. Your voice will not do what you require of it. Additionally, I imagine you will have noticed several things. Your restraints are imperative for your complete and prompt recovery. You may also have noticed feeling rather, how can I put this, er... healthy and strong under the circumstances?"

The voice came from a male dressed in a white coverall. From Symes vantage point on the bed he seemed to possess inordinate height with a hawkish face and a few wisps of grey hair on his brow. He appeared to have an extremely promi-nent forehead.

"My name is Doctor Allan Hazred, Dr Symes. It was I who performed your surgery and it appears we have a success on our hands. I have to say that it was the most important and delicate procedure I have had the opportunity to conduct. I imagine you will have many questions but at this point it is not possible for you to speak. I shall do my best to provide you with answers to the most obvious questions that would be arising for you at this point." The unusual looking man gestured to his companions.

"My associates are Mr Lucien Lazard who provided the funds both for the process you have endured and the exceptional care of which you are now beneficiary." A smaller man moved forward. Grey Symes noticed his hands seemed finer in structure than those he had seen on any man.

Long, narrow fingers extended to a small palm. Over a turtle neck sweater he wore a grey business suit which hung from his body as though it were splayed over a coat hanger, seeming not to connect with his body at any point other than

where a narrow black belt wrapped around him half-way down his skeletal form.

He smiled at Grey Symes and as he did this one of his hands came to rest on the cast that bound Grey's right leg, just below the knee. "It is my great pleasure to meet you at last, Dr Symes. Yes, a great pleasure indeed and so pleased too that the surgery seems to be a complete success." His voice was thin and possessed a troubling sibilance.

"And this, Dr Symes, is Mr Christopher Heney. He also possesses great interest in the success of your surgical procedure and enormous interest in any changes it might provoke in you. I know that he foresees great usefulness in the procedure for a whole range of reasons."

The third man moved forward into Grey Symes line of sight. He possessed a powerful physique and a heavy brow. He was dressed in the same style of coverall as Dr Hazred, though worn with much less ease. He nodded once then stepped back out of clear vision.

"Frankly, Dr Symes, we couldn't afford to lose you. Your efforts have been met with deep appreciation by an influential sector of society. It was they who approved your surgery and it is they who are depending on your complete recovery and improvement. There is much to do." The Doctor moved to the foot of the bed and lifted a square metallic chart and flipped through several pages before continuing.

"You had a massive coronary incident in your vehicle on the way home from your regular exercise. We can all be grateful that the monitors you carry as part of your role with WHO alerted authorities immediately. We were able to recover you within six minutes and have you transported to this facility."

Hazred paced around the bed, tapping occasionally on a device, taking absentminded glances into the glass-enclosed control room. Grey Syme's eyes followed his every move.

"Though you were declared clinically dead, we were able to maintain you. We kept your impressive brain functioning long enough for a heart transplant donor to be sourced to suit the

circumstance. At this point I conducted the surgery aided by the best team on this tiny planet. I have great pleasure in informing you that it appears to have been a complete success."

The doctor's shoes made a tiny squeak on the polished floor as he spun around to address his patient.

"You have however been in an induced coma for the past four weeks while your body recovered and," the Doctor paused for a few moments as if searching for the right words, "er, for your body to integrate the organ..., well the organs as we decided to provide additional support for your introduced heart... and the entire experience." He paused again and a small tic appeared at the corner of his left eye. He rubbed at it with shielded annoyance.

"However, that's enough information for the moment. I would ask you to relax with the understanding that you will be released from your restraints in less than forty-eight hours. In the meantime, this will relieve you of boredom and discomfort."

The Doctor connected a small vial to one of the intravenous lines attached to Grey Symes. He felt an instant flood of relaxation and a mild euphoria, a feeling that increased exponentially with every moment.

As the drug took its full effect Grey Symes experienced just one wink of distress. In the expression of some strange and perhaps unexpected side effect of whatever he had been administered, the three men leaving the room took on the form of a troupe of loathsome, distorted and disfigured goblins, rubbing their hands together and plotting with clandestine whispers. It was momentary but for that single moment, intense and troubling. Then the drug reasserted its assigned role and he was whisked headlong into an all-encompassing euphoria.

When next Dr Grey Symes looked upon the world he opened his eyes to sun streaming through a large glass window bound on both sides, one metre distant from the glass, by stainless steel bars. Outside were extensive gardens, managed with impeccable care. Closely trimmed hedges provided a background to several huge statues of massive humanoid beings

towering over the garden, larger than life. In the foreground, beds of crimson flowers in full bloom carpeted the ground.

All of his restraints had, at some point, been removed. He was covered by a light-blue bed sheet and a crisp, white blanket. The sheet was folded tight across his chest and tucked under his arms. His hands were resting across the top of his stomach, fingers intertwined. To his left was what appeared to be a sophisticated electro-cardiograph. Several lines trailed across to his bed. He could not see nor feel where they were connected to his body.

To his right was an enormous viewing glass. To his fresh eyes, this looked to be at least triple-glaze and once again, there was a pane in the wall on his room and perhaps a metre or two between to the pane on the opposite side. He could see two orderlies moving in the viewing room. One appeared to be using a cell-phone.

If it were true that he had been comatose for four weeks, Grey Symes knew that his muscles would demonstrate significant atrophy. To test the theory he lifted his left arm and was surprised that it took almost no effort. He tried each of his limbs. First his right arm, then each of his legs, left and right. He felt in superb health and inexplicably strong and fit. A metallic voice sounded throughout his room. It was the voice of Dr Hazred.

"Treat yourself with some care at this early point, Dr Symes. All your vital signs are in better than perfect order and you will have already discovered that your fitness is extraordinary, considering the trauma you have met in the past five weeks or so. The cuts, abrasions and bruising from your motor vehicle accident are one hundred percent resolved."

Grey Symes turned his head to look into the viewing room. Dr Hazred stood, leaning a little to speak into a long thin microphone which reached up from a metallic panel. The angle he had to assume to speak amplified the strangeness of his forehead which Symes had noticed several days ago. Last time he had made an effort to speak he had achieved nothing more

than a croak. It was time to try again. Taking a deep breath and with some consternation, he spoke.

"Where am I? What facility is this?" This time his voice was no croak. It had a depth and timbre that sounded nothing at all like the voice he was accustomed to as his own. His voice possessed an enchanting warmth and invitational concomitance that surprised him. And he still wanted answers. The speakers in the room activated once again and Dr Hazred spoke.

"You are in a secure, military, medical facility close to Zurich, Dr Symes. This facility is unmatched anywhere in the world. You have been very well tended and that will continue to occur until it is time for you to re-engage in your role at the WHO or serve the needs of those who intervened on your behalf." The speakers made a small click as Hazred disengaged his microphone.

"What has been done? What procedures occurred?" Grey Symes' voice presented a disturbing sonorous tone. Disturbing for him because it was not his voice, not the voice he knew as his own. It sounded like someone else speaking. The small click again.

"The principal operation was a heart transplant, Doctor Symes. It was, however, not a standard procedure. That was where my expertise was required. Some of the matters of complication and the outcomes from the solutions to those complications I perceive you have already noticed. Your voice is one such alteration. I believe you have also recognised that there is a significant change in the capacity of your muscular system to respond even after protracted torpidity. Namely there is not the usual atrophy one would expect after a month in coma."

"Why is that?" Symes demanded, his voice guttural and gruff.

"That, Doctor Symes, is something we will discuss in private at the right time. Now is not the time." Grey Symes shifted in his bed and realised just how capable of movement he was. He sat up quickly and tested his legs by sliding to the polished floor. He stood on both legs, a look of amazement on

his face. Several probes were attached to the left of his chest, under his arm. He pulled them out of his body, skin stretching with the withdrawn needle. He noticed that there was no experience of pain at all.

"This is not possible. What the hell have you done to me, Hazred?" He could feel anger rising.

"Please calm yourself, Doctor. You are free to move about the room and find out more about your capabilities but I'm afraid it is still several days before anyone will be joining you in there and certainly before you will be permitted to leave." Doctor Hazred spoke with a constrained authority.

"I'll calm myself when I damn well please!" Symes walked over towards the viewing glass with surprising speed. Thumping his fist on the glass he came to another realisation about his strength. The heavy glass shivered under his strike. "Tell me what is going on, you bastard. I have a right to know."

A curt nod of his head and the two orderlies immediately exited the viewing room. Doctor Hazred stood with his arms crossed, looking directly at his patient. He clicked the microphone on.

"Dr Symes, you do need to relax. If you fail to do so there are less than optimal steps that I will take in order to ensure it. Do you understand?"

Symes struck the glass once again and once again it shuddered. Anger bubbled furiously in his blood and his muscles ached to strain.

"Doctor Symes, please refrain from the level of activity you are employing. It is still several days until your body will be ready for such intensity."

"I'm ready right now and I will have my damned answers. Talk to me now!" He refrained from striking anything, prevented his hands from balling into fists.

"I can tell you some things if you remain calm."

"Speak."

Doctor Hazred reached over to pull a chair to where the microphone was stationed and sat. He drew a thin hand over his face and across his brow and crown before continuing.

"If you insist, Dr Symes, if you insist. What I have to share with you is not something that is ever shared outside of a highly specialised and elite group of people. It is likely to give you a significant shock. It would be my definite preference to leave it several more days before telling you, but you do insist." He drew his hand across his brow once again.

"Your heart stopped, Doctor Symes. You were considered dead yet here you stand. You are a very important cog in a wheel that has been a long time in planning. An inordinate amount of time in fact and there is some level of impatience from some parties. Because of this, a decision was taken to ensure that you survived so that, in addition to several other matters, your preferred outcomes for the World Health Organisation come to fruition as soon as possible."

The facial tic returned to Hazred's face. He brushed at his eye with the same mild annoyance.

"I am a member of that specialised group, Doctor Symes and since your recent operation, so are you." Hazred shifted, his body awkward in the chair. "The procedure I performed, Doctor, has and will continue to have some very powerful influences on every aspect of your being." He paused for several moments before taking a decision about the detail and extent of information he intended to share.

"The primary reason that you survived, Doctor, is because one of ours didn't. On the same day that your heart decided to relieve you of duty, a rather influential member of our number passed on. Our patrons and I are thankful that most of his body did not suffer significant physical harm though it was a violent situation. We were able to preserve many of his life-giving organs. You now share his DNA. Based on where you originated and the level that this being inhabited, you are now a kind of enhanced hybrid."

Along both sides of Doctor Grey Symes' neck, cords of fury roiled. Even as he witnessed the feeling in his body, he felt the strangeness of it, his disconnection from it. His hands now balled into fists and he lifted them both and began pounding the glass. It shook and shuddered with the power of his attack.

"I did warn you, Doctor Symes."

One lean finger touched a small metal instrument on the desk and Grey Symes fell to the floor, sagging like a rag doll tumbled into disarray.

CHAPTER THIRTY THREE

Cole woke early, still wrapped warm and intimate around Ivy, their legs entwined. His face was nuzzled into her neck. He breathed her in and she stirred as though she felt him draw out a little of her essence. The chill of the morning stung his shoulder and he twisted his face around to get a glimpse of the wet grey of the arriving day. It was pre-dawn. The dimness of the light eking into the room suggested about four-thirty am. Drops of rain pattered on the glass, soft one moment, insistent the next as the clouds scudded and boiled across a roiling sky.

"How long before we need to leave, Cole?" Ivy whispered to him, eyes still closed but in the same moment shifting her warm back and buttocks a little more firmly, reassuring against his body.

"Say what?" He moved to get a better view of her face.

"How long before we need to leave? It's a simple question." Ivy opened her eyes and turned her soft gaze into Cole's eyes and rested them there, a slight smile on her lips while the rest of her face did its best to frown. Cole was dumbstruck. He shook his head in disbelief and shifted up onto his elbow.

"What are you talking about?" he demanded in a voice that sounded far harsher than he intended.

"You've been talking to Dave. You went off and did some ceremony the other day and since then you've been wandering about looking worried. I'm guessing it's time for you to head off," said Ivy frankly, "and if I'm right, then we all have a bit of a journey ahead of us." The bedcovers rustled as she rolled over to face him, lifted her head and doubled up the pillow to rest it there, eye to eye with this strange man she had come to love.

250

"How long?"

From the time they had met seven years ago, Ivy had exhibited an uncanny talent to reach into places Cole was unaccustomed to visiting. When everything else felt as though it was crumbling in to crush him, it was the one thing that held him, bound him to her in a way he could never quite understand. The silence in their bedroom was disturbed only by the muted clatter of rain on the glass.

The rest of the morning felt somehow surreal to Cole as he and Ivy meandered through the tasks that could not be avoided, for the sake of one-year-old Robin, enclosed in Ivy's arms even as she stepped through the chores one by one. Somehow, as the rain cleared and the sun revealed itself, the light in the kitchen felt as though it were reflecting from everything. Dust glittered in the still air, the leaves on the houseplants shone and the walls of the room glared. The reflection cast a hue over everything. It was sparkling, exquisite, beautiful.

Cole kept doing. One small task after another until both he and Ivy were spent, still shrouded in silence. Tiny Robin was also silent, though wide awake and observant. When Ivy left the room, piled high with towels, linen and baby, Cole began to make tea. He sat on the lounge nursing a steaming cup, lost in some world that had little to do with family and children, lost in a world of long remembered dreams. A whole series of memories or dreams or visions assembled themselves piece by excruciating piece until it was clear for him. Ivy returned, Robin still cradled by one reassuring arm.

"You have it?"

"I do, yes I think I do. No, that's not right. I do. I have it." Shaking his head to bring himself back into the room, Cole remained immobile as Ivy refreshed his cup and got a tea.

"Dave is on his way."

"He's coming here?"

"Uh huh, he said maybe a couple of months. Of course, he's walking."

"Of course he is."

Ivy smiled and sipped her tea. "So we have some time up our sleeves." Almost a question, but it somehow felt that Ivy had gone beyond questions.

"When he gets here, I think it would make sense to travel with him. He's strong and resourceful. It makes sense."

"So we walk too. Slow and steady is the right speed for this."

"It is if we are going to rewrite the stories. It's necessary." He paused and looked at Ivy, eyes soft, for a few moments.

"You get it too, don't you?"

She sipped her tea, put her cup down and lay Robin, now sleeping, on the couch swathed in a soft blanket.

"I get it. It's time for this Cole. We are all part of it. Our one big advantage is that we BOTH know this is happening now and what it means. It is time for the stories to be rewritten. We, the three of us and Dave, are one of the new stories. You've been visioning this for long enough. You've dreamed it for years. You, me and all the others who get it are being activated right now. I heard or felt, sensed Elias just as you did. I know Robin sensed him too. We are all in this."

"We don't have anywhere near the distances to cover that some have," Cole shrugged, "so we can take some time to prepare. At least we have a couple of months until Dave gets here."

"Let's hope that's true."

"You got the message from Elias too?"

"It was loud and clear. I was nursing Robin at the time and as I say, I know she also understands. She was quiet and relaxed in a way I've never witnessed in her before. She has been like it again this morning."

"This is a pretty major rewrite, Ivy. It's almost impossible to imagine how life might be once this whole thing is done. We need to reach out to some people too."

"We do, my love and for at least the next hour or two, while Robin sleeps, that is not what we will bring our attention to."

She smiled at him and took his hand in her own, encouraging him to stand. When he was up and they were this close, it demonstrated how he towered over her. It was also obvious that even with his size, he was no match for her intention, nor did he want to be. She guided him back to the bedroom. If love was going to underpin 'all and everything' for the first time in the history of the species, Ivy was determined to express the love she felt for Cole. It was a duty of pleasure. It was the way of the future.

As the town outskirts drew nearer, Dave's mind took him back to the beginning of his friendship, first with Cole, later Ivy and just a short time ago the magnificent soul they had named Robin. It had been one of those chance meetings that defied reason or logic. A five-minute conversation had sparked a kind of brotherhood. Cole had then come with him on an adventure to clear his heart, mind and soul. It had done that. It was during this time that they discovered their common thread.

The stories must be rewritten.

The myths needed revision, the legends required a major edit and the long repeated stories that designed the world of human were destined for a complete rewrite. 'Erase and begin again' was the line upon which they had agreed.

Over the past two and a half months a lot had happened. Day in and day out, rising at first light in a different place on most days to reload the pack, make food and eat it, drink water, walk for a few hours, drink and eat again then walk into dusk. As usual, when Dave attained the rhythm of the walking day, time ceased to exist. He often prepared for a place to lay his head, only to notice he hadn't eaten anything more than a few nuts since breakfast. Now this first part of the journey was coming to an end.

Dave took a few extra steps towards an array of boulders standing like sentinels beside the path. He walked between several of them, took off his pack and sat in the shade. The hardness of the rock pressed warm against his back.

Suddenly there was a giant rush of wind. Dave was transported to the edge of a cliff overlooking a sullen and turbulent sea. It was as though the air itself was screaming, issuing a roaring howl as it buffeted him, threatening to throw him from this cliff to jagged rocks far below.

"The King's men are coming for you. For you, your wife and child. Flee! Flee this place right now! Go to where they can never find you."

He pressed against the wind and made his way, swift as he was able, to his horse and leapt onto its back. Needing no more message than that, the massive animal turned and galloped toward his village home.

"The King's men are coming. Leave your houses. Go to the cave. Flee!" he shouted as he arrived, dismounted with a leap and sprinted between the houses to find his family. The wind became even more insistent, whirling and rushing around everything as if coming from every direction at once. The carved wooden door crashed against a yellow-stained, adobe wall as he burst in. He collected his sword and, strapping it on, rushed into the second room to find her, child at breast.

"We have to go."

Nothing was moving fast enough but for the wind howling through the open door.

"I can have the horses saddled in less than five minutes. Leave everything but food and warmth."

She rose and covered her chest. The child began to cry.

"I'll be ready."

None of the healing plants, none of the potions, none of the knowledge stored in a neat row of books could come with them. Their well-worn staves leaned against the fireplace. He scooped them up as he rushed back outside to the village stables. In less than five minutes he returned. She held their child close, wrapped in her warm clothing and enclosed in a deep-green cape.

Handing his black-cowled cape to him, she shouldered a pack of food she had prepared and pushed him back out the door.

254

Outside, the urgency was all around, the entire village making final preparations to flee into the mountains and seek refuge in a complex series of caves and catacombs that had served their ancestors for more than eight hundred years.

"We can't go with them, can we?" she intoned, her voice flat, knowing the answer.

"We cannot. We go via the cliffs, you know the path," he replied as he hoisted her small frame onto her horse. He tied the bundle of food to his saddle before leaping onto his mount. In unison they dug in their heels. The two strong horses leapt away, back the way he had come, towards the cliffs and that treacherous path where surely the soldiers would not, could not follow.

The wind intensified as they rode, twisting around to blow from behind them, aiding their flight. Soon they reached the cliff's edge. They halted for just a moment, horses and humans alike lifting their heads and sniffing the air, listening for the sound of pursuit. There it was. On that fell wind, they heard the thunder of what must have been thirty horses, running hard towards them.

"They know we are here. We have to go. Ride!"

They kicked their horses and shot along a pathway which seemed to become narrower by the second. Fifty metres below, the sea was rabid, peaks cresting high, topped by brown-white foam which flicked into the air from the shape-shifting pinnacle of every wave. In the same moment, though they knew nothing of the synchronicity, both riders blessed the surefootedness of their mounts and urged them forward, adding just a little more pace to their escape.

With the wind and the ocean it was impossible to hear anything that might reveal how close their pursuers followed or even if they still followed at all. The path, though it was generous to call it that, was now strewn with small round stones and no more than twelve inches wide, yet still the massive horses moved fast, their riders enshrouded in billowing capes.

Further on, less than fifteen minutes later, their progress slowed to a walk. The wind died almost as quickly as it had arisen. In the midst of the stillness, a blanketing mist rose from the angry sea, making it impossible to move at more than a gentle walk. It seemed their pursuers had either ceased to follow this treacherous path or were so far back as to be no present threat.

Both riders halted and dismounted. Their child showed no sign of its arduous journey, sleeping still, bound to its mother's chest. The tall figure, wrapped in his black riding cape, held the reins of both horses. He looked back the way they had come and spoke in an undertone, further muffled by the blanketing mist.

"They will keep coming. They must. They are under the King's orders. We need to find the pass." His voice sounded ragged and tired.

He looked down to the pale face in front of him and saw...
"Ivy."

Dave shook to release him from the trance into which he had journeyed. The rock was now stone-cold against his back. In gradual increments the scene of standing stones became clear as the mist cleared in two worlds at once. With it, David's mind cleared as well. He spoke out loud.

"Well that explains a lot, David." He shook his head from side to side.

"Ivy, we have travelled this together before."

It was a revelation though not unexpected for David, but still a little unnerving. The picture from his... What? His vision? His dream? His time travel experience? Whatever it was, the connection was undeniable and the clarity perfect. He spoke again, to no-one but the giant stones, now grey and cold around him.

"I wonder where Cole fits into the story. He has to be there somewhere."

Dave stood and looked around. Beyond the rim of the standing stones the sun was almost past the horizon. A few remaining tendrils of light were catching the tops of trees

and embellishing charcoal-grey and pure-white clouds with a plethora of colours from a deep, dark, burnt-orange mass through to golden edges slicing the ether. Shafts of yellow light fanning out through cracks in the cloud conjured wisps of purple, indigo and pastel mauve reflecting from the higher realms. The land was shrouded in ever-deepening darkness while the stark street lights of a nearby town began to send pinpricks of white and orange across the fields to his watchful eyes. It took no longer than this for Dave to decide that this place was as good a place as any for him to set up camp, eat and rest. He could brave the clamour of the townspeople with all their 'doings' sometime tomorrow.

An hour later David climbed into his hiking tent, laid out flat on his sleeping mat, stretched his body a dozen ways to release the tension of the days walk and fell asleep. The dream danced itself alive once again.

No time to waste, the pass must be found. Scanning the sheer cliffs was impossible as mist blanketed everything, blinding all sight beyond ten feet. It must have also slowed their pursuers to walking pace. Perhaps they still advanced on horseback but more likely on foot, leading their mounts. Either way, it provided them with a little time.

"Wait here for me, Ceridwen," he said, gentle care in his tone, "I will have to search. I know that the pass is close and it is terrible difficult to find."

"Be bold, be swift, Tegid. We will not move until you return. I shall cast an enchantment for all other than you."

He moved off into the swirling mist as she began muttering strange words in a low voice. The mist clove to his cape and trousers, slowing the pace of his search but he ignored its grasp and moved with methodical thoroughness across the landscape. As he moved he dodged rocks and stones and the occasional small, gnarled tree which clutched voraciously to life in this harsh and unforgiving place. No more than ten minutes had passed when he heard movement followed by a single cry. It could have been some animal screeching in this cold, forbidding

place. It wasn't Ceridwen who called but he knew he must return to her now.

Judging the distance and the angle, he moved as fast as he was able, back to her side.

"That sound? You heard?" she whispered when he was by her side. She looked pale but uncompromising in her resolve and bravery.

"Yes. Perhaps a man, perhaps something else, we must be prepared. I will not leave your side again."

He drew his staff from the saddle and stood looking in the direction they had come, eyes and ears straining for anything to provide warning. He walked around his wife and child drawing a hard line in the earth to encircle them. They held hands and both spoke a series of strange words in unison.

Suddenly the earth outside that circle erupted around them and fire filled the air. Rocks tore from the ground, flared into a bright malevolence and cast themselves at the trio. All of them fell back to the earth, spent and cold once again, outside their circle of protection.

"They also use magic. Hold fast." Tegid called out with a power in his voice that could not be imagined. All other sound faded as his voice rose in authority, deep and strong. He invoked the spirit of the water. As the flaming rocks and stones pounded against their magical barrier, an enormous wave grew, massive in size and volume, towering above them, held there by some indescribable means. He spoke in a voice of command.

"Glanhewch ni o'r budreddi hwn".

The wave crashed down upon them, drenching everything but for the three of them in their protective circle. Pandemonium erupted as horses shrieked in fear, men screamed for their lives and all washed over the side of that sheer cliff to plummet to the sea far below.

One man emerged from the furore, still mounted on his giant of a horse. He grasped a carved yard of blackthorn in his left hand, black as pitch but for a sickly crimson light which

seemed almost to ooze from it. Tegid and Ceridwen both saw him in the same moment. He issued a forbidding malevolence.

As he raised the short staff above his head, massive rocks from the cliff behind him began to break free and float in the air. Torn from the solid ground just outside their circle, a rift formed, weaving a ragged edge from two points on the precipice around them. Giant stones moved through the saturated ether, seeming tethered by an invisible rope, moving toward a place above them.

Just then, a figure that blurred and wavered even as eyes perceived it, flashed past them and thrust a carved, glyph inscribed dagger into the thigh of the dark horseman, just above his knee. The cry he made as that knife drove home shook the air, pounded the rock and scored the ocean. Enormous boulders plunged earth-ward, the screaming of his giant horse telegraphing certainty that the horseman's mount was crushed beneath them. Somehow the rider avoided harm, though his attention and focus was lost. Nature responded with stillness and an uneasy calm.

"This way." A harsh whisper they both heard. Tegid, dragging their terrified horses and Ceridwen, bearing their tiny child, followed the deep-green blur, a murmur of sage as it or he wove a twisted path away from the sea, along the cliff's edge, to turn sharp right between towering stones. Tegid could have sworn there had been no pass in this place when he had searched for a way through. Perhaps the mist had concealed it?

On they went, chasing a blur, silent but for their footsteps and ragged breath for more than an hour. As suddenly as his presence had appeared on that cliff, he was gone. The three fugitives were stone-still, no sound even from the child. Tegid moved close and enclosed Ceridwen and child with exquisite gentleness in his strong arms.

There was no sign of their pursuers. The air was crystalline and still. The ground beneath them was covered with a soft down of leaves and warm soil. He released them and began gathering sticks, leaves and lichen. Striking a flint three times, a tiny patch

issued a single curl of smoke. He drew more of the kindling around and blew until a flame began to consume it.

In just a few minutes there was a warm fire, burning bright. Ceridwen took the horses to a patch of grass and left them there, reins tied to a foreleg for each of them. She pulled a bag from the saddle on her own horse and returned to the fire to sit in its warmth. She began tearing pieces of crusty bread from a loaf and cutting large chunks of hard cheese.

"Who, or what, was that?"

"I met him once, many years ago. He has grown in power. The King is aligned with the same evil magic he fears. His name is Uthyr."

"And who was that who intervened? He, too, must have great power."

"I don't know. But yes, he too, must hold power."

As he spoke, the flame of the fire flared a little. A tall, lithe figure, dressed in several shades of deep green, stepped into the edge of the clearing.

"Cole, is that you?"

David sat up rigid, wide awake though his eyes took a few moments to adjust to the dim, grey light of dawn. His head took longer still to discover which reality or which illusion he was now inhabiting.

CHAPTER THIRTY FOUR

Just under the rock wall covered with a screed of tumbled fragments of the same rock that made up the barrier, Wolf wiped sweat from his forehead and stopped. He and Max were perched on a small ledge of soil surrounded by long, spiny, hard-edged grass intermingled with tiny, white, native orchids. It was a space two metres across and about the same deep. Nevertheless it offered a brief reprise from the constant of stepping upward and feeling the fire in thigh muscles pushed well beyond their normal calling.

"We can rest here." Between one hard breath and the next, Wolf puffed these few words.

Max could not speak, his breath funnelling in and out almost in time with his heartbeat. As Wolf peeled the straps of his pack off sinewy shoulders, Max stumbled to the cliff-side edge of the ledge and without removing his pack he hunched against the wall. He was still breathing with difficulty and unable to speak.

Drawing his in-breath fast through flared nostrils to a count of four, holding for a count of sixteen and releasing to a count of eight, Wolf began to breathe normally with a steady heartbeat after four breaths. He was twice the age of young Max but hadn't spent most of his life in a book store. Still he knew that within a week at this pace, the younger man would be stronger than him or broken. He must trust it was the former. When the fire was a pile of glowing embers and inky grey ash, Wolf turned his attention to the young man.

"Get as much rest as you can tonight. Tomorrow morning we set out at dawn. We need to make it over that pass to the

northwest before sunset. It'll be a hard, high paced day and you're not fit but we have no choice. There'll be heavy rain the following day and I don't want to be climbing in that. Get rest."

With that, Wolf rose from his perch close to the fire, propped his jacket under his head as a makeshift pillow, covered himself with a blanket and closed his eyes. In a moment his deep steady breathing had Max assume he was already asleep. Wolf travelled to a place where he could speak with his brother.

Max sat alone under a sky suffused with a profusion of stars and an almost vertical wall of stone at his back. He considered what he had not spoken about in his experience at the bookshop.

What was the constant thrumming that now seemed to reside in every part of him? What could the images of a wandering old woman in what he imagined to be an African village have to do with anything of importance? Who was the pretty, young tourist in India, the tall greying man and young woman in what looked like it must have been Britain, the man on a motorcycle near towering, snow-covered mountains, or the girl with flawless skin and striking, almond-shaped eyes?

What was this vision now? A man sitting beside a fire, adding sticks and twigs, feeding it to keep the flame alive, became present. Max held back a little, hidden by the leaves and branches of acacia. It was not yet right that he step into that circle of light.

A little while later carrying new knowledge shared by the lone figure at that fire, Max fell into a deep, dreamless sleep.

CHAPTER THIRTY FIVE

It was less than an hour's drive to Balsam Lake though Carter took almost two and a half. He insisted on stopping to admire one magnificent view after another, even exiting the car to breathe the cool, mountain air. Katy looked too, but the book held more of her attention. She flipped the pages searching for the stilted, black-and-white pictures.

"That's him!" Carter was looking over her shoulder through the passenger window. "That looks just like the guy who came by the pizza place back in the city, the one who told me to come out here. He looks the same."

"OK, but that's not possible, Carter. This guy was a chief around this area in the 1890's. It seems a bit improbable." Katy flipped further through the little hand-published book to find three feathers lodged at page seventy-eight. "I wonder what sort of bird these feathers came from?"

"It looks like a Golden Eagle."

"How would you know that?"

"You'd be surprised what I know," he grinned and continued, "but I learned things like this because my Uncle was a bird lover since I knew him as a little kid. I found it interesting. Those are rare if they are from a Golden Eagle. Don't lose them." She turned several pages ensuring the feathers were enclosed, safe, back into the book.

Carter climbed back in and they travelled in a strange silence for the last few miles to a green, grass-covered park, dotted with ancient trees at the south-eastern edge of Balsam Lake. Once the sound of the motor stopped, both of them sat in the car for several minutes with the windows down.

The view across the lake was spectacular, not because it was more entrancing than anything else they had witnessed, but because this was the place they had come to see. This lake was the destination for which they had both dropped out of New York City life for a weekend. The simple direction of a stranger in a bar and now here they were, in wild country, listening to the sounds of wilderness, the shriek of birds held aloft hundreds of feet in the air, the titter of scrub birds, the rustle of animals in the brush beside the lake and the ripple and splash of water on the moss dusted shore.

Carter opened his door and climbed out of the SUV. He began wandering along the edge of the lake. Quite soon, he was a dot in the distance as he continued his solo ramble, stopping now and then to gaze across the surface of the lake, watching the sun play on the water. When he was distant, Katy also opened her door. She stood for a few moments beside the car, still affected by the experiences of their journey. In her hands she clasped the small book.

A voice interrupted the silence.

"I see you found it." A deep voice, the voice of a man yet Katy felt at ease. His voice was soothing and warm. She turned to see who had spoken. About twenty feet away, sitting with his back against one of the old trees was a solidly built man. His long, straight, black hair reached down to broad shoulders covered by an old, stained, woollen jorongo. His legs, in faded jeans, were crossed underneath him. He was shoeless, displaying hard-soled, bare feet. Katy somehow knew what he referred to and lifted the book up to show the cover.

"Yes, and though I don't understand how, your picture is in here. How do you explain that?"

"I'm a long way past explaining anything, my dear. Let's just say that everything that most people see isn't the full picture. I show up when there are things to do and right now, as a good friend of mine has said, 'it's time'." He paused to adjust his legs a little then continued, "Did you read anything interesting in there yet?"

"I just had a quick look through and I saw your picture, or at least I saw the picture of a man who looks like you and Carter recognised you from the bar, last night in New York. We wondered how that could be possible. Oh, and I found some feathers. Is it your book?" This solicited a smile from his serious mien.

"Well, you might say there are several roles that my consciousness has contributed in that book. Not exactly mine is the best that could be said. What you are witnessing as 'me' doesn't own the book if that makes any sense to you. But then in the local traditions there weren't, and still aren't, words for owning something or someone. That's a recent concept for the Muhheconneok people." He laughed out loud, a deep gurgling sound that seemed to rattle off the leaves of the trees and create ripples in the still water of the lake.

"Who are you then?" Katy moved a little closer to him, drawn with a magnetic intensity to his power and presence.

"That too is a somewhat difficult question to answer, Katy. It's not avoidant to fail to answer you but it has an automatic connection to 'I' and that is something that no longer applies. Let's just say that all that is going on in the world right now calls for some intervention and that intervention is happening, here and in quite a number of other places around the world. You are implicated, that is, you as a person, as am 'I'."

He brought his hands together as though in prayer, then blew on them.

"If you are reading this and it begins to make sense, pay close attention to everything that presents in your life right now. You are one of the ones we have been waiting for and the time is now."

He closed his eyes and seemed to disappear into a trance or meditation. The attraction continued for Katy. She drew closer to sit just a few feet away, crossing her legs in the same manner as he. She waited with more patience than she could recall ever possessing. Five minutes passed. The meditation extended to her. Her eyes closed with the sounds of the lake in this remote and

beautiful place. As she dropped into a place of complete peace, his eyes opened once again and he smiled to see her near him. He spoke again but it did not interfere.

"You and this young man were brought here to have the opportunity to experience the full impact of the decisions you are supporting for the beings for whom you work and their entities. These beings have no appreciation of the magic of this earth. For them it is nothing more than a source of the energy they require. They are coming to the end of an era. They will never admit it but they are quite aware of this ending. It frightens them."

Picking up a pencil-sized twig he began to scratch a flower-of-life mandala into the ground in front of his folded legs.

"They have no imagination for any alternative than to pillage the last of the resource of this earth. When all has been reaped, they have no answers at all. They are beings that arise from the over-extended dance of the crimson energy yet they are not native to this earth. Their time is almost over. A new dance has already begun yet they still cling with voracious vigour."

As the words spilled from his mouth there came the cry of an eagle, punctuating him. Katy opened her eyes to see him shape-shift – a hundred or more faces flashing before her and, at last, a magnificent Golden Eagle.

"It is imperative that humanity ceases to engage with them. Among billions of others that means you. Read this book. Learn from it. Walk this place for at least a day and see if you are not affected. You cannot be forced to choose because whether you know it or not, you always have freedom to make a choice. It is time for the balance to be restored and each incarnated soul is here right now in order to make a choice. Read this book. Experience this exquisite earth without interference and make your choice."

With this, he unfolded his legs and stood looking down on her for a few moments. Placing his hat on his head, he walked into the trees and then further until he vanished from sight.

Carter returned to find Katy in deep meditation, the small book resting in her lap with both hands laid over it, thumbs and

forefingers forming a triangle over the cover diagram. He sat down near her and leaned his back against the tree where the long-haired man had been minutes earlier. Closing his eyes to wait for Katy to complete her meditation, the rush of the city and of the journey removed by his exploration of the lake's edge, he also dropped into meditation. They met each other there. Both heard the voice of their mysterious visitor, deep and filled with a frequency which calmed them and excited them in the same moment.

"Now you are both here. Now I will show you. In the space of this weekend it is time for you to decide. I cannot direct you because you always remain in a place of freedom to choose. I can show you."

It was as though their eyes sprang open together yet both were still sitting in meditation. Startling visions came into view in that inner place as the lake and its glorious backdrop of forest and mountains appeared. A ripple of air reflected across the surface of the water as if to demonstrate the beauty of the still-ness before and after. This extraordinary scene pulsated with life even more than in life itself, a glamour dancing in their vision to show a design even more beautiful than the reality they had come to see.

Then there was a sound. A terrible sound that shrieked of pain and loss, like the wail of an animal dying, torn asunder by a rabid predator, rent the air. In the background black smoke gushed skyward far behind the distant shore of the lake. Where once there was the verdant green of mountain forests, there now rose a filthy putrescent. A writhing mass of pipes and concrete were joined together by hard, dust-filled roads awash with roaring trucks pushing dust and the black smoke of diesel into the air.

On the distant shore a stain of brown interrupted the turquoise blue of the water, reflecting from a pure, blue sky. The stain increased, reaching tendrils across the entire surface. Where there was forest just one moment ago the trees turned first to skeletons before collapsing into dust. Dispersing into

choking air, dust joined other rank and filthy fumes. The shore of the lake became devoid of trees. A dirty rain dredged the soil downward, runnels carving into the earth and staining the water. The colour changed again.

The water became a red-brown sludge. On the shore, rust-stained machines trundled forwards and back, giant tankers tearing at the ground and pouring filth into the air. The animals have vanished. Terrified creatures large and small rush and scurry to find a place of safety until there is nothing living left, not even the worms of the soil.

The water is bubbling with putrid gas, detritus of an industry that cracks and breaks the underground while it scars and scours the surface. The air is thick with black smoke from a thousand diesel engines. Smoke is churning into a viscid sky.

The gluttonous machine called 'progress' has arrived.

As the skies darken, mountains tumble into rubble as machines scratch them away, piece by piece. Acid rain tears gullies where they have never been before. Soon the land is broken and torn, the magic destroyed and a million lives overrun by industry.

As the vision progressed through their meditation both Carter and Katy began to cry agonised tears so profuse that they wet their faces, their clothing and soon the soil upon which they sat. Soaking up those grieving tears, the earth around them began to respond, as if there were magic in their grieving. Around them the scores and rifts in the earth began to heal. In a widening shroud, the sores and susurrations etched into land and water, air and ether began to repair. With their tears, as if there were magic present, the earth recovers.

Drawing down to the edge of the lake, grass and flowers replace bare earth. The water's edge now laps against the new green. Fecund moss has returned to offer a protective blanket extending further and further around the lake. The waters churn and ripple as their salty tears form a tiny rivulet trickling across a single leaf to drip into the polluted pond. At the moment of impact of each and every drop the water responds. It clears, life

becomes incarnate. Sludge which clung to the floor of the lake draws back, dissolves into nothingness and vanishes.

Machines are overtaken by rust, consumed as if by some sorcery into the ground upon which they stand. Gases bubbling and gurgling from cracked earth ease and ease and, at last, cease. The machines, pipes, pressure gauges and wire fences become molten lumps upon the slopes and the mountains reform behind and above them, clothed in rich forest, trees growing fantastically fast.

Soon the destruction is gone. The forest, its animals and all the magic and mysticism of wildness return. Yet they haven't just returned.

As they continued their inward journey, Carter and Katy began to recognise the universe inside them to be as vast as that without. They remember the power that resides in every decision, every thought, each word and every deed.

They discovered the reality that every moment is the moment of creation and co-creation.

Beyond the recovery of the beauty of the wild places there is still further to go. In this new vision everything has the opportunity to go beyond, to shine as never before.

As their sight returned to focus, the magnificence of wilderness came to a place even more exquisite than either have ever imagined. Together, for the first time in their adult lives, Carter and Katy began to witness all of existence with awe and wonder. Now tears flow for a different reason. In that final witnessing their meditation is complete. The two New Yorkers opened their eyes in unison to return to the world sitting beside this lake in the Catskills.

The sun began to set. As it did, the temperature dropped several degrees. Katy stood.

"Carter. It's time for us to go. It's time to go back to the cabin. Come with me now, please." Katy loomed over her friend, looking exhausted, yet calm and peaceful. The whole experience of her journey thus far has drained her energy. Above all else,

she needs to eat. Carter opened his eyes and drew his hand across his face to wipe away the remnants of his weeping.

"Yes, yes it's time to go. You just saw......?"

"Yes, Carter, you know that I did. Yes, come now. It's time to go. We need to go."

Katy reached down to take his hand. She lifted him to stand and join her. "It's time to go. I'll drive." They walked back to the car arm in arm. Katy opened the passenger door and helped Carter in. She pushed the door closed. When she started the SUV, she backed it up, turned the headlights on and eased the vehicle onto the road. The sun hid itself behind mountains as they drove. Their headlights lit the road in front of them as approaching night consumed the landscape in ever-darkening shades of grey.

The book sat between them, silent, yet louder than the sound of jet engines at New York airport.

Not a word was spoken in their drive home. When they arrived at the cabin Carter began preparing a simple dinner. Katy took a shower. With just a little effort the fire was soon burning bright, sending a flickering light through the space and taking the edge off the chill which descended with the sinking sun. Carter clattered pots and pans and scattered food all over the bench. Soon the aroma of roasted vegetables pervaded every nook and cranny, reaching into the bathroom. Katy emerged, followed by a waft of steam. She was swaddled in a large, white towel. Turning to greet her, Carter stared.

"What?"

"Er, nothing, food is almost ready." Still he stared.

"It'll burn unless you keep an eye on it." She turned to head to the bedroom. A small smile played at the corners of her mouth.

"Yes, yes you're right." He fussed with the contents of one small pot, scraped and stirred the pan that bubbled on the gas stove and checked the oven. "It's been quite a day, Katy. What happened? What was it that we both saw?"

270

"I don't know," she called from the bedroom, "some kind of vision is the best guess I can make. It felt a lot like some things I experienced when I was a kid. Nothing like that has happened to me since I was nine years old. I'm not sure what to make of it." Wrapped in a huge white bathrobe she made her way to the fire. She sat close to it, not so much for the warmth but because it felt safe and comfortable.

"I'm going to leave this to cool for a minute while I get cleaned up. I won't be long." He disappeared into the bathroom.

The book sat on the edge of the coffee table. One of the eagle feathers poked out a little. Katy reached for the book. Opening it to the page where the feathers lay across the stained beige paper and the sepia-tinted photograph, she scanned the pages to read,

'When it comes time to die, be not like those whose hearts are filled with the fear of death, so when their time comes they weep and pray for a little more time to live their lives over again in a different way. Sing your death song, and die like a hero going home.

Chief Aupumut'

Something about those words made Katy take a deep, fast breath, almost a sob. She turned the page several times to find a piece that had been circled and underlined in red ink.

"You have noticed that everything an Indian does is in a circle, and that is because the Power of the World always works in circles, and everything tries to be round..... The Sky is round, and I have heard that the earth is round like a ball, and so are all the stars. The wind, in its greatest power, whirls. Birds make their nest in circles, for theirs is the same religion as ours... Even the seasons form a great circle in their changing, and always come back again to where they were. The life of a man is a circle from childhood to childhood, and so it is in everything where power moves." – *Black Elk Oglala, Lakota Holy Man*

Under this, a small notation was scrawled.

Though this is not strictly Mohican, it speaks to a way that will come full circle to return and that will be quite soon. It has been included for its value to us all.

There was a signature which was quite difficult to read but Katy was almost certain it read "Negyesydd".

Negyesydd! How could that be so? This could not be coincidental? Negyesydd. From childhood, from a dream, from a lifetime she could almost not recall, how could this name be right there on the page? She made a conscious decision to allow it even though she was incredulous. Read on Katy, read on.

The book was a compendium of wisdom from the Muh-heconneok people from times long past, more recent and even through to current times. On some pages other tribes were represented. On each of these there was a notation of origin and respect. Many other pages were almost hieroglyphs, markings that meant little to Katy or to any reader who had no notion of the language. On these pages, red ink was splashed across the page. Perhaps some reader had been seeking to comprehend or make some esoteric calculation. It was impossible to tell. On each of these pages, Katy noticed that she 'felt' some kind of energy permeating the room, permeating her body. She wasn't able to determine with any precision what that energy was, but there was a significant shudder in her field with each of these red marked pages.

She turned the page to find a portrait photograph of the man she had come to recognise as Negyesydd, the writer of several notations in this volume, the imaginary friend from her nine-year-old self and the strange visitor in this unexpected journey to the Catskills. She felt a peaceful relaxation move through her. It made the unease of the red-inked pages even more noticeable.

A puff of hot steam poured out of the bathroom as Carter re-entered the room looking fresh and clean. He smiled a generous smile, a towel wrapped around his waist and his hair wet and dishevelled.

"Two minutes. Just have to get some fresh clothes on." Katy's eyes followed him into the bedroom. For just a minute, the book was forgotten.

"This is a massive bed. It has to be at least king-size, maybe even bigger. I've never seen such a monster of a thing." Carter's voice came through the open door. A few moments later he followed it in to the warm space beside the open fire. "I might have to renegotiate sleeping on the lounge. Maybe we could toss a coin for the bed." He crouched on the animal skin rug, faced the fire and almost theatrically, rubbed his hands together to warm them. "Are you ready for dinner, Katy?"

With stomachs' full, Katy went back to reading the book. Carter sat leaning against the lounge, his hands clasped behind his head, lost in thought. Both of them jumped at the sound of a knock on the door. Carter answered. It was Negyesydd. Without invitation he removed his hat, slipped off worn brown sneakers and walked in. Carter was silent. When the old man was comfortable by the fire, Carter sat to his left as though it was his natural place. Katy remained where she was, the book resting on her lap.

The old man unrolled a deer hide wrapped around multico-loured cloth. He placed them both on the floor. From several small, red bags he drew out a selection of totems. There were several crystals, some decorative stones and wooden things carved into the shape of power animals; jaguar, bear and a full antlered deer. In its own black piece of animal hide he revealed a crystal skull the size of a fist and placed it furthest from him in the centre. Negyesydd became something else, something that had a place in more than one world. He drew out the two parts of a native American smoking pipe. The long timber stem he laid to the right and the carved stone bowl to the left. Raising the two parts of the pipe into the air he spoke some words in a low but power-infused voice. He put the two parts of the pipe together, bringing the feminine and the masculine into alignment to become one, in complete balance. Both New Yorkers watched in awe as Negyesydd followed precise protocols of an ancient

pipe ceremony, calling in the powers of stars and planets, earth and asteroids. As he puffed long breaths of sweet smelling smoke in each of the directions, with prayers and invocations, Katy saw images reflected in the windows of the cabin. Standing in a long line were twelve Muhheconneok ancestors, shadowy figures who looked on the ceremony in acknowledgement, forbearance and support.

When his ceremony was complete, he was meticulous in placing every item back into individual bags and at last into the soft deer-hide. This package remained on the floor in front of them.

Long hair framing his slender face, Negyesydd looked first at Carter.

"You will go back. You will face them and you will bring to them knowledge that they have forgotten. Yours will be a journey that will test you as nothing else. You will go back and sit in those steel and concrete towers. You will do everything you can to let them know that they must stop. Most of them will not listen. Some will. This is your task."

He turned to face Katy.

"You will join me. Together we will make our way to answer the call of Elias. I know that this means nothing to you now. It will soon make complete sense. Tomorrow you will both walk into the forest to meet what the white man calls 'wilderness', though for us there has never been anything wild about it. It has always been, is now and will forever be part of us. Tomorrow you will go into the forest."

He turned once again to Carter. "Then you will return to the city. You need to leave this place by half-past-three tomorrow afternoon and be on your way back to the city." He turned his head toward Katy, "and you will come with me. I will come to collect you tomorrow at a four forty-five."

He slid all of his paraphernalia into an umber-brown, buffalo-skin bag and tied it. Without another word he stood, the bag tucked under his arm. At the door he slid on his sneakers, donned his hat, opened the door and was gone.

First to move was Katy. She rose to take a few steps to the firebox. She tossed three heavy, dry logs onto the embers glowing on the hearth. Leaning in to blow on the embers, they began to glow and spark until a flame caught. She sat down again. They watched the flame grow and begin to consume the timber, painting a billion patterns against the blackness of the grate.

"So what now, Katy? What the fuck do we do now?" asked Carter. The flames were lighting her face in much the same way as Negyesydd had lit her spirit.

"I'm going to finish reading this book. I'm going to sit by this fire. Tonight, I'm going to sleep in that enormous bed in there. If you'll join me, we can hold each other because I know that I need that. When sleep comes I'm going to sleep the sleep of the Muhheconneok ancestors. Tomorrow morning I'm going to walk some trails in the mountains with you if you will come with me." She shrugged her shoulders a little and smiled at her friend. "That's what I'm going to do, Carter. Will you join me?" Carter smiled and nodded, the firelight flickering on his face.

"Tomorrow afternoon I'm meeting a strange being that I first made acquaintance with when I was nine years old. I am not afraid. For the first time in my life I feel at home, on point and doing what I came here to do."

It was just after ten past one when sleep called an end to that day for Carter and Katy. Katy read every word of the small volume and remembered while she learned. Knowledge was contained in those pages along with myriad prompts and sigils that called in powerful remembering. Katy remembered and she became someone else, became herself again as she read.

Carter wandered outside for a while, returning to tend to the fire as it needed. He settled into reading excerpts from a book he uncovered on a small stack near the bookshelf. It was called "The Book of Secrets" by an Indian guru named Osho. He had never heard of the author but the volume kept him transfixed for hours. In it the guru spoke of a 'new man' for changing times.

When Katy finished her book she glanced at a small clock on the mantle above the fire. It was a few minutes past eleven. The fire still flickered. She watched Carter for several minutes, watching the light on his face, the seriousness of his expression, the familiarity of him. She padded off to the bedroom, removed all her clothes and climbed naked into the huge bed, pulling a soft, warm duvet over her. Less than ten minutes had passed when she called out to Carter.

"Would you hold me soon please, Carter?"

Carter placed the spark screen in front of the fire. The flames burned bright and pure. He left the bedroom door open, stripped down to his underwear and slid in beside her.

"You're naked?"

"You noticed." She hooked her fingers into the band of his shorts and pulled them down. In friendship, in love, in care and appreciation they discovered each other in a way that New York had never permitted.

The following afternoon, after they had walked far into the wild country, breathed the mountain air, felt their feet on the ground and shared the magic of that place with the creatures and the spirits of the land, Carter and Katy parted. Carter packed the SUV, wished Katy an emotional farewell speckled with tears and began his journey back to New York City. He carried with him all of his own possessions, most of Katy's, including her heavy books and a hastily penned letter of resignation addressed to the management at Rothstein and Kill.

CHAPTER THIRTY SIX

On the side of the mountain, on a bold stone outcrop, in the chill of the night air in the Canadian Rockies, Raniyah set up her telescope while the other two spoke in hushed tones together, smiling and joking, balanced in wide canvas chairs, sipping steaming hot tea from big metal camp cups.

"Hope this is worth all the bother, Ran." Toby smiled with unshielded fondness at his younger sister as she fussed and tweaked the telescope until she was satisfied with the setup.

"Make up your own mind, brother. It's all set and it's already changed again so I'm thinking you won't be disappointed."

Raniyah, her hands shaking a little, not from cold but from excitement, moved away from the scope and picked up her mug of tea. "Take a look."

Pushing out of the chair, Toby passed his tea to Brianna and positioned his eye over the eyepiece.

"Holy shit, Ran, that is amazing. Bloody hell, Brianna, you have to look at this."

Raniyah looked pleased. It wasn't often that she was able to surprise her older brother and he was genuinely surprised now. Brianna almost spilled both mugs of tea getting into place at the telescope.

"Oh. My. God." This came from Brianna as she perched over the scope. "That is truly amazing, Ran." She also looked stunned. "I don't know who else might know about this but I'm betting it's fucking significant."

What had looked out of place when Raniyah had first seen it, now looked even more startling. The colour was a distinct

green and though Toby and Brianna hadn't seen its earlier manifestation, Raniyah insisted it was much more prominent in the
night sky. Together, they packed the telescope down, removed
any trace that they had been together on the ridge and retreated
into the grotto. Toby came in last, closing the hatch and sliding
half-inch stainless steel bars into place to make it secure against
almost any intrusion.

"So what do you make of it, Ran?" Toby said as he stepped
down onto the floor of their sanctuary. Raniyah screwed up her
nose and shrugged.

"I don't know what to make of it, Toby. It's changed
again since I last looked. It looks closer again if that's at all
possible. There's no way it hasn't been noticed by NASA by
now because something changing that fast in the sky would be
computer-monitored by them for sure. Whatever it is, it seems
to be coming this way." She paused and took a deep breath. "If
it's a comet, it's difficult to tell what its trajectory might be in
the long term. I haven't heard any rumour of a comet in any
case and the public record of comets is pretty extensive and
available." She slurped her tea.

"So I'd say it's not a comet." She slurped again.

"If it's not a comet, the other possible scenario is that it's
some kind of meteor and it's a big one. I mean an enormous
chunk of space junk. The kind of mass that would make a real
mess here on earth even if it just happens to pass by quite close,
say just outside our recognised solar system. Its movement and
its mass would be... well... more than a bit disruptive." She
slurped again and smiled at them both.

"You mean dinosaur epoch disruptive, don't you?"
Brianna asked.

"At least that, yes, if it came close it'd change everything.
If it's coming direct at us, life as we know it would be wiped
from the face of the earth."

The three of them sat in contemplative silence, pondering the tiny greenish dot in the sky. Brianna was the first to exit their shared reverie, standing to announce,

"Well folks, this might seem a bit challenging and a mite depressing but let's stay on task. Someone has decided they are not too keen on us, so it makes sense for us to get some sleep so that we can get into some research first thing tomorrow, death star or not."

It bumped them all into action. Toby helped Raniyah to prep one of the bunk beds while Brianna did a double check of the doorway and hatch to ensure security. In less than fifteen minutes they were all asleep to a night of lucid dreams unlike anything any of them had ever experienced before.

It was a dreamscape though each of them were there, witnessing themselves and the others. Was this the dream or was that place they had just left the illusion? It was impossible to tell. As three and one they moved forward across a landscape unfamiliar to them, dry land as far as sight could fly, gently rising. Impossible towering white-trunked trees soaring to heaven amidst a startling blue sky and strange animals, giant creatures snuffling and shuffling at the base of these trees searching for who knows what, giant clawed paws tearing at earth and rock. Ever moving forward all three scanned to view a range of massive mountains which dwarfed everything to a minuscule place, ants on a giant ant nest, scurrying and weaving. Even the greatest of the giant creatures were made infinitesimal to the boulder-strewn range, snow whisking from peak to peak and there in the ice there was fire too, scorching the sky and painting the clouds in red, amber, maroon and violet.

A collective sigh issued from the three as one asking, "Where are we?"

Just as the question was breathed into existence, all three found themselves standing, perched on a colossal peak, impossible balance maintained in a gale, clothes whipping around them like lashes, yet they remain perched there. It is impossible to fall.

In plain sight, perhaps ten thousand metres below, the mouth of a giant volcano is spewing forth molten stone, hissing gas and flame and spouts of liquid coruscation and effulgence, looking like the fire and brimstone of the hell of any religion of tragedy.....and yet.

There in the centre of that, seeming to float in a ball of greenish-gold, not liquid, solid, air or fire, in a swarming mass that must then be ether, one sole being bearing a simple staff of wood. From this impossible height, clarity as though viewed through a telescope trained on this one entity. From here, emanates the colour green though from black skin, wiry in frame and well-muscled. The dance of this being in such a ball of green-gold light, weaves such an intricate tapestry with every movement of that simple stave of wood as though it might be infinite, never ending, eternal and momentary all at once.

As their vision is captured so that it is witnessed as one experience, a vast contraption soars above them. Was it some ancient bird, some antediluvian dinosaur, creaking and groaning through the fire-tortured sky above this gigantic portal to the centre of the planet? Not of flesh, bone and spirit, this bird is a machination, an abomination reaching downward to that green-gold ball of light, tentacles extending down, fixing to attach, yet unable to connect. Screaming with frustration the giant machine tumbles out of the sky, plummeting down into that pit of fire, weapons activated, intent on tearing the tiny figure limb from torso, breaking the light, bringing darkness.

Without effort it is repelled, a sordid blast of liquid fire emanating from the portal, towering three thousand metres to shift the energy of that weapon into a mass of molten steel and through to molecules of gas and light and thus it is transformed. From far below, a wooden, ceremonial staff plunged into solid bedrock that is no more solid than the air on which that green-gold ball rides. In the perfect centre of the fire, green flame, dark-skinned being, sinews straining yet at peace, contained within that green-gold ball, without words and yet words form into their collective mind and those words are comprehended

by three and one. There can be no denying, no turning back, choices made and none too soon. The words that form in the minds of these three, sent in sigils and cuneiforms, yet words nevertheless, in a voice as old as time itself,

"It's time, my friends. Be bold and come."

Then, something more for these three, a sigil that speaks direct to them as separate to any others that are called on this journey, an instruction and a command.

"This is the way you must travel. From where you are, walk to visit the village of Aniak on the Kuskokwim River. There you will find hope for life. There also, death will visit though fear shall not. Find a Yu'pik elder named Kopanuk Mountain Dreamer. She will know you. Seek her wisdom."

Next morning, inside the grotto, safe in the folds and hollows of mountains seen to be a world away, three souls woke in unison. It's not the light of morning, nor the sound of birds calling in the day that disturbs them from slumber, just the end of a dream that couldn't be a dream.

Brianna, Toby and Raniyah lifted their heads from their pillows as one. Each looked toward the other, not a word spoken, yet inherent knowledge present that the guidance they had all been seeking, unspoken, had been provided by who knows what or whom. In their collective mind, in the games they play with soundless communication, they know. Elias has called them.

Brianna rose first and padded to the stove to prepare coffee. Toby began packing down everything that needed to be stored, safe and dry. Raniyah found a place for her telescope, just behind a giant standing stone to the east of the grotto. She began to choose what few things must come with her on this journey of lifetimes. Soon the aroma of fresh coffee is drifting through the space. They all pause, Toby and Raniyah side by side on a deep soft leather lounge and Brianna carrying cups and percolator, honey and milk on a carved timber tray.

"We'll set out just after midday. I think we can have every-thing done by then and it seems we were late in receiving the call, so we have a bit of catching up to do." Toby laid a map out

on the table and smoothed it down. "We will need to go north and we need to be well prepared for some extraordinary, tough conditions. If there was any time of year that it was good for us to travel it's now, so for that we can be grateful. Ran, I'm guessing you have all the usual stuff you carry. Compass, lights, camp stove and so on." He checked in with her with a glance and she nodded tersely.

"Great. Bree, can you handle everything communications?" Bree also nodded as she snapped a battery onto an old Nokia cell-phone. "I'll handle strategy, sustenance, defence and protection. After those dudes at the house, we have to assume that we continue to be a target. They weren't amateurs so they aren't going to vanish. More likely, they'll be better prepared next time. We need to have them in awareness from the moment we leave this place."

He switched into their soundless communication. 'Guys, whenever we connect about what we're doing and what direction we are going, let's choose to use our new found skills, huh? I'd say it's best to put it to use from this moment and good to be in practice as much as possible. As far as we know we can't be heard or traced in any way when we communicate like this, so it's the best security we can offer each other. It'll be good to be skilled too if we find ourselves in a confrontation of any sort.' They all connected eyes as he concluded.

"I want to name it, Toby. As far as I'm concerned it's "soulspeak" that we're doing. From now on it needs to be called soulspeak," Brianna shared.

Raniyah smiled a huge broad smile, 'I really like that, Bree. Do we need to do something with sigils to make sure we know who we are soul-speaking with? Something to identify each of us, so we know any communication from one to the other is intentional and genuine. Who knows whether we are the only ones who have opened this particular doorway?'

'Good idea, Ran. We can't be too careful.' Brianna picked up a small stone pyramid with an arrow etched into each plane. 'This is mine. I'll package mine with this every time from now.'

As if to punctuate her statement, both Toby and Raniyah sensed her sigil as she spoke.

'Mine is this, guys.' She transmitted a green light with a long tail. The moving stellar object she had located days ago and to which she had begun to feel a vivid attraction.

'Nice choice, Ran. This will be mine.' Toby sent a Japanese symbol that looked something like a stick figure house but drawn in calligraphy, the symbol for 'Ai', harmony from his beloved Aikido.

'That's so perfect, Toby, no mistaking any of us. I'm so glad we're all doing this together. It couldn't be better.' Raniyah was beaming.

Just after noon, the three of them began their long walk, heading due north to their first connection with a township at Garibaldi. They walked with steady, measured steps as they all felt the need to familiarise themselves with travelling on foot.

It was four days walk to Garibaldi.

From there they would restock and replenish.

CHAPTER THIRTY SEVEN

When Kesari first arrived in Cairo she had been amazed by the intensity of the dry heat that sapped every last remnant of moisture from everything. It had been the middle of the hottest summer on record in this place where hot was already taken for granted. It had etched a memory that would stay with her forever. Max seemed to love it, running and sweating and drinking huge draughts of fresh, cool water from smiling stall holders in the Khan El Khalili. Not one of them ever hesitated for a moment to pass over large glass flagons or worn brown leather pouches, full of water, to quench the boy's thirst. Somehow he was born to the heat and to these brown men who seemed willing to do whatever he bid.

Now that the third year had passed, she was able to bear the soaring temperatures of summer with greater ease. She had changed how she dressed and began learning to move with slow efficiency through the sun-drenched streets to and from the home she had established for the two of them in the second storey apartment of an ancient shopfront on a backstreet near Gohar Al Kaed.

The apartment hadn't been much to look at when Kesari first negotiated a price with a very old Egyptian woman whose wrinkles gouged channels into her sharp-featured face. She had the brightest eyes Kesari had ever witnessed. In the intervening time, both of them happy with the arrangement and Kesari always six months ahead in rent, they had become friends. Her name was Hotep.

On a glistening, still and hot morning in the middle of July, Max disappeared. Even the call to prayers of every nearby

mosque, belting out from dawn in deafening competition, hadn't woken Kesari. She slept through until after eight am when the street hawkers began shouting their offerings of fresh fruit, vegetables, fish and meat to all that would hear. The fog just wouldn't clear from her eyes, nor the cotton wool that seemed to have lodged in her ears. She arose from her low mattress in her stone-walled, tapestry-laden bedroom and padded to the makeshift kitchen. A portable gas stove sat at a precarious angle on a rough-hewn wooden bench near a single, rusted water tap. Kesari poured cold water from a porcelain jug into a tall, silver beaker. After downing all the contents at once, she shook her head and tried to fathom what it was that felt so wrong this morning.

Max! She hadn't heard anything at all from Max. No question about it, that was abnormal.

"Max. MAX! Are you there?" she called as she pushed her way through a thick cloth that sufficed as a door for the tiny cubicle that was a private space and sleeping quarters for her ten-year-old son. Twisted and skewed at the foot of the low bed was a swatch of bright, decorated cotton that was Max's bed sheet. The bottom sheet which featured a golden Anke inked into its design was crumpled and a little damp with sweat, the pillow pushed up hard against the wall, doubled over so that the pillowcase didn't quite contain it or the russet-brown stain of its overuse.

She cast her gaze around the tiny room, not a second glance for the strange Egyptian decorations that constituted Max's own version of the superheroes present on the bedroom wall of any ten-year-old boy. To a western boy it would have been hieroglyphics. To Max it was normal.

Max not being in his room was not.

Mind racing, Kesari dragged on enough clothing to be considered decent and flew down the steep, steel stairs to rush into the street.

"Max," and then louder again, "MAX, MAX!"

Heads turned here and there, but so much happens on the market streets of Cairo. The sight and sound of a woman calling for someone in the street doesn't attract attention for long. Kesari paused. She took several deep breaths. Her son was quite capable in these streets. He spoke the language. Ten years old and a calm, thoughtful boy, though still active and engaged with everything around him.

"Walk and look, Kesari," she said. "Just slow down, breathe, walk and look."

Moving with more sureness now, Kesari went from shop-front to shop-front, market-stall to market-stall with the thoroughness of a mother. Remaining calm, she called his name. She controlled the rising fear she had that Max was lost to her. That must not be so! The day was warming fast and the streets becoming busier, bustling with markets, hawkers and languid knots of every shape and colour of man, smoking brown cigarettes and drinking pitch-black coffee. There were flurries of well-wrapped women, pointing and bargaining on everything from swatches of bright-coloured fabric to a massive array of fruit, vegetables, animal-flesh and large, fly-covered, foggy-eyed fish.

Turning sharp left, Kesari was now just a few hundred metres from the market square. Her poise almost left her as she considered the mass of people and traffic in that place. How would she ever find him there?

In that same moment, she felt something, some presence that, just for a moment, meant that the sounds, sights and smells of the street dulled just a little and she thought of Tisa. She shook her head. Keep looking, woman. She began to make her way to the market square, to that rush and tumble of humanity, searching for her son. From that moment, she could not dislodge from her mind, "Tisa is coming. She is on her way now and drawing closer each day. Prepare for her. Life is about to make a dramatic change again".

It was taking all her self control not to slip-slide into panic. Kesari took a moment to remember Max's capability in Cairo.

'He is a part of this place where I still feel alien.' She continued her search. The noise of the markets rose as both customers and marketeers thronged into this place of trade, peddling wares and buying the everyday needs of life. The streets are awash with the odours of rotting garbage, perfume and incense, sweat and smoke. Carts laden high with fish and blood-red slabs of the carcasses of sheep, goats and cattle are surrounded by the blackened movement and annoying burr of tens of thousands of flies.

A hundred male voices rise above the clamour to tell whatever each purveyor of goods has to sell. In the midst of all of this there is the sound of religious chanting. Somehow the sonorous chants cut through the noise. Issuing from every mosque and temple dotted along this road, the sound is juxtaposed with this orgy of everything earthly.

Taking a moment to reconsider, to catch her breath, to calm her anxiety, Kesari leaned against the cold, smooth stonework of a temple doorway. From this temple it seemed the chanting of prayers has ceased and at first she thought there was silence inside. Waiting just a few moments longer, she held her breath. A mother can always hear it, there can be no mistake. The sound of her child was, to anyone else, almost indistinguishable amidst the ocean of sound in the street, but 'almost' meant Kesari needed just a few seconds to recognise the voice of her son. His child-like soprano is stark, apparent, interspersed with several other voices, questioning and challenging. One voice arises harsh and loud, the sound of frustration, the sound of anger.

She pushed away from the carved stone wall to take a few steps inside the doorway, noticing the coolness of the air, the echo of voices from the high arched ceiling and a relative peace from the squalor and disturbance of the market. Without thinking she continued to walk inside, drinking in the coolness, the scent of incense and the shuffle of her shoes on the ornate, marble floor.

Max's voice is quite easy to discern now, his soprano bright amongst the rumble of Imam's and priests. It both ushered her

inwards and slowed her pace. She slipped unnoticed into a hushed alcove a short way inside the cavernous prayer space. It seemed to Kesari, as she recovered her wits in the cool mosque with its walls echoing the silence of stone, imbued with the prayers and sins of a thousand years and a million souls, the men in here were genuine in listening to her son. Robed and bearded, they sat almost in a circle around ten-year-old Max, some nodding, some grunting, some looking wide-eyed and surprised. One looked livid and agitated.

A man's voice cut through, booming in Arabic something that Kesari could not understand, but concluded was directed at her. She turned to face the sound and saw a large, bearded man, heavy-browed, moving with more haste than his size seemed willing to permit, toward her.

"You cannot be in here," he hissed at her in English as he came close. "This is not a place for women."

"I came for my son."

"You cannot be in here."

"Mumma." Max called out to his mother, stood and walked, calm and composed, taking her hand. "We can go now." He smiled at the large, fierce-faced, bearded man and stepped a few steps, drawing his mother with him by the hand out onto the flagstones in front of the mosque, down the stairs and onto the bustling street.

Two streets toward home and Kesari stopped. She lowered onto one knee to look into Max's face.

"What on earth were you doing in there?"

"I was telling them some different stories, Mumma. Stories they hadn't heard before." He looked a picture of innocence.

"Max, I was frantic. I didn't know where you were! I thought I had lost you!"

The words tumbled out of her. She allowed relief to reach her and she sobbed.

"I was fine, Mumma. This is my place. I can't be lost. This is what I have to do."

"You have to let me know where you are, Max. I don't care if it's what you have to do, you cannot just disappear. You have to let me know!" Even as she spoke, Kesari realised the words falling from her mouth were a product of her fear, love and relief bundled together into words. She threw her arms around him and held him close. He squirmed a little to encourage her to release him.

"I am safe here, Mumma. This dance has just begun and there are some things that I have to do. I'll make sure I let you know where I am."

Max was the picture of earnest.

Kesari held him at arm's length to gaze at her son. "Don't leave me behind, Max. Don't leave me behind. We travel together, my darling."

"I won't, Mumma. Like Tisa said, one day we'll go on a great adventure."

Kesari nodded. "She is not far away right now, Max. Our adventure will begin quite soon."

"I know, Mumma." Max's eyes shifted for a moment and he pointed. "Look Mumma, over there is a man from the Mosque. He was with the angry man."

Reaching out to hug him, Kesari lifted the boy into her arms and turned around to see a small, black-robed man showing great interest in a market-stall full of colourful fabric. His clothing made the sight incongruous though the merchant seemed unconcerned, flitting to his side, willing to ply his wares to anyone who might take a look.

"We best get home." She spoke in a whisper, her lips close to her son's ear and began striding through the street, Max clung to her like a limpet, while she turned random corners here and there in an effort to lose their theological tail. When she reached the stairs to the apartment, he was nowhere to be seen. Kesari relaxed a little. Max had fallen asleep in her arms. She placed him back into his tiny sleeping cubicle.

It had been a torrid morning. There was so much to be done which had received no attention at all. She began with normal

tasks of the household, making an effort to bring normality to her day. Glancing at the ornate mirror which concealed a smudged stain on her bedroom wall, she laughed out loud. Her hair resembled a poorly attended bird-nest, her face taut and pinched, large shining eyes notwithstanding. The cotton robe she wore, loose-tied at the waist made her appear plain and without shape. In this place, that last matter was a good thing but the whole picture? No wonder she was ejected from the mosque. She looked a complete wreck.

Untying the cord at her waist, Kesari slipped out of the loose fabric and padded on the cool floor to her shower. The sound of the water drowned out the sounds of Cairo and her mind and body found the relaxation that had been evading her since noticing Max's disappearance. Her thoughts moved to Tisa and the strange message she had received while she was searching for her son. It was a message that even the hubbub of Cairo's market streets couldn't quiet. As the water ran over her body, cleaning and cooling her, Kesari closed her eyes to search that other landscape for her old friend. She searched with something that might have been her mind or might have been another thing within her, not identified with such ease.

It was a single moment that passed as Tisa came.

At first it seemed a visual thing. A moving picture projected as a dream, a small figure walking with dogged steps along a long dry road, the dust flicking up in whorls and wisps, coating everything in a red-brown patina, including the solitary walker. Soon however, perhaps just a few seconds as time seemed somehow unimportant in this realm, it was as though Kesari were able to 'zoom in' so that she was gazing into Tisa's face. She could see that although she had some hardship in her travel, Tisa was relaxed and at ease, a hard staff in her left hand providing support as she walked. At first, she seemed not to notice she was being observed. Then her eyes brightened and a satisfied smile began to etch its way into the contours of her face. Tisa looked at the space from which Kesari observed her. She broke the silence.

"Kesari, darling I'm so pleased you are here. I'm on my way to you now. I'm walking most of the way, my dear. It does seem unnecessary at first, but understand this. The walking is essential. I have to walk. I won't be too long. No hurry for you but when I get there, we will need to go without pause. All of us." Her voice and words matched the pace of her steady steps as she walked that dry, dusty road in central Africa.

"I heard you, Tisa, when I was looking for Max. I lost him this morning but he is found again. He was in the mosque. I brought him home." The water from her shower ran over the crown of her head, past her lips, across her breasts and belly, down her slender legs and gurgled away. Kesari continued to soulspeak with her teacher and friend.

"I felt your discomfort though I couldn't work out what was going on. So I just called you."

"What is this thing we are doing? How are we......?"

"It's wonderful, isn't it? Somehow it has in recent times become a simpler matter to communicate in this manner. I believe it has to do with the time I spent in a village where the people are connected with others all over the world. They connect like this. Better than this! In any case, it's wonderful to be able to speak with you in this way, Kesari. It is the communication of our souls and it feels like home. I intend to practice it as often as possible. Elias told me this would return to us one day, when we woke to our genuine potential." Tisa paused for a few seconds. "Will you give me one minute, darling?"

As Tisa walked, she came by a small cart on the left of the road, attended by a small man who had a vague familiarity. Though it seemed improbable in this place he appeared to have Asian ancestry. In spite of this, he spoke the local dialect without accent.

"Will you have some fresh things, mother?" He slid a small drawer out at the rear of the cart and drew out some fresh greens and a mixture of bright-coloured fruit. "I always have some special things I grow myself."

In the shower, so far away, Kesari watched, both physical eyes closed as the water doused her but with her third eye, her spirit eye wide open. Tisa reached out to take the produce from the small man's hands. His gnarled and hard-worked hands reminded her of her own. She had known well the working of the soil to provide the food for her village. His were honest hands. His presence here and the goods he had for sale were surprises too. Goods and produce like this, before the rains in this harsh and unforgiving place, were miraculous.

"Thank you. Yes, I'll take all of this." She handed him some coins which he pocketed with one movement of his brown hand but with a smile he proffered a small amount of change.

"That's not necessary, thank you". Tisa smiled in return and pushed his hand away.

"Then take this please, mother."

With his left hand he offered her a small wooden box accessorised by a silver clasp and two tiny, silver hinges. On the lid there were some simple carvings that looked like some kind of strange animal. Tisa took the box gingerly. The man looked satisfied.

"May I open it?"

"It is yours now, mother. You may do as you wish." He took out the makings of a roll-your-own cigarette. With an air of long term practice he rolled and lit his cigarette. As he puffed with obvious contentment, he behaved as though Tisa had already moved on. She lifted the miniature, wooden lid, fashioned with a craftsman's skill to hug the rim of the box and gasped when she saw the glistening emerald-coloured gem inside.

"I can't take this. It must be worth at least five hundred times what I have just purchased from you. I can't take it."

He turned back to her and held out his small hands, palm up.

"You already have, mother. It is yours. Remember me and use this when freedom is the most important thing you desire and require." He held her wrist. Tisa felt an unusual tingle in her arm. Any thought of returning the emerald-hued gem vanished in that same moment.

"I will. Thank you."

He puffed again on his cigarette and sat down behind his cart on a much larger wooden crate. He was shaded from the bright African sunlight by a huge green umbrella. She felt it odd that such a thing had missed her attention.

"You are going to make it, mother. She is waiting for you there with the little one." He took a long drag on his cigarette. "Sometimes it will seem there is no hope and we have wasted our time. I can say that this is untrue. What is coming will not be prevented. It will not even be significantly changed though monumental effort will be made to deter us. Know that it will be difficult sometimes and many will feel as though it's going nowhere, but I say to you now that it cannot be stopped."

He pushed the last remnant of his cigarette into a corner of his crate and began the makings of another.

"Remember, Mother, when you want freedom more than anything else."

"When will Tisa get here, Mumma?" Max's voice broke through her reverie. She shut the water off and wrapped her nakedness in a simple sarong.

"You know she is coming, don't you, Max?"

"Of course I do, Mumma. I see her in my head all the time. She spoke to you like she speaks to me while you were having your shower. She got a little box from that man she got food from." Max looked almost bewildered that his mother seemed unaware of his capacity to see what he was seeing.

"Could you hear us too, sweetheart?"

"Yes, but I didn't start listening until she got food from that man. She is coming soon."

"She is, Max. She is walking from her home. She set out a little while ago but it will take her quite a long time to get here. Still, we are going to need to be ready because once she gets here, we will all be going on an adventure together."

"Yes, she told me. And then it will be good to see Elias." Max was matter of fact.

"There's not very much I need to tell you, is there?"

Max smiled at her, then moved in to wrap his arms around her hips.

"It's time, Mumma."

"Yes baby, it really is." They held one another, the boy and his mother for a long time. Max drew back for a moment.

"Mumma, do you feel that?"

"I do. I don't know what it is?"

"It's Elias. He wants to speak with us."

It was insistent. Across all the realms, Elias, Dirawong Juwir commanded an audience with his peers and his circle. Each of them knew they must answer.

Kesari held her son tight and loose so that he would travel with her to the ceremony. As her boy grew in age and wisdom, she wondered who was leading whom in these journeys.

Together they travelled into a realm available to everyone and attended by precious few. Before they had an opportunity to take the first steps of their long walk, Kesari and Max came to communicate with the listener in the centre of their circle. He sat by a simple campfire near the remnants of a stupendous mountain, under a sky glittering with billions of stars to speak with his circle, to empower each of them to make their journey.

Kesari and Max waited in turn to speak with love to the earth wizard.

CHAPTER THIRTY EIGHT

Tisa sat on the dry ground, brushing sticks and stones away to make it clear and comfortable. She noticed a small scorpion scurrying under a piece of bark and took care not to disturb the opening of a nest of tiny, black ants. Unfurling her pouch of soft, tan deerskin, Tisa crossed her legs and perched just south of the centre of the circle she had made.

Surrounding her were twelve stones, four large rocks in the cardinal directions and between each, two smaller stones set close to even distance apart. Each of them had been tapped with her crystal studded wand and she had uttered prayers to the energies of the direction. In the centre place, a deeply embroidered cloth laden with Celtic, African and Australian indigenous motifs supported a low-set, soapstone plinth of intricate design. Atop that, a fist sized piece of perfect, clear amber with what looked like a tiny, ecstatic, human form captured inside for eternity.

Tisa placed the emerald coloured crystal gifted to her by the old man there in the centre too. To the right or eastern side of the centrepiece, a knife with a simple wooden handle. To the left or western side were three small carvings, a kangaroo carved from Australian ironbark, a griffin fashioned in Welsh pewter and a sleek, black jaguar carved in African onyx. To the north of centre, a Lions Paw shell bore a smoking smudge stick emitting the sweet smell of sage and eucalypt to the still, warm air. Lifting her eyes and her arms to the sky she called out in a loud voice.

"All that is blue, all that is green, come to meet one another. It is your sister Tisa Emem conjuring at this time, in this reality

so that I might advance your will and intention. As above," she lowered her arms now and placed both palms flat on the ground, "so below, I call you into balance with one another. In this joining I command that you remain at peace so that I might have the freedom to journey and share communication heart-to-heart with those who would guide and assist me."

Mumbling an incoherent and ancient language, Tisa shuddered and her eyes rolled upwards till all that could be seen was white. Through this her back remained ramrod straight. Her connection to the earth demonstrated itself to be solid and grounded. Her hand crept out as if guided by sight, yet if sight it were, it was not through Tisa's earthly eyes.

"Hear me sacred powers of the coming tide that have been, are today and will always be. Through the powers of original source, I hereby banish from this sacred space into all thirteen directions, above and below, back and front, left and right all energies, powers, spirits, entities and beings, in every dimension, every reality, both incarnate and disincarnate that are not in alignment with lore and are not present for my well-being and care. I command it to be so, it is so and shall remain so until my return. I speak with the authority of the source of all and so it is." Her hand gripped the hilt of the knife, drew it towards her and slid it into the folds of her skirt.

As the incantation ended, an eerie silence descended on the land. The rocks and stones had heard her and they imbued their billion years of silence from the earth, so that even the birds and insects became still.

Tisa began to travel in a place few imagine, much less visit but she was at ease. Floating in an immense and ice-cold bleakness, Tisa navigated her way without fear. She had done this many times before and though this early phase was disconcerting, experience relaxed her. She did however, remain vigilant. This was not a place to drop your guard. Sensing an imposing malevolence moving towards her, Tisa shifted direction a little. The creature was not seeking her. It was nothing more than present, living whatever its life constituted in this dense place.

Time ceased to be relevant, light began to infuse her experience though in this place she had nothing that could be described as eyes. It informed her that she had almost completed traversing what Elias and Victor often called "ngandir jagun". Soon she would emerge into the place where her conversation could occur. Both Elias and Victor would already be aware of her journey and her need. They would be there.

Tisa became aware of her body. Glancing around she saw the circle of twelve stones were repeated exactly as she had arranged them, though the surroundings were new. She was seated in the centre. To the north-west was Victor, draped in a long green gown and to the north-east, Elias clothed in nothing more than a red cotton wrap around his waist tucked between his legs and into the back. His skin was dotted with white and red ochre and he was smiling a broad welcoming smile.

"It's good to see you, sister."

Victor smiled now too.

"Brother speaks for me. We see far too little of you, Tisa."

She grinned back at them both for a few moments, feeling their genuine love and care.

"I love you both too but I came here with a very specific goal," she intoned.

"I have seen the gathering of the villages who speak without speaking. I have met a man who gifted me with the very crystal I lacked to make this journey. I have heard your call, Elias and I am still a long way from you. I need greater guidance. I have walked far already yet I am still a long way from Kesari and Max, let alone reaching you in the physical. I have to admit that I'm a bit lost, Elias. I don't have the sight of my brother Victor and I don't share in all of your knowledge, Elias. Do I walk on, find Kesari and Max and ask no questions?" She gazed a few seconds at them both, "Well, it's too late for that. I'm here asking questions."

Tightly held shoulders, hunched forward, showed the intensity of the moment for Tisa. She could not monitor her physical form with ease from this place and had not found time

to appoint a door guard for her medicine circle. Someone could find her at any moment, straight sitting, surrounded by rocks with eyes rolled back. It was not ideal for her safety or how others might perceive her sanity. Some might even see voodoo in her behaviour. That would not turn out well. She shuddered a little and the hair stood straight on her forearms as she recalled events from another circle long ago.

Vincent shifted in his seat but spoke not a word in response. His grey eyes sparkled. Above his head shone an almost golden light tinged in radiant green. The light brightened as she finished speaking.

Elias nodded and fished out a short cigarette from his red lap sash, which began to glow as he touched it to his lips. Soon a sweet smell filled the space and Tisa's nostrils reminding her of gentler times spent with this wisdom keeper.

"I'm sure you do that to show off, Elias," said Tisa, allowing a small smile and perhaps for some of the tension to ease from her shoulders just a little as she felt the effect of the smoke on Elias.

"There's nothing I know more important than a sense of humour, lady." He took another deep drag and blew the smoke skyward. "But I do want to answer your questions the best I can. So hear me."

He shifted on his seat and flicked ash at the fire.

"I feel your caution and your reservation yet I have to ask you to trust and keep on. You're right to say that I have the good fortune to know more than many so let me share my insights. Perhaps you can decide if that makes any difference at all. For me it doesn't but that means nothing except I say that it's so in one moment and let it be or not be in the same moment."

He smiled a brilliant smile at his friend.

"It's a kind of tightrope, Tisa, this knowing. As I know what I perceive I also know that every other possibility remains equal in its validity. So, what is this 'knowing' I possess?" He took another lungful and released it with a long sigh. Then he spoke soft words in a sing song manner.

"Some will not answer. Some will not come. Some who seem to have nothing to do with us will come without comprehending why. Some will interweave with us as though they could be part of the foundation yet will wash away like a sinking tide. There are those who will remain steadfast and will keep on. When all these come together it is pivotal, though neither you, nor I, nor anyone could have determined it would happen this way."

As he spoke the sky above them crackled and sparked as though stars were falling to earth. "I have had the dreams and travelled to the places that watch and hold us all. This will unfold in perfection no matter what your decision. You will become one or the other or the other. Though I know you made your choice long ago you continue to have the opportunity to choose again. May any commitment we have entered into with one another mean nothing as of this moment. As far as it is ever possible Tisa, decide if this is the wave on which you ride or whether you wait until the change of the tide. Pause as often as you want. Doubt as much as you want. Nothing is wrong."

Elias shut his eyes and sat as still as stone.

"Here is something specific that may satisfy what you are asking. You will find Kesari, though in a manner very different to that which you have imagined." Elias took a deep breath.

"Max will not be joining us in any way that you have dreamed or seen in your realm adventures, yet Max will be there and will have a role that only he can play. I say keep on, Mother Tisa. Each step adds to this movement in the way it is intended, no matter whether you step in or step away. How you perceive it is the only way in which anything will change. Do you hear me, Mother?"

The air around him crackled and wove a dance like that of a fierce flame on a tinder-dry desert night. Vincent too seemed to have expanded into a giant mass of sparkling blue-green flame. As Tisa observed this, Vincent spoke.

"Mother, what you see in us is also in you. Both of us here witness this truth for you. The door has opened. We are nothing

299

more than the wedges that ensure that it cannot blow shut in an errant breeze. Keep on, yet know that whatever decision you take it will lead us where we are going. That doesn't help much I know too well, yet notice it is we three that sit here to have this conversation."

Vincent brought his hands together as though in prayer. He rubbed them seven times then held his arms as wide as he was able.

"Have faith in that, if that is all you can find. It is significant in itself. Now I would suggest we return. I am the appointed guard at this gathering and I see you appointed no guard at your wheel. Return. It is important to return now". He winked at her, crossed his hands over his chest and vanished.

Looking toward Elias she felt an enormous surge of energy pour through her torso. Elias too crossed his hands over his chest, across his heart and vanished. Somewhere in the ether she heard.

"Keep on, Mother Tisa. A new beginning is upon us." Elias' chuckle echoed behind that and the sweet smoke lingered.

The presence Tisa had felt on her journey was far greater and acute in its malevolence as she returned. In the consummate darkness, she felt it coming. She could feel its hunter. She felt the force of its ravenous hunger. This time it was hunting her. She would need to assemble her skills. The first onslaught came from too far distant and gave her warning. She felt the first prickles of fear begin to sweep over her as tendrils of red-orange fire. They wound their way into her protections like the grasping roots of a twisted, ancient willow wending their way through soil and rock.

Tisa knew that her protections and banishing would hold against this. With that knowledge the fear diminished and was gone. Such a belligerent first approach demonstrated the immense power of this being. It was off-hand, almost dismissive, palpably confident of success and Tisa was warned. As it withdrew, shaping itself to reach her again, soaring off in a wide sweep, Tisa made ready. Her pose in this dank place

matched that in her circle, yet here her eyes were now wide open, pupils dilated and brimming with golden fire. As the creature completed its arc and it began to spew itself toward her, she moved her hands in an intricate, swirling design. Tisa Emem conjured and spoke, with clarity and surety, an ancient ensorcellment.

"Fuente tuláakal, diseñador yo'osal áantajil, Tene' juntúul wéetel. Accedo u páajtalil asab te'elo' u u páajtalil, je'el asab te'elo' u u páajtalil, yaakunaj asab te'elo' le yakunaj utia'al mantener in in salvo, utia'al permanecer ti' u k'abo'ob, utia'al u suut in encarnación, utia'al táanil in meyaj ti' u diseño".

Source of all, original designer, I am one with you. I access power beyond power, might beyond might, love beyond love to hold myself safe, to remain in your hands, to return to my incarnation, to continue my work in your design.

The gigantic beast showed no sign it recognised who or what it was dealing with and descended on Tisa Emem raging and ravenous, tendrils of scorching orange fire roping around her, surrounding her with excoriating flame and lava. In this Tisa sat calm and seething with power. As the beast enclosed her, she began to expand her aura, pressing back, relentless on the giant maw determined to engulf her. As the tempest raged all about her, she remained still but for this almost delicate issue of power that emitted from her every fractal, every pore. Where the two powers met was a seething, sizzling berm, yet not a single tendril disrupted her tiny sanctum and she continued to expand.

When her space had grown to almost three times its original size, a phosphorescent green-tinged, lemon-white flame issued as a deluge into the very structure of the enormous creature's tendrils and talons of crimson-orange, discomposing them without effort. A gigantic, silent implosion shook the fabric of the realm and Tisa's challenger was met and categorically overcome. The massive creature faltered, shuddered and withdrew, issuing an anguished, shrieking scream. Some distance away another traveller sighed with relief and wondered about the entity which could overcome such a creature with ease.

Tisa was safe. She relaxed, power still eking its way out of her diminutive frame, washing the near impenetrable blackness around her in a coruscating light. More than any riddle shared with her by Elias, this confrontation reminded her of her place in this tapestry, this matrix of indefinable futures.

Now she was in her circle of stones facing north, seated on a brushed seat of dust. Her attention returned to the earthly realm. She checked on each of the stones of her wheel, one by one. The circle was intact. The instruments of ritual on her mesa were unsullied and benign. The blue-green gem in the centre of her wheel shone and shimmered, casting a cool light on her and everything within the circle. Inconceivably, that light halted at the perimeter.

The old woman began to draw her ritual to a close, collecting each of the tools she employed with her left hand and placing them one-by-one into a bag of soft deerskin. When she came to the gifted stone and the soapstone plinth, she hesitated for just a moment to change hands. This stone she collected with her right hand to place it gingerly into its box. She clipped the tiny silver clasps into place and slid it into a pocket hidden in her clothing.

As she concealed the gem, four men stepped into full view in alignment with each of the cardinal directions. Each of them wore a long sharp bush knife and carried a submachine gun. A fifth man, with a powerful build and a triangular tattoo on the back of both of his hands grabbed the old woman from behind. Before she could react, he plunged a fine, hypodermic needle into her neck a little below her ear.

A few moments later her struggling ceased and Tisa Emem lost consciousness.

CHAPTER THIRTY NINE

The rain began as Flynn turned back toward the city. By the time he reached the city limits it had drenched everything in a cold lustrous glamour. Grimy creeks and dirt-caked ditches poured with a brown and grey torrent pocked with plastic wrappers and bottles. The road became a quagmire in the places where tarmac had been stripped from the surface. Flynn rode with little caution, confident of his skills, dodging potholes and errant rubbish strewn everywhere in his path.

The thought of the home of the disconcerting woman Chodak and her great-granddaughter Jungney became genuinely attractive, even if it were for the chance to escape the saturating deluge and the creeping cold. Splashing fountains of dank, cold, brown-stained water to each side Flynn gunned the motorcycle to arrive sooner, faster to the place on his map that Chodak had marked. The cold was beginning to edge its way even through his waterproof clothing though the drenching wetness remained unable to penetrate.

Flynn was reminded of his homeland in the high country of Scotland. He could almost smell the hint of coconut from uncountable stands of yellow gorse. It conjured memories of his grandmother, collapsed into a rough-hewn, kitchen chair near a giant, iron woodstove, passing out remedies and tinctures to everyone in the village of his childhood.

Without warning, a thin, black dog charged out and dropped to the ground in his path. Flynn veered sharply to avoid it. His front wheel slipped and made an erratic twist to the left. There was nothing to be done. He was going to fall and fall hard. It felt like slow motion as his shoulder crashed to the saturated

road and he and his bike slid, side by side along the slippery tarmac. He thumped hard into a deep pothole filled with murky, muddy water. The bike continued to slide another ten metres or so then stopped with a crunch, its bright-orange indicator flashing, making the raindrops around it sparkle and flare.

"Stupid, damn dog." He muttered and cursed. A sharp pain in his right shoulder warned him of the physical damage. A strange, dank dizziness warned him that there was more than just physical damage at play here.

"Fuck!"

Struggling to gain balance, Flynn half stood, half crouched. His right arm dangled loose and the pain became sharper and deeper as he brushed dirt and grime off with his other hand. The shaded dizziness would not shift. Through the fog of his discomfort he scanned the space around him. The dog slunk off to the side of the road to hide, tail between its legs.

'At least I didn't hit the stupid thing.' Flynn thought even as he winced with the pain in his right shoulder and arm. He rubbed his good hand across his face in an effort to clear the fog which seemed to be deepening in his consciousness. He turned with a pain-guided care and caution to his bike. The bright, orange, indicator light still flashed intermittently. There didn't appear to be too much obvious damage. He'd been travelling less than fifty kilometres an hour on the wet streets. He reached down to the bike and lifted it a little with his good arm, double-checking for damage. From this point he wasn't sure he could continue to ride. His right arm was becoming agonising. The pain continued to increase. He staggered, releasing the bike and toppled to the ground, just managing to save himself a little with his left arm. The pain of the impact sent an agonising stab through his damaged arm and shoulder.

"What the fuck have I done?" He spoke out loud as the rain continued to drench and drown. The cold inched further in. The strange, dizzy sensation crept through him and he noticed with some surprise that, as it did so, the pain began to ease.

"Shit, no. I must not faint. I must stay conscious." He felt the dizziness intensify. Staggering forward a few steps, he shook his head and gave his face a vigorous rub in an effort to become clear.

"There is nothing to be afraid of, Mr Flynn. You are going to be fine. Just come with me."

The tiny woman, Chodak, was at his side, clutching his left arm with that claw-like grip he had noticed at their first meeting. In her grasp he could not fall. As she led him shuffling away he turned his head to see a small figure, dressed in black, lift his bike back onto two wheels to follow behind. The indicator continued flashing orange for a few moments. He lost consciousness. The last things he recalled were light returning as soft candlelight, a rush of warm dry air and a hand on the back of his head pushing down.

Chodak pushed Flynn's head downwards to ease him through the door of her home. Jungney wrestled his motorcycle down a narrow alley beside the stonewalled house and through a rusted steel gate. She propped it against a tidy mound of neat-stacked firewood that she had held sole responsibility for collecting throughout each spring, summer and autumn. She backed out of the space and bolted the gate behind her taking a minute to balance several old earthenware pots in such a way that they would fall with a loud clatter should anyone venture in.

When she was satisfied, Jungney pulled open the rough timber door that was at the back of her great-grandmother's small, stone house and went inside. She could hear the old woman rustling and fussing over their guest, sometimes muttering under her breath as she tended to him.

As Jungney came into the room Chodak turned to her, a look of deep concern on her face.

"Jungney, come here. Bring that cloth and dish of water."

"Dhoo, Chen Mo-La." The girl collected the steaming bowl and the soft cloth beside it and brought them to the bedside. She placed the bowl beside her great-grandmother and knelt down on the yak skin that covered the floor at the bedside. Her face

still ran with droplets of chill rain and her straight, ebony-black hair was plastered down the sides of her face, dripping onto her black-shirted shoulders.

"There is more at work here than meets the eye, great-granddaughter. I knew of this when this man agreed that he would come to find us. The rainstorm was not a normal occurrence."

She closed her eyes and rocked from side to side, her lips mouthing incomprehensible words of invocation.

"There was a black dog. It is my knowing that we would not find that dog now if we were to look for it. There is much more at foot and it is important for us to be awake to every part of it."

Chodak wiped a warm damp cloth across Flynn's forehead, cleaning away some of the mud and cold rain. She looked up and motioned to the girl.

"Jungney. This is not my task. It is yours. Undress him, cleanse him and then use your body to warm him."

"But Chen Mo La, I am afraid." Jungney's eyes resembled a small animal caught in bright light.

"There is nothing to fear, Jungney. Remove his clothing and cleanse him with this cloth and water. I have added some tinctures that will help him. When you are done, take your wet clothes off and lie with him to warm him. I will be here all the time but I must take a journey to see what we are to do next." The old woman looked with fixed intensity at her great-granddaughter. "Will you do this, Jungney?"

"Of course, Chen Mo La as it is what you ask of me." Modest, she dropped her eyes, drew the cloth out of the steaming bowl, twisted water from it and began to clean Flynn's face.

"His clothing, Jungney........?"

The girl blushed. "Yes, Chen Mo La. Forgive me."

The young Tibetan girl began to remove Flynn's heavy motorcycle clothing. As she lifted his damaged arm he flinched and groaned but made no further objection. Soon his heavy jacket was on the floor with thick waterproof trousers, windcheater,

shirt, jeans, underclothes, boots and socks. Flynn lay for a few minutes naked as Jungney collected extra wood for the fire. It took just a few moments for the dry wood to catch and the room warmed a little more.

Jungney began to tend to him, cleansing every part of him. She began with his good shoulder and worked her way across and around his body, moving downwards by increment. Chodak had instructed her to be thorough and she was obedient to her teacher. Nothing about the task was unfamiliar to her. Her grandfather had needed this care for the past three years. The primary difference was that she did not know this stranger, this white man travelling from China. The other difference was that she had never tended to such a huge human being. Summoning all her courage and the healing ways of her people, she submitted to the task.

While Flynn appeared to be unconscious he was aware of his predicament and equally aware that some power, strange to him, was present. Thankful for the absence of pain, Flynn was unnerved to discover that other entities had influence here. There seemed little he could do about it.

Though there was no sense of having a body, something moulded and shaped his consciousness into a simulation, the illusion of a body. Something was all over him, sinuous and somehow malignant and enticing. It felt like a hundred small hands touching him everywhere at once, teasing him and encouraging him to feel the pleasure, to deny anything and everything else.

Soon the touching began to move inwards from the extremities of his simulated body, creeping unerringly from feet and hands and head to envelope his torso in a seductive stroking and pressing, moulding and squeezing that was pure ecstasy. It was a welcome release from the pain he had felt, the memory of which lingered still.

The sensation increased in intensity and focus moving with infinitesimal patience toward his genitals, urging him to erection, teasing and stroking him. Now a change came.

The sensation felt like one small pair of hands, ever so gentle, touching him in a way that he had never felt before. As he dropped into the unnameable, excruciating pleasure something else called him. He was rushed back into the world of pain, his arm shrieking at him, he screaming in agony as he floated for a few moments back into a small room, his injured arm sending shooting, tormenting pain throughout his body.

He opened his eyes to see the innocent sweetness and beauty of the oval face of Jungney, gentle yet firm as she moved him to continue the sponge bath. His eyes swam in an ocean of agony. He faded back into blackness which felt sweeter for the pain it left behind. All that remained was a picture, etched in his mind, of Jungney's flawless face and soft almond shaped eyes.

The pleasuring returned. By now the simulation was focused on his genitals and his erection. Whatever had invaded him perceived the image of Jungney. The entity grasped her, stripped her naked and began to push his engorged penis between the lips of the girl. In his unconsciousness and despite the ecstatic pleasure the entity imposed through the illusion it had created, he moaned and moved, uttering just one word over and over.

Jungney paused her ministrations. She put the warm cloth on the bench beside her, ignoring his tumescence and called for her teacher.

"Chen Mo La, he speaks. Come please. He is speaking." Jungney cast her eyes around the room, searching for her great-grandmother. There was no sign of her. She leaned in closer to Flynn's face to listen. A whisper issued from his lips.

"No, no, no, no, no, no..............."

Suddenly Chodak was beside her. "Leave him, child. Light that bundle of sage and bring it to me. Put a pot of water on the fire and bring more wood. Quickly now, Jungney, the sage, hurry girl." Chodak spat out the last instruction and with a brusque shove, pushed the girl away. She leaned in close to Flynn.

"I'm here with you, brother. You are safe." She turned her head and hissed at Jungney. "Bring it here, girl, quickly."

Jungney held the sage stick over a candle flame to light it. She moved swiftly yet her great-grandmother's harsh whisper hadn't fazed her.

"Here it is, Chen Mo La." She pressed the smoking sage into the old woman's hands and stepped back a pace, watching.

The old crone began at Flynn's left foot, waving the smoking sage just above the skin. She moved steadily upwards, taking care to be thorough. Up the left leg and across his torso left to right, over his head and back down across the torso then down his right leg and repeat, forming an infinity loop. As she did this she muttered words that might have been prayers over his prostrate form then passed her right hand through the same passage across his body. His muscles and sinews relaxed. His erection subsided. He began to breathe more steadily. Chodak rose from his side and gave the smoking sage back to Jungney.

"He has been under attack as I expected. I have provided him with what protections I possess the ability to provide. You may now continue." The old woman walked away, muttering under her breath and moving her hands about to complete the ritual of some ancient blessings and banishing.

Jungney removed her damp clothing until she too was naked. She reached out to collect a flawless, unadorned, pure-white, silk shift and drew it over her head. Shivering a little, perhaps from fear, perhaps the chill air, she climbed in beside the naked, unconscious man, snuggling her body in close to his, to warm him. A coarse and heavy woollen blanket was their only covering. Jungney tucked it in around his torso, careful with his injured arm. Flynn shifted a little. The shapes of their bodies melded closer. Chodak stepped up beside them and adjusted the blanket to cover their shoulders. Fussing with the fire, she added a faggot or two to the glowing embers. She blew long and slow until the new wood flickered into flame.

She whispered, perhaps to no-one in particular, perhaps to some audience that no-one else could discern.

"This sleep will change these precious ones. Now there will be healing of the journeyman, in physical body and also

in soul. He will awaken to the precise knowledge of why he is here with us. This is also the gift for my beloved Jungney. It is her activation to full presence in this world. I will watch over them until they wake and for eternity."

The old woman perched in an armchair near to the fire. She lit a small block of incense that smelled of lemons and lime. Reaching for a small volume that rested beside the chair she began to read, not in complete silence but whispering each word, making them manifest. As she did this, on the other side of the world, Victor felt her. He double-checked the clasps on the box that contained the red marked volume he had found in the library. All the sigils on the box emitted a fiery glow. The container remained sound. Victor replaced the box and its book deep in his pack.

Flynn returned to his dreamscape. The ecstatic pleasure was still present but he was aware of the source of the illusion and with access to his consciousness, spoke to the dream.

"I am aware of these things in me and I will not be drawn into this path. This is not who I am, nor who I choose to be. You will cease this abomination now." And the stroking, cajoling and fondling stopped in that instant. In the dream, the sound of hissing as if air escaping and the entity was ejected.

Flynn relaxed into a deep healing sleep. Beside him, Jungney shifted in still closer to his sleeping form.

When Flynn woke he was surprised to find the girl curled in beside him. He was immediately aware of his nakedness and the light silken shift between his body and hers. Contrary to the desire that had been so palpable in his dream, now in this waking world he felt nothing but an immediate and overpowering protectiveness toward her. He wrapped his arms around her and felt a pulsating, all-encompassing, healing energy exuding from her slender, diminutive form. She opened her eyes.

"You are healed, Mr Flynn?"

It hadn't dawned on him that he had drawn her close with both arms. There was no pain at all.

"It seems that I am, Jungney. I'm not quite sure how, but I am very grateful."

"We have quite a journey to make together, Mr Flynn. My teacher told me that this must happen before we began. Now we can travel together as we are destined to do." Jungney extricated her body from his arms, lifted the blanket away and stood.

Flynn felt healthier and more at ease than he had for many years. He watched the tiny Tibetan girl walk across to the fire, lift the silken shift over her head and begin to dress in the day clothes that her great-grandmother had arranged to dry by the fire. Chodak was wide awake, still sitting in her chair. The book she had been reading aloud sat on a cushion just to her left. A dried flower extended from the top of it, marking the page where she had completed her readings.

The sensation of imbalance and confusion that Flynn had experienced previously in the company of these two women had vanished. He sat up, wrapped only in the rough blanket and looked around. Though it seemed impossible, the room reminded him of his own grandparents' house in Scotland. He could almost smell a hearty vegetable stew bubbling on the stovetop and the sound of his grandfather's boots scraping on the mat outside as he bustled his way into the kitchen for a late lunch.

"You have been here many times before, Mr Flynn," said Chodak from her perch beside the fire, "So many times." She chewed on a piece of the branch of a neem tree, from time to time rubbing it across her teeth and gums. "We have known one another in other lives. That is why you are here again. We have both returned to this plane for a very good reason and for this short time at least, our paths are aligned."

Jungney walked the few steps to sit on the sleeping platform beside him.

"Your daughter will travel with you. Do you remember her?"

Flynn put his arm around Jungney. "Of course I do. How could I possibly have forgotten?" His face became a mask of exhaustion, anxiety and shame.

"I had such a strange and troubling dream. I have been so lost. Perhaps I managed to find myself within that dream. I hope so."

"There is no need for shame or any such nonsense, Mr Flynn. Both Jungney and I know what you dreamed in every detail. We witnessed your process, your temptation and how you dealt with it. You have remained in your integrity. That is so important to the way forward for us all. Today you and Jungney must prepare for what will be a challenging journey. It is a journey which will test you as you have never been tested. All that has happened thus far has equipped you for what is to come. Even this woman you feel slighted by, this Mara Lin, has her prescribed place in this transformation."

"Yes, even her," replied Flynn. He released Jungney and smiled. "But right now there is just one mundane thing on my mind."

Jungney stood, collected a bowl and spoon then drew three large ladles of steaming, vegetable stew from the pot on the fire. She brought it to Flynn. He thanked her and began eating with gusto, blowing each spoonful a little cooler before slurping it down.

"Will you be able to do that with everything from now on?" He asked between spoonfuls. "Know what I'm thinking?"

"Yes, Mr Flynn. And so will you." The girl replied.

"We cross the mountains into Nepal and travel onwards to India, yes?" Flynn finished his stew. Jungney nodded and rose to get him another bowl of stew. He took it and thanked her. "I would say that it is quite a dangerous journey."

Chodak spoke in a voice that sounded like it may have come direct from the mouth of Elias.

"This is a journey that must be taken brother, dangerous or not. Between the two of you there is little you need fear. Stay alert and present to one another. Bring all your focussed

attention to the outcome you know to be the perfect outcome. Trust yourself and you will be worthy of trust. There will be protection from all of us that are aware of the journey. You are well watched and we are sentinels that guard your passage and the passage of those who might seek to thwart you."

By midday Flynn's motorbike was in good order and packed with all that was necessary for their travel into the Himalayas. Jungney added just one small bundle tied with a strong, hemp rope. It contained a few items of clothing, several small, clear crystals and a ceremonial knife sheathed in soft leather.

At one o'clock Chodak came out of the house with Jungney and Flynn, hugged them both and bestowed a soft-worded blessing over each of them. She paused a little longer with Jungney. She threw her arms around the child.

"Go swiftly, my precious one. He came to assist you once again as I said he would. Now fly! Elias and the others need you and the story you write. Remember, first find the other. She is in India. She has no knowledge of her place in this so it will be up to you to bring her into alignment. Then continue the journey for there is much more to discover as balance is restored." She gave the girl another fierce hug though there were no tears from these two women. "Now go."

It was precisely eleven minutes past one when the goodbyes were complete and Flynn steered his way down the street with Jungney perched between the pack and his leather-clad back.

Chodak went inside, sat beside the fire and began a simple ritual. In just a few moments there was a smoky image of Elias hovering in the warm air above the fire. The old woman looked at him with a mixture of warmth, love and the deepest respect.

"It is done, my brother."

The image of Elias bowed its head to the old woman and said, "Then your work is complete, ancient one, and I thank you."

The old woman's clothing fell into the chair in a crumpled heap.

The smoky image of Elias and the physical body of the crone, Great Grandmother Chodak both vanished.

CHAPTER FORTY

Ambika's meeting went well. Rouseabout Advertising, thanks to a combination of savvy, skill, reputation, research and relative anonymity acquired their latest new client, Verity Global. The meeting had revealed that Verity Global was about to take the element of water by storm and Rouseabout was their choice of marketing and advertising agency.

Alone, that one client dwarfed all of Rouseabouts other accounts.

Though the meeting went well, for some reason she couldn't determine, Ambika did not experience the exhilaration to which she was accustomed with the gaining of a powerful, new account. What was present was more like a feeling of dread. Sitting on the terrace, gazing out across the city she sipped from a glass of chilled water provided by room service on her return. Ambika was drinking water, not champagne. That sealed it. On any normal day like this she would have been partying with anyone who would keep up, celebrating her good fortune. Today felt more like a water kind of day. No real excitement, just rolling with the flow. It felt weird.

Tapping on the screen of her phone, by accident she activated a news service app.

'French President Missing In Action'

The headline sent a chill through her. She read on.

'Early reports from our Paris newsroom suggest that President Henri Beauchamp and his family have vanished. His absence was first noticed at nine this morning when the President failed to attend a meeting where the leaders of five nations were to vote for the Secretary-General of the United

Nations. In his absence a letter indicating to the other leaders that he would abstain from the vote means that nominee Anita Claesson has been elevated to the role by the remaining four votes and is the new Secretary-General.

The French Police have begun a massive investigation into the missing family but at this time have not been able to indicate that there are any significant leads in the search...'

Ambika could not read any further. She made an immediate and troubling connection with her conversation with Anita Claesson.

CHAPTER FORTY ONE

Time passed quickly for Cole and Ivy, caring for Robin and preparing for their journey. They gave away, sold, packed and stored everything, piece by piece. The house became a little barer each day. Forty eight hours before Dave arrived that they were down to the bare essentials. He walked the final kilometres on a Friday afternoon and arrived as the sunset sent an orange hue into the evening air. Cole greeted him at the door, calling to Ivy to join them with their daughter.

"You took your time, old fella." Ivy and Dave hugged, the little one pressed between them.

"It's a whole lot further than you think when you're on foot." Dave left his pack near the door and with his arm around Ivy, pushed his way inside.

It was almost four hours later when Dave's storytelling began to subside. There were stories of long, hard trudging through rain and sleet, feeling as though there would never be a dry day again. There were stories of long days of brilliant sunshine, white clouds and not a single soul to speak with, resulting in deep meditations hour upon hour. Interspersed with these were tales of tiny, flickering campfires and the visitation of creatures that are rare to see, just a little off a dirt track that may never have been for motor vehicles. There was quite a long and detailed story of leaving home, packing the last of that precious library into safe storage and walking away, with light playing on the windows.

There were the stories of his dreams, the dreams that felt so real, the dreams that seemed to have such an impact on his every waking moment. These were the most power imbued

stories. These were told with slow precision, in a halting fashion, not so much because he couldn't recall but because recalling awakened them, taking him into a kind of trance. Yet as the story grew long, silences interrupted Dave's cadence. Robin had fallen asleep long ago but began to stir as though the silence was more disturbing than the sound of voices she knew and trusted.

Cole spoke now, soft and distinct in the hollow room.

"Tell us more about those dreams, Dave. What do you think they mean?" Dave looked up and shook his head a little.

"I can't be sure. They were so lucid, so detailed that they could be right here and right now. I have not experienced anything like them before, at least never in such vivid detail by far."

"But you say that you recognised us all in the dream, that the characters in your dream you recognised as us? All of us?"

"I did. We were all in it together, that's certain. How we go about breaking it down from there I can't be sure. It felt like we were, I don't know, facing tyranny yet representing freedom somehow?"

He paused for a long moment then continued, "It was... as though it was some kind of model for us, a first response. Facing overpowering odds the sensible thing to do is run. As a first response, get out of harm's way. Choose to find a safe place to be able to stop down, consider, strategise."

Dave used a breath technique he had learned as a boy. Five times he took a deep breath. Each time, a short, strong in-breath for a count of four, held for a count of sixteen and out for a count of eight, one breath for each cardinal direction and one for the centre. Cole and Ivy knew him well. They waited.

"It felt like the dream demonstrated that as a first response. Gain time to take the first step. The feeling when we found that passage, came through it and were in a peaceful place was exquisite. The fear had vanished, the fight had vanished and there was a chance to relax the senses a little, clear the soul. Come into peace." He lifted his shoulders one at a time,

stretching and breathing. Twisting and rolling his neck from side to side, a cracking sound came from his tired bones.

"From that place and only that place is it possible to imagine the first step to different outcomes. The first step after that, well as far as I can tell from the dream, is to share the story, tell what happened and begin to write new stories together from a place of peace. Yes, that feels right."

He stopped, sipped his tea and added, "Well, it seems there was a story waiting to be told about that dream. It just wasn't in my mind. It felt more like it comes from my soul."

Cole piped up, "You say I was the strange being that rescued us all?"

Dave nodded, "You were. I came out of the first dream and couldn't understand why I hadn't recognised you, but then he appeared. I still couldn't say exactly what he was but he had some tricks I'd be happy to know. And later I could see, without doubt, that he was you."

"Well I'm a bit pleased about myself then." Cole beamed a big smile, stood and moved to the kitchen, clattering pots and pans, opening and closing the fridge and cupboards. His voice carried over the sounds.

"I'm going to make some dinner for us all. Then we can do an experiment if you guys are up for it. Best if Robin's in bed I'd say because she might not be able to drop in for the experience. She'll be tired." Then the cutting and clattering continued.

Ivy spoke to Dave in a quiet voice as the three of them sat there. Robin's eyes wide open in a steady gaze at the older man as her mother spoke.

"We're coming too, Dave."

"I imagined so, Ivy. There's not much that you are going to miss when it's swirling around in the ethers, let alone this little muffin. I guessed that you would have heard the call, probably both of you did. Am I right?"

She nodded.

"How soon before we need to set out, do you think?"

"I wanted to speak with you all about that. I don't know how ready you are exactly, so let's leave that until we can all speak together. Not long though, Ivy. Not long. We need to get started as soon as we can. That is what activates all sorts of things in the matrix once the call has been made. So it's quite important that we begin. Elias doesn't get impatient but he also doesn't tolerate being ignored. Everything we are doing revolves entirely around the fact that The Call has been made by him so all of us can be assured that those who have heard must get ourselves into action as soon as we are able. No excuses."

He grinned, rubbed his face and stood.

"Where do you want me to put my stuff? Right now I have to get some rest."

"Food first, my friend, then you can consider your bed." Cole presented him with a bowl of rice and steaming curry. They ate in silence. Cole clattered the dishes into the sink and left them there. With that, all three retired in that echoing, empty house, filled to overflowing with each of them and their thoughts. As they slept, the dreams and visions came. Elias reached out to them with a knowledge that left each of them distraught and confronted. Summoned to a small campfire, each of them now needed to garner hope where hope had been obliterated.

By mid-morning the following day, nursing thoughts that encompassed their likely failure but with emboldened will, they set out to complete the roles assigned to them since the beginning of time. Nothing must interfere with that.

Each of them but for tiny Robin placed one plodding step in front of the other, driven by a heart fashioned from lead.

The child continued to sparkle. All she had in this life was the future.

CHAPTER FORTY TWO

"It's happening all over the world, Petra. It affects everyone to some degree or another no matter where your consciousness was when Elias made the call. That action has made a bold intrusion into a whole other realm, a different dimension you might name it. Elias has made a call that cannot be ignored in that realm and across many realms. It has the capacity to accelerate us, interact with us and entice us to take a necessary step into our own destiny, our own expansion and enlightenment. We all knew it had to happen someday but so many of us cannot quite believe it is right here, right now and we are the ones we have been waiting for."

Maria stopped and sat back. "Oh, I get quite excited don't I?" She looked at Jose then laughed out loud. "It is the most exciting time it could possibly be – to be alive." She laughed again. Pushing down and rubbing one leg Maria stood, groaning as circulation revived her muscles. "Oh, I've been sitting in one position far too long. I'll make another pot of tea." She moved stiffly toward the fire, humming a love song between almost inaudible groans.

"So you knew that we were supposed to meet? You stopped for me because Elias sent you?" asked Petra. Jose answered but she couldn't be sure whether he was speaking or communicating with 'soulspeak'.

"It is not so simple, Petra. No part of this has anything to do with being 'told' what to do. No directions are given from anyone else. It is quite certain that Elias would not instruct in such a manner – but yes, there is a certain type of knowledge. It is a kind of heightened discernment as to how things are

moving so as to go with that flow as they unfold. It has been such a privilege to spend this time with you." He reached his hands out to clasp hers,

"You are travelling for us all and we for you." This, he spoke out loud.

Maria turned to the two of them as she fussed a little with the cups and pot. With a big smile she said, "There is no longer 'you' and 'me'. It is time for 'we' and you have already witnessed and experienced some of the possibilities of that. Evita Huamani will open you to a great deal more. She is more than capable of doing such things. She would not interrupt your journey unless she had some very empowering intentions for your visit."

This was another surprise revelation.

"You know her too?"

Jose smiled a knowing smile.

"Of course you do." Petra began to comprehend the enormity of the connections in her journey. The matrix that was forming felt key to the energy of The Call, she did not have to, must not, walk alone.

Being held by this family was just the beginning of the way of community being heralded into reality across realms.

They continued to commune together, drinking tea, sharing stories, laughing and surprising each other. The children slept, assured of their futures in the hands and hearts of these elders who love them.

The following morning, though late in the morning, they woke. By eleven minutes past one, the sun high in a brilliant azure sky, they completed their farewells. Petra couldn't help but notice the coincidence of the time. Jose and Maria and the two children rattled away in the old Peugeot. A little blue smoke billowed across the road and into the surrounding hills as the vehicle disappeared.

. Petra shouldered her pack and set off to the south-west, to meet Evita Huamani, to discover more of this exquisite unfoldment. With each step she took she felt energy rising in her rather

than diminishing. The walk took her almost six weeks. On the fortieth day, Petra realised the tremendous fitness of body she had achieved by walking in these mountains with her pack. With an almost magnetic quality, the ancient ruins of Machu Picchu drew her onwards and, it seemed, forever upwards. She stepped forward each morning, up and down yet another towering rise and fall, rise and fall, her legs strong, her breath steady, her heart beating sure, steady and slow. In that same six weeks there were many other aspects of her fitness of which she was much less aware.

In many ways, each day was a repeat of the day before. She rose at seven without the use of any alarm other than the body clock which stirred in her with increasing accuracy. By week two she was checking the time each day. Without exception, every day her waking time was within two minutes of seven o'clock. By week four it was on the dot of seven.

Every day began with meditation. Fifteen minutes emptying her mind and scanning her body for strength, aches and any messages it might have for her. Breakfast followed, each day selecting a piece of fruit which she carefully and methodically prepared. Though she didn't make a personal note of it, she ate just as methodically. As she did this, oats and dried fruit that she soaked overnight warmed on the small stove she carried. This soon became a thick porridge that made a perfect slow release meal to serve her well for the coming hours of effort. By eight-fifteen, she had cleansed her spoon, bowl, knife and pan and packed them, her small tent and sleeping gear into the allotted place in her bag. It was a discipline that served her. As she walked she discovered the true beauty of discipline applied with intention and focus.

Each day, no matter what the weather, she shouldered her pack, adjusted everything for maximum comfort, and walked. At first, though she had always been proud of her fitness, picking up and putting that pack on her back was heavy and difficult. By the second week it felt light and easy. Now, it was part of her.

It had been forty days of uninterrupted, unaccompanied walking. The connection that Petra had both sought and experienced was these wild hills. She had skirted all the major roads on purpose and found her way through country that was not visited by anyone except those who were indigenous to the region. The silence and solitude made a more significant change in her than she had expected. Forty days of self-reflection while treading the songlines of the country, reached into the depths of her soul. She could feel the significance of her upcoming meeting with Evita Huamani.

Sitting beside the road close to the ruins of Machu Picchu, Evita waited for Petra to arrive. She looked like any one of the indigenous women that lived in the region. Her once black hair was pulled back into a ponytail, tied with a deep green hair tie. Draped across her shoulders was a multicoloured blanket covering an off-white shirt and a full-bodied, olive-green skirt tied at the waist with a wide, brown, leather belt studded with rhinestones and blue-green glass. Eyes closed, her head moved from side to side as if she were listening to music.

The most striking feature about this small woman was her round face. Even with eyes closed and a film of red and brown dust fanning out in deeply etched laughter lines, her face still held a kind of shining radiance that was impossible to ignore.

It had often been described by others as perfect peace.

In a time long past all of those who knew her perceived her as a striking beauty but the beauty of her latter years outshone that physical appellation with ease. For some reason, when passing her on this road it was impossible not to observe who it was that possessed such magnetism. Quite often the local people, in particular the women, would sidle up to squat beside her. Short conversations most often but sometimes longer, many of these women would nod their heads and smile.

Some found themselves with tears streaming down their faces as one truth or another was spoken and shared. All would clasp their hands together as their own conversation ended, stand, bow and leave small gifts and coins as they gathered up

their few belongings to continue on their journey. As a consequence, Evita was surrounded by a scattered mesa of simple treasures, dotted on the roadside up to two metres from where her skirts rested in the dust. On some occasions a child would wander a little closer. Evita would motion for them to take the coins, which they would, shy eyes shining, clutching pieces of copper and silver in grubby hands sporting big smiles as they chattered their way home.

This is how Petra found Evita Huamani.

Stepping along this road to Machu Picchu, strong back and strong legs pacing out the final few kilometres of this first part of her long journey, Petra felt her, well before she saw her. It was a clear, cool morning when she strode up yet another rise. As she reached the top, she stopped and turned to look out over the mountains, stretched with graceful solidity to every horizon. White streams of mist rose from the valleys to drift and float in the cold air. They looked like spirits and sprites, dancing an elegant dance with the solid mass of tree dotted ranges.

It was then that she felt her.

At first, it was nothing more than a tingle behind her brow, between her eyes. The sensation then erupted in her root chakra, sending a raging fire upwards through her spine and connecting with that same point behind her brow, before continuing through the top of her head like a bolt of searing lightning in reverse. Her whole body shuddered and she was forced to sit down. Her backpack was still attached, but her legs gave out and she collapsed onto the grass near the road. A guttural "hrrrrmmm-mmm," issued from Petra's lips, sourced from a deeper place than she had ever experienced.

The whole encounter took less than a minute. Petra remained motionless, eyes half closed for more than ten, feeling her body, down to her cells, adjusting to a different vibration. Beyond her fitness and form, Petra felt more alive and vital than she had ever imagined possible. When ten minutes had passed she unstrapped her pack and tossed it to one side. She lay on the sharp stones on the shoulder of the road, feeling the sharpness

of each and every pebble pressing against her. Then she sat up and loosened her hair from the rough braid she had fashioned that morning.

Petra shook her head and dragged her fingers through that unruly mass. The wild woman made its startling appearance for the first time. Not just untamed but wild, as a rabid predator, fierce and frightening. Stretching out, arms spread wide Petra faced the sun and issued a piercing scream across the valley to the surrounding mountains. It echoed back to her, over and over.

That was how she first felt this woman. A woman who had known Petra had a journey to make even though she was so far distant. There was no way she could comprehend such ability. This sensation was no explanation but sent a clear message about the power of this diminutive woman, this Evita Huamani.

Shouldering her pack once again, drinking a long draught of water from the steel bottle she carried, Petra walked on, legs still quivering, her eyes glowing, no longer hazel but a luminous, startling green. When she reached the top of the next rise she could see her squatted beside the road with two children laughing and chatting with her, their mother sitting quiet beside them, hands clasped. Each step closer excited her body a little more. Petra felt wave after wave of what could only be described as "bliss" with every pace. Soon she was standing at the edge of the mesa of coins and gifts looking down at her. With a broad smile, face beatific, Petra spoke.

"You are Evita."

The small, mesmerising woman looked up at her and smiled.

"Welcome, Petra. It is a deep honour to meet you." She stood and walked the few steps to Petra and took both her hands, her head bowed. Stunned by the actions, words and astounding aura that surrounded this diminutive woman Petra simply stood, motionless, and allowed her to hold her hands. Healing, restorative warmth surged through her body as she did so. After perhaps thirty seconds Evita released her. To Petra it might have been an hour and the energy of her remained palpable within.

"You wrote to me." Petra said. Her green eyes flashed and twinkled as she stood with Evita Huamani.

"I did. You came."

"Yes. Somehow it felt right. I'm not quite sure why, but it felt right. How did you know about me? Have I met you before?" Petra was beginning to regain her senses or perhaps it was nothing more than returning to what she considered 'normal'.

"We have a very significant friend in common, Petra. He lives in a land far from this one, yet he reaches out and influences people all over the world. You and I have both been affected by his influence. I'm happy that it is so." She turned and stepped back over the scattered items surrounding the place she had been sitting. "Let's not speak too long here. Come, I have shelter not too far from here. We can drink tea, eat some food and find out more about why you are here."

Without pausing a single second for an answer, Evita collected her few possessions and began to walk in the same direction Petra had been travelling. "It's not very far. Besides, by the look of you, walking isn't something that frightens or exhausts you. You look very alive. Perhaps Maria and Jose have also had an effect." She walked on as she spoke, leaving Petra little alternative but to follow.

'Not very far' for Evita was still an hour and a half of steep terrain, the first hour of which was tarmac and gravel road, the last thirty minutes, a winding path that wove through low scrub between small farms and cluttered woods. Petra marvelled that Evita seemed to be able to set the pace, making even Petra's strong legs falter. 'She must be much stronger than she looks,' thought the younger woman as they picked their way through the hills to Evita's dwelling. They stepped into a clearing. The ground was hard, packed down by years of feet trampling and compacting the soil into a hard surface that no longer yielded dust. It looked as though it had already been swept.

As Petra looked around she saw a young woman on the far side of the clearing brushing a crude straw broom across the surface. The young woman didn't appear to notice them

and simply kept up a methodical stroking of her broom, back and forth. To the left of the pathway from which they emerged, perhaps five metres away, were row upon row of green things in a thriving vegetable garden. Stakes in neat rows supported beans and vines. To the right a clear space was populated by four chairs, two of them solid, old-fashioned deckchairs with faded canvas slings, one a tattered chaise lounge. The last, perhaps more incongruous than them all, appeared to be some kind of golden throne. All four faced in the direction of mountains stretched to the sky in the place on the horizon where Petra imagined the sun would rise.

In the centre was perched a humble house. Stone and mud packed hard against one another formed solid walls supporting straw thatch for a large portion of the roof. The remainder sported shining, new corrugated iron. As they walked towards the front porch of the house, Petra noticed bright flowers decorating the two facing window sills. Earthen pots surrounding the front door were filled with a huge variety of herbs. Some of these she could identify. Many of them were strange to her. Down each side of the house the herb gardens continued, pressed against the walls from front to rear.

Extending out both sides at the rear was a low stone wall draped with multicoloured woven cloth, perhaps airing or drying. The scrape of the straw broom sounded from the back yard as the young woman continued her task. From inside issued the delicious aroma of food, signalling preparation for dinner.

Without warning the front door burst open. A tiny woman wrapped in multiple layers of cloth and skirts emerged. She spoke rapidly in a dialect that Petra had no chance of comprehending. The effect of being in close proximity with Evita was profound. Heightened senses in every way meant that Petra experienced each moment as though time had decided to pause and restart, pause and restart, so that every encounter might be savoured.

The woman spoke to Evita, wagging her finger and chuckling, waving a wooden spoon which still dripped with the

contents of her cooking pot. Petra noticed that the same strange comprehension that she had experienced with Maria and Jose began to return. While the woman spoke in her strange dialect, Petra understood first that the tiny woman was talking about her and as she brought her full attention to the brightly swaddled cook she began to comprehend words and phrases.

Activating her mind Petra framed a phrase of her own and 'sent' it to the little woman with intent.

'After all my travels, Senora, I am very much looking forward to the meal you have been preparing.'

The woman shook her head with vigour and turned to gaze at Petra.

"You understand me?" she asked, her eyes bright with surprise. "How can this be so?"

Without moving her lips Petra answered.

'I do, much to my surprise. I don't know how.'

The woman shrugged and turned to Evita to say, "Is this the one you spoke of?"

Evita replied in the same dialect. "She is the one. Now let us make her welcome rather than prattling. She has had a long and arduous journey to get here."

"Of course. My food will be my welcome." She turned and walked back inside, her spoon held aloft and her clothes rustling.

"Follow me, Petra. There is a room prepared for you." They entered the house. Stepping around a low table decorated with a striking crystal array, Evita took Petra's arm and guided her to the rear of the large room. All around the walls of the house were pictures and icons depicting beings with what could only be described as 'light activation' up and down their spines. There seemed to Petra to be no fixed path, school or religion favoured, yet at a glance, every mystery school she had ever investigated was represented.

Amidst this, adjacent to each image, a crude drawing of a circle depicting thirteen beings gathered together. As she noticed this, Petra studied the room to discover this pattern repeated in many different ways throughout the space.

"Come now, Petra. Let's get that weight off your back and give your legs a break."

Petra felt the weight of her pack and her legs call for rest. She grimaced and soulspoke.

"Did you just do that to me?"

Laughing out loud, a deep guttural sound from this extraordinary woman, Evita spoke in return.

"You are quick to notice, which is fitting. Yes, perhaps a little. Forgive me. I simply allowed some channels to open that you have learned to control. I opened you to your fatigue."

They walked together into a small, yellow-walled room. A tiny sash window half-open let in cool, fresh air from the shaded side of the house. On the floor at the rear of the room a thin mattress lay, covered in woollen throws and multicoloured bed covers to make an inviting resting place. Tossing her pack to one side, Petra collapsed onto the bed with a loud sigh.

"Rest, Petra. You have worked hard to arrive here to see me. Thank you for your effort and your trust. Rest now. We will speak again later today. There is much to be shared and much to be learned but now is the time for you to sleep." Her voice was sing-song, irresistible and entrancing. Evita intoned each word with supreme gentleness to bring about a sense of complete relaxation. All Petra could do was ride the wave. She felt a creeping warmth and comfort in her bones. As she allowed relaxation to overtake her she saw images of the beings from the main room floating in the air around her. Intertwined with them was a circle of thirteen. All but one of them was located on the rim of that wheel. One sat in the centre. No more than a few minutes passed before Petra fell into a deep sleep.

Evita reached down to her backpack and zipped it open. She drew out each of the items inside and placed them in a green cupboard, filling the shelves one by one until the pack was empty. She hung the pack on a brass hook. Evita turned to gaze at the young woman on her low bed. Petra's face was relaxed, her lips parted. She looked young and vulnerable. Her breath came in gentle puffs as she slept.

"Such a responsibility for one so young," Evita whispered into the room. "I trust I can aid you. I will do everything in my power."

She left the room. The catch clicked into place as she closed the door. Petra stirred and rolled over. A shadow crossed her features as she did so, the shadow of a dream.

The sun was spending its last few moments above the horizon when Petra emerged from her yellow room. Hair dishevelled and wrapped in a colourful blanket she walked through the empty house, taking her time to examine each and every little thing she could. Though the house was simple she felt 'held' and at home. It was as though the walls and roof were blankets on a cold night, a breath of fresh air on a hot, steaming day. She ran the tips of her fingers along one wall, enjoying the roughness and coolness all at once. The aroma of food simmering seemed to pervade every pore in her body, reminding her of the ravenous hunger she had been repressing for several days.

Through a half-open window above the stove where three large pots bubbled, Petra could hear muffled voices, discussing something unintelligible. She had a sense that the conversation involved her. Impatient to speak with them about what was to come yet reticent to join them, enjoying her solitude, Petra made her way toward the front door. On a rough-hewn wooden table near the door were five metal containers, identical in size and design yet each marked with distinctly unique sigils. Two of them she found strangely attractive. The other three were plain and uninteresting.

She ran her fingers over the lids of the two boxes and felt a tingle that extended to her elbow. 'Something significant in there, it seems' ran through her mind as she reached the front door and opened it. Stepping onto the porch she watched long shadows stretch across the fresh-swept yard, the mountains painting themselves as landscape for a second time.

"Come join us, Petra. We have been making some simple plans which will involve you if you permit. Come, we have a seat for you and a spare shawl for when the sun is hidden."

Evita looked fresh and clean. She was dressed in muted grey with a startling, pure-white shawl around her shoulders. Beside her was the tiny woman who had been preparing food. On her right, one chair distant from her was a wiry, dark-haired, South-American man with long braids, oiled so that they seemed to emit a slight glint in the last light of the day. Petra joined them. She sat in the only vacant seat between Evita and this man she had not yet met. As she sat she felt a strange sensation. It was as though she were leaving her body to drift somewhere above the heads of her three companions. She made a focused effort to reconnect with flesh and blood, to come back to earth, back into her body.

"This might take some getting accustomed to, Evita. I just......."

Evita interrupted her. "I saw you up there. It is quite normal, in particular if you find yourself between Basilio and me. Congratulations. You reclaimed yourself with ease. That alone is no small feat considering the two of us and where we positioned you."

Petra considered where she was and how she had arrived.

"Perhaps it is time that you filled me in on how and why I am here, Evita. My connection with Elias was unusual enough but this is even more random. Yet here I am, having come in the opposite direction to that which I would take to meet with Elias."

The sun dropped behind the mountain, engraving trees and tall, stark standing stones against an immense flotilla of multi-coloured clouds painted across a blackening sky. In the same moment, a chill washed across the land, dipping into every corner. Smoke rising from the stone chimney of the house wafted and wavered in the dusk inspired breeze.

Evita's white shawl glowed as if illuminated by the last rays of sunlight. The four of them sat for some time in companionable silence, Petra's words poised expectantly in the chill air between them. Petra shivered. She shifted in her seat to draw a woollen shawl about her shoulders. Evita spoke in an almost secretive undertone.

"This is the culmination of an era, Petra. It must be plain to you by now that you have a significant part to play in what might be called the final drama. You and others like you form a kind of bridge between the world in which most reside in this current paradigm and a world where the bindings are loosened, even cut away." She paused and took several slow, deep breaths. A multi-coloured butterfly visited, landing for a moment on Petra's shoulder before fluttering away.

"It is very important that you and all others who feel the new era arising embrace it, allow it and encourage it. To some we will appear flawed and misguided because we have all been in this old programme for such a long time. It has a strong hold. Yet you and many others have already begun to feel and sense that change is present. The impossible has become possible." Again Evita paused. The chill deepened as the four sat in the encroaching dusk.

"Still, I don't understand what that means, Evita." Petra interjected, wrapping the shawl tight around her shoulders.

"That is why you are here, Petra. That is why you are here. Basilio and I have prepared for your arrival for the past weeks. Now that you are here we can begin. I know that you have already had some experiences on your journey that have altered your outlook."

"You mean Maria and Jose?"

"Yes. They were provided to you in order to begin the process. They were part of your education. You would have noticed some things that were not what you would describe as normal in your journey here with them."

"Like my ability to understand a language foreign to me."

"Yes that and more yet. There was more if you recall." Evita looked enquiringly at her.

"I could hear them without words. Jose in particular "spoke" to me without sound, yet I could hear every word he had to say. It was a kind of transference from his mind to mine." Petra recalled. Her excitement bubbled.

"This is what is available to those who embrace the impossible with vigour. It is time to investigate those things that we have been conditioned to perceive as impossible. The time has come for them to be not only possible but a natural part of our new reality."

"And there is more to learn?"

"There is so much, child. From tomorrow Basilio and I will take you on some journeys that will alter your perspective on what is available to you and others in this life." Evita smiled. As she did so Petra felt warmth coursing through her body, erasing the evening chill.

"But for now, perhaps it is time to enjoy some of Mora's delicious dinner. Will it be ready yet, Mora?" Evita turned her head to the tiny woman who nodded once.

"Basilio, will you join us for food, my friend?" He also nodded and placed his hand on his heart as a gesture of thanks and acceptance.

At this point conversation stopped. Darkness embraced them and the air stilled. All sign of cloud dissipated in the night sky and a billion stars shone above them. Each of them leaned back to take in the glory of the night sky. Each of them, without speaking a word to one another, conveyed their awe and wonder at the beauty above them. Each of them too made a personal note that somewhere in their perception a single star emitted a faint green in that expanded infinity.

Each of them saw an ending and a beginning in that night sky.

Evita was the first to move. She stood, made a movement with her hands clasped together in supplication to the magnificence of the heavenly realms and walked inside. The others followed. Petra was last to move, feeling a change in her as Evita and Basilio went into the house. She offered up a silent prayer,

"Creator of all things, speak through me, act through me, protect me, guide me, enlighten me, inspire me, provide for me, heal me, strengthen and empower me for I am completely in your hands."

It may have been a trick of the night or it may have been that as those last words echoed in her mind that the stars shone just a little brighter and that faint, green light moved a little closer.

The morning dawned bright and cool. Though there was still a chill in the still air, Petra opened her eyes into a warm and comfortable room, rainbows dancing on the wall refracted from three small crystals dangling in the open window. It must have been at least an hour before she arose, the flickering light show capturing her attention and hypnotising her. She threw the duvet off at last and stretched her long legs straight and strong from her walking adventure, her stomach taut and body slender. Her hair, loosed the night before, had grown long during her journey, a little tangled and knotted but framing her suntanned face.

Though she had little idea what Evita might have in store for her, there was excitement bubbling in her. She hummed snatches of songs as she dressed. A smile lit her face. Whatever had guided her to this place, Petra could feel the potency, both of the place and these people. There was nothing else to do but embrace what would happen today. Petra was ready.

"Good morning, Petra," Evita turned her head from the pot on the stove and her face exuded a warmth that was impossible to describe but was infused with love, "I imagined you would have some questions this morning so I arose early so we might have some time together."

"What's that you're cooking?" Petra asked.

"This? Nothing more than buck-wheat porridge with a thing or two added to make it a little more interesting. I do recommend that you have some this morning because I will be asking you to water fast for the coming three days, to prepare yourself for a different journey than the physical one you have been experiencing."

"Water only, for three days? That'll be a challenge knowing how much I can eat." She smiled. The prospect of three days without food was not too difficult as she had fasted with some regularity during her walk. Though the energy she had been

expending on those days had been significant, three days with water or some fruit juice had been manageable. By the third day, Petra recalled that there had been some alterations to her perception.

"And there will be some very significant alterations to your perception in this experience too, Petra. Basilio has been preparing for your arrival since Elias made the call, so as you would imagine, he has quite a journey prepared for you by now." After several previous experiences, Petra was becoming a little more accustomed to this communication without speech. She answered through her mind.

"Preparing me a journey? I thought I was already having a pretty major one."

Laughter bubbled out of Evita. Petra thought it was perhaps the most beautiful sound she had ever heard. "Well, yes you are. Once again you surprise me. Do you have any idea how long it takes many very gifted people to soul share in the manner you just used? Basilio is a very powerful shamanic teacher and practitioner and he is still unable to do much more than make a sound that gets my attention. You, on the other hand, are already able not only to converse but even I cannot close myself to you." She shook her head, still smiling. 'Ah Elias, you always did have a way of knowing exactly who to include in this giant leap we are taking.'

"He had a profound influence on me, Evita. I felt I had known him for a very long time. When he called for me to set out I had no doubt at all that I needed to begin. Yet I still have so many questions. What is this 'giant leap' anyway? What exactly is so important? I'm like a ship without a rudder. I know that I'm on a journey that must be taken but I don't have any real notion where it is taking me. Will you help me with that?" Petra spoke this as she looked into the pot that Evita still stirred.

"That is precisely why you are here, Petra. Basilio and I have several rituals planned for you to open you to the knowledge you will require for the rest of your journey. But for now, eat."

She spooned out two large bowls of the dun-coloured porridge, drizzled honey all over them from a large jar filled with the amber fluid then splashed fresh milk on them both. Bowls in hand, the two of them stepped out onto the porch where they ate in silence. Steam rose from their bowls in the cold morning air. Puffs of mist danced in the light with each and every mouthful.

Saffron

S affron brushed her hands through a rainbow of colourful fabrics while Marcelle followed her, sometimes silent and pensive, sometimes animated, talking, touching and laughing. Wandering through the stores along the beach was Saffron's favourite pastime. Her new friend, Marcelle seemed happy to join in the adventure of a million different colours. Pushy and insistent salesmen did their best to find a way to help the girls' part with some money while flirting with relentless candour, in particular with Saffron with her long, blonde hair. On occasion one of them would make a sale. Some flitch of cloth or a new sarong, bracelets, bangles or charms shaped like Ganesha and Shakti to rattle on a tanned ankle.

The two girls enjoyed each other and the excitement of Arambol Beach preparing for one of the transcendent parties of the year. Saffron and Marcelle explored and laughed as the sun sank into the deeper brown of a perpetually smoke-stained sky. As nightfall overtook the beach, millions of tiny fairy lights began twinkling at every place of business, each store aiming to outshine the next. Draped in a sheer, almost see through, flowing silk dress Saffron spun about and posed for Marcelle, pouting her seduction like a catwalk model, lewd as she exposed her breasts to her.

Marcelle was spellbound. Entranced.

"You are so fucking beautiful, Saffron," she whispered, her voice husky with desire, "Let's get out of here. I'm done shopping. Let's go to yours."

"Great idea, I'm done too." She smiled and winked at her friend. "Though I think I will get this. I love the colours and it feels good on my skin."

"Yes get it. You look amazing. I'll wait outside." She spoke over her shoulder to say, "I've got all our stuff."

She turned and took the few steps to open air. Her phone beeped twice. Marcelle checked it and tapped a quick reply. A minute later, Saffron joined her, wearing her new silk dress. Hand in hand they set out for Saffron and Ethan's rented house, less than a kilometre away. Every eye was on them as they wove and danced their way through bright-lit, crowded streets and hurried through darkened laneways.

The persistent noise of Goa fell away as they pushed the heavy wooden door closed. Ethan and Saffron had found this haven after meeting a crew of well-connected young Indian men. The father of one had an array of real estate options across Goa. Saffron loved this one, adobe pressed into straw bales, making the walls more than half a metre thick. It was hidden behind two multi-storey, wholesale storage units. Splayed about were six other similar buildings arranged in a rough circle. Once, all of them had been occupied by a single, extended Indian family. Now all were leased to foreigners.

A small orchard was visible in the gloom behind the house and each tree was laden with almost-ripe fruit.

Inside the house was cooler. Saffron flicked a switch and the room was illuminated by white lights directed at startling wall hangings and multicoloured strands of fairy-lights trailing around the room.

"Wow, Saffron, this place is amazing."

Marcelle looked around open-mouthed. It was a single, large, round room painted white but lit in such a way that it was multi-coloured. On the west wall to her right was a kitchen featuring solid timber benches piled high with pots, pans, metal dishes and timber trays containing cutlery, serving spoons, ladles and an array of kitchen knives. A deep washing tub served as a kitchen sink.

Above this two large framed photographs of a flawless, white-sand beach devoid even of footprints. A third photograph showed Ethan surfing an enormous wave. In front of her, on the south wall, several low cushioned seats extended from the wall in a broad half circle. Tossed with random abandon over these were swathes of cloth striated with gold and silver thread. A large window was draped in more ornate fabrics, though some light could be seen twinkling between the folds of cloth.

In the centre, a low coffee table supported a shallow bowl full of the biggest stash of weed Marcelle had ever seen. Surrounding this was an array of impressive looking crystals. Several large coffee mugs, unwashed and in disarray, featured various Hindu gods and goddesses. The centrepiece was an ornate hookah with a long turquoise and black pipe shaped as a unique and sinuous snake.

To her left was an enormous king-size bed, draped in luxurious fabrics and cushions. Suspended above the enormous bed were a myriad of Hindu deities and several images of Gautama Buddha. Marcelle tumbled onto the bed and rolled around.

"This place is divine, Saff. Did you decorate it?" She rolled onto her belly and rested her chin in her hands as she watched Saffron's slender form flitting around the apartment, setting lights, opening the window, preparing a platter of fruit and filling two tumblers with water and ice. Just as she was about to bring her platter to Marcelle, she reached into a cupboard to collect a small decorative porcelain bowl. She added it to the platter.

"Viola, my beautiful new friend, here's some snacks and drinks for us. I thought you might also enjoy some of these for later. Saffron pushed the porcelain bowl a little closer to her friend.

"What's in here?"

"I'm not sure but lots of fun things. It belongs to Ethan. There are a couple of different things. His special weed, some hash, acid, mushrooms, dmt and..." She drew out a small bag containing brownish crystals and tossed it back into the bowl. "This looks like MD."

Marcelle fished around in the bowl for a minute or two then drew out the tiny zip sealed bag of brownish crystals. She rolled over and laid her head in Saffron's lap, looking up at her with the bag clinched between finger and thumb.

"How about we have some of this right now?" She smiled a sweet, cheeky smile at Saffron and her eyes glittered. "It'll give us a kick start for tonight."

Saffron smiled in return, also cheeky.

"Why not, just a little bump huh?" She suddenly looked even more impishly elf-like.

"Yes."

Marcelle rolled over. She reached over to get her phone, opened the bag and poured the brownish crystals onto the face of it. She shuffled them around and chose two crystals.

"Does that look about right?"

Each of them placed the crystals on the tips of their tongues, washed them down and French kissed.

Less than an hour later the substance took effect.

Saffron stripped naked. "I'm going to take a shower. I won't be long. Wow, this feels delicious."

She disappeared into the bathroom. Marcelle stretched like a cat, ironing out the tension of the day. Her long, auburn hair strewn across the bedspread and her legs splayed as she sank into a gentle feeling of wellbeing. Saffron emerged, cleansed and naked but for a towel bunched on her head like a turban.

"Can I take a shower too?"

"Yes of course, sweetheart. Just a minute, I'll get you a fresh towel."

By the time Marcelle emerged from the bathroom, Saffron felt ecstatic. Lying across the massive bed, her eyes glistening in the soft light, she ran her hands with gentle tenderness over her skin, touching and teasing as the drug took hold.

"May I do that, Saffron?" Marcelle stood at the end of the bed, wrapped in her towel, with a soft smile and sparkling eyes. Lifting her head and pausing in her ministrations for a minute or two, Saffron nodded.

"Yes, please. Oh this is so lovely. Do you feel it too?"

"Mmmmm. Oh yeah, I feel it."

Marcelle ran her hands over Saffron's feet and legs, stroking her skin with a touch like air and scratching like fire with her nails. Saffron quivered a delicious shiver, entranced by the sensation. As the substance deepened its effect they discovered far more than a physical experience. Marcelle explored every inch of Saffron's body and used her energetic body to penetrate her, lost in an ecstatic bliss. Saffron bathed in the caresses of the petite French girl and relished in receptive submission.

In a kind of slow-motion swirl, soft skin on soft skin, lips and tongues and hands and exquisite, gentle kisses they found themselves strewn on the bed, side-by-side, holding hands.

As she gazed at the coloured lights playing across the ceiling and felt the shining buzz in her every cell, Saffron turned her head and whispered.

"Can I tell you something, Marcelle?

"Uhuh. Anything."

There was a pregnant silence but for the almost imperceptible sounds of them both breathing, both conscious in their awareness of each and every breath.

"I'm not quite sure what I want to say." She breathed out. Then while watching every nuance of every sensation in her body she breathed in. Marcelle followed her breath then breathed out, issuing a soft, cat-like purr.

"Mhhhhmmmmmmmhhhmmmmm. Oh this is so yummy, Saff. Mmhhhmmmmhhhhmmmm." Marcelle snuggled into Saffron's body, laid her head on her heart, her arm along her belly, her hand tucked between her thighs. Saffron shifted a little to allow their bodies to meld even more closely together.

"I love Ethan and... I don't think I'm going to be with him for much longer." She spoke the words into the room as if to avoid disturbing the air, the dust, the shifting, waving colours weaving patterns into the ceiling. Marcelle remained silent but held her a little tighter and stroked her neck and shoulders.

"It's just a feeling I have." A long pause ensued and both girls lay back, bathing in the ecstatic comfort of the amphetamine. Saffron added.

"It came up about a week ago and it feels fine. That is, I'm not going to 'leave' him, but in another way, I am."

"Why? What's happened, Saff?" Marcelle leaned up on one elbow and trailed her fingers through Saffron's blonde hair, down her cheek, along the line of her neck to her chest and breasts. She continued to her stomach and again came to rest between her legs. Both of them were quivering. As if answering, Saffron pulled Marcelle closer and kissed her, gentle, deep, soft lips against soft lips, tongues exploring.

When that kiss ended, Marcelle drew back and began to kiss her new lover from head to toe until those butterfly kisses evolved into a passionate exploration of their fresh, new intimacy. The energy between them continued to rise as Marcelle brought her full attention to Saffron's inner thighs and the moistness of her sex, bathing her with her tongue, using her soft lips to pleasure her lover.

Saffron shuddered. Her body writhed and shook as she reached a powerful climax, her fingers entwined in Marcelle's mat of silken hair, pressing her inwards, moaning and shaking. Aided by the drug, the power of Saffron's orgasm also imbued Marcelle's body. In seconds, the two of them were writhing and weaving their energies together, one being, enmeshed in ecstasy.

As the experience continued to possess them, they entered another realm. Here it was calm though the ecstatic feeling was constant, their bodies embraced in exquisite, vibrating energy. It was in that place that Saffron answered Marcelle's question, not with words but with a lucid, shared, visual experience.

Hands clasped together, they flew. Without effort they soared above treetops, over wide-open, desolate places and amaranthine expanses of green and growing farmland. Goa faded to a tiny, haze-ridden spot on the horizon. In this place the air was crisp and crystalline. The Himalaya's towered before

them, white with snow and ice, stretching into an azure sky into the gold and silver realms of heaven.

Soaring above the wind-swept summits, the two girls were drawn downwards. Still clutching hands, Marcelle to the left, Saffron to the right, they raced between towering peaks, refreshed in the icy air, gambolling and cavorting on updrafts and plummeting ground-wards to capture another pocket of warm air to toss and rollick them deeper and deeper into the highest mountains in the world. In this way they arrived above Tibet.

Hacked through these imposing palisades and their silent, massive stillness, was the road from China to India. On that road, something was moving.

In their interconnectedness, one thought became instantaneously real and their trajectory shifted. Down and down they plummeted, racing so fast that a shrieking whistle sounded through the mountains and a spacious echo rebounded from towering vertical faces of stone and massive ledges of ice and snow.

They hovered above that moving thing.

A lone motorbike was making its way along the road through this frozen landscape. The rider seemed not to notice them, wrapped in leather, oiled cotton and animal skin. His focus seemed to be captured by staying upright on a road hatched with rocks and rubble. His diminutive female passenger seemed underdressed, yet not suffering in any way from the bitter cold. She stared straight at them. There was no doubt she was witnessing their visitation. She shook the rider hard and moved on the pillion seat. Her agitation caused the bike to wobble. He shrugged his irritation. Gripping his right arm near the shoulder, she pointed at Saffron and Marcelle. He had no sight of the realm she perceived. His concentration was disturbed. He kicked the bike down a few gears and drew to a stop on a wider part of the shoulder of the road. Here the cliff dropped over one hundred metres and the travellers were surrounded by towering snow and ice enshrouded peaks.

As the travellers climbed off the bike and began an arm waving exchange, Saffron and Marcelle peeled off to the right and vanished around an ice-covered abutment. They ascended above the highest peaks and flew south.

Marcelle and Saffron opened their eyes in the same instant. Saffron burst out.

"Did you see? Did you see them? The people on the mo-torbike?" She looked into Marcelle's entrancing eyes. "You did, didn't you? You saw them."

"Of course I saw them, sweetness. Clear as day. Is that somehow connected.......?" Saffron interrupted.

"It's because of them. They are why I won't be with Ethan for much longer. They are coming to find me. I know it. I can feel it. I have not the slightest notion why, but I know it's true."

The pretty French girl gazed back at Saffron. With powerful intent she probed into her energy body. Saffron shook her head once, shuddered twice and looked at her new friend, a question lingering.

Marcelle spoke.

"I felt it too Saff. I felt it too and it was awesome. If they don't have any mishaps, they'll be here quite soon. That was the Himalayas, right, Tibet or Nepal or somewhere? I'm sure they are coming to find you and on that motorbike it won't take long." She peeled away from their entangled arms and legs. She retrieved her cell-phone, wrapped a sarong around her and returned to the bed.

"Well, I could stay here for much longer, my beautiful friend but hadn't we better start getting ready for Ethan to come by?" Marcelle turned her phone towards Saffron to show her the time and in that same movement took a photograph of her.

"You don't mind do you? I would love to keep this to remind me of this time together." The French girl smiled a beguiling smile.

"Of course that's OK. May I take one of us?" Saffron reached for her own phone.

"Yes do!" They posed together, holding each other close. When Saffron had taken the shot they both looked at the result.

"What is that?" squealed Saffron.

Extending from the top of the photograph into the crown of Saffron's head was a shaft of rainbow-coloured light that completed in pure white at the point where it entered her head. Above Marcelle in a similar way a beam of crimson light entered her completing in a cloying maroon which faded into black.

"It must be something to do with the lights in here, Saff. Maybe it's a trick of the light because of the fairy lights and candles and such." The slim French girl stood up and ran her hand over the crown of Saffron's head.

"I'm going to have another shower. Want to join?"

"Yes, I'd love to," replied Saffron, reaching for her towel and heading straight to the bathroom. Marcelle cooed after her.

"You start then. I'll be a minute. I've gotta send a message or two."

"OK. Don't be long." Saffron disappeared into the bathroom and the sound of water tumbled into the room.

Sitting on the end of the bed in just a light sarong, hair dishevelled and body still thrumming from the drug, Marcelle composed her message.

"She is one of them. That is certain. She seems to have no idea. I can't take hold of her energetically. She just removed me without effort. There is also another coming. The one you told me about with a tiny Tibetan girl. They are on a motorbike riding through the Himalayas. The Tibetan girl could see us both in the other realm." She added the picture of Saffron.

Marcelle pressed send, tossed her phone on the bed and dropped her sarong. "Coming, Saffron." Steam rushed out as she opened the door and disappeared into the bathroom.

Just one minute earlier Saffron had reached to turn both taps off at once, searching the space around her.

"Who's there?" she hissed. There was no answer. Saffron could smell acacia smoke.

346

In western China a phone pinged. Mara Lin read the message and forwarded it.

On his bedside table a cell-phone buzzed. The big man grunted and rolled over to reveal a small naked figure curled in foetal position on the bed. He picked up the phone and read the message, harsh light from the screen etching deep lines and ridges in his face.

"Damn it. Fuck them all."

The Cardinal slapped the child on the backside.

"Go back to the dormitory, boy."

When the boy had gone he tapped the screen of his phone once and put it to his ear. It rang just twice before it was answered with silence. The cardinal spoke.

"One termination and two extractions as we discussed. The extraction is at Goa in India, the female. Do not harm her male friend nor our agent. You have data on both. In Tibet, on the new road, facilitate termination for the male and extraction for a Tibetan national – a young female. Do not harm the two extraction subjects under any circumstance. Understood?"

"Yes, understood." The deep, resonant voice was almost irresistibly and immediately hypnotic. It purred just those two words in the cardinal's ear. The line went dead.

CHAPTER FORTY THREE

The first shipment of Verity Tibet water had arrived from China. There was a box of it behind each chair in the Verity Global boardroom. At each place at the massive table stood a water-filled crystal decanter and a fine crystal tumbler. Simon Chant surveyed the room and nodded, satisfied that he had covered everything necessary for the presentation and induction of each of the board members. He retreated to his personal space, flipped open his tablet and pored through the notes and emails he had been exchanging with Anita Claesson, Secretary-General of the United Nations and his new advertising agency, Rouseabout Advertising. He had insisted on dealing with the agency principal, Ambika Rouse. Together they had strategized the release of the new Verity branded Tibet Water.

The campaign would be a success, he felt sure of that. The agency had a raw creative edge he liked. The board meeting today would introduce the board to Ms Claesson and connect them with the strategy utilising Tibet Water to provide a genetic tag to every living human on the planet. It was brilliant and it was going to be the source of incredible profit.

Verity Global shares were already up eighty-three percent on the rumour of today's announcement. Without the use of artificial intelligence or injection of anything at all, a whole new realm was being created, beyond nano-technology. Humanity would be marked and monitored. Verity Global would be the international hub. The advertising and marketing campaign that he and Ambika Rouse's team had designed meant the future for Simon Chant and his company looked bright.

"Alva Irving is here to see you, Mr Chant." The intercom chimed with the voice of Simon Chant's new PA.

"Ask her to come straight in, Lisa," he replied, "and as the board members arrive, show them into the boardroom and let me know when they are all present. Make sure Ms Claesson is shown to the executive suite, the same for Ms Rouse."

"Yes of course, sir. Ms Rouse is already there. I've had a call from Ms Claesson's PA to say they are on their way from the airport." The intercom went quiet. Simon Chant stood and walked towards the door. It swung inwards.

"Alva, welcome, it's so good to see you. Can I get you a drink?"

Simon was effusive. Alva looked less than impressed, her face revealing her discomfort.

"Stop it, Simon. Just... stop it." She walked with a stilted gait to the vast window that overlooked the city, stopping just short, her hands twisting and twining a small white envelope she held.

"I need to speak with you, Simon." She didn't turn but began to talk, deadpan to the pane of polished glass, her face a mask.

"Of course, Alva, we have never done anything else, have we?" He joined her in surveying the city far below them. She turned toward him.

"We haven't exchanged a straight word since that night, Simon. Not a single one. You know that I don't approve of us proceeding with the launch of this. Yet still you move it forward without any genuine consultation whatsoever. It's a flawed product, Simon. It had enormous potential but we haven't perfected it yet. It should not be released." She turned now to face him eye to eye. "I nearly fucking died, Simon. You have to stop!"

"You are over-dramatising, Alva. On that night, you had nothing more than a bad reaction to some dirty cocaine that you decided to imbibe. The amount you consumed was, shall we say, significant. As you were in my office at the time you will

recall I accepted full responsibility for the unfortunate events that followed. I considered it was my fault because it was in my quarters."

Alva maintained a stony silence as Simon preached. His face reddened in several large blotches as he spoke.

"That's why you are now a wealthy woman, Alva. There are not too many people in the world that have over five hundred million American dollars in their personal account. I am also responsible for that, if you recall. Your shares in Verity Global continue to rise, meaning your wealth increases every day. You need never do anything you don't wish to for the rest of your life, Alva, but for one thing. You need to change your attitude. I will not permit it inside or outside this building. The matter is closed."

His appearance was calm but it was impossible to miss that he was seething with anger. "I need to bring my attention to the boardroom and our guests, Alva. I expect you to be under complete control during the meeting. You know that I will not stand for it to be anything other than a united front as we launch the most exciting advance in medical history. With this technology that we perfected in Verity Global facilities we have changed the face of medicine across the globe."

"You mean the most significant weapon ever foisted on an unsuspecting public, you fucking madman." Alva was livid. "You have weaponised what could have been an incredible gift, Simon. You have perverted everything I worked for."

"Nonsense, Alva. Once again you are stretching the truth in an irresponsible manner. I will not permit that to continue. You need to regain control of yourself."

He reached for a small item on the glass table nearby, hard matte-black plastic and polished chrome about the size of a finger drive. "And I will have this handy little item with me at all times. Everyone present has already been informed that you haven't managed a complete recovery from the trauma following your spectacular presentation nine months ago. They will not blink if you become less responsive than normal in the course

350

of the meeting. I imagine you would prefer that I don't have to use this." He held the unit up for her to see before slipping it into the pocket of his trousers. "Shall we join our fellow team members?"

As if on cue, Simon Chant's cell phone buzzed once and the intercom sounded.

"All board members are present, Mr Chant. Ms Claesson is in the executive space with Ms Rouse."

"Thank you, Lisa. Alva and I will be there in a moment. Please take Ms Claesson and Ms Rouse into the boardroom and show them to their seats at the table. Please then take your lunch break and don't return to the office today. Take the rest of the day off. I have arranged for you to enjoy dinner at that restaurant you and your partner love so much. You have an unlimited tab on Verity Global account and a balcony table for two booked for seven this evening. I do hope you will enjoy, Lisa."

"Thank you so much, Mr Chant. I'll leave now with your permission."

"Permission granted. Get out of here." The intercom clicked into silence.

Alva placed the small white envelope she had been holding on the glass table in the centre of the room.

Throwing both doors open, Simon Chant strode into the boardroom like a triumphant Emperor. Alva trailed behind, looking far less strident. Rather than taking his seat at the head of the enormous oval table, he directed Alva to sit. Aiming a fine steel pointer at the wall furthest from him, he pressed once. A screen lowered to cover almost the entire wall. He pressed again and the lights in the room were extinguished and all windows blacked out. After a few theatrical seconds in the pitch dark and silence the Chairman of the Board of Verity Global pressed once more. A kaleidoscope of light, colour and sound burst on-screen.

The first thirty-second commercial for Verity Tibet Water filled the room, surround sound almost deafening, extolling the virtues of "pure bliss from the top of the world".

When the commercial finished there was complete silence for several long seconds before the room erupted into applause. A few cheered. The infomercial followed.

"From the towering Himalayan Mountains of The Chinese province of Tibet, Verity Global is proud to offer 'Verity Tibet Water' - the purest source of water in the world." Shot after shot of sweeping mountain ranges and untouched glaciers preceded images of attractive people of all ages drinking from one hundred percent recyclable bottles of Verity Tibet Water, sporting new artwork and label, the Himalayan ranges, snow and ice free under a crimson cloud-filled sky.

The infomercial rolled on extolling the virtues of water from the freshest source of pure water in the world and asking how better to bring that to every nation in the world but through a truly trustworthy international company, Verity Global.

When the infomercial ended Simon Chant pressed his controller several more times. The lights came up, screen rolled away and blinds retreated. Every member of the Verity Global board was varying degrees of stunned. Simon Chant was triumphant. Anita Claesson checked her Cartier watch. Ambika Rouse was unreadable. Alva sat immobile, head tilted forward as though reading notes on the desk, though there were none.

"Distribution of Verity Tibet Water begins this weekend. That is, there are stocks already in position at every major distribution point in the world. The final retail distribution occurs from this Friday." Simon paused and decided to pass the baton. "Ambika Rouse, principal of Rouseabout Advertising, will brief you on the advertising and marketing footprint to cover the launch. Ambika?"

"Yes, thank you, Simon. The decision has been taken to launch in a similar manner to a high-end perfume. That is we will spend fifteen times the projected annual profit of the product in the first three months." Simon lowered the screen again and dimmed the lights. A series of graphs and diagrams flashed on screen, prompted by the flash of Ambika Rouse's laser marker.

"We will dominate every major online platform for the coming three months, every major sporting event worldwide, every free to air and cable television channel, press, magazines, even radio. We'll be all over the online audio platforms, major apps, billboards. It's blanket coverage. We've also been able to negotiate an arrangement with the principal social media platforms, video platforms and search engines to maintain exclusivity during the launch period." Ambika flipped to the next image of her presentation.

It was at just this moment that Anita Claesson's telephone buzzed, interrupting Ambika's presentation. The Secretary-General answered. She listened for a few moments then said.

"Understood. Yes, of course. Yes, within the hour." She hung up.

"Please continue, Ms Rouse". She put her phone in a black clutch bag and clipped it shut.

"Thank you. Now, just before I cover off some numbers I'd like to add that it seems that we will be able to maintain that exclusivity benefit into the future. Your Chair informs me that Verity Global has made arrangements to provide Verity Global Tibet Water for the principal offices of each of those platforms. He is therefore confident that we will not have any difficulty continuing our dominance."

She gestured to the images on the screen.

"Our models show that we will reach over ninety percent of the population of the world in that three-month period and we'll have a frequency of impact exceeding thirty-eight. In our industry it's known as a brainwash plan."

She flipped to the next image.

"The expected take-up of Verity Tibet Water is estimated at sixty-five percent within the three months of the campaign and ninety-three percent of the human population within nine months of launch, on the basis that the launch is coupled with a marketing strategy that will provide comprehensive delivery. There has been approval from the Chairman of your board for

a distribution of four billion complimentary bottles of Verity water, most of which is already stockpiled."

This drew some murmuring from several members of the board. In the dimness of the room one voice said, "Can we afford that, Simon. That's a fucking substantial comp allocation? Did you consider that it may have been a good idea to bring a decision such as that to the whole board, would it not?"

"That's where I come in, I suspect." Anita Claesson's voice cut the room to silence. "Your chairman had the very good sense to connect with me about the incredible technology that is inherent in Verity Tibet Water. Those first four billion bottles, including every step in production and distribution have been covered by a contribution from the United Nations and the World Health Organisation. There will therefore be zero investment from Verity Global for that very significant part of the marketing of this extraordinary product. In fact, I suspect that your Chairman has managed to achieve a small profit from the arrangement. I'd be disappointed if he hadn't." She turned to face Simon.

"Would you please bring us back into full light, Simon? I'm tired of this and I now have another appointment very soon so I'd like to complete." She turned to address Ambika.

"Thank you, Ambika, I'm sure you have been as thorough and professional as your reputation suggests." Ambika sat down masking a sigh of relief as she sloughed into the leather chair.

Anita Claesson picked up her crystal tumbler and reached into her personal bag to retrieve a labelled bottle of Verity Tibet Water. She twisted the lid off and poured a substantial portion into her glass then with practiced composure, closed the bottle and returned it to her bag.

"I propose a toast. To the most significant advance in medicine ever achieved. This alliance between the exciting and unique technology of Verity Global, the Tibet Water product and the influence and agendas of WHO and the United Nations will achieve outcomes that we have been seeking for the past forty years."

She looked around at each member of the meeting then raised her glass.

"To Simon Chant, the brilliant research of Alva Irving and her team and to the inspired board of Verity Global."

She upturned her glass and drank all the contents. Each of the board members in the room followed suit from their ready filled tumblers but for Alva and Simon. Alva didn't move to touch her glass. Simon took a single gulp after checking that it was his personal beaker. Ambika Rouse reached for her glass and lifted it to her lips, but drank nothing at all before placing it back on the table.

In his private quarters following the board meeting Simon Chant and Anita Claesson each lifted a glass filled with a different liquid, eighteen years aged. Neither of them had consumed nor would ever consume Verity Tibet Water. Each of them was secure in the knowledge that they just launched the most powerful medical monitoring system on earth. The primary purpose was less well publicised but would serve them well. This breakthrough represented a level of control of humanity that some had been dreaming of constructing for generations. It was a breakthrough representing the solution to some of the world's greatest challenges, from global warming, international trade and the ever-present threat of war between nations to the quelling of mass protests and burgeoning overpopulation.

Until this moment the dream had seemed almost impossible. This development however, this modified water, meant that a long publicised agenda could be met sooner than projected.

"Congratulations, Simon. That went as expected. As I mentioned, you will be required to attend a top level meeting this Friday in Brussels. There are some people who will need to see the secondary process played out with equal success." She threw back her cognac and placed the glass down with theatrical care. "You have subjects chosen for the demonstration?"

"Yes of course. My European division has been working with several universities in Brussels. We have a crop of volunteers from the social science divisions of each of them. They

have already been participating in comprehensive studies and the results have been nothing short of perfect." He walked to the huge window that overlooked the city. "Your people will have complete satisfaction, you may rest assured. I fly tomorrow so will be spending several days in Paris prior to the meeting. In that way I can be reached with ease if there is a need."

"Good. I'll show myself out and see you in Brussels."

Anita Claesson left the room, cell-phone pressed to her ear to alert her driver and security team. She descended to the foyer of the Verity Global building and left the building through a smaller door to the side of the fascia, flanked by three heavy-built, suited men. They delivered her to a grey Mercedes with blacked-out windows.

Though Anita Claesson could demand priority in almost any circumstance, there were still a few figures in the world who could command her. Her next appointment was one of these figures. She did not like to be kept waiting. Based on the other side of the world in a remote castle in Switzerland she had sent the single message that had interrupted the Verity Global board meeting.

Less than half an hour later, Anita Claesson was in her private United Nations jet. Upon boarding she connected the intravenous syringe installed in her seat. The cocktail within restored her energy as nothing else could. It was more than important that she was at her best when she made her appointment with Valda Balaz, a woman who was known never to meet anyone face-to-face.

This private audience meant that Valda Balaz had either taken a personal interest or had a task for her, perhaps both. In either case, the world was about to meet a very different future than even the Secretary-General of the United Nations could imagine.

CHAPTER FORTY FOUR

At the end of their first afternoon they had trekked just over fifteen kilometres. They set camp in a shallow gully surrounded by low scrub and scattered stones. Choosing caution, they lit no campfire but managed a bowl each of hot stew, prepared by Toby in a single pot on his tiny camp stove.

As the first fingers of cool, slate-grey light stretched across a troubled, leaden mass of clouds tossed to and fro by unpredictable gusts of freezing wind, Toby, Brianna and Raniyah packed their camp and set out. Less than an hour later a sleeted drizzle started. Fine pinpricks of almost frozen rain slashed their faces and hands and wet everything with chill dankness.

Ice cold droplets splashed their faces as they trudged along a winding path tangled and twisted with vines and sharp, spiked thistles. The spines caught and tugged on their socks and trousers, pestering every step.

Toby led the trio, brown and tan backpack weighing heavy on his muscled shoulders, his aikido jo looking like an antenna extended from his left shoulder. The ex-military man was difficult to make out in a grey and green, lightweight rain-jacket and thick jungle-green trousers bustling with pockets. He shoved, cut and pushed his way along the track, clearing as much as he was able for his two companions, slashing and swinging with a huge machete. He swore when thistle spikes pierced his trousers or prodded their way through his gloves.

Raniyah was next, walking in silence, her mind still weaving a story about her 'green star' discovery. Her slender figure appeared barrel-like, swaddled in a long, oversize oilskin, buttoned to the neck. In several places the sheepskin under-jacket

357

poked through, dirty white puffs of wool sagging with muddy wetness. The hem of her trousers dragged a little under the heel of her boots. A wide-brimmed oilskin hat kept her hair and head dry. Her dirt-stained green and orange backpack prevented her from appearing comical, like an old fashioned seafarer.

At the rear was Brianna. Her entire outfit, pack and hood included, a dense olive-green trimmed in disarrayed black. Her wet face was framed by the drawstring of the hood. In these conditions she was difficult to see even twenty metres away. She moved in a catlike fashion, smooth and sinuous, alert and watchful. She had her aikido jo in her left hand, ever ready.

At the end of the next day, their first full day, they set up camp in a natural alcove surrounded by trees and shielded from view by the same vines and thistles they had been carving their way through all day. Everything was saturated. Even in this shielded place the ground squished and squirmed under their sodden boots, mud and slush darkened their trouser legs and the surrounding trees dripped large cold drops that made muffled splashes as they hit sodden earth. A thick mist surrounded the travellers as the last light of day faded to gunmetal grey and a cloistered, viscous darkness descended.

Once their tents were up and packs offloaded, Brianna took a flashlight to search the area for any semi-dry sticks of wood she could find. She returned with a small armful, though most of it was wet. Raniyah stacked the driest of the twigs and leaves and a little paper on the wet soil. Flicking the top off an antique brass lighter she touched a flame to the paper. The thirteenth time she tried, the fire began to burn. Toby fiddled with his handheld GPS, silent but for an occasional expulsion of air that signalled his frustration. Soon the fire burned bright. Brianna tossed the sticks and small logs beside Raniyah and without a word headed back into the scrub for more.

As Raniyah added the wet timber, the fire smoked and sputtered but the flame continued to grow. The logs hissed, water boiling out broken ends, sissing and fizzling into the coals.

When Brianna returned with another load, Toby looked up.

"That's enough, Bree. The fire is a bit of a risk anyway but in this weather, some comfort. I'm guessing if anyone is following us they're as miserable as we are." He looked at the contraption in his hands.

"I can't be sure this thing is working properly but if it is, we haven't managed to walk very far today." The tiny screen flared a little and lit Toby's face in a pale greenish light.

"What does not very far mean, brother?" said Raniyah as she fussed and fiddled with the fire.

"It looks like we've come about eighteen kilometres. We made better speed yesterday afternoon." Brianna looked aghast. Raniyah added a few extra twigs to the flame.

"If that's so, I'd be suggesting we take a few more risks and use the roads a lot more or we'll be walking for the next twenty years." Toby tapped the screen of his GPS in annoyance.

His words did little to improve their mood. After a cold hour and a half, Raniyah working to keep the fire burning while Toby fired up his lightweight camp stove to cook three dried food packages, they crawled into their damp tents in damp clothes with the hope of warmth and sleep.

Neither was available that night.

Toby woke as though disturbed by sound. Still blurry with sleep, he reached for his bush knife and opened the tent on the side away from the cold remnants of their fire, cautious. The night had become even colder. The rain had stopped. Now a dank fog blanketed the three small tents and hid all of their surroundings but for the closest trees. These hung low, wet and sordid over their doubtful haven. He felt around at the edge of his tent and found the 'jo'. It felt familiar and reassuring in his hand.

Casting his eye all around, Toby extracted silently from the tent and pressed against the trunk of the nearest tree. All looked quiet and peaceful but there was something indescribable that niggled at his senses. He knew the feeling. It placed him at full alert.

Lifting his body minuscule by minuscule movement at a time into a standing position, he made his plan to ensure safety for Brianna and Raniyah. Until this moment he forgot to reach out to them in 'soulspeak'. That was remedied before he moved. Fashioning his sigil he sent a bright white arrow of intention to them both.

"Wake now. Be silent. Something's wrong and I don't know what. Be ready."

Brianna responded in an instant, her sigil bright and just three words.

"I'm with you."

It took Raniyah just a moment longer and her soulspeak was a half-awake mumble, but sufficient. Toby scanned the space again, intent on protecting the women in the tents. It was still almost impossible to see more than a few metres. He waited, not breathing for a full minute. He heard nothing but low muffled sounds of the night. Just as he breathed again a loud report shook the night. It sounded like a branch breaking and was followed by a yawning roar.

A pair of black bears shuffled into the lair of the travellers. As Toby watched he dropped his guard a little. Any danger from these guys was manageable. The bears showed little interest in the tents. Scratching and scraping on a gnarled trunk or a fallen log, they ambled through camp and continued on their way.

Toby soulspoke once again, sending his sigil in a cool, green colour along with a simple message.

"It's a couple of black bears. Stand down guys."

Brianna unzipped her tent and stood beside it, still poised and ready with her aikido jo in hand. Raniyah emerged a moment later, her hair a tousled mess and her boot laces in the mud. She looked around as though confused, saw Brianna and peered through the thinning fog to locate Toby.

"Over here, little sister. Man, you wake well then. Not." He chuckled. Brianna turned to face Raniyah and also let out a little laugh.

"Been a bit of a torrid night, Ran?"

Running her fingers through her hair, Raniyah looked piqued but answered, "I've been having the weirdest, weirdest dreams. I've hardly slept at all. Probably just dropped off when Toby bloody yelled at us. What time is it?"

"Two thirty-five," said Toby as he walked into the centre of the camp. "There's still time to get some sleep, so that's what I'm doing." He climbed back into his tent, placing the jo and the knife in easy reach. Brianna took a step towards Raniyah.

"You OK, sister?"

"No, not really."

Bending down to her open tent she drew out a thermos.

"Want to drink a mug of hot tea and see if we can get that fire to throw a little warmth?"

"I'd like that."

Ten minutes later they gave up on the fire and sat companionably beside cold ashes in muted torchlight, sipping hot tea from metal mugs. Her hands cupped around her mug, Brianna sipped another warming mouthful, swallowed and said,

"Do you want to tell me about the dreams then?"

CHAPTER FORTY FIVE

Walking with a steady gait, appreciating everything in his immediate surroundings, communing with the natural world as he walked, Elias padded homewards. There was still the rumbling of something troubling in what he had sparked, some sense of responsibility for others. Then his reasoning mind reminded him that he was a cog in an infinite wheel. He was playing his part. In his heart and deeper still, in his soul, he was at peace. The greatest clarity was always gained at a soul level and he had trained every day to access that soul since the age of nine.

"I accept my place in this, none greater none lesser," he intoned into the whirr and flicker of cicadas and birdsong.

As he walked, one steady step after another, a golden, late afternoon light shikkered through a billion leaves. For those with the ability to release their learned limitations, another dimension became visible. A huge circle of 'stands behind' ancestors, family ancestors, clan ancestors and enlightened ancestors could be witnessed walking with him at the same pace, relaxed and steady. Each and every one was proud to walk with him.

The rumble and cough of an old diesel motor disturbed him.

"Jingiwalla, mate. You want a lift?" An older woman perhaps in her late sixties, a farmer by the looks of her, drove a truck covered with dust. Elias stopped and squinted through the side window facing a red, setting sun. Though he couldn't see the woman's face he replied,

"Boogelbeh, sister, I'm fine. I've only got about fifteen kilometres to go."

"Get in. No need to walk if I'm going that way."

It was an instruction and an invitation. Elias shrugged, smiled and grabbed the door handle. He opened the back of the truck, tossed his staff in, slammed it shut and climbed aboard. His backside dropped into the passenger seat in the same moment that she shifted the truck into gear with a grind and a crunch. The old motor roared and the truck moved off with a massive plume of black smoke.

"Jingiwalla, brother. Name's Awhena. You can call me Aphee." She reached out a gnarled brown hand across the steering wheel and shook Elias' hand.

"Elias. It's good to meet you and thanks for the ride, Aphee."

Though they had just met, both fell silent without awkwardness. Elias returned to his ancestors. Five kilometres further on, Awhena spoke again.

"Strange old world we're in, eh? When I was a kid I came here from Aotearoa. There were lots of people walking about here and not so many cars. If a car came past there was always a lift." She shrugged. "Just how things were once upon a time, I guess."

The gears ground and clunked as she shifted them and continued. "If you ask me I'd say there's a big shift going on right now, Elias. I saw some goings-on a few nights ago over on the mountain. It was a bit like lightning but different. It was a lot more colourful and a lot less momentary. Same sort of power though."

She nodded in solitary agreement.

"Yep. There's big stuff going down right now. It's time eh?"

Without warning Aphee swung on the wheel to avoid a deep pothole.

"The original people from around here have some stories. They say when that sort of light shows up from that particular mountain, massive change is on the way. They speak of big change to shake the foundations of just about everything. They say it's from their Dreaming. The stories I've heard go that the last time there was a big show like the other night was just

before white man landed here. That time, the original people knew it was coming but they didn't have any idea what to do."

She coughed, cleared her throat and spat out the window.

"The story finishes off saying that the next time there would be enough people who knew what to do so it would work out good for the mountain and all the lands and everything in it, in particular, the rainbow serpent."

She shared a genuine smile.

"It's quite a story, huh?"

She swung hard on the wheel again. The truck thumped into a pothole and Aphee swore. She changed down a gear.

"You got a long ancestry here, Elias?" When Aphee raised her eyebrows her forehead curled into a sea of sun etched wrinkles.

"Sure do, Aphee. I go back a long time." Elias smiled in return. "And I know that story pretty well."

"Yeah, thought so."

She glanced in the cracked and spider-web-grimy, rear-view mirror and added,

"Seems to me that a man walking would be at about the place I picked you up if he walked down from that mountain just after the light show."

Elias looked straight ahead.

"You're right, Auntie. There are a lot of strange things going on. Me, I just want to get home, get myself a good wash and eat some food cooked at my place. I been walking a long time and I'm tired. I'm grateful for this ride, like I say."

Aphee noticed the change in Elias' address to her. Calling her Auntie was a sign of respect. She looked to the road ahead and remained silent for several minutes. Then she spoke to him in a strange hushed tone, almost sing-song whispering as though to encode the sound of her voice with the somnolent drone of the truck engine.

"A time might arrive soon brother when staying at your place isn't the best decision for your health and happiness. The Grandmothers have an eye out for you and they want you to

know that you always have a safe haven with them. They asked me to find you to let you know that there are some old hidden ways around here. You can use those paths to travel where you can't be sensed, tracked or followed."

She changed down another gear for the rise in the road.

"On this physical plane, on this land, there is also my place. It's humble but it's comfortable, well-stocked and you can come whenever you want and stay as long as you need."

As the truck slowed with the rise, Awhena reached out to collect a small scrap of paper from the dashboard of the old truck. She passed it to Elias. He unfolded it to see an address scribbled under Awhena's name.

"Boogelbeh again, Auntie. I'll keep this in case I need it. My place is just around this next corner, on the right. There's a purple flag out the front near the mailbox."

Aphee pulled the truck to the side of the road with a squeal of brakes long overdue for repair.

"You make sure you keep that, Elias. You make sure you come see me if you have a need. Don't forget now, brother."

As he climbed down and retrieved his staff he smiled a broad smile and said,

"Yoway, you can be sure of that, Auntie Aphee. I am thinking, or maybe hoping it won't come to that, but I can't be sure, even with lots of good clear foresight. Thanks for the ride and for the offer. I'll be there if I need to be and you make sure you reach out to me if you have need. Boogelbeh, Auntie."

"Boogelbeh, Elias. Nice to meet you. Catch up soon, one way or another. Nynboo."

She ground the old gears again. The truck lurched forward, blew thick smoke and began to rumble and sway its way along the road.

Elias shook his head. The niggling doubts about whether he had chosen the right moment had vanished. Now was, without question, the right time. Of course, if the Grandmothers had such a direct line to his work and what he had done, then others

would have paid attention too. Maybe he would need to take up Awhena's offer.

The Grandmothers had a long-recognised story of activity across many realms. They had a habit of showing up at just the right time to bump a thing or two in a new direction. They kept things on track. But they were not the most powerful beings that visited there or gleaned messages from that place.

Far more malevolent beings would already have been searching for him. The work he had done would have left clues behind. That was impossible to avoid. Some of those beings would hunt him down, once they comprehended what he had set in motion.

The ride those beings would offer him would take him straight to hell.

CHAPTER FORTY SIX

W hen the three days of fasting had passed, Petra felt light-headed, in particular when Basilio was close. When both Evita and Basilio were present together it was impossible. On the final day they packed warm clothing and a sleeping bag into backpacks, slung them across their backs and set out into the hills. It was difficult for Petra to determine which direction they had taken. The path wound through dense forest and the sun was obscured by clouds roiling in a sullen sky. The result was that she had no idea where she was but she was with two beings that held her in ways she had experienced once before. The last time she had felt this way had been during her 'chance' meeting with Elias. She felt safe and on the edge of a precipice all at once.

At the end of the hike, Basilio led them into a clearing. In the centre of the clearing was a small log cabin. With little fuss the three of them collected firewood and soon had a fire burning bright in the centre of the single room. Basilio and Petra warmed their hands. Evita sat motionless in one corner, eyes closed in meditation.

Relaxing into a deep inner peace was second nature to Petra by now. The walking had been profound in bringing her to a place where her mind could be empty. She went to that place as the fire warmed her hands and from there dipped back into thought to send an unspoken message to Basilio.

'What is in store for me here?' This time she was able to recognise that she had sent her message in the shaman's native language. He responded in a soft voice.

"Evita has asked for me to be your guide in meeting the medicine of the plants and animals. I agreed, knowing your

connection to my brother in that other land. The jungle has much to teach. This jungle has been calling for our awareness for many years now. I am at your service, respetada senorita."

He bowed his head a little and rose to his feet to collect a blackened pot. Returning to the fire he placed the pot beside the flame, nested on a bed of glowing coals. At that precise moment Evita opened her eyes and spoke in a language that Petra could not understand at all and yet there was familiarity in the sound.

"Ngali na jugun, ngali narima mala jugun, wana junjma mala gunu gala jugun, ngali wana junja mala jugun, ngali na mala jugun. So we begin."

When the water began to tumble, Basilio reached into a small hessian bag, drew out a grey powder and dropped it in. Five large pinches were deposited in this way, each followed by a few words, prayers invoking earth, water, air, fire and ether. The pot bubbled and a cloying aroma filled the air in the hut. Basilio lifted the vessel from the fire and placed it on a flat stone to cool.

Rising to his feet once again he walked a few steps to the eastern wall and adjusted a stone painted yellow, turned it once then lit a smoke-stained yellow candle. Muttering as he walked, he stepped to the wall in the south, turned a red stone three times and with three fingers stirred water into a shallow, red bowl. He stepped around the circle to the west, turned a black stone twice and dipped two fingers into a bowl of dark soil. As the final step he moved to the north wall, turned a white stone four times and placed four feathers on a ceramic platter.

He returned to the centre fire and dropped a powdery substance into the flame. Their faces glowed with an eerie light as the fire flared and hissed. Taking his seat once again beside the fire, he reached over to collect a wooden ladle, dipped it into the liquid five times before drawing it out to fill two engraved, bone tumblers. Steam rose from the cups. Muttering something unintelligible he picked up one of the cups, placed it to his lips and drank. When he had emptied the cup he placed it back on the ground and passed the other to Petra. She followed his lead

and drank all the contents of the second cup then placed it down beside the first.

"Growing in the shadowed, wet places this medicine teaches us that new life emerges from death and decay. Travel with me on a journey into hope. Travel with me on a journey where life asserts its endless courage. Travel with me in the knowledge that nothing will harm you, where clarity comes in the knowledge that beings from many realms are walking with you, my sister, Petra". He began to sing in a low deep voice, chanting with a steady cadence and rhythm. To Petra his cadence seemed to keep perfect time with the flickering of the flames of the fire.

The warm liquid sat uncomfortably in her stomach. Petra felt she might vomit. She looked across at Basilio. His face was calm. He nodded and said, "At first it feels uncomfortable, senorita, but stay with me. It will soon change." They sat in silence for almost thirty minutes before the journey began. The shaman began to sprout wings, eagle wings shining with glossy, brown and black feathers. As she watched all of his body took on the shape of a majestic eagle, firelight dancing on every feather. He spoke once again.

"Look to yourself."

Petra looked down and saw that she too had transformed, though her colour was pure gold. She lifted one arm to witness a magnificent golden wing spread outward at least three metres. This time, without words, his voice sounded in her head. 'Yes, we are one and two, now come with me.' With a single movement he rose from his place beside the fire and took to the air. Petra stretched her wings and in a moment was soaring above the hut beside the shaman. The mountains called them. Basilio and Petra answered. The earth raced beneath them until they had risen far above the tree-line, giant wings suspending them in the cold air. Their fine-tuned senses collected every tiny shift in the movement of air so that the earth raced beneath them as they danced the thermal breezes.

'Where are we going?'

'There is a place deep in the jungle. First, we go there. Now ask no more questions. Stay with me.' Basilio plummeted from the sky beside her, wind whistling through his wings. Just a single movement of one giant wing and Petra followed. Beneath her she could see fine details of trees, forest, roads, streams and rivers. Where people gathered, the roof of every building gouged holes in the landscape and lights shone incessant and blinding. From each of these a crimson thread stretched to the next township. To her eagle eyes these threads seemed somehow malevolent and incongruous with the balance, peace and freedom of the open spaces between. She determined not to concentrate on the crimson matrix.

Her eyes were drawn to the beauty of the dense forest. A billion trees towered from steep slopes, each one of them reaching up to her, asking her to choose them as a place to land, a rest for the golden eagle. Each of them had a voice that sounded or felt older than time itself. The result was like a song sounded by a choir of millions. Petra scanned the sky to find her companion, that other giant eagle she knew as Basilio.

She saw him, a tiny speck heading towards the cleft of a deep valley under a colossal mountain. She followed his lead, dipping a mighty wing to race through the cold air. Down, down to soar one hundred metres above a raging river rushing across rocks and stones, pooled in giant waterholes writhing with muculent, sinuous eels and wet scaled, darting, silver fish. The two giant eagles circled here, glinting eyes scanning every tiny detail as though they enjoyed the full light of day.

From this tempestuous, untamed wilderness, Petra could feel a throbbing pulse, a frequency deep and strong. Floating on this frequency infused her with infinite energy. Her golden wings quivered with its potency. The trees continued their song for her, yet here, the river also sang, so too the rocks and stones, the water joining in with impossible falsetto.

Every creature, every tree, every stone, every drop of dew or tumbling stream, every mass – everything – joined in the song. As they did so, the frequency of the sound ascended, the

energy of the song compounded. Petra, Golden Eagle Dancing absorbed the magic of the song, felt power surge through her in an unquenchable ecstasy. Eagle sight was surmounted as an even greater clarity ensued. She could see life coursing through everything, flowing through even the rocks and stones in an irrepressible stream, joyful in being witnessed. In her mind a phrase formed.

Everything... Everything is immutably alive.

Everything pure boundless energy, pressed into being from the space in between which was nothing but energy itself, ready to be expressed into matter.

'Basilio, I......' She could not find words, not even in soul-speak. Instead a shrill, shrieking whistle emitted, echoing up and down the valley. It was perfect. Petra Golden Eagle Dancing was the perfect soloist in the magnificent, multitudinous choir of life.

Again she called, this time with full intent. The sound that issued wheeled and danced between the mountains before crashing against towering cliffs and resounding deep into the valleys. As her call returned to her she felt every living thing in that place amplify their life force. This conglomerate of energy was then thrust, in a giant surge of power, direct into her golden eagle heart. She shrieked again, this time in exquisite joy and ecstasy, the energy flooding through her, strengthening her wings and her will, making her eyes keener still.

A rush of errant wind buffeted her. Her attention returned to presence. Floating on widespread wings in midair, she heard her eagle brother, Basilio.

"It is time to go, little one."

Basilio wheeled and danced around her on thermals lighter than air, calling her to fly with him. He too exuded an aura of power and life that defied description. Petra Golden Eagle Dancing followed him as they waved their power-filled wings to climb from the valley, up and still further up into the realms of heaven. The entire landscape became life in miniature.

From here a bright green-gold beam shone upwards from the place they had been. From the shadows of that deep valley,

pure life-force thrust far into the heavens. As the two of them climbed still higher, similar glows could be discerned across the surrounding regions, Basilio's shamanic brothers and sisters at work. The valley from which they had come outshone them all.

'Why is that valley we journeyed so bright, Basilio?' Soulspeak had returned. She turned her majestic head toward him. 'You can see that too?'

'Of course I can, little one. It is as she suspected, sister. Evita has been imagining that you will be a profound influence in this drama that is unfolding. She has assigned me to take these journeys to assist both you and her in proper discernment. It seems she was right, as she usually is. You received a greater blessing from that sacred place than I have ever witnessed or had the opportunity to share. It is a very significant thing. Now come. We must return.'

With that the eagle that was Basilio flapped his giant wings and began to climb even further into the heavens. Petra Golden Eagle Dancing followed suit and soon they viewed the entire continent. Though the air was thin and cold, both grand eagles breathed with ease. Warmth that could not be overcome coursed through their bodies extending even to the tips of their massive wings. As they sailed in the frail air, to their right they became aware of a single, shining thread of multicoloured light, glittering fragility as a rainbow infused with icicles.

'This light, this shimmer is the connection with the place you will go as the time becomes right, sister. This is the land where the balance hangs teetering on the brink. It is there that all will come to be or everything will come crashing down around you and all of humanity. The great southern land is fundamental to everything that is now your reality. When your teachings are complete here, you will walk again. In perfect timing that ancient dominion will be your landing place.'

Basilio's soulspeak was potent and self-assured in this realm. None of the halting uncertainty was present. It was as if he belonged and was at home here rather than in the world in which Petra had met him several days earlier. She asked him.

'Is this your place, Basilio? You feel more real here.'

'It's true, little one. Again you demonstrate why Elias has selected you. It is unusual for me to stay long in the relative dimensions. My journey has been on other planes since my teacher took me when I was thirteen years old. Now let us return to Evita. You have witnessed the power of the energy of life and have perceived the interference. This teacher plant has imparted the body experience, the genuine knowledge that we came here for you to learn. Time to return. Come.'

The great, brown eagle dropped one wing and the sound of rushing wind called Petra Golden Eagle Dancing to plummet from the stratosphere, down, down, down until she was rushing and wheeling above the tree-line. The earth was close now. The trees cried out to her as she flew by. She saw the tiny hut, smoke drifting from the chimney. Feathers sheared off in a flurry behind her, her face shifted into human form. She felt a warm hand on her shoulder.

"Petra Golden Eagle Dancing, welcome back. There is hot tea beside you. It will warm you after your journey." It was Evita. The sound of her voice was soothing and welcoming. Petra's body shuddered as she opened her eyes. The fire flickered in front of her. She felt a magnetic attraction.

"Take your time. Don't fall into the fire. Bring yourself back here with me, Petra. Congratulations on your sacred name. Do you recall it?" She gripped her shoulder with a reassuring firmness.

"Golden Eagle Dancing."

"Yes my darling, Golden Eagle Dancing. It suits you so well. You were, and are, magnificent my dear.

Tears flooded Petra's cheeks and spilled into her lap. The light of the fire danced across her face. In that shifting light she morphed once again into the magnificent bird she had become.

"What have we done, Evita, what have we done?" She sobbed her grief and her whole body shook with those sobs.

"Nothing we cannot attend to, sweetheart. That is why we are all here. It is all in perfect time. You and I and everyone

who has begun the journey are the ones we have been waiting for all these years. Concentrate on the power you felt. Focus on the energy you received. Drink tea."

She lifted the cup and held it in front of her until Petra wrapped her hands around it, drew it to her lips and took a deep draught. Evita stepped around her to a small pile of timber. Selecting a few logs, she placed them on the fire and blew a little. The flames soon doubled in size and brightness. Petra noticed that Basilio was opposite her, a satisfied smile on his face, hair dishevelled. Evita leaned in to kiss him on the crown of his head, smoothing down some of that chaotic, windblown thatch with hands that glowed with their own tender light.

"Thank you, Basilio. You are a blessed soul, my friend." Once those few words had been uttered Petra could have sworn that Basilio vanished. She shook her head, rubbed her eyes and looked again. A crumpled pile of blankets and animal skins moved against the wall. She noticed that the head protruding from the mess of blankets was his.

In silence, Evita and Petra sat with beakers of tea in cupped hands until light shone through the window announcing a crisp, clear, sunny morning. In unison they rose from their place beside the fire, traversed the few steps to their beds and lay down to sleep a dreamless sleep.

Later that day, Evita was first to wake. She checked on Petra, adjusting her blankets and tucking her in a little, as a mother might. Brushing her hand across Basilio's brow, she sent him energy from hands that shone as they moved across his forehead.

"Rest, my friend, we can take a break today and journey with the mother vine tomorrow. Tonight I'll prepare us a broth with which Petra and I can break our fast without upsetting the mother." With that she left him to collect a large cast-iron cauldron from the bench under the window. She placed it by the fire, set a tripod above the flame and suspended the cauldron of broth over the flickering flames. She reached into the wood-pile and added five faggots to the fire to heat their dinner. Petra woke

in the midst of this and observed Evita with fondness. A flash of realisation came. Evita emitted something with remarkable similarity to that which she had observed in Basilio. She looked even closer. Evita was somehow not quite solid.

'You are right, Petra. Both Basilio and I have already taken the quantum leap that all of this is about. We are assigned to guide and assist as we are able. This is what we are doing with you right now. It's a genuine honour to be ordained to this because you are so elemental, so fundamental.'

Petra shuddered and drew the blankets a little tighter about her shoulders.

"It makes me quite nervous when you share that you see me this way, Evita. I don't feel fundamental. I feel surprised and confused about almost everything that is happening. I know that there are some incredible shifts occurring but I don't understand what is going on, nor what I have to do with it." She sat up and leaned on one arm, a quizzical look on her face. Evita smiled her gracious smile and replied.

"Be patient, little one. In just a few days I believe you will have much greater insight. Now come and have some broth. It will provide you with much needed sustenance." Petra sat near the fire and took the deep bowl Evita passed to her. Steam rose from the bowl and a delicious aroma pervaded the room. They ate together in silence, firelight flickering on their faces. Tomorrow would arrive soon enough and could not be visited until it became today.

When Petra finished the warm broth she felt better. She wandered outside to gaze upward at a shiver of shimmering stars while they, in turn, gazed down. To the north in that fantastic, expansive sky she noticed one bright light was a gleaming, glittering golden-green.

Petra perceived it as it moved in infinitesimal increments, closer with every second.

CHAPTER FORTY SEVEN

In the foothills of the Rocky Mountains the morning came clear and ice cold. A bitter wind had cleansed every last vestige of fog. Every in-breath was sharp. With every out-breath an opaque nebula rushed away on the chill wind. Brianna and Toby rose first and bumped everything in the camp but for Raniyah's tent and Toby's tiny camp stove. Perched on that and just beginning to bubble was a small percolator. The smell of coffee washed away on the wind.

"Ran it's time to go, kiddo." Toby shook her tent a little to rouse her. "Coffee's ready."

No response. No movement at all.

"Raniyah. Are you OK? Time to get moving, sis, come on." A long, slow groan sounded from inside. "Ran!"

Silence.

"Oh shit, Ran, are you OK?"

Another quiet, agonised groan. Toby moved fast, crouching down to unzip her hiking tent. The zip caught on fabric. Toby tore at it until it gave way and the zip flew open. One more zip to go and Toby was in. Raniyah was contained in her sleeping bag, unnaturally still.

"Bree, get the first aid, top of my pack." He unzipped the bag and rolled her onto her back. She was pale as snow. Toby pressed his hand to her forehead and picked up one of her hands. Both were cold. He leaned down to put his cheek next to her mouth and nose. She was breathing, but only just.

"Fuck! Raniyah, what the fuck! Bree, have you got that kit?"

"Here."

"In the left-hand side foldout there's smelling salts."

She unlidded the small brown bottle and passed it in. Toby slid his hand under her head and positioned the mouth of the bottle near her nostrils. As Raniyah breathed in the smelling salts had an instant effect. Twisting her body as though in pain, Raniyah raised her head a little to see her brother looking ghostly-pale, dark-browed and worried.

"Toby? What's happening...?" She whispered. Her voice slurred as though still in half-sleep.

"I don't know, Ran. Just relax. We'll get you sorted out." Raniyah attempted a smile but it turned to a grimace. She closed her eyes and sank back, wavering in and out of consciousness. Her body shuddered a little each time she woke. To Toby's relief her breathing remained steady and even. He soulspoke to Brianna.

"Bree, can you grab everything? Put it in one place. Check the GPS. Nearest road with any traffic is about three kilometres from here. I'm going to carry her out."

In less than five minutes they were moving. On his back a light daypack contained a few essentials. Raniyah was caught in Toby's arms like a child, still wrapped in her sleeping bag. She continued to breathe shallow breaths but showed little other sign of life. Though she was quite a significant load, as she was deadweight, Toby carried her with ease. Some of that was due to his discipline in maintaining his strength and fitness. Much of it was the knowledge that his sister needed him – was dependent on him. He would not let her down.

Brianna too was loaded, Toby's pack strapped to her chest and her own on her back, more than forty-five kilograms in all. Strength was also part of her daily regimen but on this day, need drove her further and faster than muscle.

In a little over an hour, half jogging, half walking, Toby pushed through thick undergrowth and thistle to emerge onto a well used, well maintained, gravel road. Lowering his sister to the ground, Toby emptied the daypack to unfurl a sleeping mat. He slid her onto it, bunched a towel into a makeshift pillow

and slid it under her neck and head. Icy wind continued to unnerve the day, pouring through the tunnel of the road with more insistence than in the scrub. Beads of sweat from his effort froze on his face.

Brianna appeared less than two minutes later, a determined look on her face. She unlatched the two heavy rucksacks and deposited them without ceremony at the edge of the road. Sweating profusely she sat on her own bag. Exhaustion etched the contours of her face. After loosing her water bottle and taking a long draught she proffered it to Toby. He took it and drank.

"What now, Toby?"

"We call for help. We wait." He looked concerned with the helplessness of his own response.

"How is she?"

"It's hard to tell. She's staying warm and her breathing is weak but steady. Her pulse is the same. I have no idea what has done this. She has no wounds and she's been with us the whole time. Same water, same food." He retrieved a cell-phone from one of the pockets in his trousers, pressed it once and waited for the screen to light. He paused a moment and spoke to Brianna.

"This is going to bring us way into the open, Bree. I hope I'm doing the right thing."

She nodded and said, "Call."

Toby dialled 911. It was answered in seconds. He reeled off the answers with military efficiency then hung up.

"Twenty minutes."

Ten minutes later as Toby was tending to his sister with water and yet another vital signs check, there was the sound of a motor. Brianna heard it first as she had wandered five hundred metres up the road to provide an early warning. Since the attack at their home they remained cautious and vigilant. She sent a brief message in soulspeak. 'Vehicle coming' and both Brianna and Toby stood in a 'ready' pose.

What greeted them was nothing like the two possibilities they had both imagined. An old farm truck came trundling along the road toward them. Brianna had hidden from view so the

truck roared past her, ground down several gears and stopped beside Toby, motor rumbling.

"Need some help?" Her strong Canadian accent made it clear that she was a local farmer. Toby peered into the cab of the old truck to see a woman, perhaps sixty years old but maybe a little older, her skin browned by years outside in sun, wind, rain and more. Toby paused for a moment then replied,

"My sister has had a turn of some sort. We've called for an ambulance. It should be here in ten minutes or so."

The woman coughed, cleared her throat and spat out the window onto the road before continuing.

"Yes. The ambulance. Good. Trouble is, young man, it's not going to get here before those damn folk you messed with the other day. Your call informed them precisely where you are. It's a good thing this wind is blowing hard or they'd have been here by chopper. Put her and your girl there in the back and you jump in here. Quick now, no time to waste."

She smiled at him and motioned with a flick of her head for him to get started. It was an invitation and a command.

Once a decision had been taken and he moved into action Toby was competent and systematic. He unhitched the rear tray of the old truck and dropped it down to reveal a nest of blankets and cushions where Raniyah would fit. There would also be sufficient room for Brianna to stay to attend to her. Toby walked back to collect Raniyah, lift, carry and lower her into the rough bed. He shot a soulspeak message to Brianna to let her know that all was well and that she would travel in the rear of the truck. She shot back.

"Are you sure about this, Toby? Who is this?"

Both of their jaws dropped when their soulspeak was interrupted by the old woman 'soulspeaking' to them both from the cabin.

"Get in the truck, sweetheart. You too, handsome, there's no time to waste. We need to go now."

It was enough. No further discussion was necessary. Brianna tossed in her pack and jumped in beside Raniyah,

placing her aikido 'jo' at the ready as she went. Toby slammed the back hard, grabbed his pack, tossed it in the cabin and climbed in. The old woman already had the old truck in gear and took off with a roar. She spent almost as much time looking in the cracked, spider-web-grimy, rear-view mirror as she did watching the road ahead. The truck roared and retched its way to its top speed as the old woman ground and crunched through gears. At forty miles an hour it was not a getaway car. It was no more than a thought entering his mind when the old woman said.

"We're not going far, handsome. Don't you worry, we'll get away. I've got this covered." She swerved the old beast hard to the right into a rough creek washout. While the old truck rattled, groaned and sputtered, it kept on. One hundred metres along the creek between a stand of firs on both sides a wide doorway opened into an immense tunnel, chiselled out of solid rock. The woman slowed the truck to a crawl. There was just enough room for it to fit in that space. As she moved it forward the mirror on the passenger side caught a little and cracked again.

"Damn it!" She spat the word into blackness as behind them a door slid shut. The cold wind stopped. All light was obliterated.

Toby reached into a pocket to find his torch but by the time his fingertips touched the cold aluminium case, the old woman lit a yellowed cabin-light. Blinded by the glare he held up his hand to shield his eyes. The old woman's face came into view, her green eyes shining.

She reached a gnarled brown paw around the steering wheel and shook Toby's hand.

"Nice to meet you, Toby. Name's Awhena. You can call me Aphee. We'd better get those two out of the back, huh? We don't want to keep old Kopanuk Mountain Dreamer waiting too long. She gets more and more impatient the older she gets and she's four times my age so she's getting pretty long in the tooth."

She chuckled, climbed out and slammed the truck door behind her. Almost in the same instant her brown face was back, looking at Toby through the open window.

"Come on then. Pick up your jaw, pretty boy. Your girls are keen to get out."

It wasn't quite true. In that instant both Toby and Brianna disengaged from the reality of the cold mountain cave. Eyes glazed over, they journeyed to a dimension they were called to by Elias. Raniyah too lay inert, not present either, eyes dull but drawing soft, short breaths.

Outside that womblike cave, in a sky bedazzled by stars, one green star shone brighter still.

And drew closer.

CHAPTER FORTY EIGHT

The more Valda Balaz pondered what she had gleaned from her visit to that etheric realm, the more furious she became. It was transparent to her that the damned old wizard, wisdom-keeper Elias had made the Call.

That changed everything.

One fucking ceremony which Elias and perhaps three other beings on earth had the capacity to conduct, had been activated. It meant this physical world and several of its surrounding dimensions were now on high alert for more significant change than had been experienced for many thousands of years. It was the very change she had vowed to prevent.

The last cycle ending had been a debilitating, stultifying turmoil. Upheavals had occurred which were now so ancient that the only memory of them, with the exception of one small circle of individuals, was bound in stasis and mystery. Giant and impossible stone structures, pyramids of immense power stationed all over the planet marked the detritus of that dominion. The reign of power that followed, which had consumed an expansive, exquisite, ancient era was the reign she was bound to.

Through thousands of complex ceremonies and labyrinthine ritual she had gained her authority, immense influence and ascendancy. With his one damned, simple ceremony, delivered at the right moment by the only being on earth with the gall to deliver it, Elias Dirawong had started a chain of events that would require all her skills and training to overpower. If that were possible at all.

It was so much more than that. The reign that had been defended for millennia by the powerful being to which she was

indentured was therefore under direct challenge. Her instructions and guidance were unequivocal. She intended to carry out her instructions with extreme prejudice. She was cognisant of the old story in visceral detail.

She had learned through pain and fear that the being which guided and empowered her was determined to prevent the cycle taking its natural course. The infinity loop, the spiral of life, the torus of energy and power was to be subverted. She had been appointed to spearhead the subversion. Long ago she had given her heart and soul to become a servant to the will of that being.

She would not, must not, permit the likes of Elias to interfere.

Standing straight, swaddled in a majestical, patterned, traditional, silk kimono, Valda Balaz stood in front of a flawless, stainless-steel panel. Her iris was scanned in less than a second. A smooth, polished-stone door slid aside with a sibilant hiss. She walked into the enclosure to stand in front of a gigantic picture-window overlooking the township of Thun and the beautiful Thunersee. The Swiss Alps towered in ancient majesty as a monumental backdrop.

A small portion of her citadel bustled with tourists. The activity provided an appropriate cover for the perfect condition in which the castle was maintained. Billions had been spent to convert the remainder into an expansive, secure and private fortress. It was the perfect location for Valda to conduct her business, secure in the knowledge that, in this place, there was nothing that could touch her unless by her will.

Valda rarely chose to be touched. When she did choose so it was in order for her to do what was necessary to maintain her youth. All her other essential needs and desires were supplied in her absence during the four hours each day when she retired to her inner sanctum and locked the door behind her. If she still had access to human emotion, she would have found her existence to be an unbearable loneliness. As it was, she revelled in her solitude and power.

Sun poured liquid gold into her operations room as it peered between Swarzhorn and Ritzlihorn. She spoke the word "screen" and the intensity of the light diminished as one of the internal panes of polarised munitions-grade glass moved infinitesimally. A paler light played on her flawless skin but that could not mask the very real anxiety that sat within her every thought. Knowing that she must contrive a strategy for dealing with Elias and doing it was the matter that consumed her.

She knew him to be a powerful and significant being. He had demonstrated his confidence and authority by making the Call. Many others across the generations had considered taking such a bold step.

Each of them had paused and thus faltered. His audacity, his bloody impertinence must be dealt with. She paced the room, backwards and forwards in front of that massive window, under the eyes of those incredible mountains underscored by a network of underground tunnels that connected her with anywhere on earth she desired to be.

None of the grandeur, nothing of the exhaustive underground matrix of her subterranean labyrinth, none of her own skills was bringing her any closer to determining how to eradicate the being called Elias. Through all of time Valda knew him by many other names. It was time to bring an end to his influence.

The scent of coffee signalled that she could partake in her morning ritual. She broke the pattern of her pacing and padded with bare feet almost silent on the golden-hued hardwood floor. She recalled with satisfaction the moment she had ordered her floor to be cut from the last three trees of their species. Those trees had survived everything that more than a thousand years in a remote dense, wooded valley on the Australian island state of Tasmania could deliver.

They hadn't survived Valda Balaz. They were now no more than the subject of the soles of her feet.

A bitter smirk crossed her perfect features as Valda considered her own bleak humour. Valda took her cup from a

purpose-built niche and sniffed the fresh coffee before touching the rim of the polished-bone cup to her lips. As she did this something conjured others into the tapestry that bound her every thought on this morning.

Others that had the capacity to create complications would also need to be dealt with, though the loss of Elias would cast them into disarray. She knew that she was, as yet, unaware of all of those that conspired for her failure, but she had identified several of them.

A chime sounded. Turning to an expansive oaken table that served as her private desk she said "on". An image appeared.

What is it, Hazred?" she demanded, piqued to have her silence and solitude disturbed. The image wavered. Dr Hazred sniffed before speaking.

"The subject has come through the operation success-fully, Madame." He replied in a simpering tone. "A complete success has been achieved in physical terms. There is still some resistance at a mental and emotional level but that was to be expected."

"When will that resolve, Doctor?" Valda said. "He's of little use to us until then."

"Well, the DNA altering inoculation from Verity Global has been effective. When he loses control I can settle him instantly and comprehensively. I am unaware whether that method will continue to be effective considering his, er......., 'hybrid' nature. It will be perhaps another week or perhaps two before I can be certain."

The doctor scratched his nose then tweaked it, aware that his every movement was monitored in every detail by this woman.

"You can control him?" She spoke this as though to herself rather than to the doctor.

"Yes. In proximity the result is instant. I haven't had the opportunity to trial it at distance."

"The insert was added too, yes?"

"Of course, Madame, as you required. It is placed at the base of his skull. It has also appropriated perfectly."

"So theoretically, I can influence him from here right now." She smiled. The beginning of a solution began to present itself.

"Theoretically yes," Dr Hazred replied, "though I wouldn't recommend it at this stage."

"I don't give a damn what you recommend, Doctor. Are you in the clinic now?"

"No Madame, I'm about to go into a meeting on the other side of the city."

"Cancel it. Go to the clinic now. Wake him, disturb him. Make him angry. I want to see what he is capable of. I want to see what I can do with him and what use I can make of him. Rouse me when that's done."

"But............"

The image disappeared as Valda said "off".

Encouraged, Valda strode across the room, stepped into a small alcove and said "up". The lift moved until it vanished, leaving no trace that the alcove existed. She emerged into a pyramid-shaped room fashioned in the ziggurat of the chateau. On every surface was painted a myriad of symbols and sigils that spoke of antiquity, designs long forgotten by all but a few. Valda smiled. She intended to be at her very best. She intended to remove the challenge of Elias. She would access a massive dose of adrenochrome. She would not underestimate his power.

The convolution of tortuous, strange and beautiful symbols caught her attention as they were intended to do. She was reminded that these symbols in this arrangement were capable of conjuring power beyond the imaginings of the rabble this world called 'humanity'.

"No better than cattle, a plentiful resource." She muttered incoherently as she dropped her kimono to the floor and walked forward to adjust the numerals on a display. She set it to twelve litres.

"Just to be sure," she whispered.

In the centre of the room stood a plinth of solid quartz supporting a sarcophagus-like box, made from gold, silver and copper. Like the rest of the room, it was inscribed with a myriad of etchings and hieroglyphs. She climbed five stone steps to stand on top of the plinth beside the coffin, then stepped into it and lowered her body to lay on a soft, down mattress lined with silk, her head facing directly east.

Using a small circlet of rubber tubing to stop the flow of blood beyond her bicep, she struck the inside of her left elbow six times with the first three fingers of her right hand.

Reaching for two catheters installed on small gold hooks, she first inserted one long, superfine needle into a vein at the top of her inner thigh. Once in place she inserted the other slender needle into the upraised artery at her elbow. She released the tourniquet and placed it on the rim of the sarcophagus.

Her head lay on a cushion that morphed as a living being to shape itself around her, embracing and enfolding her shoulders, neck and head. She closed her eyes. Several of the sigils on the exterior of the sarcophagus began to glow. Her presence in the space activated them.

A warm, viscous, carmine-hued fluid began to pump through the needle into her arm. The blood she had been using for the past week began to ooze in an amplifying stream out of her body, through the catheter attached to her inner thigh.

CHAPTER FORTY NINE

On the third day, Evita rose an hour before dawn to bustle about, setting the fire and the room. In every single nook and cranny a candle was placed and lit until she had one hundred and sixty nine candles burning.

They flickered and fluttered with her every movement.

Around the fire she first placed charcoal-grey, woollen blankets, three deep, covering every centimetre of bare floor. On top of this, whilst mumbling incantations, she spread multicoloured runners a metre wide, one for each cardinal direction. In between each of these she placed two long triangles of coloured fabric, the point towards the fire and the wide end making the circle, bound by stones placed to the north, south, east and west for the previous ceremony.

"That's so beautiful, Evita." Petra woke as Evita completed the final processes in the setup of the room.

"Thank you, darling. Yes, beauty has quite a lot to do with it. The number of candles is important, the number of divisions in the circle also significant. It is very important that we tend the fire consistently from this moment on."

She stepped away from the centre to view her handiwork.

"The centre of the circle, the hub of the wheel is critical to the alchemy we are creating. It is the place of the element of ether, the place where the life force of all and everything is contained. Can I ask you to be my fire chief and keep our fire burning today?"

"I'd love that." Petra enthused.

"The wood stack is there under the window. Keep the fire alive but it doesn't need to burn the house down." She smiled

a small smile and made her way to Basilio's sleeping place, collecting one blanket at a time to fold and deposit in a neat pile beside his pillow. Petra selected a few small sticks from the wood stack and added them to the fire.

"What do you have in store for me today, Evita? I can feel something reaching out to me. It feels like the jungle. A sinuous feeling, inescapable....."

Petra's description took her by surprise.

She turned her face her and said, "As all of this unfolds, Petra, as all of these happenings and adventures confront you, please bring all your awareness to the clarity of your intuitive perceptions. They astound me. You have just begun, yet you exhibit skills that shaman with decades of training are unable to access. Respect your gift and you will enhance it."

"Yet still I am not sure what you have in mind for me."

Laughing out loud, Evita finished her tidying. She stepped up to grasp Petra by her elbows.

"In a little while we will be asking the mother vine to teach us, Petra Golden Eagle Dancing. She is called ayahuasca. For this journey, in order to fashion and create a leadership circle, I will be joining you, as will several others. Your intuitive sense serves you well. She is the jungle and she is sinuous and she does reach out to those for whom she has a message. If you are feeling her with such clarity as I begin the preparations for the ceremony it is likely she will deliver you a powerful message. It is likely she will call you into remembering."

A little after midday, the fire burning bright and each of the candles adding light to the room, Basilio returned to the room accompanied by a startling, beautiful, South-American, teenage girl and a handsome young man around the same age. They bore a large pot of viscous, brown liquid in a steel pan, blackened by fire. As they entered the room Basilio took a moment to bow to Evita. To Petra's complete surprise he turned to her and bowed once more, touching his forehead to the ground in front of her. She stepped forward to hug him.

"Basilio, I should be bowing to you."

"Nonsense, Golden Eagle Dancing, the honour is mine."
They hugged a long deep embrace.

Over the next hour more young people arrived. Not one
of them was more than twenty years. Each of them seemed to
Petra to be more beautiful than the previous one. In all, the
company became thirteen, including Evita, Petra and the wraith-
like presence that was Basilio. Five beautiful young women and
five handsome young men moved into place, finding their way
to the edge of the circle. Each lowered themselves onto small,
ornate cushions, their legs folded under with hands clasped
loose on their laps.

"Who are these beautiful, young people, Evita? What are
they doing here?" Petra whispered to Evita when they had all
filed in and settled around the fire.

"They are the future, Petra. They are the reason all of us
are here. What other possible reason could we have for bringing
these new days into place? They are the future and we must all
travel together."

Basilio beat a round, flat drum five times. He sat close to
the fire and passed the drum and beater to the young woman
sitting in the South-Sou-West of the circle. She took it and began
beating a soft, steady, heartbeat rhythm. Motioning to Evita and
Petra, Basilio called them to take their place on the wheel.

Evita was directed to sit in the East where a space and
cushion had been left for her. Petra looked around to find that
the remaining place and a larger cushion had been left for her
in the direction of the South-Sou-East.

On the left of her place sat a petite curly-haired girl draped
in a mustard-coloured shawl. To her right, a shirtless, muscular
young man with vine tattoos, leaf and branch, in a broad curlicue
extending from his left hip, across his back and extended in
whorls to the centre of his chest. Basilio directed her to walk
thrice around the circumference of the circle and claim her seat.

As she did so and the circle was completed, Basilio began
to chant in a language that Petra had not heard before. It took
several minutes of the chant before she began to understand.

She glanced across the wheel to Evita who nodded and offered a small smile in return. The girl beside her rested her hand on Petra's knee, then drew it along her thigh until it rested in the crease between her leg and torso. The young man sitting in the south place of the circle did the same. Petra felt held with a powerful intimacy. She reached out to the left and right and copied them, resting both her hands in their laps. In this way the whole circle was connected and complete. The drumbeat increased pace. Basilio's chanting followed.

As she gazed into the fire Petra was astounded to see the vision of another, similar circle. In her vision there were also thirteen participants but they sat naked. Each face morphed and changed with every passing second. The vision transported her back through time – and yet there was a constant. In the centre of each of those wheels sat Basilio. He looked younger, that was certain, yet he still bore an impossible presence in each of those circles and this one. As she witnessed, she realised that she was the sole other continuous presence.

'You have a powerful awareness, Petra Golden Eagle Dancing. Welcome back. It has been an age. I have been waiting for you with patience for all this time. When we have completed this ceremony, our journey together will also be complete. I welcome this time.' Basilio soulspoke to Petra while continuing his chant over the fire. She gazed at him, surprise in her eyes and replied,

'We have done this before. We have, haven't we? We have done this many times, Basilio?'

He nodded his awareness of her response and of her newfound understanding. He continued his sonorous chant. The drum and his hypnotic drone ceased. The sound that remained was the crackling of fire. Basilio spoke to the encirclement of souls. Petra couldn't be sure if he spoke in English. In her entranced state she might have been hearing any language. She understood every word.

"The mother vine has made her union with chacrona and calls you to hear their message from the plant world. You are

391

called and welcome as you come in peace, seeking knowledge. So now, as you will, partake."

The first to rise was the young man to her left. He walked to Basilio, took the wooden cup from him, held it to his forehead in supplication, muttered a few words that Petra couldn't hear and downed the contents of the cup in one large draft. He thanked Basilio as he returned the beaker and resumed his seat. Basilio refilled the cup, drank it and began to chant again as he dipped it for the third time. The drum restarted and a wooden flute wove its sound between the beats.

One by one the young people of the circle stepped up for their cupful of ayahuasca potion until there were none but Evita and Petra to drink. Evita stepped up to drink and was soon back in her place, eyes shining as she looked towards Petra. At last, Petra stood. As she did she had a strange sense of every stitch of clothing falling away so that she stood naked. The drumming and chanting swirled around her. She remembered the last time she had been here, over two hundred years past, in intimate detail.

Basilio saw her.

He filled the cup and spoke to her in his resounding baritone.

"Welcome home, sister. It is my honour and privilege to serve you once again. Drink deep. Allow me to bring my waiting to an end."

He handed her the cup. She drank. He refilled the cup and passed it to her once more. She drank. He refreshed the chalice twice more and he too drank two serves of the dank liquid. Petra resumed her seat, brushing her hand across Basilio's forehead and crown as she passed, as a mother comforting a child. Tears flowed down her cheeks to drip on the cloth beneath her. In a few minutes her journey commenced. The mother vine recognised her, wrapped her arms around her, coddled her, reassured her and rushed her to the place she chose to reveal.

In this circle the mother was well-known. No-one became ill, rather each of the journeyers sat in ease with this powerful

plant medicine. Though she had a little warning of her place in the circle it soon became clear that Petra Golden Eagle Dancing was intimate with the mother vine and her journeys. She and Evita moved as one in the dreamscape, Evita in flowing white robes and Petra in thirteen shades of green. Each of the young people became representatives of ancient knowledge gathered together in the circle for aeons and aeons.

Together they danced in a realm into which the mother transported them, weaving and wheeling through myriad generations to the beginning of the sacred plant world, accessing lessons otherwise beyond human comprehension. When that journey was done they sat together once more, the chant and the drum holding them each in a place of perfect peace, in balance with all that was green and growing.

The young man to the left of Petra now appeared to be the bearer of the vine. She wound and bound, sinuous and snake-like around his torso. A long tendril extended to the figure that had been Basilio who now appeared as a gnarled and aged tree-trunk, bound to the earth with deep, strong roots. A collective soulspeak began, emanating from the organism that was Basilio. Each of them knew they heard the same words though no language could be identified. The voice was deep, boundless and warm and in the same moment soft, gentle and sweetly persuasive, a maternal coddling.

'Your circle is welcome in my realm and we thank you for your ceremony and your willingness to visit.'

A long pause.

'You are called to usher a new era for this planetary being. You are called by we, the givers of energy to this place you call earth. You are called as many and as one.

It is time for change on this earth, it has been so for some time and it will continue to be time.'

The vine weft and wove around the wheel, writhing and wending its way into every space available in the ceremonial circle.

'It is time to tend to the earth humans, it is time to cease your destructive ways.'

As one, the thirteen souls in the circle began to ascend. Up and up and up they went, perched in the pregnant, impregnable arms of the mother vine. First the valley came into full sight, cold, clear water rushing down the cleft where two ranges meet, charging through the valley to become a mighty river weaving its way to the sea. Every tree, every bush, each blade of grass sang to them from its place on the earth, reached for them, implored them to hear the song, to dance the dream into wakefulness.

The animals joined them.

As they climbed into the sky an omniscient chorus enveloped them, issued from every wolf, bear, mouse and dove, every singing cricket, worms of the soil, bats and bugs, cattle and sheep, tiny flitting sparrows and finches, murders of crows, flocks of starlings and swirling of swallows. Each added voice to an amaranthine choir calling humanity to its blossoming and maturity. Rising still further, the rocks and stones, sand and mud, mountains and deserts sang to them too. Still they rose further until they looked upon the earth to see it as a magnificent blue and green sphere funnelling through space, trailing a brilliant sun, past stars, supernovas and impossible celestial clusters in an infinite void.

Returning full circle, their attentions were drawn with gentle insistence back to the planet they had been gifted to experience. As they observed, wound in the passion of the mother vine, the vision became one of millions of people gathering, dancing, singing and chanting in a kaleidoscopic mandala – intertwined in the mother vine, an endless matrix of leaves, lithe branches and sinews to coalesce every soul with the veritable source of life.

The image deepened and amplified as the mother vine made her final connections to form an endless, perfect pattern, a flourishing flower of life extended to every living being that possessed an open heart and soul. With this final connection

there was a cataclysmic explosion of light. The blue and green planet called earth transformed, released itself from its confines and expressed itself in a realm beyond the confines of physics, of the physical, of the morbid mundane.

Alongside it, the sun was dim.

The mother vine soulspoke once again, this time each of the other twelve perceived Petra to be the messenger. This time, Petra was the mother vine.

"It's time, my friends. You are the bold ones. Come."

Stars glittered, fragile in a pitch-black sky. A wisp of grey, fragrant smoke rose from the tiny cabin. When Petra was able to discern her body and embrace the illusion of separation once again, she and each of their circle of souls were still bound together as they had been when they drank from Basilio's wooden cup. Each hand was caught in profound intimacy, resting in the crook of the legs of those beside them. Her first visual image was Evita smiling the broadest and warmest smile she had ever witnessed. The next was Basilio who still appeared to her as the strong, grounded trunk and roots of mother Ayahuasca but for his extraordinary, bright, shining eyes and swatch of rich, black hair sensually entwined with the sinuous tendrils of the mother.

An hour later the young people left. Each of them took a few moments to thank Basilio and to leave with him a simple gift. Fresh, round, baked, rye and buckwheat loaves, home-grown tobacco, fragrant sticks of herbal cuttings bound together with colourful twine. These gathered at his feet as they blessed him with their offerings. Each sat for a few moments with Evita to share nothing more than a few words and receive a simple blessing. One by one they came to Petra. All bowed, foreheads touching the ground near her feet. She found it incomprehensible that they honoured her in this way and was thus speechless.

As Petra sat with Evita and Basilio that evening, breaking chunks of gifted fresh bread with their hands and dipping it into a thin but spicy vegetable soup, she raised it with them.

"I don't understand why they bowed to me." Evita cast her a piercing look.

"Yes you do."

"But I...."

"Silence, Petra. Look deeper but don't waste my time with this. Eat. Be silent. Tomorrow, we have one final ceremony. Eat now then rest."

Basilio broke another piece of bread, dipped it in his soup and munched, deep in thought. When he was finished he reached out one hand to Evita and one to Petra. Petra felt the mother vine inside her, holding her and taking root in Basilio. In the same moment the mother extended delicate long tendrils of green and brown to Evita. From Basilio, she felt a power like water and minerals rising. From Evita she felt the gifts of air and light descending. In that moment the supplication of the young people in their circle became apparent. The shaman released them both.

"Thank you, Basilio. Quite right." In acknowledgement, Evita offered the shaman a gentle bow.

Next morning dawned bright and fresh. Basilio rose and collected more faggots of aromatic timber for the fire. As Petra woke she realised Evita was not present in the room.

'She is outside, Golden Eagle Dancing. She is engaged in a morning meditation I believe. I'd recommend that you too venture outside. Breathe some fresh air. Perhaps take a walk in the forest. The two who sat either side of you with the mother, Maria and Paolo, are out there too. I am sure they would enjoy your company.'

In her spoken voice Petra responded to Basilio's soulspeak.

"Thank you, Basilio. That sounds so good." She wrapped a woollen shawl around her shoulders and opened the door to step into brilliant sunlight and fresh, cool, mountain air. Just to the left Evita sat in meditation, legs curled beneath her and face exuding perfect peace.

At the edge of the clearing were Petra's two young companions. She realised that she felt a connection with both of them far deeper than their short interaction could account. When

Maria looked over she waved and beckoned her to join them. As she reached them Maria spoke to her.

"Good morning, Petra Golden Eagle Dancing. Welcome to a beautiful day."

"Thank you, Maria."

"Paolo and I are going to the waterfall for a swim. Would you like to come with us?" In the midst of the fantastical journey she had been having it was such a normal thing. Petra felt her whole body respond with a resounding yes.

"I would so love to join you, Maria." She turned to the young man. "Good morning Paolo." He had the kindest eyes Petra had ever seen.

"Good morning, Golden Eagle Dancing."

"Let's go."

Maria took her hand and led her into the jungle via a track that wound through trees and undergrowth as a vine wound its way to the light. Paolo followed. Petra could feel the vigour of them both as they traipsed and tumbled along, Maria chattering without cease and Paolo sharing an occasional thought, his soft baritone sounding too old for the picture of his youth.

Ten minutes later they stepped into a clearing surrounded by towering stone. There was no sign of water but for its sound. Maria led them to a cleft in the rock.

"You'll need to lean down to get through." She edged forward and the walls of stone closed around them. Bending down they moved forward through a tunnel a little more than a metre high and less than a metre wide. Twenty or so small, careful steps and they were through. When Petra looked up she released an involuntary gasp.

Cascading water crashed and splashed from a towering cliff, sending spray and mist throughout the space, dancing and tinkling in dappled sunlight filtered through fresh green growth of trees, tree-ferns and interwoven vines. Native flowers shone blue, orange and gold in the branches of the trees and on the floor of the forest, blossoms of red and violet carpeted

the clearing. The pool was enormous, unfathomably deep and crystalline.

"Come on."

Maria threw off her clothing and plunged into the pool, sending waves across the surface that bounced back from the opposite shore. Paolo followed her, hooting as he dived from a boulder, his suntanned body shining in the dappled light. Petra dropped her clothes on the shore and stood for a moment, naked in the shimmer of mist. She dived into the water. It was cold, not so cold as to shock but cold enough to enliven, to refresh. Underwater, she opened her eyes. Though the water was clear she could not make out the bottom of the pool. As she broke the surface she shrieked in pure joy. For a little while they swam and played as children.

In time the sun-heated shore called them to warm their bodies once more. Petra's shawl provided a perfect blanket. She spread it onto the ancient granite flecked with channels of verdigris serpentine. Maria lay to her right with Petra in the middle and Paolo to her left, just as they had been in the circle. Petra dozed in the warmth of the sun, relaxed and at ease. She came out of her half sleep to the sound of a soulspeak question from Maria.

'May Paolo and I touch you, Golden Eagle Dancing?'

'Yes, of course, Maria. Yes.'

All three made the most exquisite love Petra had ever experienced. After her long journey, her self-imposed hermit lifestyle on that beach in Colombia and the rigours of the past week of fasting, ceremony and plant medicine, she yearned for sensual, sexual, physical touch. As Maria kissed her deeply, gently, sweetly – Paolo entered her. The mother vine returned to worship the magic of their union, connected to earth and water, air and fire. Together they were the centre of that circle of life. They were ether. They were life itself. They were the element from which everything is created and everything destroyed.

Evita found them curled around each other, asleep on the shawl.

"It's time, little ones." Then she laughed. "Well, almost time..." She shed her clothes, stepped onto the same boulder that had been Paolo's launching pad and plunged into the pool. Surfacing on the opposite bank she turned and swam back to them and onto the shore, water sliding and splashing off her body.

"Oh my god, Evita, you are the most beautiful person I have ever seen." Petra could not look away.

"Well thank you, Petra," replied the older woman without the slightest hint of self-consciousness. "Now move it along all three of you. One ceremony remains. These two will experience it with you, Petra. Basilio is waiting."

At the fire Basilio looked as though he hadn't moved at all. His frame was as potent as the wood and his spirit was as ethereal as the wisps of smoke that rose to the roof and trickled upwards and outside. Once they had seated themselves, one placed halfway between each of the cardinal directions, he spoke.

"This is our final ceremony together. We have journeyed with the mycelium, the beings that compose their song from decomposition. We have learned what they teach. We have communed with the mother who weaves her way through the soul of every member of the sacred plant world. She has bestowed her gifts. Today we venture into the dreaming of the sacred animal world. We will witness their message, hear their song and embrace that which we have forgotten in our arrogance and our myopia."

He reached into his pouch and drew out a black, powder-like substance which he deposited, one at a time, into four glass phials set before him. When he was satisfied that the perfect amount had been added to each of the phials, he screwed them into a short, wooden pipe. One by one he did a simple blessing over each pipe and passed them, first to Paolo, then Maria and Evita. Finally, a pipe was passed to Petra.

That too was the order in which the ceremony progressed. When Paolo breathed in the medicine of the toad to the intermittent chanting and flute that Basilio procured and played, he thrashed and tossed and swore and cursed then dropped onto

his back on the cushions lying there to receive him. He emerged a little later, unscathed and wide-eyed. Respectful. Humble. Astounded.

Maria was next. As she drew in the smoke her eyes rolled back. She tumbled to one side and lay motionless. Thirteen times in that journey she sat up without warning. The first three times she laughed out loud. The next three she wept and three more times she babbled in what seemed a nonsensical language. In the last three her eyes opened but what she was seeing was not in the room but in some other place. She lay back and issued a satisfied sigh.

When she sat up the thirteenth time she was silent, arms extended outwards above her head and a beatific smile on her beautiful face.

She emerged from the experience a little later, unscathed and wide-eyed. Respectful. Humble. Astounded.

Evita sat ramrod straight as she drew the smoke from that glass phial deep into her lungs. Throughout her journey that didn't change at all. When she emerged a little later she too was unscathed and at peace as when Petra first met her.

It was Petra's time to journey. In the exact same moment that she had this realisation she sensed the man Elias reaching out to her from beside a small campfire in a ceremony of his own.

"Breathe out, Petra Golden Eagle Dancing, remove all air from your lungs. When you have breathed out every breath of air bring the pipe to your lips and I will set the fire to the phial. Then inhale as you have never done before."

Petra sat still as stone, nervous as hell. She took a long slow in-breath. She expelled it with equal patience until her lungs were empty of air. She looked into Basilio's eyes. He gazed back and soulspoke to her.

'Farewell, Golden Eagle Dancing. You are my greatest honour.'

Petra began to breathe in as the shaman touched the torch-like flame to the glass phial.

By the time she had taken the last of the smoke of that potent substance deep into her lungs, Petra Golden Eagle Dancing was gone forever.

CHAPTER FIFTY

He had to lean down a little to step through the front door of the rustic home he'd built on a small, vacant parcel of the traditional land of his forebears. He'd received clear guidance that it would be a safe haven, a place to call home for long enough. That had proved to be good guidance. He had not been troubled by anyone or anything while he had been here these past eight years. The vegetable garden thrived as though the divas of the plants had been invoked, which of course they had.

Elias wasn't quite sure what it was that sat in his solar plexus after his unexpected ride home. Setting a gas burner aflame, he shifted a stainless-steel pot already quarter-filled with brown liquid onto the blue flame. To his left, beside a small steel framed bed, stood a row of books, propped on a shelf fashioned from a plank on bricks. From this makeshift bookshelf he selected one small volume that emitted the slightest yellow-white glow as he held it. As he opened it and began to shuffle through the pages it flared a little. A curlew feather fluttered to the floor as he found the page he sought, reminding him of fishing on the sand-flats as a boy, listening to the sad call of this mysterious bird.

He spoke into the empty room.

"I hope you got those books put away, old friend and I hope you are on your way. I know we can't talk right now but I'm impatient to say some things to you, so you get here. You bring Cole, Ivy and Robin and you come, brother."

A shrill whistle announced that the water had boiled. He slid the small volume back into place, collected a chipped blue enamel mug from a hook above the cooker, blew in it to clear

out some dust and poured a cup of steaming chai. Lowering his head once again he stepped outside, sat at the base of an acacia tree, leaned against the trunk and began to sip his tea. His face became a picture of serenity as he shifted from tea to meditation, folding his long legs under him.

Three hours passed. The warm breeze became a chill wind. When he opened his eyes to the approach of dusk he made his decision. He would also walk. He would walk this sacred land to inform it and to enquire of it. This land always had a story to share. None of those he had called were even close yet, so he could be absent from here. Thirty-nine days before the equinox he would walk.

He would walk with respect for three days for each of those he had called. He would walk with respect, three days for his own soul.

He would walk a whole new story in a giant wheel around the mountain.

Elias shivered in the chill air. Ducking his head once more, he went inside and placed his mug on the bench. In the same dusty clothes, he fell into bed and slept.

When he woke he set out to find Awhena.

CHAPTER FIFTY ONE

The soft mechanical hum which permeated the entire crucible of the pyramidic room, clothed in solid stone, became a little louder and a little more insistent with every moment. It signalled the completion of Valda's sarcophageal ceremony. While she had looked youthful and flawless prior to the ritual, now everything about her was glowing. The instant she opened her eyes the alarm ceased.

She sat up and winced, perhaps with pleasure, perhaps with pain, perhaps both as she removed first the catheter from her thigh and then the other, replacing the fine hollow needles on their golden hooks. She stood and stepped out of her sigil-embossed coffin.

The kimono which lay akimbo on the cool tile floor was swooped up as she passed. As she wrapped the silken garment around her she stepped into the lift. The door hissed shut with a silky, sibilant whisper. Her voice was equally silken as she spoke just one word.

"Down."

Refreshed, Valda moved into action. Her first call was to Dr Hazred who informed her that their patient was ready.

"Good, connect me to the videocom."

Doctor Hazred did so.

"Go ahead Ms Balaz."

The man in the enclosure still bore a powerful resemblance to Grey Symes but his musculature revealed an influence which summarily surpassed the effects of the regular jogging programme he had adhered to prior to his heart stopping. His musculature appeared to be rippling whilst in complete relaxation.

Facially he was identical, though he appeared significantly more vital. His eyes bore no humanity. That part was now absent.

"Hello, Dr Symes, welcome to your second chance at life. Can you see and hear me without difficulty?"

The creature looked up, part crazed and ready to rage and destroy, part frightened and dangerous.

"Who the hell are you?" Symes demanded.

"My name is Valda Balaz, Doctor and I approved all the machinations that were put in place for you to be subject to a radical and unique surgical procedure. That procedure means you are still alive."

"What have you fucking done to me?" he snarled. A repetitive tic flickered under his left eye.

"It's a process we have been imagining for some time now but you are the first human who has undergone the full procedure with success. You have become a hybrid human being. We replaced your damaged heart and several other organs with organs from a race of beings that have a significant responsibility for the current state of our civilisation. We were determined to retain the skills and abilities of the individual that is now part of you – or perhaps you are part of it. It's difficult to forecast which will take on the dominant role in the long term."

"You've done WHAT?" he growled, "Under whose authority? Who and what is this being? You fucking experimented on me?" His voice progressively shifted to become a deep yet sibilant gnarr. Valda Balaz remained silent for a few moments then also spoke with a similar sibilant tone.

"Pghtsich' it is I. Do you not recognise me? You need to awaken now. We have urgent matters to attend. You are required."

Dr Grey Symes shook his head, fell to all fours, howled in utter anguish and vomited on the polished floor of his reinforced prison. When he looked up there was no physical difference in the man but for those who could see, his auric emanations had become a lambent, florid crimson.

"Do not dare to interfere with me, human." His voice took on the ominous sibilance as he addressed her, eyes locked to hers in rabid fury.

"It's a little too late for that, my old friend. You have been interfered with though you will have no memory of it. Suffice to say that I had need of you and all those things of which you are capable, but I also needed to have control. I have achieved that."

She proffered a small, sepulchral smile.

"I am never controlled by another. When I am out of this place I will find you." He hissed, stood and strode to the glass. He began to pound it, exerting every iota of his enormous strength. The glass shuddered and the pane began to show hairline cracks in three corners.

"Enough, Pghtsich. Stop it! Pay attention."

"Fuck you, woman. You will suff........." He was unable to complete his threat. Clutching his belly, he slumped to the floor writhing and moaning in excruciating pain. Valda caused the frequency to abate and the hybrid who had been Dr Grey Symes lay on the cold floor, rage seething.

"I told you to pay attention, Pghtsich. It was not a request. I require your services in a very important convocation. I remind you that I have taken the initiative to ensure that you comply with my designs. You will stay here for a little more than one month. I would prefer it to be sooner but the timing of this particular convocation must be precise. The timing is paramount for ensuring the power to which we have both been indentured is maintained. Now, old friend, listen closely. I have arranged for you to be able to walk the grounds of the clinic. Do not attempt to move outside the perimeter however as you will feel much the way you did a moment ago, though the impact is substantially higher."

She licked her lips and turned her attention to Doctor Hazred.

"Thank you, Doctor Hazred. That is all I need of you today. Please ensure our friend has the freedom of the grounds as he needs or desires. Make his stay as comfortable as possible and

remember to remain vigilant. You have my permission to restrain him to prevent harm to the property or to himself. Be quite sure he is not harmed."

The Doctor replied, "Yes Madame, understood."

Her image vanished.

The others would be so much less trouble to summon. In each case however, she would be required to carry out the task personally. Valda Balaz made a mental note to discipline Adiputera. Her people had reported that he had changed nothing of his behaviour since their conversation. That was not to be tolerated. A similar strategy to that which now controlled Symes would bring him into line. She smiled at the thought. Yes, that would be satisfactory.

Sitting at the oak table in her fortress apartment she said, "screen".

Once it appeared she said, "Mara Lin".

One by one she summoned each of them. The creature that had once been Dr Grey Symes, Cardinal Ruslan Adiputera, Mara Lin, Simon Chant, Ethan Wahasha, Akashi Agola, Anita Claesson, Abel Rothstein, Rurik Murdek, Chen Jiao-Long, Agnes Adholok and against the will she no longer possessed, Alva Irving.

She instructed them to be present in her castle fortress at Thun three days before the approaching equinox.

When that day arrived, the creature that had once been Grey Symes was transported in a container of solid steel riddled with holes that permitted him air but gave his enormous strength no purchase. Alva Irving was forced to comply under the manipulation of the man who had once been her friend and associate, Simon Chant. Akashi Agola was escorted by two active agents of the CIA who were then executed.

Each of the others arrived cognisant of the role they would play in this subterfuge, this master play.

When they had gathered she drew them into a ceremony of immense complexity and corruption. Following a full day of reciting the ancient texts aloud she arrived in the three-sided

pyramid room and arranged them to align with the structure. Each of them but for Grey Symes was dressed in voluminous robes of dark crimson and blood red. At the base, one to each corner, she positioned Cardinal Adiputera, Anita Claesson and Agnes Adholok.

On the first level, perched three metres above was Chen Jiao-Long, Abel Rothstein and Simon Chant. Each of these held broad bladed swords standing on their points in front of them, their hilts covering heart, chest and face. Their hands bled onto the blade where they clutched the finely-honed cutting edge.

The next level was four metres higher. These three stood first on a narrow platform and were then required, one by one, to step onto a raised plinth gouged out of the pyramid's edge. Mara Lin looked determined to add whatever influence she could, her face set like the stone that surrounded her. Akashi Agola was compliant. Alva Irving was also devoid of free will. Valda Balaz held their controllers on a lanyard, dangling between her breasts.

These three each held an intricately decorated and burnished chalice fashioned from gold, silver and copper. Their heads were held high in a circlet of gold that made it impossible for them to look down without spearing six large needles further into their necks and shoulders.

In the centre of the base, the abomination that had been Dr Grey Symes, the hybrid Pghtsich was wheeled into place in a glass cage half a metre thick. He was naked and rampant, unashamed of his erection. His face was a mask of pure, unadulterated rage.

Above him, at the same three-metre point stood Rurik Murdek. Perched four metres above, his dreadlocks making him appear out-of-place yet potent was Ethan Wahasha.

At the very pinnacle there was gold, shaped like a barely-revealed, crescent moon. In this container stood Valda Balaz, clothed in a crimson-black fabric that was, in the same moment, enchanting and a nauseating putrescence.

In this configuration they desecrated what had once been a sacred and magnificent technology. It was the technology of

exceptional beauty catalysed and sanctified during the last dance of the green. Valda Balaz had spent an age corrupting that power. Now it served her and her master.

Each of the twelve members of their alliance were connected into the pyramid by twin catheters, one in the carotid artery at the base of their necks and one in the femoral artery in the inner left thigh. One small movement of Valda's hand and adrenalized blood began to flow through each of them but for the beast called Pghtsich. He raged inside his glass prison until Valda pressed once on a titanium panel in front of her. He slumped to the floor of his cage, whimpering and shrieking as one hundred and forty four hypodermic needles emerged through the floor to pierce him for the sole purpose of generating excruciating agony.

At the height of his fear and pain the woman began her incantations in a language never borne of planet earth, a language steeped in the fire of a prison planet roiled in interminable war for a thousand millennia. When she fell silent the floor of the pyramid had transformed into a flagellated, fiery, howling vacuity.

The agonising, blistering abomination of abhorrent ritual that Valda Balaz foisted upon Mother Earth excoriated the very substance of the planet. Earth shook and thrust with all the power she could muster to deny the thrall of this heinous ritual but she was unable to prevail. With the sound of a rushing, raging gale she submitted.

Across the surface of the world wherever ancient suppurations had once spewed forth molten rock to feed and bless a youthful earth, an unholy incandescent eruption thrust into the ether, smoke and ash and blood and stone bursting into a smoke-impaled sky.

Yet each of these was nothing compared to the pestiferous conflagration that emanated from the massive caldera within which Elias, Girawong walked for the circle of thirteen. In one hundred and forty-four realms at once the massive, heinous, crimson fire tore stone and earth, air and ether, crystal and

magma in one profane explosion of immeasurable fury to destroy the earth wizard that had dared to make the Call.

Their execrable ritual turned Mother Earth upon herself and upon one of her favourite sons, drawing her fury and her fire, bloodstone and molten magma howling in protest to fuel a fire that had been dormant for aeons.

Their target was Elias, Girawong – sorcerer, earth wizard and deepest of the knowledge keepers. His obliteration would ensure the dominion of her master for millennia. The ritual called for Valda to reach to the very precipice of her power, risking everything to access the searing, mordant venom of her master.

One day before the solstice they completed their rite. Elias, the wheel he walked, the pathways to the hidden labyrinths of the grandmothers and the entire caldera in which he had made The Call was obliterated.

The next day, on the equinox, as never before in all of time, malevolence commanded omniscience and earth wept.

Elias Girawong, the caller of a new earth was engulfed in a fire spanning one hundred and forty-four dimensions.

His passing would be mourned in realms beyond imagining.

CHAPTER FIFTY TWO

Retrieving the scrap of paper that Aphee had given him, his staff and the small book from its place on the shelf he first performed a simple ceremony to bring his awareness to the sacred nature of the journey he intended. When the eucalypt smoke had cleared he began the short walk to the address scratched on her note.

The decision not to carry any belongings came from his personal intention of travelling with minimal supplies so that the earth and the heavens could provide for him without interference. Perhaps choosing the hidden way that Aphee had told him would be available was a kind of interference in divine support, but he had already forgiven himself for the choice. He wanted them to know, wanted them to feel him and be reassured. The passage in the labyrinths and catacombs which she had offered would ensure their knowledge. He found her, tending to a garden brimming with vegetables and herbs, her hands dirt-stained and hair tied in a loose bun on top of her head. Without looking up she greeted him.

"Welcome, brother. I thought it wouldn't be long before I saw you. Come on in. We'll go in the house and I'll make you some tea."

"Bugelbeh, Aphee."

He leaned his staff against the wall outside the front door and followed her in, screen-door creaking behind him as it slammed shut. The truck she drove had created a particular picture of this woman for Elias. The home in which she lived painted a different story. Everything was where it belonged. Elias shuffled his feet on the mat inside the front door.

411

Aphee smiled a big broad smile and said, "Don't you wear a hole in my good mat, young man. Come in and sit down. Don't fuss."

Elias grinned, flopped into a large, green, lounge-chair and looked around. Aphee disappeared into the kitchen. There was a clattering of cups and kettles as Elias discovered a wall covered in books and a myriad of artworks full of story, painted in a traditional way from central Australia, near Uluru. Sash windows, immaculately clean, looked out on her vegetable garden and compact orchard through flowers and innumerable herbs growing in pots lined along the sills. When Aphee returned she was balancing a tray of cups and teapot on one hand and had something else clutched in her other hand. Elias jumped up, took the tray and deposited it on a tiny, round table. They both sat.

"I want you to take this with you, brother. It is a simple thing but it will make me feel a lot better if you would be willing to keep it and wear it."

She opened her hand to show him a pendant made from silver and malachite tied with a leather lace. The green of the stone appeared almost luminous in the sunlight filtering through the windows. She handed it to him, held his gaze for a moment and cupped her hand over his.

"I know what you are about to do. I have the deepest respect. Let us not speak about these things where all that we say and do can be overheard and overwatched." She lifted the teapot, pulled aside a knitted, woollen, tea-cosy and poured steaming tea into two deep mugs. Awhena soulspoke to him.

'Brother, I feel the weight you have to bear at this time and I do not envy you. Few comprehend the import of the work that you have done and continue to do. I am one of those few. You have many allies, many friends who will do whatever they can to aid this transformation that you had the duty and the responsibility to set in motion. The Grandmothers asked me to give you this gift. They asked me to seek your assurance that you will wear it at all times. Will you do this?' Aphee lifted her mug to her lips and slurped.

Elias responded in kind, surprised at how little effort it had taken for Aphee to move from spoken word to soulspeak, though it had been foretold that such things would be remembered and become widespread.

'Of course I'll wear it and bugelbeh, Awhena.' He looked quizzical as he also picked up his mug of hot tea and soulspoke again. 'You say you know what I am about to do. That seems strange to me, Aphee, and nothing much feels strange to me. How can you or the Grandmothers know? I only just came to the decision a few hours ago.

'Did you know your course after some time dreaming?' He nodded.

'There is much that we can still affect and learn in the Dreamtime brother. We are all very close to you. Your journey is ours. You will not and do not walk alone. Many of us walk with you every single moment.'

Awhena shared many things. Elias stayed in her home longer than he had imagined and discovered that even a learned man can learn more if he will take the time to listen. In those few hours Elias became the consummate listener.

"It's time for you to go, brother. Let me show you."

He retrieved his walking staff and she led him back through the house to the back door. Awhena paused to collect four fist-sized stones, one black, one red, one white and one yellow which she dropped into a leather bag. It already contained a large portion of bark from the black wattle trees which grew close to the river. She gave the bag to Elias.

They wove their way through her garden and the orchard to emerge into a paddock of swaying grass lined almost a hundred metres further on by a row of the perfect, white, straight trunks of enormous flooded gums, regimental in the neatness of their array. They walked together through the grass, Elias tapping the ground ahead with the tip of his staff to warn any snake brothers and sisters to get out of the way and not be stood upon.

When they passed the first row of trees the temperature dropped several degrees. Five rows in and the light was so

dimmed by these giants that it took some time for Elias eyes to adjust, though Awhena moved as she had in bright sunshine.

Without warning, she stopped.

"It is here. Place the stones in each of the non-cardinal directions with three metres between them. Sit in the centre place facing west. Hold your staff tight. Are you wearing the stone I gave you?"

Elias nodded and lifted it off his chest for a moment to show her.

"Good. Now then....."

Awhena began a long and complex summoning.

"It is I, Awhena, for all time a member of the thirteen grandmothers. I call all of the sacred ancestors of this man called Elias, all through his grandmothers line going as far back as the beginnings of human on this land, I call especially the dreamtime weaving of the crystalline python that stretches across all of this land and to all of those ancestors woven into the fabric of earth and trees. I call goanna who comprehends the value of patience and inspired action. I call also to..."

The summoning wove on and on as Awhena called Elias ancestors and all the enlightened ancestors of humanity.

Awhena called out next to the dream teachers. She called them as those who guide and direct with wisdom beyond the mind and who reach out to us in the dream, both day and night. The daydream, dreams offered in sleep and the dream in which we all reside were summoned into presence. In a hushed and cautious tone Awhena took time to recognise that universal frequency had taken a Quantum Leap from the imprisonment of one hundred and forty-four to the liberation of one hundred and sixty-nine.

She paid deep and potent respect to the sacred green, the energy-being claiming its right to dance. She paid deep and potent respect to the sacred blue, the sky and the waters reflecting beauty to one another.

Standing still as stone itself, the old woman then reached out to the life-circle dwellers assigned to give and receive

knowledge to Elias. Those who watch and wait, the other twelve sitting forever in circle were asked to bring all the knowledge and memory of all those who had already come into this dimension to learn.

In the final invocation she summoned all the selves, hosts and stands-behinds that wove the dream awake for Elias, from the highest self in this one man to the myriad of representatives that remained alert in previous incarnations.

It took such time that all light left the space. Still she continued. By the time she concluded and spoke to Elias, it was impossible to tell from which direction her voice emanated. It was potent, direct and omnipresent.

"Now speak, brother. Speak to those for whom you walk. Speak of each of them and speak of yourself. As you speak of yourself a doorway will open and you will be granted access to catacombs that are navigated only by those who must. Today you are, without any doubt, one who must. Speak now. Begin, so that the gateway can be revealed to you."

415

Epilogue

Elias stood stock-still for several minutes. Stepping forward he began to gather leaves and sticks, the spilling and offerings of the acacia. Using some of the paper-like bark to spark the kindling into flame he tended the fire until both flickering flame and thick smoke danced into the darkness.

When he was satisfied the fire was as he wished, he began his own invocation. In a deep, pellucid voice he conjured the drawing together of the oneness of every participant of this profound dreaming, this thing called life, this all as one. Circular in design, never ending, building upon the talents, contributions and passions of each and every being who chose it to be so would co-create an irresistible movement into a new humanity.

"I walk with my old and valued friend and confidante, Victor. Brother, what can I say that we haven't already spoken about with one another? May you bring the greatest weaving of this exquisite tapestry that you have ever delivered for you weave the ascension of consciousness as no other. With your enormous heart and soul you affect each and every living being on the planet, raising consciousness so that everyone and everything may walk closer with the divine."

Not far from a dissembled fort, beside a river that had seen some of the foundations of humanity set in place sat Victor, his legs crossed underneath him and a cloak draped across his shoulders. As he sat, soft tears flowed down his ancient face, drawn by the knowledge of his brother that he could discern even now.

"Ah, my brother, we have walked long in these many incarnations, side by side through the ages. I witness your design, your implacable mystery and the love that permits you, nay,

encourages and supports you, to take the next bold step where others would surely falter."

Victor took a deep breath and was transported to a place where he was seated beside that small, ceremonial fire. Elias sat to his left, washing smoke from the fire across his chest and arms and breathing its power into his lungs. Elias spoke.

"Each and every other step in this walk we have had together has been to lead us to this one, my brother. There is no alternative but to embrace what is coming. We have known for some time that it would require the acceptance of enormous upheaval. Do not mourn. Of all those I love, you truly do comprehend the scale of what is occurring here and now. Remember there is no ending. We shall spiral onwards forever. Pray that we recognise one another when next we walk, side by side."

At this Victor was able to conjure a smile through his warm tears.

"I will always recognise you, my brother. I will always stand beside you and know you."

Elias poked at the fire with a stick and looked up at his old friend. "I hear you friend and offer this insight. Some things are beyond our ken. Some things will be strange so that this whole tapestry might unfold as is intended. Though we will always be brothers, there may be times where your denial of me and all that happens here serves the outcome we all know must eventuate. Farewell, my friend." Beside that fire they embraced. As they drew apart, looking into one another's eyes, Elias took a deep breath. As he breathed out, Victor was transported back to the bank of the river and to the fort sitting stolid there, ridden with the stories of ages past. He drew his cloak about him against the damp cold.

"I walk with my beautiful sister, Petra. Ah, Petra, there have been so few who remembered with as much ease as you. I recall when we first met. You dropped in so deep to the magical web of life with me. Few can claim to have such an empowered connection to life and all the sacred humans."

"May you weave divinely the wheel that teaches us how to listen, to observe, to give, to guide, to accept and weave us into unity. As consciousness leaps from me to 'we' may each and every human witness and claim the power of each of us in cohesion, dreaming our collective heart and soul together in uncharted dimensions."

From Petra there was no reply. He waited. The whole realm waited without breath. No sign of her. Elias scanned across all of the realms available to him. There was still no sign. He could not find her. As tears welled then tumbled down his cheeks he called out across every realm he knew,

"Petra, where have you gone? It cannot be so. Can I take my own advice? How can I not mourn? You are lost to me. Though I know much that is concealed from others, this I did not foresee. Petra, if there was another way right now I would choose that course. Petra!"

All remained silent, though the stars shone with a startling incandescence.

It was some time before Elias found the will to continue his ceremony. The flames of the campfire diminished almost to nothing before the soft glow of fading embers reminded the earth wizard to add a few sticks of dry wood. He placed them on the hottest place in the coals and blew until a flame ignited once more and flickered, hypnotic in the gloom. Elias returned to his ritual; salt dried on each of his cheeks. In a voice softened and quivering he persevered.

"Hey my little brother, Cole, grand soul that you are, you know I walk side-by-side with you no matter what might transpire. With you come those other souls who sustain you, the magical Ivy and your little one Robin who will be so vital to the ongoing story. I have the very good fortune to know that each of you is an integral part of this tapestry we weave together. Every day we dream of the gentle intimacy of knowing one another. I know this is your dream and this is what you bring."

"For so many in this strange world we have permitted to be fashioned around us, disconnection is the source of the suffering

we endure. You, Ivy and the soul you have drawn into this reality are the weavers and teachers of intimacy and conscious relating so that we can remember we are one thing gaining reflection. This, so we might let them dissolve away to co-create true connection woven into the tapestry of all life."

In the dream Cole heard him and answered.

"My strength and resolve is with you, my brother. With me, as you know, comes my family who ride with me through all time."

Just as that was communicated another incarnation of Cole became present. Elias smiled a greeting.

The lithe figure of Cole, as he had appeared in Dave's dream, glided towards Elias' campfire and stood in the flickering glow, not quite in full light, bearing a straight staff of elder wood capped with a knot which formed a face of indescribable gentleness. In that light it was also possible to discern his face appearing as the waft and wend of the leaves of an ancient oak. Elias spoke.

"All of our people, yours, mine and all of the kindred of human-kind, extend backwards and forwards in a giant wheel beyond time. It is a great honour that in these changes we walk together. The green arises to dance, my brother, and we have the task of heralding that arousal. Dance the new story into time and space, Cernunnos. We have waited long enough."

"Aye, that we have, Dirawong Juwir. Where go you now, brother? Why do you reach out to us at this time?" he soughed through lips of leaves.

"I cannot tell. I am called to walk the songlines around this sacred mountain. That is all. In doing so I know not what I will awaken, only that it is required of me. I reach out to call our circle into the round. I also call upon the millions whose eyes, ears and hearts are open, whose souls still live to incite them to hold firm. Rally right now; follow the guidance that has been patient and waiting. I reach out to say that the time of waiting is over. I know nothing more than the irrefutable certainty of this."

"The awakening is right here and right now. It is the most exhilarating and frightening time to be incarnate. These are the times. We are the ones we have been waiting for. Gather together. Bring your unique offerings to your circle. Do not hesitate. Be bold. More I cannot say."

Elias Dirawong Juwir looked at Cernunnos Cole and smiled a smile so warm that the flickering campfire ignited and shone with respect.

The leaves disguised as a face spoke again. "There is something about this conversation that troubles me, old friend. I cannot say what it is, only that underneath it lie secrets that even I am incapable of revealing."

"Petra is lost." Elias' tone was dour and forlorn.

"That is sore news, brother. Yet there is still something more. I cannot tell. I shall let it rest and wait to see what transpires. Farewell, brother, and thank you for checking in. May your walk for us around that giant caldera inform us all of the next steps we must take."

The entity vanished leaving Elias sitting motionless beside his fire. Cole slept on, yet turned and tossed a little, disturbing the dream so as to gain the rest of unconsciousness. Ivy and Robin were not disturbed, bound by the bonds of freedom engendered by faith.

Elias walked out of his clearing to collect extra wood. He encircled the space with silent footfalls. In a few minutes he returned, laden with an armful of sticks and logs. He added several smaller faggots to the fire and looked up to see another of his companions settled beside him, his face made ghostlike by the blue-grey smoke which engulfed them both.

"Aha, there you are, Wolf. Welcome, hunter and hunted. You and I have walked together so long, my ancient accomplice. So many times you have been the one that stood with me, old friend, firm in the knowledge of who you are. In that knowledge all around you feel your strength and your ability to remain steadfast and true."

"Walk with me again this time, Wolf, for this time is more significant than at any other in our remembered history. It is you who weaves sovereignty, self-expression and the power of being in masterful balance and control of our emotions, letting them move and shift so that we respond rather than react to all that presents in this world. Walk close by my side one more time, old friend. I need you right there."

As one they turned to each other. Wolf held out his hands, one palm up, the other down. Elias curled his fingers into those of his brother and they gazed at one another as their faces shifted and morphed into a thousand faces, each one equal until the ancestry was complete and the two of them sat in the image of their first incarnations.

It was Elias who soulspoke first.

"Here we are again, old friend. Where do you see this taking us this time?"

Wolf grinned and chuckled. "This time, Elias you know better than almost any soul where this leads."

Elias smiled a gentle smile and said, "Would you remind me?"

This prompted Wolf to become present and serious. He rumbled a reply.

"This has been dreamed, imagined, breathed and spoken for millennia and thus it is real. This is the awakening of one of the giants to dance again in the spiral called life. It is thus the awakening and the ascendance of humanity. It is the trembling of anticipation of a magnificent dance that will span millennia and catapult us into realms beyond comprehension. Nothing must be done but to choose to ride the flow of that which calls us for that is what fuels the dancer with renewed energy.

For those who have grown into adulthood and those who continue to seek that maturity, pioneer humanity into a whole new realm. Every soul called here at this time, every person drawing breath has a role to play in this cataclysm, this trans-formation, this rapture."

Elias sat still as stone. Wolf mirrored him. Across Wolf's face rode a flicker of sadness, momentary and momentous. Elias nodded and Wolf returned to his cliff-side eyrie.

"I walk with you too you, dreamer from the stars, Ilith named Raniyah. There is much to learn by dreaming the impossible and you weave this with consummate ease. Continue to seek extraordinary ideas and imagine improbable wonders. Connect with the immeasurable possibilities in every moment, for this is your weaving as you explore galaxies that others dare not dream, so that we can make that quantum leap in consciousness and experience through the avatars that live among us."

Elias inhaled then emitted a small gasp as if surprised.

"I feel you, beautiful child." He drew another deep breath, collecting his thoughts.

"Saffron, you surprise me yet we can both trust your confusion and your certainty. You are so welcome on this wheel, in this tapestry, and I wonder why we have not travelled together before. Some things remain closed to me. I must reside with patience and forbearance. Welcome home, young one. You are crucial in this weaving though it remains a mystery to me where you weave."

Ilith named Raniyah spoke.

"Elias, earth wizard, well met, brother. It seems I have other realms in which to venture. I know this feeling well. I am at ease. Perhaps our paths will cross sooner rather than later in this cosmic dance across the stars."

Elias laughed. "Is the mothership calling you home, Ilith, old one?" She laughed with him.

"I am always at home. Farewell. All appears to be in place."

Elias called out, "will you speak to me of Petra?"

But she was gone.

Saffron stood naked under her shower in her house in Goa, western India. Gushes of sun hot water washed her clean of the saliva, sweat, scent and skin of her lover. She reached out to the taps and shut them both off at once. "Who's there?" Connection

established. She vanished. Elias smiled, satisfied that she was on her way.

Elias turned a little on his perch beside the fire as a curlew wailed its mournful cry.

"Hey Toby, seems the grandmothers are busy with several of us. I walk with you brother, you designer of structure, hard as steel, soft as feather down. When you weave your magic we can feel solid on this mother we have named Earth. Your weaving is practical, measurable and strong. Thus you are pivotal to a future where all that has come before is not discarded but rather reassigned so that the tapestry we are co-creating stands for the millennia it must. Walk with me and help me build the bridges that we will need to cross a chasm that has been affecting mankind for far too long."

Toby stood opposite Elias at the campfire. He inclined his head and spoke.

"I have no fucking idea where all this is leading old friend, but I know it's a journey that must be taken, so here we are. Walk in beauty, Elias, walk us all into the fabric of a new existence. I'll carry on no matter what. We have been assigned to visit..... ah but you already know....."

Elias replied. "I do. It warms my heart that you will meet with Kopanuk. She will inform you and prepare you for what is to come. This is a time of great turmoil. They will want to hunt you down. You and Brianna hold a connection with this earth that none other possess. If that is severed, all our work would be for naught. Be sure to carry on." Elias paused for just a few moments before speaking.

"Your sister......."

"I know. Already I grieve yet still she breathes."

"If there is anyone who can offer her assistance it is Kopanuk Mountain Dreamer," Elias intoned.

"Thank you, my brother," said Toby, "though I sense she is already well beyond even Kopanuk's skills and talents."

"And you, how are you?"

"She is my sister and yet so much more. I see her lineage too, so have spent many years preparing for this. Still I grieve."

Elias ran his fingers through his hair, pondered a moment then reached into a small calico bag and drew out a small tourmaline crystal, half radiant blue half verdant green.

"Will you give her this?"

Toby reached across the flickering flames of the fire to take the stone from Elias. He examined it and slid it into a pocket.

"Depend on it." He paused and tilted his head. "Why didn't you give it to her? You have already spoken with her."

"Yes." He hesitated as if considering what to share. "It's important that it comes from you, connected to the earth as you are. You or Brianna but no-one else, you hear me?"

"As I said, depend on it. Always just a little mystery added, huh Elias?"

"There is always much more mystery than anything else, Toby. I haven't even begun to fathom it all and I have been studying for aeons. Now go. Return. You are needed."

He turned to face Brianna who sat cross legged beside where Toby had been. She was in the west of the wheel, facing Elias in the centre.

"Brianna, you magnificent soul, your weaving is so important. For as we live in this physical world you weave the skills and the beauty of growing things, creating a home, nurturing our physical bodies. Above all, you guide our human family who know that we can do it, must do it. You ground those who are willing to hold the ground that is this mother we have named Earth."

"It's good to see you, Elias. It feels like it's been a long time yet in some ways you are always present to me. Right now I thank you for your ceremony and I choose to return to Raniyah. She needs me."

"Yes, she does, though her journey and yours are on opposite sides of this wheel. You, who are so grounded, remember to set her free."

"What does that mean?" she asked.

424

"It will become apparent. Remember to set her free even after it seems she has done so herself," he rumbled.

"You have always spoken in riddles to me, Elias."

"It is the way I must, Brianna. I am not your guide but I can sprinkle some breadcrumbs if you would pick from them." Elias leaned forward and placed the palms of both his slender hands on the dry earth in front of him.

"Remember Bree. Set her free."

She faded from the scene and woke, cosseted with Raniyah in the back of the old truck in a cold cave in Canada.

Now Rena was present. She stood straight as she addressed him. "I see you, wizard. In fact I've been watching you for some time."

Elias chuckled then snapped his head up and gazed into Rena's sparkling eyes.

"Welcome to you, Rena, daughter of my beloved Ariah. Let us walk together so that your weaving will find a way for us to release the trauma that causes all those things we perceive as illness, for you are the divine weaver of our collective and individual healing."

He moved his torso as if to call in her skills for his own body.

"Thank you for your faith in Victor. It's a rude introduction to your place in this but I witness you embracing your gifts. You bring such extraordinary power for our collective healing. With that in alignment we are all able to embody this communal dream at our highest potential. That is crucial in cohesion with the healing of this planet and all life upon it."

Rena snorted.

"Just a minor role for the new soul eh, Girawong?" She winked at him.

Elias broke eye contact and shook his head. "You know me by that name?"

"Some things are still a mystery to you, brother. It could just be that I am one of those mysteries." She grinned at the quizzical expression on his face. "Don't worry too much. All

will become clear as this whole drama unfolds, no matter where you happen to view it from. Farewell, earth wizard. I'm seeing some things that you cannot, yet it is not my place to share. I will tend to the well-being of your friend, Victor. All is as it is meant to be."

She raised one hand in farewell, smiling as she slipped back to the fort beside the river, leaving Elias to ponder her words.

Elias continued his ceremony after drinking from a flask beside the fire. The water cooled and refreshed him. He placed the flask back onto the hard ground. When he looked up, he saw him.

"Dave, my old friend."

Elias stood and walked the few steps to embrace him.

"We have walked together so long and have seen so much. You retain our collective memory and allow us to learn from lessons that have gone before so that we avoid making the same mistakes. The library is secure?"

Dave nodded, "Rest assured, Elias. Ordered, categorised and locked down. Safe as it can be."

"You are with Cole and his family?"

"Yep, I just arrived. It looks like the whole crew is going to come walking."

"That was always going to be." Elias had a brief shadow cross his brow. "Look after them, Dave. As we hold the knowledge and memories it's important that we remember that it can stir old stories. Those old stories can hold more power than most would imagine. Some of them may try to misguide us."

Dave reached into his pocket and drew out a leather pouch. He rolled a cigarette, lit it and puffed blue smoke into the air.

"I'd say that has already begun. I dreamed in an old story just the other day. We were all in it, even the little one. I'm not sure what I need to do with that but something is directing me to Wolf. Somehow he has acquired answers that I'll need to access."

Elias searched Dave's gnarled face and said,

"The book?"

"What book?"

"He has a book. He discovered it. It looked like pure chance. He knows it is significant. It is contained."

Dave's features softened as he looked at Elias.

"Are you going to walk three days for me, brother? That makes a change."

He tossed the leavings of his cigarette into the campfire. Elias replied,

"I am. My purpose is to walk your vast knowledge immutably into this story. With the memory of all our learned knowledge we can move forward with hope. Stay strong my friend."

Dave smiled and offered a mock salute. He reached into his pocket and tossed a small knife across the fire to Elias.

"This might come in handy."

Dave walked off and faded into the gloom.

Elias paused for several minutes to listen. A creek burbled in the distance. A night animal scratched on rough bark. The rustle and swish of branches and leaves dancing prompted the earth wizard to take three deep breaths, breathing each out with an intention that his prayers be heard and empowered, that the ancient grandmother spirits carry his prayers through the treetops and onto the wind into the dreaming.

He shifted a little to ease an ache in his leg then continued.

"Am I permitted a special tribute to you, my sister Tisa?"

He shifted from his spot in one lithe movement to drop onto his knees.

"We have walked together, co-designed this exquisite tapestry for so many lifetimes. It is my great honour each and every time. You are the humble master who resides with us. You hold knowledge in one hand so that one hand is free to discover that which is wisdom and that which is scattered distraction. No matter how I might fare as this quantum leap occurs, I know you will always be there to exercise your wisdom. Thank you for being with us all, magical sister."

Tisa was not present to his ceremony. Elias knew the power of his sister from a thousand lives and was not concerned.

"You are busy then. Never mind, you are forever in my circle." Though he revealed nothing on the outside, something in the pit of Elias' stomach twisted.

The completion of his rite drew near. He lifted his eyes and cupped hands to the stars.

"May you also walk with me, stranger. You sit on this wheel and yet even I know not your name. I feel you. I sense your challenge and the journey you are taking. I welcome you into the place of teacher, the place of learning. Walk with me, you who walk in two worlds at once. I assign you to choose co-creation, the balance of the infinite, inner and outer, peace and freedom from all the rules and regulations that inhibit our divinity."

There was no reply but a ghostlike presence bowed and vanished.

"Ah, and there you are, Kesari, soul sister. You've brought your boy." He stated this in a matter-of-fact way, without surprise. "Thank you both for walking with me. Kesari, stay strong. There will be challenge for you. Don't lose hope. It is you who brings the greatest of beauties."

At this, Max sat straight in her lap and gazed into Elias' eyes.

"You are, on this wheel, all of our creativity. You are art, artistic expression and the infinite opportunity to create in every moment of the tapestry we call life. The impossible is possible because we are the tools of the divine. You bring awe and wonder and so dance life into a thing of impeccable beauty. Thank you for choosing to walk with me as this new reality manifests."

Kesari bowed her head to him and said, "Elias, you know I have little idea what is going on. I will do everything and anything to ensure my son is brought to an adulthood of hope. Tisa will have answers, yes?"

Nodding, Elias said, "Yes, speak at length with Tisa. Find each other as soon as you are able."

"We have been communicating. She's close. And you, brother, what is this you are doing?"

"It's time for me to walk the wheel. Three days for each of you, three days for me," said Elias, "to complete a circle."

"So around and around we go, Elias. Well, you know I'm on board because it feels like time for me too. I'm up for having a choice. It takes a leap so it's said. Every ending's a beginning. Do you mind if I paint a picture of you near that campfire? From memory is fine, nothing more invasive." Kesari grinned at him.

Elias chuckled, "Of course you may."

"Great. Thank you. Walk your wheel, brother. We'll be on our way to you in no time."

Kesari and Max returned to their home near the markets to wait for Tisa.

Elias stopped again. A cimmerian cloud crossed his brow as he invoked the last of his wheel. He spoke once again but this time rather than speaking in a voice of power it was imbued with a deep reverence. His voice quivered as he spoke and tears once again wet his cheeks, dripped from his chin, splashed on his legs and the soft, dry ground.

"Walk with me, you centre holders. I know your journey better than all others. I know what it brings, the confusion, responsibility, and yes, sometimes what feels like agony. Yet with that is complete liberation. Listen well. Speak from your heart and soul. I welcome you into this wheel. You are two and one. Your union entwines me as we. I will not name you into this wheel at this time for there are those that would hunt you down should they know of you and what you bring."

"It's time, my friends. Be bold and come!"

Sitting in complete stillness and silence for each of them, each invocation, each prayer; Elias listened. He made no attempt to move. As he sat, still as an owl – listening – the inky blackness of the night swirled around him, engulfed him, drew him

into catacombs seldom explored, save by those who wove close with the thirteen grandmothers.

As he walked through that doorway Elias began a journey that walked a giant wheel about the sacred mountain where he had plunged wood into stone, fire into ice, air into water.

He began a journey of thirty-nine days, to bring form into the wheel of thirteen souls to whom he was inextricably connected. He walked each of the twelve for three days, wefting and weaving songlines with leylines until he came to walking the last three days, the hub of the wheel.

It was on the third day of that hub, the thirty-ninth day of his weaving, that hell-fire came.

On the thirty-ninth day, when the wheel Elias walked was all but complete, Mother Earth screamed terror, agony and frustration as a ritual of blood and fire, pain and separation, greed and lascivious hunger emanated from a castle fortress half a world away. A blistering force shook that same mountain from which Elias had made the call.

Molten stone and six-thousand degree magma drawn from the very centre of the earth by powers misused and enthralling in their arrogant confidence became an all-engulfing, crimson fire.

Moments before he could complete his ritual, his walk for the green and blue planet upon which hinged so much, in a galaxy of stars near its exquisite completion, Elias Dirawong Juwir, Sorcerer, earth-wizard and deep knowledge-keeper was obliterated in each and every one of one hundred and forty-four realms and the night became preternaturally dark.

Not the End

We have only just begun...